FILE UNDER FORTUNE

Geraldine Wall

Geraldine Wall has asserted her right under the Copyright, Designs and Patents Act 1988 to be identified as the author of this work.
2019 – Geraldine Wall
ISBN:9781079447262

Books in this series:

    File Under Family
    File Under Fear
    File Under Fidelity
    File Under Fathers
    File Under Fortune

*For my sons, John and Daniel, with love and gratitude:
no matter how far away, I'm always by your side.*

5

Why do you stay in prison when the door is so wide open?

Rumi (1207-1273)

1

She found the bell-push but the door was flung open before she could press it and a shiny young woman was beaming down at her. 'You must be Anna, come in, come in, dad's washing his hands – he's been playing with his new toy in the garden.'

'It's not a toy,' he said, joining them in the hall, 'it's an economy measure. Good to see you.' He smiled at her but she saw how tired he was and not the kind of tired that a decent nap puts right. 'I just can't get the thing to obey its own instructions – it's wilfully disobedient and far more human than I'd hoped.' He pushed open a door and ushered Anna in. 'Let's go into the living room, the garden doors are open and it's pleasant in there.'

'He's bought a lawnbot,' Elizabeth murmured into Anna's ear with that assumption of intimacy that only people sure of their own charm use on strangers, 'but don't get him started on it. Tea? Or something cold?'

Anna sat down. The last time she had been in this room she had been drunk and crazy and had just assaulted the security guard in the supermarket. Andrew Dunster had rescued her that brazen summer day two years ago as she had crashed and burned and by confessing his own guilt had, by some alchemy of the soul, exorcised hers.

Now his daughter, Elizabeth, wanted a favour from her.

From where she was sitting the garden beyond the open doors fell away across an acid-green stripe of lawn into a black hedge of leylandii tall enough to reveal nothing of the houses nearby. Just outside on the patio a robin peered in at them from its perch on a pile of bricks, cocking its head one way and then another as if trying to get the most telling angle for a snap. Difficult to find robins so cute now we know what thugs they are, Anna thought. As the drinks were being distributed she wondered why they were inside on such a fine day but then she heard voices.

Andrew took a step out on to the patio and called, 'I think the marguerites would be perfect for you – just down the end on the left – take as many as you want.' He turned back to the room. 'I'm doing their wedding next Saturday. The bride wants an informal white look, apparently, and her mum's on the scrounge.' So, Andrew must want privacy for whatever Elizabeth would be asking. Anna girded herself up.

'I'm getting married myself in September,' Elizabeth said, leaning back into the sofa and smiling to herself, 'and I'm hoping you can help me with my wedding gift to my new husband.'

She had Andrew's long, lean frame but her effervescence was her own – it was as if she was forever on the brink of leaping up and clapping. Anna sipped her iced tea warily knowing that her skill-set did not include thoughtful presents. Diane, her dad's partner, had been so affronted by a birthday cache of toiletries (last minute grab from Boots) that the fall-out had only just settled. It hadn't helped that Diane often did smell quite bracing from her animal rescue work. Your subconscious is rarely your friend, Anna reflected. But the armchair was comfortable and the sweet amber tea slipped down pleasantly and if she was at home now she'd be sweating it out among the brambles so why hurry Elizabeth?

'She's engaged to a violinist,' Andrew put in, 'a very talented young man. You may have heard of him – Thomas Budas?'

Anna was just about to shake her head when the name pinged a neural receptor. 'Didn't he just release his first album? I think there was an article about him in the Sunday Arts section a week or so back. Very good review. Yes, they said he'd studied at the Royal Birmingham Conservatoire. But I'm afraid I'm not really musical, I mean, you know, I like music, of course...'

'Oh no, no,' Elizabeth interrupted, shaking her bright hair, 'nothing like that. I'm hoping you would be willing to try to trace his family. Of course, it would be paid work if you'll take it. Look, let me explain.'

It seemed that Tom Budas was, as far as he knew, alone in the world. His mother, the only relative he'd ever known, had died ten months earlier when the Cessna Citation Mustang her client had sent to bring her to his Channel Island home had ditched in a squall in the turbulent waters between Jersey and Guernsey. Anna rummaged in her bag and brought out a notepad (always available and never prone to loss of function, this was still her favoured device in this kind of situation). Giles Budas, Tom's father, had disappeared shortly after his son's birth and set up home with another woman (details unknown) but might well be alive and traceable.

Anna had to interrupt Elizabeth to ask, 'But would he want him found, do you think? It's an unhappy history.'

Elizabeth had thought this through and replied briskly that she hoped Anna would find any relative, even half-siblings, and hopefully grandparents on both sides and then she could decide whether to approach them or to hand the information over to Tom or do nothing at all. 'It's what he most wants in the world, you see,' she said, 'connections, roots, bloodlines, you know, a family. To belong to people.' Anna nodded, meaning she understood what Elizabeth was saying, but years of professional and personal experience had taught her that finding your tribe can be a very different experience from the one you imagine.

'Tom knows that his dad was a doctor and his grandparents were doctors, too, but apparently they went out to live in some African country and his mother lost contact with them,' Elizabeth went on. 'Naturally, she would want nothing to do with them after their son had abandoned her or perhaps, more tragically, they had little interest in her or Tom.'

Oddly, Tom knew even less about his mother's family. He had understood from a very young age that questions about them would be met with silence or a rebuke. The only clue he had was a photograph taken in a field somewhere on a sunny day. His mother, then a little girl, was perched on a pony and squinting proudly at whoever was taking the photo. At the pony's head stood a man in a white shirt with his sleeves rolled up, a cigarette in his mouth.

As a teenager Tom had been helping Loretta pack up their belongings in yet another house move and had come across it among some baby photos of himself. His mother had taken it from him, he had told Elizabeth, and stared at it angrily and then said, 'My father and me long ago. My pony was Skip-Along-Docie.' He hadn't dared ask her anything more about it but he had kept the photo and Elizabeth had asked to borrow it to get it framed and had made a print for Anna which she now passed across.

'I didn't realise she was so difficult,' Andrew said, 'she was pleasant when your mother and I met her.' He was seated in the shadiest part of the room, sunk deep in the armchair. Anna studied him for a moment but he only smiled at her.

Elizabeth turned to him. 'Actually, he was, is very proud of her and she was of him and mostly she was a good mum in a practical sort of way but maybe not overly cosy. I think she was a very private person. She certainly never confided in me but she always made me feel welcome.' If Tom and his mother only had each other, Anna wondered what the older woman's feelings would be about this super-confident woman sweeping like a tidal wave into their lives.

'Do you have her dates?' she asked, pen poised, 'And do you know what she did for a living?'

Elizabeth bent sideways and picked up a single sheet of paper from the coffee table, handing it to Anna. 'I want all this to be a surprise for Tom so this is what I've managed to wheedle out of him without giving the game away. I hope it's enough. I had to be a bit devious which is against my nature as you know,' she winked at her father, 'but it's all in a good cause, isn't it?'

Anna scanned the few lines of data: Loretta Snow Budas, born 6.2.1975, married Giles Budas 1992, died 12.8.2017. 'She married very young,' Anna noted, 'so he must have been considerably older. It takes years to qualify as a doctor. Do you know her maiden name?'

'No, Tom doesn't. After her death he searched for documents because he needed to tell the Registrar for the death certificate but he couldn't find anything.' This was even more unusual.

'Was it not on his birth certificate?'

'He couldn't find it, he said, and I couldn't press him.'

'So, what did Loretta do for a living?'

'Well, that's one reason why Tom was so proud of her. Obviously, she was a teenager left with nothing: no qualifications, no money and a baby to look after when Giles went but she got some kind of an administrative job in an accountant's office and then went on to take courses and day release and so on to qualify herself as a financial advisor. She was very good at it, it seems, and by her early thirties she had set up her own consultancy which became successful.'

'So the client who sent a plane to pick her up wanted her financial advice?'

'Yes. He must be one of the 1%,' Elizabeth said with a grin.

'Probably one of the 0.1%,' Andrew added, 'if he can afford his own plane.'

'She worked long hours always,' Elizabeth went on, 'but Tom never resented it because he knew she was doing it for him. He wasn't the kind of boy to get into mischief and I think the violin became a friend so practising was never a chore.' Elizabeth picked something else up from the table by her side. 'This is the three of us at a concert where Tom was playing at Symphony Hall two years ago.' She passed the photograph across.

It took Anna several seconds to drag her gaze away from the central figure. Tom was not just handsome, he was mesmerising. The shining eyes, the brilliant smile, the sheer animation of him commanded attention - certainly it was commanding hers. He shone, in the photograph, even more brightly than Elizabeth who stood beside him. 'He's nice-looking,' she said neutrally, forcing herself to look at the two women flanking him. Really, if you wanted a made-to-order celebrity musician, Thomas Budas had the full kit: romantic looks, exotic name and clearly a considerable talent, too. It seemed unfair somehow that he could tick every box.

His mother, Loretta, was smaller and less glamorous with a neat figure which she had dressed carefully although Anna noted the deep crease between her brows and the tension in her jaw and found herself warming to her. She had succeeded in a difficult world without privilege or connections to help her and had made it financially possible for her talented son to follow a notoriously precarious career. Their relationship may have been undemonstrative but she had built a good life for him. Envy took a stab at Anna right under her ribs but it was a familiar thrust so she winced and ignored it.

She stood up. 'Thanks for the tea. I'll see what I can dig up and get back to you. It's an interesting challenge.'

'We haven't discussed your fee,' Elizabeth said, rising to tower above Anna, a situation all too familiar to her.

'Your father has already paid,' Anna said, smiling at Andrew. 'You don't have to know any more than that but I will bill you for expenses, if that's ok. It'll mainly be the cost of certificates if I need to order them but I'll check with you before I go ahead.'

Elizabeth walked with her to the door. 'I'm excited now,' she said, 'please order anything you need. I can't wait to hear what you find out.'

As Anna walked away down the drive the afternoon sun burned the back of her neck and she registered a rising pulse of adrenalin at the challenge ahead of her, a challenge all the better for not being constrained by Ted's fiscal sensitivities.

Thinking of Ted reminded her that he had emailed her to see him in his office first thing on Monday morning in his idiosyncratic argot: *C me min soonest*. Ted had fat fingers and often hit a neighbouring key. Texts were even more cryptic. It could mean something or nothing and she refused to worry since for once she had nothing on her conscience, at least at work. She strolled down her own road and turned into her drive to squeeze past her dusty car musing that by the time she had changed into shorts and a T shirt it would surely be too late to start gardening, if hacking back brambles and tearing up nettles could be described as such .

It was quiet in the house and her resolve to do nothing but sip something cool and wet in the back garden and sink into her book strengthened pleasurably. Ellis was at the tennis club and wouldn't be back till later and George was helping Diane with something at Safe 'n' Sound animal rescue. Normally she would have got ready to amble down the road to spend a couple of hours with Steve but he was away climbing in Scotland and his little niece, Alice, was in Derbyshire, no doubt bossing her grandparents about. Anna didn't want to think about Alice right now. The afternoon colours were deepening and she wandered outside through the cluttered utility room to the back garden with a glass of elderflower cordial in one hand and her book in the other and settled on their mildewed recliner so she could watch the sky flicker through the branches of the sycamore tree.

It was very likely that Giles Budas was still alive. Even if he was older than Loretta, as she guessed, he might still be only in his fifties. There might well be half-siblings for Tom. It was also possible, but slightly less likely, that both sets of Tom's grandparents may be alive. It was strange that there wasn't a maiden name for Loretta but it should be easy enough to find.

Probate work such as her company, Harts Heir Hunters, took on went straight to the deepest secrets of family relations and they did it by finding facts. Dates, authentic names, assumed names, war records, addresses, births, marriages and deaths and so on made short work of family myths and legends. Often, within a few days a researcher like Anna could find out more about a family than closest friends knew or even the person involved. Usually ignorance was not because of secrets and lies, though, it was because people hadn't asked about their own heritage when they had the chance, when old people in their families were still alive. Illegitimacy, desertion, bigamy, criminality were routinely exposed as were heroism, generosity and altruism. An astonishing amount of data is on record.

Elizabeth naturally wanted a fairy-tale result for Tom but it was obvious to Anna that Tom's father's abandonment of his wife and son was only one schism in his family. What had caused Loretta to turn so fixedly from her own people? Of course, she could have been in care most of her life and felt she had no family.

Tom's lack of an extended family, and especially a father, must have affected him deeply Anna reflected as she half-closed her eyes against the spangles of sunlight piercing the leaves of the old tree. She knew that because she had been abandoned herself as a toddler. Lena, her mother, had simply walked off one day without a word of explanation. No father, no person, could have been kinder or more supportive than George and yet there was still that small fumarole emitting sadness from her heart that comes from a vital absence – the perpetual shame of having been inadequately loved. Did he feel the same? Of course not, she decided, given his stellar career and his dazzling, self-confident appearance – he was clearly, at the very least, rising above it.

She shifted in the recliner and found her place in the book. After all, Elizabeth had only wanted the usual factual information but it was always a little thrilling to start that search, especially when mysteries were involved.

2

Ted didn't even ask her to sit down. 'Guthrie Cromer,' he said, 'the police can't be bothered with it so it's come our way. I'm not complaining. There's no foul play, obviously, he blew a gasket – straightforward aortic aneurysm – must have been waiting to happen for years. It was eight centimetres. Can you believe it? No symptoms, none at all, and he was only thirty-five.' Ted massaged the space below his own sternum reflectively.

Anna sat down anyway, choosing the straight-backed chair Ted normally used for his in-tray overflow but which today was clear. 'Don't people at work have some clue about his next-of-kin? Surely he would have chatted to colleagues?'

Ted stifled a yawn and rubbed his face, which was particularly mottled today, Anna noted. She guessed that a sleepless night was making him irritable. He had chosen to take the angle that his impending divorce was merely an arbitrary gladiatorial combat in which he found himself a reluctant and perplexed participant. But the office all knew the truth. There had been one affair too many. He had brought it on himself.

'You'd have thought so but even his line manager, a guy called Chris Barton, said Guthrie would just change the subject if anything personal came up. All Chris knew was that he dated sometimes and followed the Wasps. Oh, and that he grew up in Stratford-on-Avon.' Ted's next yawn made his jaw click. 'No will, no solicitor, but then, at that age, who would think?' He opened the office door and Anna stood up. 'You've got the stuff you need so crack on with it would you? He's in the morgue waiting to be claimed. The Council won't pay for a burial for a guy with his assets as you know. He must be worth a bit, you don't get too many paupers in merchant banking.'

As she passed Steve's door Anna wiggled her fingers at him and he beamed back mouthing, 'Lunch?' so she nodded. In the moments it took for her computer to wake up Anna pondered the coincidence that within a couple of days she'd been asked to investigate two men with no known next-of-kin, one dead, one alive, but at Harts it hardly counted as coincidence since it was so commonplace - except that usually the disconnected or estranged were old.

She had spent some time on Saturday evening looking into Tom Budas's family and had been hooked almost at once by an intriguing discovery. Loretta had not been married to Giles Budas as she had told Tom but to someone called Teller Budas who was certainly not a doctor. She had checked the UK professional registers and not found him. To find his occupation she would need Loretta and Teller's marriage certificate, since no father had been recorded on Tom's birth certificate, and she had ordered it immediately. She had already found that Loretta's maiden name was Smith which had made her groan. But, when she had gone back to the GRO Birth/Marriage/Death Indexes she had found that not only were Loretta's parents probably alive but, thankfully, had unusual first names which would help the search enormously. Loretta's mother was called Queenie and her father Rakes, a name which Anna could never remember having come across before. It might be difficult to find any address for them, though.

Overnight she had had a brainwave. In 1939, at the outbreak of World War 2, a register had been set up to record the population in the United Kingdom who were not in the military and that register listed occupations and addresses. It was a snapshot of the civilian population and, unlike the censuses since 1911, was available online. Rakes Smith, Loretta's father, might well be listed on it as a child but if not, Loretta's grandfather, Lorel, might be and there was a chance that he may not have been redacted when records were published online (when the identities of all people still living were erased with a thick black line) because he might have already died. Blessing the Smith family for having such distinctive first names, she had brought up the website and typed in Lorel Desmond Smith and there his details were. Lorel Smith had been born in 1918 and lived, at the time of this snapshot census, at the same address as his brothers, Chip Valentino and Stanley Miller Smith, who were two and four years older respectively.

Sitting at the kitchen table on Sunday morning with the sound of rain tinkling on the window and George's espresso percolator popping on the stove, Anna had frozen in the act of biting into her toast. The address for the Smith brothers was Apple Orchard, Middleway Farm, Gloucestershire. Butter dripped on to the space bar and Anna had hastily replaced the toast on its plate and run for kitchen towel.

Occupations were listed as hawker (Lorel), field worker (Chip) and for the oldest, Stanley, horse dealer. They were Travellers, Gypsies. They must be. Tom's great grandfather could have been Romani rather than Irish with a name like Smith she remembered from a unit on surnames she had covered for her Diploma. Quickly she brought up The National Archives (Army section) and searched under Campaign Medals. Her assumptions were that a Romani conscript would be more likely to be put into the Army than the Navy or Air Force and most people who served did get a Campaign Medal. She found him. Private Lorel Smith had been killed in 1941 during the Battle of Gondar. When she looked it up on Wikipedia she saw he would have been fighting alongside Commonwealth troops in East Africa. Rakes was his only child. She knew that many Travellers were conscripted during both world wars and, to the consternation of the families, many of their horses requisitioned, too. Since for the most part the horses, which drew everything from the decorated Vardi caravans to plain trailers, were the only way families could get from one source of agricultural work to another (as well as being treated almost as members of the family) this must have been devastating.

Anna thought about Tom's dark good looks and that photograph Elizabeth had given her of the little girl on a pony with the black-haired man at its head. That must have been Rakes Smith with little Loretta. But weren't Travelling families supposed to be fiercely loyal and protective of each other so why would Loretta have been left so isolated and vulnerable at such a young age? She was seventeen when she had Tom. Whoever Teller Budas was, he had clearly not stayed around when Tom was born. Why had her family not supported her? Or, had she turned her back on them? More research was desperately needed but Sunday had become crowded with events and there had been no time.

Ellis had been playing in a junior tennis tournament and she and George had gone to cheer him on and then Faye and poor Jack (as Anna always thought of him) had allowed her to give them dinner to celebrate three months of cohabitation or some such thing. Previous dinners had marked the acquisition of a sofa from the Heart Foundation and Faye's move at work to a desk with a view. Anna didn't mind – the couple were often out of cash and this was her way to catch up with their lives and check on how they were doing. In return for Sunday night dinner (deal unstated but understood) Faye and Jack had entertained Alice by taking her to the fairground attractions at Cannon Hill Park after Steve returned from his trip. Anna, remembering how she and Steve (tired but more than willing) had spent those precious hours, smiled to herself. Now it was Monday morning and Guthrie Cromer was in the morgue awaiting her enquiries.

'Ok, what are you grinning about, young lady? You look positively smug. I never feel that way when I see Ted – who's he given you?' Suzy placed a crackling paper bag with a cellophane window on Anna's desk. 'Brain food.'

'I wasn't actually thinking about work,' Anna said, peering into the bag. 'Cinnamon Danish – thanks.'

'Spare me.' Suzy pulled up a chair and dropped into it. 'I don't want anyone to be loved up so wipe that smirk off.'

'Why?'

'Dispensed with Rob's services. He stood me up again at five minutes notice so he's got to go.'

'Ah.'

A little while later she was able to start work and found that Guthrie Cromer's next- of- kin, unlike Tom's, held no surprises. His mother, Bella Cromer, was not married it turned out but that was far from unusual especially for an eighties' relationship. Bella was very much alive and her address, according to the Electoral Register, was still in Stratford-on-Avon, in fact, the same one as was written on Guthrie's birth certificate. Anna made a note of it and picked up her office phone to call Ted. 'Do the police just want the contact details of the next-of-kin,' she asked, 'or do they want us to notify Mr Cromer's mother?'

'They haven't said so let's just do it and invoice them,' Ted replied but added quickly, 'Where is she?' Anna told him. 'Ok, that's not far away, go and see her tomorrow, it will be a nasty shock for the poor woman, and make sure you log every minute plus mileage.'

Not a pleasant task, of course, but the researchers were all trained to deliver this kind of sad news. Set up a professional but caring relationship, reveal the facts simply and slowly to give the recipient time to absorb them, offer condolences and then move on to practical matters. Of course, some people hadn't known the deceased and were secretly or openly delighted to find they had unexpectedly become beneficiaries. But, in the case of a close relationship like this one, a mother and son, even if they were estranged as seemed likely, it would be bound to be more emotional and Anna would take as much time as she needed to conduct the interview.

Of course, she might arrive at the address to find Bella was out or on holiday – there was no way of checking for a mobile and no landline could be found from her internet search. In that case she would have to call on neighbours or in the final resort leave a note with her business card asking Ms Cromer to call her. If that failed Ted would just have to hand the case back to the police and if he hadn't been so eager for business he would have done that in the first place. Surely detectives could find her? But Ted belonged to many social clubs of the kind that were good for business and the giving and receiving of favours was one currency members employed. Not for her to delve into the murky genesis of this case.

Tuesday's weather was clear and dry and a trip to a pretty town like Stratford-on-Avon was always good if only to get out of the office. Anna felt that a quick refreshment stop at Huffkins on Bridge Street was perfectly in order, especially since Bella lived a short distance from the river across a pedestrian bridge and the famous café was almost on the way from the main car park.

She wondered what the throngs of chattering teenagers made of all this Stratford and The Bard stuff. She could imagine how excited they would have been to come here from France, Hong-Kong, Germany, the USA to visit the hallowed ground but now they were here what were they thinking? The gift shops bulged with slow-moving groups of them peering at mugs and tea towels and outside they sat in herds on railings or on the ground with their faces bent to their phones.

She found the bridge by the lock between the River Avon and the canal (which had started its life in Birmingham's Gas Street Basin only metres from her office) and strode over it checking directions on her phone. Ten minutes later she turned into a quiet side-street of 1920's terraces with their narrow fore-courts no longer given to little gardens with neat brick walls but now made ugly with wheelie-bins. Bella's house was at the end of the block and Anna slowed her pace to take in first impressions. The shallow bay window was cluttered with New-Age bric-a-brac and on the door was a sticker suggesting that callers *Give Peace a Chance*. Next to the door, mounted on the wall, was a sprung cast-iron bell. Anna tugged at it and rapped twice sharply on the door. She glanced down to see a fraying coir mat which when new would have been a vibrant rainbow but which was now obscured with dirt shaped rather like a nimbus rain-cloud, Anna thought whimsically.

The door was snatched open by a florid woman dragging a scarf from her head and twisting a rope of grey hair into a knot. 'You're early, darling, but that's beautiful! Come in, everything's ready, no need to take off your shoes, we have no materialistic ways here, carpets are made to be walked on, aren't they, through here, that's right, I'll be back in a jiffy.'

Having not had the chance to say one word, Anna looked round. The room was crowded with objects of every kind as though Bella was about to open it as a junk shop, the sort Anna had loved when she was young but you hardly saw any more in Birmingham. On the table was a chenille cloth and on that a set of tarot cards. A joss stick had just been lit on the mantelpiece, the match-head still sending up a spiral of smoke from where it had been dropped a moment ago into a ceramic cabbage leaf.

Bella came back carrying a tin tray with two mugs. 'Nettle tea,' she announced, 'nothing like it for cleansing the chakras.' Clearly Bella's therapeutic techniques were as eclectic as her décor.

'Mrs Cromer,' Anna began, giving her an honorary marriage licence, 'I think you're expecting someone else.' She pulled out her business card and offered it to the older woman who, she noticed, had popped on some chunky beads while she was in the kitchen as if it would be a breach of professionalism to be seen without them. 'I'm here about Guthrie.' Bella didn't drop the tray but she slopped the tea by putting it down too quickly.

'Guthrie? My son, Guthrie?'

'Can we sit down?'

Bella sat as clumsily as she had set down the tray. Anna watched as she read the Harts' card and saw her draw her brows together in confusion.

'I don't understand – this says you work on probate for people. Has Guthrie come into money?'

Anna stalled, wanting to gauge how close this woman was to her son. 'How long has it been since you saw him?'

Bella flushed a darker red. 'We're very close – you don't have to be in each other's pockets. Look, just tell me what this is about. Why have you come here?' The doorbell jingled and Bella leaped up and rushed out but after a few seconds Anna heard the door bang shut and she returned. 'Are you looking for him, I mean, to trace him?' She stared at Anna. 'Is it a bequest from a grateful client? I wouldn't be surprised, he's so clever.'

Anna couldn't let this go on. 'No, Mrs Cromer, it isn't that. I'm afraid I have some unwelcome news for you. Your son Guthrie suffered from an aortic aneurysm of which he was probably unaware and a few days ago it ruptured.' Bella continued staring. 'He was alone at the time in his office and when he was found by the night security guard it was too late to save him.'

Bella blinked. 'He's dead? Are you telling me Guthrie is dead?'

'Yes, I'm so sorry.'

'Why aren't you the police? I thought they always send the police?'

'They asked us to find you.'

Bella's eyes narrowed and she thrust her face forward towards Anna. 'We were soul-mates,' she gasped, 'soul-mates! I loved him more than my own life.' Then, to Anna's alarm, she tipped back her head and began to wail, a sound so eerie and atavistic that Anna wondered if she would also start to tear her hair. She had never experienced such a reaction before and it was scary. Then, as suddenly as she had started she stopped, leaped up and pulled Anna to her feet. 'Come and look,' she ordered, 'you have to come and see.'

Anna found herself being hauled up the staircase by a strong arm and then thrust into a bedroom. 'Look!' Bella commanded, 'Look how he was loved! My boy, my baby, Gus!'

The paraphernalia of a teenage boy's bedroom was scattered about, the bed unmade. If the boy concerned had not now been a thirty-five year old banker, even if he was lying cold in the hospital morgue, there would have been nothing odd in the scene except for its lack of modern technology but none of the objects could be of interest to anyone older than an adolescent. There was a poster of Luke Skywalker on the wall, some cheap sporting trophies on a shelf together with a portable Radio/CD player and assorted stacks of books, magazines, DVDs and CD's. Boots and trainers were thrown in a corner and a hump of shirts and sweaters hung from a hook on the door.

Bella had stopped the clock. Whatever had caused the rift was so unacceptable to her that she must keep this room exactly as it had been, not even putting on clean sheets, so that normal life could, in fantasy, be resumed at a mythical future point. The Miss Havisham reaction to shock and loss. Perhaps this was how his room had been before he went away to university. Perhaps he had never come back.

Grief doesn't only come with a death. The room, the time capsule of Guthrie's childhood, was soaked in the yearning of a mother for her lost son. Maybe there had been some hasty words instantly regretted, some foolish ultimatum that had caused him to break all ties and for him, maybe, that had even been a relief, but for her – well, that would be a different matter. Anna turned to Bella who was standing in the centre of the room looking from one thing to another as if bewildered to find herself there and placed her hand gently on her arm. 'I am so very sorry,' she said, 'can I phone someone for you?'

Bella shook her head vehemently and demanded, 'Where is he? Where's his body?'

'In the Queen Elizabeth Hospital morgue.'

'You're going back to Birmingham – take me with you. You have to take me to my son.'

Anna didn't know what to do. Bella seemed so agitated and almost wild that Anna was a little afraid of the intensity of her reaction. 'Is there a friend I can contact?' she asked again, 'A neighbour?'

'I have to do things, don't I?' Bella now said helplessly, sagging at the thought. 'I'm his only family. His dad's dead – there's no-one else.' She grasped Anna's hand and repeated urgently, 'There's no-one else,' as though she must make Anna believe it.

'The hospital chaplain and the police will help you through the process and the Register Office people are very understanding.' She paused, noting that Bella's expression had changed to something fiercer and more guarded. 'Bella, let me phone someone for you. I can let the police know you've been located and informed.'

At this Bella became very still. 'Yes,' she said coldly, 'you do that. I'll make my own arrangements.' Anna was now hurried back down the stairs as quickly as she'd been dragged up and almost pushed out of the front door. She managed to say, 'You've got my card, call me anytime,' before the door was slammed behind her.

She walked slowly away feeling that she had handled things badly and yet she was unable to think of how she could have done it differently. She had had to pass on news of a death many times during the years she had worked for Harts and usually, if people were connected emotionally with the deceased, they received the information quietly, the seismic shocks reverberating through their hearts and minds with little showing on the surface. She remembered an elderly woman who had been told of the death of her estranged younger sister sitting very still for several moments and then offering Anna a cup of tea as a tear made its way down her cheek. She had allowed Anna to call a friend who arrived quickly and had then thanked Anna as she left as though she had brought her something good, not something devastating. People were often excessively polite and it was not a lack of feeling, Anna knew, but the opposite.

Bella's reaction, although extreme, was certainly understandable. It was clear that there had been a rupture between herself and Guthrie and Anna could only imagine with horror the pain that such a thing would bring. If Ellis were ever to cut away from her – she shook her head as if the very acknowledgement of such a possibility might make it happen. Faye, although far more provocative, would be unlikely to sever herself from her family if only because she would be cutting herself off from a source of household items and petty cash. She hadn't so much left home as taken it with her when she set up with the sweet-natured, long-suffering Jack in their little flat. But, having met Bella, Anna could see that her world-view and that of a banker might be poles apart and it would be easy to imagine a clash of personalities. Perhaps Guthrie despised his mother who seemed to be stuck in the seventies. Perhaps she had insulted him?

Making her way back across the bridge towards broad lawns knotted with picnickers, Anna found that she was unable to shake off the unsettled feelings that the awful shrine of a room and Bella's pain and hysteria had stirred up in her but she called Ted to tell him the mission was successful and she was on her way back.

'It's a messy business,' Ted growled, 'I thought it would be straightforward, but now they've delivered some boxes of his papers so you'd better look through those – why, heaven knows. Most likely too lazy to do it themselves so you've been dumped with the job.'

'Thanks, Ted,' Anna said sarcastically. 'Who's got his devices, then? I hope they're not bringing us those, too.' She was thinking of Steve who was always busy and didn't need that kind of time-consuming task to add to his support of the researchers, to say nothing of his government work.

'No, they picked his laptop up from his flat and they took his phone from the hospital.'

Anna slipped her phone back in her pocket and sat down on a bench to enjoy being outside for a moment and to let her emotions settle. She noticed a group of tots feeding the swans and squealing with mock-fear when the big birds moved towards them. She was just about to get up and go to the car park when her work phone trilled and she saw an unfamiliar number.

'Is this Mrs Ames from Harts Heir Hunters?' a breathy voice asked.

'Yes. Who is this, please?'

'You're sorting out Guthrie Cromer's death, aren't you? It's so awful – I'm just devastated and no-one told me – I only just found out when I phoned the office to talk to him. You can imagine the shock...'

'I'm sorry,' Anna interrupted, 'could you give me your name and explain your connection with him, please?' She was rummaging in her bag for the notebook and pen.

'Connection? I'm his fiancée! I'm Mel.'

'I didn't know he was engaged.'

'Look, we have to meet, we have to talk. I've been to the morgue but they won't let me see him.' There was a glottal sob. 'I'm the only one he's got, Mrs Ames, he has no-one else!' The very same words Bella had used – *he has no-one else.* Of course, Guthrie Cromer wouldn't be the first person to compartmentalise his life.

'But he has family,' Anna said, feeling that this was hardly confidential material.

'Oh no, he wouldn't want that evil bitch Bella to have anything to do with his body or get her hands on – anything else. He hated her. He hadn't seen her for years. There's only me. We adored each other.'

A difficult situation. Mel, as his fiancée, had no real legal connection to Guthrie whereas Anna had herself verified that Bella Cromer was his mother but her intuition hinted that there was more to this case than met the eye and on a basic human level she didn't want to coldly reject Mel who was obviously distraught. What could she lose by meeting her? She suggested Harts' lobby and Mel immediately demanded that it be first thing the next morning but Anna put her off until later in the day. She wanted a chance to go through the boxes of Guthrie's documents first and she had no idea how long that would take.

3

When she saw three large cardboard boxes, one on her desk, two on the floor, she was sure it would be a much bigger task than she had imagined given Guthrie's age and her assumption that he would have stored almost everything digitally, backed up by the Cloud. She sat down at her desk and pulled the lid off the top box which held out-of-date bank statements, receipts for purchases, warranties and so forth of no interest. She gratefully placed that box on the floor with a brief list of the contents written in black marker pen and lifted the next one.

Her spirits rose as she saw the Wasps rugby team fixture list on top. Clipped behind the list was a group photo of a team, from their strip a rugby team, so she turned it over and saw that the name of each player had been carefully printed in biro in the same formation and the group was headed 'Avon Avatars' with the date April, 2000. Guthrie Cromer was in the second row in the middle so she peered intently at his face not having seen a photo of him before. It was a pleasant, gleeful, almost triumphant face thickly topped with black hair. Perhaps he had just scored a try or something?

This box could be quickly dispensed with, too, she hoped, setting aside the photograph with a notation. Nevertheless, she should be thorough so she lifted out the brochures and membership information and so on until there was a small tower of papers next to the box. She had to stand up to delve deeper and saw that there were layers of travel documents: flyers, brochures, print-outs of airline tickets (who keeps this stuff?) and insurance papers. She put most of the material on the heap but extracted the recent e-tickets and the insurance papers just in case there was anything of interest. She then replaced the tottering pile in the box and set it back on the floor with a notation on the lid.

The third box was the heaviest so she didn't lift it up but slipped off the lid. Joy abounded when she saw that it contained only newspapers – the weekly Avon Courier. The most recent one was dated only two weeks ago so Guthrie must have had a subscription – she couldn't imagine him popping down every week to get one given the circumstances with his mother, and the oldest one, at the bottom of the pile, was from January this year so it seemed as though he got them regularly. Perhaps he followed a local rugby team and might even have played in it, like the Avatars. Maybe he recycled them after a certain time but in any case she certainly didn't need to go through these and she replaced the lid and wrote a label.

'Hey, how was Stratford?' Steve was standing in front of her with his bag slung across his chest and she glanced at the office clock. It was an hour to home time for her but he left early to pick up Alice which was one of the favours Ted granted him to keep him on board.

'Full of kids gratefully soaking up culture,' she said and he smiled.

'Right, I believe you. Hey, do you want to come to dinner at mine tonight? I've got a Norwegian friend who's at a conference at the university and wants to catch up. He'd love to meet you.'

Anna thought of Alice. 'He probably just wants to chat with you about climbing,' she said.

'No, he asked to meet you. It seems his mother's family were British and I think he wants some pointers about how to trace people.' Steve's steady smile held more than the words and she knew it. 'It will give Alice a chance to apologise and she might behave a bit better with another person there.'

'Oh, honestly Steve, let it go.'

'No, I can't. We have to get past this. She was very rude to you and I can't let her think she can behave that way. Per understands, I've explained to him. He's got kids of his own. Please, Anna.'

He was right and the truth was she often thought he wasn't firm enough with Alice so she could hardly object. 'Ok, then, I'll bring a bottle. You get off and I'll call dad and let him know I won't be dining *chez moi*.' It was as light a comment as she could make given the circumstances.

Ever since six-year old Alice had understood that Anna and Steve had a special relationship she had been jealous and rude towards Anna. There had been no problem when Faye was still at home because the little girl adored her and had been distracted by playing with her but once Faye had moved out it was as though the scales had dropped from Alice's eyes. Her uncle Steve had, as far as she knew, brought her up since she had no memory of the parents who were killed in a car accident when she was a baby and she was fiercely possessive of him as far as Anna was concerned since it was

Anna who was, the child surmised, the threat. It had been causing problems for months and no amount of patient explanation and reassurance had improved things.

In the most recent incident Alice had escalated from words to actions and had tried to physically push Anna away from their front door, yelling for her to go away when she had called round for a coffee. Steve had been shocked by the scene. Anna had been hurt but had, as usual, bitten her tongue. It was natural for children to go through jealous phases, of course, she told herself, but there seemed to be an intensity about Alice's hostility to her that was surely unusual?

She watched Steve weave his way through the office desks and waited for him to turn, as she knew he would, at the door and give her a wave and a smile. He was a lovely man and she sometimes thought of a time when they could make a home together, maybe marry. But while Ellis needed her and Alice was feeling so insecure it couldn't happen. She was in no hurry, anyway, if she was honest with herself, as one of their houses would have to be given up and she didn't want it to be hers.

Glancing at the clock, she remembered the papers on her desk from Guthrie's box and rather than check her emails (which always produced more work) she decided to look through them so that they could be put back in the box and the job completed. The flight schedules were mainly to New York, Washington and Brussels, repeated visits over the last two years. She wondered if he had a system where he kept paperwork for a fixed period, maybe for tax purposes, and then destroyed it. She turned those over and looked at the next bundle of papers stapled together. These were his worldwide travel insurance policies to include the United States which had been renewed annually. She glanced over the details and noted his address was a smart, city-centre apartment block and that he had said he had no declarable medical conditions. Poignant. Then she saw the entry for next-of-kin. The name was Mrs Bernice Sitwell, not Ms Bella Cromer. She stared at it. It was the same name for all five years. Guthrie was not married and never had been and had no siblings. Who was this woman? She picked up the office phone.

'Oh, bloody hell,' Ted said, 'just a minute, let me think. What date is it, this insurance policy?'

Anna checked again. 'They go back five years. How about asking Mary about it?' Mary Willis was the company solicitor.

'I'd rather not involve lawyers. But we can't just ignore it. Look, I'll phone the DI and see if it matters. Can you just see if you can find this woman while I do?'

'I was hoping to get off on time, Ted.' The least she could do was have a shower and try to make herself look decent for Steve's dinner.

'Yes, well, just a quick look, eh?'

She had no date of birth for Bernice, of course, but there was a mobile number on the insurance policy and she rang it. Not in service. She checked back and saw that the same number had been used for all the policies so did that mean that Guthrie had no contact with this woman and didn't know that her number was discontinued? In that case, if there was no close relationship, why did he give her as next-of-kin? Legally, he could give a close friend as next of kin, but it did complicate things potentially. Guthrie's estate was probably worth quite a bit of money and he may have wanted this woman to inherit, not his blood relative. The last insurance policy was only months ago and Mel was certainly not mentioned although Anna should check for her full name. She could, in theory, be Bernice Melanie Sitwell, couldn't she? Odd to have an out-of-date phone number, though.

She brought up the 192.com site to sift through electoral rolls but before she could enter Bernice Sitwell's name Ted was back on the phone. 'Just go home, Anna, I can't get hold of Malcolm and quite honestly I don't want to stir stuff up unless we have to.'

It was a dry evening but cool and Anna decided to wear the slinky jersey dress she had recently pounced on in a charity shop on the High Street. Usually she couldn't find anything since she was so short and, as Steve charitably said, curvy, a term she preferred to the obvious alternative. She had been with Joan who was taking a lunch break from the Nowack grocery and had found a pair of red sandals so their hunter-gatherer expedition had yielded trophies.

Steve opened the door and gave her a brief hug, the only physical intimacy they allowed themselves in Alice's presence, and she followed him into the kitchen which was far newer and smarter than hers but, she thought, nowhere near as comfortable. Good smells were coming from the stove so she placed the wine on the black granite worktop asking what he was cooking. 'Just simple.

Spinach and ricotta tortellini with baked salmon and roasted veggies.'

'Mm. Lovely. Pud?'

'People don't eat puddings any more, you know, Anna,' he said mock-seriously, flashing a smile.

'So what is it?'

'Specially for you – panna cotta and caramel sauce with strawberries.'

'Fantastic. I like those puds with no calories.'

'Ha.' He closed the oven door and stood up looking more serious. 'I'll go and get Alice. It might be embarrassing for her to do it with Per as a witness and they're in the living room at the moment.'

When he opened the door to the hall Anna heard Alice's high, clear voice explaining to Per that each worm is both a mummy and a daddy and she had seen them making babies in the glass wormery they had in school. Per was making suitably amazed noises in response. Anna composed her face into a welcoming smile as Steve came back into the kitchen holding the angelic-looking little girl by the hand. What an ethereal child she seemed to be with her silver hair floating around her milk-white face. Adults were always clucking over her and asking if she was anaemic but she had the disposition of a Hun.

'So,' Steve said gently to her, 'here's Anna. You know what you need to do.'

Alice stepped forward and smiled at Anna and her heart melted. It had been months since the child had looked at her so sweetly and Anna gladly responded by widening her own smile and nodding slightly. 'I'm sorry I was rude.' Alice whispered.

'Oh darling, I'm sure you didn't mean to be, but thank you.' She glanced up at Steve who was beaming with pleasure and relief and who then went to get Per so they could eat. Anna held out her hands to Alice, hoping for a reconciliation hug.

But as Steve left the room Alice's face turned to stone. She folded her arms and narrowed her eyes and put all the spite and contempt she could muster into the look she gave Anna. When she heard Steve and Per coming she ran towards them and called gaily, 'Can I help you, Steve? Can I get the plates out?'

Anna stood still, stunned. If Alice had put out her tongue it would have been childish and bearable but she hadn't, she had looked at Anna with pure venom. It had been bad enough when Alice was rude but it was understandable because children do go through these awkward phases, but this duplicity was almost frightening from someone so young. Had she planned it? Had she known that Steve would insist on an apology and this was her way of subverting it without making him upset with her?

They sat down at the table and the food was served and Anna managed to chat along so conversation seemed to flow easily. Alice herself contributed, sometimes turning to Anna for confirmation of a remark in what could be seen to be an endearing way. She even asked how Big B (the enormous hound formerly known as Bobble) was doing at Safe 'n' Sound. 'He's a very nice dog,' she told Per, 'but you sent him away, didn't you, Anna? He was too much for you.' Steve was obviously delighted. Alice hadn't been this sociable with Anna since Faye had left. Newly sensitised, Anna only saw the implied criticism in Alice's comment, but of course she smiled and responded agreeably because it was impossible to do otherwise.

While Steve supervised Alice's bath and bedtime, Per and Anna cleared up the kitchen and he quizzed her on the best ways to find out information about his family. She was happy to be able to help and relieved to push away the shock caused by Alice's poisonous look earlier. When Steve came down they chatted for a little while and then she left them to it knowing they would want to talk about climbing. It was a good excuse to leave; her face ached from the effort of being cheery.

She dragged herself up the road and back into her own house. With a bit of luck Ellis might be around and, sure enough, he was, but still deep into his homework with his headphones on barely looking away from his laptop to smile at her when she went to find him. She put an arm round his shoulders and kissed the top of his head anyway. His looks were changing now that he was fourteen. He had had such a close resemblance to Harry as a child that she had assumed that he would always look like him but now his copper hair had darkened and dulled into the soft brown of trodden autumn leaves and his eyebrows, which had been ochre were almost black. It made him look quite different and more striking since the gold-green lion's eyes (unmistakeably his father's) were still thickly fringed with black lashes. Faye had commented that he was trying to morph into Andy Murray and had overdone the dye job. Ellis himself was startled by the change in his appearance and the frisson of female interest it had ignited.

In the kitchen she poured herself a glass of wine and sat down at the much-abused oak table she and Harry had bought from the Treasure Trove junk shop on the High Street so long ago. Its surface was a palimpsest of decades of use. In this corner was the ink blot was from Ellis' calligraphy project when he was ten and the deep grooves on the side were from Big B's claws when he wasn't yet tall enough to simply scan the table top with all four feet on the ground. That brought back Alice's sly remark and she sighed as George bustled in from his shed in the garden.

'Hello Annie, back so soon?' He switched on the kettle.

'Oh, you know, they wanted to talk climbing. I'm ready for an early night, anyway.'

George pushed his glasses back up his nose. 'I don't like to boast, but I had a bit of a triumph, today.' Tufts of grizzled hair stood out around his balding head but it seemed the whiter his hair got the redder his face grew and the brighter his eyes shone. Faye had taken to calling him The Smurf. The breast pocket of his pilled flannel shirt bore three safety pins.

'That's great, sit down and tell me about it.' It turned out that one of the more prestigious poetry magazines had picked his poem on asylum seekers for second prize in a national competition and wanted him to read it at their annual shindig in London. He was gleaming with gratification but anxious to play it down. She hugged him. 'That's amazing, Dad, can you take Diane?'

'Um.' He deflated.

'What?'

'Says she's got nothing to wear which is true, probably, but she just doesn't fancy it, I suspect. You know how she is about what she calls "your versey stuff" at the best of times.'

'Take Joan. She'd love it.'

'I know you can't come – it's in the week.'

'Ask her. Jakub would give her the day off – there must be some perks to sleeping with the boss.'

Anna had met Joan during her first major investigation for Harts and they had become friends almost immediately. Joan's neat little house and garden was a home from home and Anna took delight in the contrast between the pensioner's rather conventional appearance and her often outrageously shocking observations and world-view. She was as near to a mother as Anna could imagine and she could write, too. Her poems were hard-hitting and passionate. It was a mystery to Anna that there had never been any romantic interest on either side between Joan and George but there it was. If anything, they were slightly prickly with each other, more like competitive siblings than friends.

'I'll phone her tomorrow. So, how's things with you?'

Anna wrinkled her nose. 'Ok – not brilliant, but I don't want to go on about it right now.'

George sipped his tea, probably waiting to see if she would change her mind and launch into off-loading whatever was bothering her but when she stayed silent, he said, 'I've got something for you since you've become interested in Travellers' lives. I popped into the library today and found a few books, I mean autobiographies, not academic stuff. I've had a look online and there are quite a few more if you're interested.'

'Thanks, Dad.' It would be a relief to think about something more exotic and interesting than being rejected by a jealous child. 'Have you dipped into any of them?'

He pulled a tissue out of his back pocket and blew his nose. The pollen was very bad. 'As a matter of fact I have. You know they call their caravans trailers, well, when someone dies they really do burn their trailer, or at least they used to until the sixties, I think, but that's not all. Before they set it alight the men of the family remove anything that won't burn and go off into the woods or somewhere secret to bury it. Often it's valuable Crown Derby or Royal Worcester china or expensive glass but it all goes. In one account I read, the husband of the woman who died walked away from their home with absolutely nothing. They all stay, the extended family who've come from miles around, they stay until the trailer is just ashes and they don't sleep. Their friends from other families take it in turns to sit up with them and drink tea. Sometimes it's a couple of days or more.'

Anna remembered how she had felt when Harry died and how bizarre her behaviour must have appeared to others although in her case it wasn't getting rid of stuff, it was obsessively gathering together everything she had left of him. She had covered the long wall in their bedroom which every scrap of paper, photographs, even strands of hair that she could find, often crazily working through the night. 'I wonder what they do now that the trailers are metal.'

'I don't know.' George got up and made himself a snack of cheese, crackers and grapes. 'It's the Appleby Horse Fair soon – it's not far from Penrith – and it's where a lot of the families get together now that they're not travelling so much, I saw a documentary about it on tv a couple of years ago. Why don't you go? By then you might have some more names to ask about and besides, it would be fun, wouldn't it? You could do with a change of scene.'

'Yes, I could try to trace some cousins of Tom's, grandchildren of Chip and Stanley, that's a great idea. I'll send for their birth and marriage certificates. Then I really would have some names to work with. What's with the pins?' She pointed to his shirt pocket.

'I wanted to remember a quotation about ocelots.' She let it go.

By the time they'd talked it through and George had brought her the small pile of books to take up to her bedside table she was feeling better. Now she had calmed down she could see that Alice, intelligent and pro-active as she was, was simply trying out a new strategy to outwit her foe. Anna decided that it would be a good idea for her to arrange to spend some time alone with the girl since she couldn't use the new ploy when it was just the two of them. She would take her out to Kimi's farm to see the glamorous Briony who was the child's idol since she had been a bridesmaid at her wedding. It would look odd for her to say no, given that she was supposed to be friends with Anna again and she genuinely loved going there. There would be plenty of time for Anna to have a talk with her, or maybe there wouldn't even be the need for it if the visit went well. There was something Anna wanted to ask Kimi, too, while she was there.

4

Mel was waiting for Anna when she arrived for work. She sat perched on the visitor banquette like a flamingo with her long, thin legs and coral wrap-around coat. Josie hardly had time to nod Anna in her direction before she was up and tapping the short distance across the atrium. 'Oh please,' she cried, 'please tell me you're Mrs Ames! I've been here ages!'

'You signed in five minutes ago,' Josie said acidly. 'Hardly ages.'

'Please call me Anna.' She led the woman back towards the banquette, glad of the strict rule about members of the public not being allowed in the upstairs offices.

'Is there somewhere private we can talk?' Mel begged. Did she have a dusting of talc on her face to make it look that pale, Anna wondered, as she opened a small interview room leaving the door ajar. Whatever it was, it didn't look natural, but set against scarlet lipstick, what would? Maybe she was going for a punk look although her clothes certainly didn't support that theory. She was so tense it was as though she might screech off at any minute if there was a sudden shock.

As soon as they were seated Mel thrust out her left hand. 'Look!' she urged, 'my engagement ring. He only ever wanted the best for me.' A large sparkling crystal perched unsteadily on her third finger but for all Anna knew it could have been glass. She covered her mouth with the hand making large, tragic eyes.

'Could you tell me your full name?' If it was Bernice Melanie Sitwell the whole problem of Guthrie's next-of-kin could be passed to the lawyers to sort out.

'Melanie Fisher. Do you want me to write it down for you?'

'I think I can remember,' Anna smiled, 'but just confirm the way you spell Fisher, please?' Mel did. 'I'm sorry for your loss but I don't see how I can help you, Melanie.'

Pink spots appeared on Melanie's cheek bones and her eyes seemed to pop out. 'What? Of course you can. I'm his next-of-kin, aren't I? You can tell his lawyer or the police or anyone. Look,' she opened her blush-coloured tote, 'I've written down my contact details for you.' She pushed a piece of card towards Anna.

Anna took the card out of courtesy and stood up. 'As I said before on the phone, Guthrie has family, a mother, who is his next of kin. The authorities will be working with her.'

Mel actually grabbed Anna's arm pinching it quite tightly. 'No! I told you he wouldn't want that! She hurt him so badly!'

Anna looked pointedly at Mel's hand on her arm and Mel let go. 'Nevertheless, in the absence of a will stating otherwise and any spouse or child, his mother is the legal beneficiary.'

Mel stared at her, rage now blotching her chalky face. 'You haven't heard the end of this,' she spat, 'I'm taking this to the top!' Then she was out of the door, almost knocking Anna sideways, and could be seen pushing her way out through the glass doors muttering.

'Charming,' Josie observed. 'Nutter?'

'I don't know,' Anna said, watching Mel run down the outside steps, 'but I'm glad she's gone. A bit intense, anyway.' Poor Guthrie, having two highly-charged and very possessive women in his life, unless, of course, he liked it that way which apparently some people did. In any case, she was no nearer to finding Bernice Sitwell.

'So when's the big day?' The pale oak surround of the reception desk framed Josie's eager pose, breasts forward, eyes shining.

'What?'

'You and Steve! Don't deny it.'

'Oh, not for a while, if it happens.'

'Why?'

Anna didn't want to tell Josie it wasn't any business of hers but she didn't want to discuss it all either. Suzy was her only confidante at work and she knew how to be discreet.

'Oh, you know, just stuff. Look, I'd better go, I've got stacks to do.'

The office was crackling with activity when she walked in and Suzy only gave a brief wave before getting back to her screen so Anna settled in to her desk and brought up the search website. She noticed that the boxes had gone but then saw them piled up in a stack by the coat tree so she would need to sort that out with Ted. Her work mobile rang.

'Oh Anna, I'm so sorry, so sorry, I was just upset! I didn't mean to be rude…'

'Melanie?'

'You just have to believe me, I'm the only person he loved. He would be devastated to know that I'll be cut out by that horrible woman! She won't even let me arrange his funeral, I know she won't!'

'Maybe you can talk to her?'

'What? I've never met her, why would I? He hated her, I told you. Please, please believe me!'

Anna had had enough. 'Melanie, it is completely immaterial whether I believe that Guthrie hated his mother or not, just as it is irrelevant how much he loved you. There is no will and his mother is his next-of-kin. Nothing you can do or say would make any difference.' A thought struck Anna. 'You're not pregnant, are you?' The call was cut dead.

She brought up the Electoral Registers on 192.com (hoping that Bernice Sitwell hadn't opted out) and found three people of that name. One in Southampton, one in Berwick-on-Tweed and one registered on the same street in Stratford-on-Avon as Bella Cromer. 'Hey,' Anna said out loud, 'what's going on here?'

It didn't take long to find out from the Indexes that Bernice was Bella's sister who had married Richard Sitwell when she was twenty and he was four years older. Guthrie's aunt. There were now three women who might think they had claims on Guthrie's estate and only one of them could be easily discounted, it seemed, which was Mel. Anna picked up the phone and called Ted but it seemed he was away somewhere for a couple of days so she decided to get on with her other work. After all, it was perfectly natural that Guthrie would turn to his aunt after a row with his mother, especially if he knew her well since he had grown up within a short distance of her. It was above her pay grade, she felt, to contact the police to see if Melanie Fisher had left any revealing messages on Guthrie's mobile so she put a note to Ted in the internal mail since he always read pieces of paper before checking his emails.

It was a beautiful gold and green evening when she and Alice set off for the farm where Kimi and Briony lived, which was lucky as Anna planned to get Kimi to walk with her across the fields and through the woods so she could enjoy being out of the city. Steve had, as part of the plan, not been able to go with them he'd explained to his niece, as he'd promised Ellis they would watch football on Steve's big-screen tv. To add to the allure for Alice, Briony had told Anna that a rich colleague had given her a box of clothes that her own daughter had grown out but which should fit the little girl.

The minute the child was belted in she had plugged in her head-set and bent her head to the tablet screen but that was ok. Anna wasn't sorry to drive without having to make difficult conversation; it had been a tiring day what with one thing and another. At least Melanie Fisher had been dealt with.

Kimi was in the yard when they arrived with a saddle over her arm. She looked sharply at Anna as she got out of the car. 'Why aren't you wearing your jodhpurs? You can't ride dressed like that!'

'Actually, Kimi, I was hoping we could go for a walk instead. Do you mind?'

'Hi kid, she's inside. Go ahead.' Alice ran off. She turned back to the tack room and Anna followed her. 'I can't believe you'd rather walk than ride – I was looking forward to it.'

'I don't think we'd have time, really.' Anna said feebly, 'I have to get Alice back pretty early as it's a school night. Sorry.'

'Well, in that case,' Kimi said, dropping the saddle over a pole, 'let's go up to the wood – I think I saw smoke coming from there last night and I don't want squatters. I can check it out.'

The evening sun gilded the hedges and striped the fields with dagger shadows. Anna breathed deeply as she walked, narrowing her eyes against the glare of the western horizon and inhaling the sweetness of the breeze.

'Briony is really getting on my tits,' said Kimi.

They had been married for less than three months but Anna wasn't surprised. The two women had strong, uncompromising personalities and now the period of mutual deception, as someone had once called courtship, was over there were bound to be disputes until they sorted out which battles to fight and which to step around. 'Why is that?' she asked, trying to hold on to the scene before her and not give Kimi too much of her attention.

'I know she's ambitious but she doesn't have to take every damn conference she's asked to, does she? She told me today that she's off to Brussels next week for four days! Some-one else has dropped out, some senior partner, and she's actually thrilled to be invited. No word to me, no discussion, just, oh, by the way... '

'Mm,' murmured Anna, noticing how prettily the sprays of red campion were set off against the lime-green hawthorn hedge. Is it, she wondered, that observing nature forms our ideals of beauty or that nature conforms to some innate template? Kimi was not the person to philosophise with so she shelved the speculation.

Both Briony and Kimi had demanding jobs but Kimi worked as financial director for her family's company so pretty much had things the way she wanted them. Briony had worked her way up to being a criminal lawyer by sheer ability and dedication which was an even more remarkable achievement given that she had been in prison herself not that long ago. Kimi didn't like her family, it was true, and with good reason but she had never had to struggle like Briony had.

'I never go anywhere,' Kimi said irritably, kicking a clod of earth from one of her horse's hooves off the path. Anna focused her attention. This was the perfect opening for what she wanted to ask.

'How do you fancy Appleby Horse Fair, then, next weekend? Just you and me?' As she began to explain Kimi stopped walking and turned to face her, the springing coils of her hair lit up into a fiery crown by the setting sun behind. 'So,' Anna finished, 'we could spend a couple of nights up there if you like. I can look into accommodation.'

'I didn't know that happened,' Kimi said, 'it sounds fantastic. Do they really buy and sell the horses?'

'Well, yes. The main thing is social, I suppose, a chance for people to catch up with each other and have some fun, but the horse dealing is a big part of it.'

'What would they be?'

'Well, different kinds of Travellers, I expect. Romanies, Irish, New-age, I don't know. We'll find out.'

'No!' Kimi snapped, 'What breed of horses?'

Anna laughed. 'What was I thinking? I don't know, Kimi, the only kind I've seen in photographs and on the television are brown and white or black and white.'

'Skewbalds and piebalds,' Kimi said thoughtfully, 'what they call paint horses in America. The Spanish took them over there and the Native Americans loved them. They're strong. Cobs, really, the perfect breed for all-round work and good with families.'

They walked on. 'I'll need to be wandering about talking to people trying to find out what I can about the Smith family who I'm trying to find,' Anna said, 'but you'd be ok with that?'

'This is great,' Kimi said as they entered the wood, 'one in the eye to Bri and a weekend looking at horses. Count me in and don't worry about the accommodation, I'll fix something up for us and I'll drive.'

In the farm's living room Alice was modelling another outfit. Clothes were dumped on the floor and Briony was lounging on the couch sipping a large glass of wine. As they went in she was instructing, 'No, darling, that isn't your colour, it's too garish. Put it on the no pile.' Alice looked pink and sweaty with all the excitement and decisions.

'How are you doing?' Anna asked, glancing at her watch.

'Almost done,' Briony said, understanding the situation. 'Just one more. Look, darling, there's that pale blue dress with the flounced sleeves. It's very you. Pop it on and we'll call it a day. The others are too big for you just yet.' She unfolded herself from the couch and raised her glass to Kimi and Anna. Kimi nodded but Anna shook her head. 'I'll find a bag for the things she wants,' she said, drifting elegantly out to the kitchen.

'I've got heaps,' Alice sighed, her fine hair sticking to her forehead with her exertions. 'I'm wearing this for Daisy's party and this one for when our class goes to the Safari park.'

'That's great – they're very nice, but we'll need to get off soon. I promised Steve to get you back by eight.' The fact that Alice didn't make a fuss proved how spent she was.

Anna planned to stop on the way back by a farm gate which gave a calming view over the valley and have a word with Alice about how happy it made Steve that they were now friends (she had decided to just ignore the nasty look she'd been given) but when they got to the place and she glanced in the rear view mirror, Alice was fast asleep.

5

Ted was still away, Josie said, and may be gone for a further day so Anna decided to take advantage of his absence and visit the mysterious Bernice Sitwell, Bella's sister and Guthrie's designated next-of-kin.

It was quite possible that Ted would have preferred to hand the whole thing over to someone else, although Guthrie's estate was substantial and the finder's fee would be very acceptable. That would be Anna's motivation, if asked, but Harts' involvement to this level was questionable and she knew it. Bella Cromer's name was on Guthrie's birth certificate, after all, so there was no doubt that she was his next-of-kin. The fact that Guthrie had cited Bernice was almost certainly because of the rift between himself and his mother and would have little legal standing when it came to probate. She quietened her conscience by checking her To Do list and scrolling through her emails with half an eye and coming to the conclusion that another visit to Stratford would be the best use of her time. It was a glorious day of blue skies and cute little alto-cumulus clouds scudding along – far too nice to be in the office.

An hour later Anna drove into the street where both the sisters lived and parked outside the Sitwells' house feeling relieved that she had parked in town before so that Bella, if she was around, would not recognise the car. The difference between this house and Bella's was instantly obvious despite the architecture being almost exactly the same. Where the outside of Bella's house at the other end of the street was decked out with an eclectic confusion of what Anna could only think of as 'stuff', this house was neatly arranged with mangers of scarlet pelargoniums nestling under the windows. The tiny front garden was planted with a stylish palette of evergreen shrubs edged with slate chips – conventional but pleasing. Someone had a good eye. At one side of the house ran the entry or access to the back for that row of houses so Anna guessed that the wheelie bins would be up there, out of sight. Was the front step scrubbed? Anna found her eyebrows had shot up at the thought.

What would she say to Guthrie's aunt to justify her visit? The interview with Bella Cromer which she had thought would be straightforward, if emotional, had ended in a bizarre and hysterical scene. Anna had imagined that Bernice and Richard's place might have been Guthrie's cosier alternative home where maternal histrionics could be avoided and comfort sought and, looking at it now, that might well be true but, if it was, they must be in a state of shock and grief. She thought about leaving and turned back to the car but was halted by the sight of a cavalcade hurtling towards her down the pavement.

A muddle of dogs of assorted sizes was surging beside a woman in a motorised wheelchair who was calling instructions to a couple of teenagers jogging to keep up. 'Jude, tell your mum that we've watered the veg but she needs to wash those bloody green-fly off the roses. Detergent.' She stopped by Anna. 'Thanks so much, sweethearts, you've been brilliant, any time you can spare a few minutes, I'm so grateful.' The teenagers, one male, one female, beamed and the girl bent forward and kissed the woman in the chair at which the dogs went mad. The woman turned to Anna. 'Hello, darling, let's go round the back, they're in the greenhouse.'

Anna dumbly followed remembering how Bella had also assumed that she was someone she was not but nevertheless allowed herself to be swept along out of guilty curiosity. There was an access gate to the garden out of the alleyway and someone had rigged it up to be weighted and balanced so that the woman in the chair (Bernice?) only had to push it to go through. The dogs dashed in. Anna followed wondering what had happened to Bernice that she needed the chair.

'Richard? Are you in the kitchen? Are you making tea?' She pointed to a bench for Anna and positioned the wheelchair opposite. 'You must be new, I haven't seen you,' she said, 'but it's kind of you to collect the cuttings. There's more than I'd planned so you don't have to take them all, but they usually sell well.'

'Do you want it out there?' Richard, presumably, called.

'Yes, bring it out, we've got a visitor.' She turned to Anna. 'I've been at the allotment, it's going mad with this weather but Paula's kids are a great help. Do you know Paula? Hi, I'm Bernice, of course.' Anna got back up to shake her hand but Bernice leaned forward and enfolded her in a hot embrace. No wonder Guthrie would have felt closer to his aunt than his mother. She was warmth and generosity personified whereas Bella, for all her declarations of peace and love, was an uncomfortable mix of spikiness and gush.

But Anna was becoming uneasy because Bernice's cheery demeanour could mean that she didn't know that Guthrie was dead and Anna was wishing she was anywhere else at this moment. 'Hi, I'm Anna Ames. Um, I'm not who you think I am, Bernice.'

'You're not from the Stroke Association?'

'No. Sorry.' So, that's what it was.

Bernice suddenly burst out laughing. 'Richard? I think I've kidnapped a passing stranger!'

A man appeared in the kitchen doorway balancing a tray with three mugs and a sugar bowl on it. He nodded to Anna. 'Well, you can have a cup of tea while you're here,' he said quietly. Bernice chirruped to the dogs. Could she pretend that was what had happened and leave, Anna wondered, but what if in the future she had to meet this couple again?

She took the mug offered to her, shaking her head over the sugar, and said, 'I wasn't outside your house by accident, Mrs Sitwell, I had come to see you.' She decided not to present her card at this point since that had not been a great move before. 'I'm sorry to say, I have distressing news to give you unless you already have been told by your sister.'

Both Richard and Bernice stiffened. 'Bella?' Bernice asked, all jollity gone from her voice, 'what do you mean?'

'Who are you?' Richard demanded, peering at her through thick glasses and bobbing his head down in a curious, tortoise-like movement.

Anna introduced herself and saw that, like Bella, they were confused as well they might be. She had to say it. 'I'm here about your nephew, Guthrie.'

Richard sat down as though his legs had given way and when Bernice spoke, her voice was almost inaudible. 'What?' she said, 'What do you know about Guthrie?'

'I'm very sorry to tell you that he recently died. He had a ruptured aortic aneurism which he probably knew nothing about.'

A profound silence greeted this. Bernice was staring into space and gripping the arms of her wheelchair with white knuckles while Richard's head was sunk deep on his chest. Richard was the first to speak. 'Where did he die?'

'In his office. He was working late and was alone which was why no-one was available to help him – I mean, to call an ambulance.' Thinking that the idea that he could have been saved was unbearable, she added lamely, 'It may not have helped, though.'

'No,' Richard said urgently, 'I mean what country was he in? Where in the world was he?'

Anna couldn't stop a gasp. Now, both of them were staring at her with white, slack faces, waiting for her answer. 'He was in Birmingham. He was at his office in the city centre.'

Then Bernice screamed and it was like the scream of a seagull, high and sharp and went on and on as though she had gone mad. Richard stepped towards Anna and she rose from her bench, alarmed at the expression on his face. 'Go away,' he yelled, 'go away and never come back!' He was pulling and pushing her, his fingers biting into the soft flesh of her under-arm as she was thrust through the door to the alley and stumbled towards her car.

Her hands were shaking as she tried to get the key into the lock and as soon as she was inside she took deep breaths and drove only a short way away until she could stop and try to take in what had just happened.

She was looking at a small suburban park but seeing nothing as she gripped the wheel and stared ahead. Certainly, Bella had not told her sister, who lived yards away, about the death of her son so the rift, whatever it had been, must have included them and it must have been a very serious quarrel since it must have lasted for many years if Bernice and Richard didn't even know that Guthrie was living and working only forty miles away. But how could they not have known? If Guthrie used Bernice as next-of-kin, he must have, at the very least, preferred her to his mother so why would he not have kept in touch?

But Anna was not just puzzled, she was upset. Bernice had struck her as a kind and warm person (Richard, maybe not so much) and she had been cut deep by Anna's announcement. And why, after all, had she gone? Just to follow up an intriguing loose end was the truth and now two perfectly decent people's lives were shattered. She sighed, started the engine and drove back to Harts feeling chastened and unsettled.

But, as the miles spun past she knew that the truth was that this information did need to be followed up. She sighed but as she turned off the motorway to drive into central Birmingham she thought instead of the jobs that waited for her at Harts and how she would describe this episode to Ted and whether Steve would be free for lunch. She decided to dwell on the last possibility and smiled in anticipation. That kept her happy until the traffic slowed and her thoughts swerved to the upcoming weekend and the trip to Appleby.

There had been a flurry of phone calls and emails and Kimi had, of course, taken over organising the whole thing which was fine with Anna. They would drive up to Cumbria early on Saturday morning and spend the bulk of Saturday and Sunday at Appleby before driving back. Anna had hoped to be there longer but the reality was that neither of them could spare the time from work. Anna could just imagine what Ted would say if she asked for time off from the day job to pursue her own private research. It was rather nice to take a back seat and let Kimi get on with arrangements since Anna's interest was only in trying to glean information while they were there. But the more she read of the books written by Travellers that George had borrowed for her from the library, the more she thought that it wouldn't be easy. A stranger, a *gorgia*, going in and asking questions, possibly questions about sensitive matters, how would that come across? All she could do was try.

But there were other avenues for gleaning information that she had discovered through the magic of the internet like *The Travellers' Times*, an online magazine, and a charity, *Friends, Families and Travellers* as well as a section on *Rootschat* for Travelling People under *Special Interests* where she could place a discreet message, which she did. Loretta and Teller's marriage certificate had arrived and she read with interest that his occupation was described as Fairground Entertainer. Appleby may be a waste of time for her research for Elizabeth but still she found she still wanted to go very much and in her case it had nothing to do with horses.

Josie was simmering with indignation when she walked into the lobby at Harts. 'It's not my job to deal with nut-cases,' she announced to Anna the minute she got through the door. 'You'll have to do something about her.' It turned out that Mel had paid another visit and had been, Josie said, abusive and threatening when she had been told that Anna wasn't in. Harts didn't have security as it would so rarely be needed so this was a nuisance.

'Ok, I'll contact her and tell her she's banned and that you'll have to call the police if she so much as sets foot inside the door uninvited.'

'And I will!'

'You definitely should but let's hope she gets the message.'

At her work computer Anna found that Melanie had sent six emails over the weekend and, when she checked, twenty five text messages on her work phone. Sighing, she started a log saving the emails and messages from Mel as evidence if they needed to charge her with harassment or some such thing. She felt more sorry for Guthrie than ever assuming none of the weird female behaviour which seemed to dog him was welcome although it might be that he had become used to it through a childhood over-heated by dramas and he might have found female adulation to the point of obsession normal so Mel would have been a fit. If not, the cheeriness of his aunt must have been a relief. She wrote to Mel telling her that there must be no more visits or phone messages or action would be taken and copied this email into the file.

The good news was that Steve was available for lunch and not just a quick sandwich at the café on the quay but a full hour. They walked quickly along the tow-path down to Brindley Place and the Café Rouge enjoying the fresh breeze and the sun on their faces. When they were seated and had ordered she was about to relay to him the encounters with Guthrie Cromer's family when he leaned forward and said, 'Something a bit odd has happened.'

'Go on, then.'

The waiter appeared and took their order but then Steve continued, 'You know the accident that my sister and her husband were in – the one that orphaned poor little Alice?' Anna nodded. 'Well, Jen's husband, Alice's dad, had a sister, Julie, who married and went to live in Birkenhead.'

'Ok.' Anna had had a long morning and was ready for some soup and crusty bread. Her stomach growled. She looked over Steve's shoulder hopefully.

'Well, I had an email from her this morning asking if she and Simon, her husband, could come and visit. They asked if they could see Alice and could I book a lunch out for everyone and they would pay.'

'Nice,' Anna said.

'Well, of course, I said I'd put on lunch and they were very welcome and suggested some dates.'

'Ok,' Anna said, wondering if she would be asked to go and hoping not.

'They said they want to talk to me about something important.' Steve sat back in his chair and ran his fingers through his hair giving a little root massage for good measure much like Suzy did when she wanted to look wanton. But in Steve's case, Anna knew it was a gesture implying frustration.

'So what's the problem?'

'It's just that Julie hasn't been in touch with me since the funerals, or with mum and dad. It upset us all a little at the time but we thought she maybe wanted to move on and not be reminded of the tragedy. She got married a year later and left the area.'

They discussed possible reasons for the visit and then their food arrived and as Anna trowelled butter on to her crusty roll she briefly reflected on yet another breakdown in family communication. Tom Budas' parents seemed on both sides to have split away from their families and then there was Guthrie Cromer having nothing to do with his mother and, possibly, his aunt. Such fractures held a painful fascination for her. Her own mother, Lena, was dead now but even so, the rejection she had experienced from her had stayed with her like a small but deep open wound that refused to scab. She choked a little on her bread.

'Ok?' Steve asked, getting ready to thump her back.

'Mm. Fine. Do you want me to come?'

'To the lunch? Better not, I'll just see what they have to say. Anyway,' Steve went on smiling at her, 'you might have run away with the raggle-taggle gypsies, oh, by that time.'

'Mm. I somehow can't see myself skinning rabbits over an open fire although sadly they seem not to be allowed to travel and live freely as they want much anymore.'

'Pud? You deserve it.'

And that was another nice thing about having lunch with Steve.

6

Kimi phoned at six on Saturday morning to say she was outside. Anna had packed a small bag the night before, tucking her tablet into it in lieu of the bulkier laptop, and had woken half an hour earlier so she had time for a quick wash and toast and coffee. She felt a little groggy but the minute she stepped out of the front door she was fully awake, breathing in the clean, fresh air sparkling with diamond dust. It was going to be a fine day.

Kimi was driving her Range Rover which Anna had expected her to do. What was unexpected was that behind the four-wheel drive was a horse box. She climbed in to the passenger seat and buckled her belt.

'Are you dropping that off somewhere?' she asked tipping her head backwards.

'No. Why?' Kimi was wearing a white T shirt and jeans, both freshly laundered, and had therefore made an effort which Anna appreciated. Her arms on the steering wheel were muscular and deeply tanned and Anna didn't need to check to know she'd be wearing her snub-nosed, all-weather work boots. There was something of the legendary Amazon about Kimi – something untamed and untameable which both amused and alarmed Anna but she knew from past experience that if you needed someone by your side in a crisis (as long as it wasn't an emotional one) Kimi would be there ready to fight to the end.

'What's it for, then? It is a horse-box, isn't it? I'm not hallucinating.'

Kimi glanced at her as she negotiated out of the side road and on to the main drag. 'It's for us, of course! It's where we're going to sleep.'

'Your idea of accommodation is to spend the night in that?'

'Yes! It's perfect, I've done it loads of times.' She registered Anna's glowering lack of enthusiasm. 'I've put in a bale of straw and a gallon jug of water. What more do you want?'

Anna stared out of the window at the passing traffic. 'A loo?'

'Oh, don't worry about that,' Kimi said airily, 'we're going to be in a field and there's a hedge.' After a few miles of silence, she added, rather whimsically for Kimi, 'It's like the Gypsies, isn't it, sleeping under the stars and cooking over a fire? We'll be in tune with things.'

'I doubt very much that Gypsies sleep on straw,' Anna said, trying not to sound as sour as she felt (she had assumed a four-star country hotel), 'and I don't think we'll be allowed to make a fire. Where is this field anyway?'

'Oh, friend of a friend. He keeps Shire horses near to Appleby and says we can use a field of his by a stream so we'll have washing water, too.' She glanced at Anna, clearly feeling that the next item would swing the decision in her favour. 'You won't have to gather sticks and all that, I've got a camp-stove, too.'

'Right,' Anna said grimly, 'bring it on, but we should maybe pick up a bottle of whisky or something on the way to take the edge off the joy of it all.'

Kimi laughed. 'You are such a townie,' she said. 'It'll be fun!'

It was motorway for hours and they chatted a little but mostly listened to music since Kimi had no need for constant conversation and Anna was mulling over what had happened the previous evening.

Around seven Faye had turned up and begged the remains of the chicken and apricot tagine George had made (and which he had hoped would do him and Ellis for Saturday dinner) and then sat moodily at the kitchen table twisting her hair in her fingers, sipping tea. Anna had been cleaning up the kitchen and stacking the dishwasher. She would have liked to pop down to see Steve for an hour or two but felt she couldn't leave her daughter in this unusually morose state.

She brought her mug of coffee to the table and sat down. 'Pops has made a carrot cake, do you want some?'

'You know I hate carrot cake.'

Anna noted that Faye's usually perfect creamy skin was now breaking out on her forehead in tiny pimples and that her hair, such a point of vanity with her and rightfully so in her mother's opinion, was pulled back in a greasy ponytail.

'So,' Anna tried, 'is Jack coming along later?'

Faye groaned and put her head down on the table. 'What night is this?' she demanded of the scarred surface. She pulled herself abruptly upright and went on, 'And what is every other sane young person in the world out doing?'

Anna sipped her coffee knowing a rhetorical question when she heard one. She was beginning to guess the source of Faye's mood.

'Partying!' Faye went on, 'Or at least out for a drink, clubbing, something FUN after a long hard week at work. Where am I? Bloody nowhere doing nothing! Where is Jack? Working, he's working!'

'Well, if he's been asked to do overtime,' Anna put in reasonably.

Faye jumped up. 'He's not doing overtime, Mum! He's doing a second job, that's what he's doing!' She slumped down again. 'Welcome to the world of young professionals, twenty-first century.'

'I didn't realise things were so bad for you,' Anna said. 'I thought you'd be ok on two wages. Has something happened?'

Faye had put her elbows on the table and cupped her chin in her hands. 'We're supposed to be saving the deposit for a house,' she said. 'Fat chance. It's not easy now like it was for you and dad, you know.'

'Mm,' Anna murmured.

She had thought of those early years before the children were born when she and Harry were both working and yes, it was true, that they had been able to buy this house, quite a large house, on what they earned but there were a couple of things Faye didn't know. One of them was that the house had been almost derelict. It had been neglected for years and was in an area which at that time was considered too close to the city centre to be desirable. Over the years they had put in central heating, new floors, new windows, a new roof and re-wired throughout. Harry had done much of the work himself with a friend who was also doing up an old property and Anna had helped where she could and decorated each room in turn as it became habitable. It had taken every penny of hard-saved cash and every hour of their spare time for years. Faye wouldn't remember that there had been no holidays and that most of their toys and bikes came from car boot or jumble sales.

The other thing Faye didn't know, which was probably as important as the relatively low price of the house, was that Harry's parents and George had given them the deposit. Without that they would never have been able to save the amount needed. Nevertheless, it was true, it was very hard for young people now. 'I didn't know you and Jack were thinking of buying,' she said.

'We're just treading water renting, and the place is a dump.'

'You've made it look so much brighter and more colourful, love.'

'It's still a dump.'

And really, Anna couldn't disagree.

At eight o'clock Kimi slowed and turned off into a service station on the M6 in Cheshire.

'Coffee?'

Anna nodded, mentally adding a chocolate croissant.

Even so, by the time they got to Penrith Anna persuaded Kimi to pull into the large car park of a garage so they could grab a sandwich. It was ten o'clock so they'd made good time and Kimi could relax for a few minutes. The reason they'd made good time was that, despite the extra weight of the trailer, Kimi drove like a demon and Anna was beginning to feel the strain of automatically jamming her right foot down on the car mat every time Kimi roared round a truck.

'I hadn't expected you to be a nervous passenger,' Kimi commented as they sat down at a tiny chrome table. She bit into a wrap, 'You're almost as bad as Briony. I could hear you gritting your teeth.'

'I didn't say a word.'

'You didn't have to. So,' she wiped her mouth, 'what's the plan?'

'I honestly don't have one,' Anna said. 'It's supposed to be really crowded in Appleby itself when they bring the horses down to the river and maybe even a bit dangerous but I know the campsites are a little way out of the town, well the village, and I wondered about going up there and seeing if there's anyone I can talk to. I don't really have any idea of what to expect except the pictures I've seen of the kids riding the horses in the river.'

'We don't need to stick together, though, do we?' Kimi said candidly. 'I'm interested in the horses and you want to find some people and we don't have all that much time.'

'No, ok. Let's just do a quick walk round and line up some possible meeting places so that we'll know where to head for when we want to get back together. You'll have to unhitch that thing, won't you? We can't take that into the village, there'll be nowhere to park it, I imagine.'

'No need,' Kimi said happily, 'the field we'll be in is only a mile away – we can walk down and back.' She stood up. 'Come on, time's wasting.'

It was a relief to leave the motorway and move at a different pace through the lanes towards Appleby. As they rose up into the hills, Anna gazed out of the window at the fields speckled with buttercups where cows grazed, hock deep in lush grass, and glossy horses stood nose to tail flicking flies from each other's faces, while hawks hung above them in a sky dappled with sudsy clouds. Broad, shallow rivers with gravelly beaches meandered through the valleys and the hedges they passed were studded with dog roses and elderflower. Where the earth was exposed in fields freshly ploughed, it was the colour of paprika. Kimi drove, of necessity, more slowly and they both turned their heads to left and right to inhale it all.

They got to the farm with no trouble, Kimi phoned the owner from the car and within minutes they had their instructions and were coasting down a narrow lane. Anna jumped out and swung back a wide galvanised steel five-barred gate tied only with a loop of orange nylon rope. Kimi rumbled through with the trailer and pulled it up a few metres from the hedge under the shade of an oak tree. The minute she cut the engine there was peace. Only crows croaking in a spinney down by the river and the rattle of leaves broke the silence.

Kimi came round the front of the car and grinned at Anna, lifting her face to the sun. 'See. Beats a motorway motel, doesn't it?'

Anna smiled back, shading her eyes and gazing up at the ripples of cirro-stratus stippling a huge sky. 'Tell you in the morning.'

'Let's get going, we want to get there before the crowds.'

But the crowds were already assembling on the steep banks of the river Eden with their picnics and dogs and children and blankets. A few ponies were in the river with their young riders but every couple of minutes another horse would skitter down the wooden slip-way and be ridden into the shallow water. Along the main road of the village, parallel to the river, the police had marked out a lane for sole use of the Travellers' horses and traps with plastic barriers, broken at intervals to form crossings for pedestrians. On the river side of the road in the shade of trees a rope had been stretched for about fifty metres to form a hitching line for the horses pulling light traps and there were already a dozen of them, some colourfully got up with bright blue and yellow harnesses.

'Look,' said Anna, 'there's a Methodist Church – that could be one of our meeting places – it's very central.'

'Ok.'

'There's a gospel tent right by it,' Anna added, 'and look, it's opposite the booze tent! Let battle commence!'

At that moment a large skewbald slid to a halt right by them, its rider, stripped to the waist and immaculately waxed, leaning hard back. The horse reared a little and people swayed away.

Kimi called up, 'Nice horse!' but the man didn't seem to hear.

They walked across the ancient hump-backed bridge and did a short tour of the little town noting St Lawrence's squat church built of the local red stone and set apart by its graveyard on the other side of a shady portico. 'It's getting hot,' Anna said.

'Let's sit a while and watch from the banks,' Kimi suggested, turning back to the river. They had both brought water in thermos flasks and luckily a space under the shade of a thorn bush was vacated by a family with a toddler and pushchair as they looked for somewhere to sit.

From here they could see the deepest part of the river just before the bridge arches and some of the horses were being urged into it by their bare-back riders. It was a swirling pageant of men, women, boys, girls, horses and ponies, not just skewbalds and piebalds but many colours including dapple greys that came out of the water shining like polished pewter. If a giant hand had scooped up the pedestrians doing their Saturday shopping in any market town, Anna reflected, and plonked them down here in the river they would be indistinguishable from these Travellers: all shades of hair colour (mostly brown) and the usual range of skin-colour except that the children were perhaps rosier and more freckled than town children, and all dressed in immaculate smart-casual or sporty outfits.

Kimi was watching a man on a large speckled animal ('strawberry roan,' she muttered when Anna asked) who was repeatedly making the horse swim through the deepest water where it couldn't keep its footing making it plunge and struggle. At one point its head went under and the man tipped off. The crowd laughed but Kimi put her hands round her mouth and yelled, 'Asshole!' when he lumbered out on to the shore. Heads turned in her direction and not all of them were amused. Anna was relieved they would soon be parting.

The people in the river seemed oblivious to the tourists enjoying the spectacle and she wondered how they felt about this invasion of their time and space. Perhaps much like the townspeople felt, maybe, about the Fair. She was more concerned about the little children who ran unsupervised between the legs of adults and horses on the small exposed beaches of the river but no-one was getting hurt and the expert youngsters on horseback handled the animals confidently. How many city lads and girls, marooned in their adolescent deserts, wouldn't want this, she thought, this roistering, physical freedom that had nothing to do with screens and shopping. Romanticising, she chastised herself, and began to think about how to make contact with some people.

'Well, I'm off,' Kimi announced. 'I think I've seen some sales going on over there, bunches of blokes shouting and slapping each other on the back, anyway, I want to have a look. Give me a couple of your business cards in case I come across anything for you. It's Smith, isn't it, the family you're after. You ok?'

'Yes.' Anna stood and brushed dried grass off her jeans. 'I'll just see who'll talk to me. See you later.' In her backpack she had photocopies of birth certificates and a couple of marriage certificates from Tom's cousins on the Smith side, descendants of Lorel's brothers, Chip and Stanley. It was scant information: names, dates, location data which vanished when she tried to follow it up. Her primary interest was, of course, in his grandparents on his mother's side, Queenie and Rakes. She had had no luck with finding anyone who fitted the name of Teller Budas and she was beginning to wonder if it had been made up.

But when she walked up the pavement side of the marked-out road away from the river to where some horses were being held and traps examined, she found she had become invisible. At first she approached a beefy man in a check shirt who was holding a pretty two-tone donkey (Kimi would know the term) but when she smiled and greeted the man his eyes went past her. There was no reason for any of them to talk to her, nothing was being sold and no trap rides were being offered.

Next, she tried a woman who was with a couple of friends, all drinking from bottles and laughing, but they spoke over her to each other. The last time she had experienced being snubbed like this was when she had been at a party that Harry had had to go to because of some sponsorship deal the school was after. Most of the people there were older, louder, privately-educated and sleek with money. They simply didn't 'see' Anna and Harry, they only wanted to mix with their own tribe and they knew their own tribe by their markers – expensive clothes, yes, accent, certainly, but mostly an aura of unassailable entitlement. It was a bit like that. It wasn't that the Travellers were rude, they simply didn't want anything to do with outsiders, *gorgias*. They were there to see each other, that was all.

As Anna moved on hoping for a better reception somewhere else, the traffic of smartly trotting (and cantering) horses pulling traps up and down the marked-out lane was slowing and thickening and people were calling to each other and laughing. Every few seconds a rider would dash through the melee on a horse with its eyes rolling and flecks of foam flying from its mouth. She wasn't going to get anywhere here.

Disappointed, she re-crossed the road carefully and walked back to the centre of the bridge where the crowd watching the display in the river was now three-deep and spilling on to the narrow strip of tarmac where cars crawled nose to tail. A gleaming new silver 4x4 edged along, packed to the gills with sunburnt men laughing with each other. She found herself pressed up against the bridge's stone parapet and peered over it at the swirling scene below which had changed little since she had left except to become even livelier.

She was wondering whether there might be somewhere to buy an ice-cream (most shops were closed) when she became aware of a man speaking close to her ear into his phone. His accent was Welsh and his voice pleasantly musical. 'I'm not bringing my *grys* down,' he was saying, 'it's too dangerous now. There's been one accident already. No, no. It was a *gorgia* with a *chavie* and a buggy not looking where she was crossing, on her phone, taken to hospital.' Anna turned to look at who was talking and saw a good-looking young man with a sharp haircut and an immaculate sports shirt.

'Excuse me,' she said, 'could I have a word?' But the man bent his face to his phone and went on talking, moving away.

7

Anna threaded her way through the crowds away from the bridge and towards the quieter centre. A pub was open but was already raucous and anyway she wasn't after alcohol. Then a small A frame sign told her that there was a craft market in the community hall and she slipped down a narrow passageway to explore. One swift look round was enough for her to realise that there was nothing approaching an ice-cream or a drink on offer and that most of the stalls were the kind of gifts which she either didn't want or couldn't afford. But, at the back of the hall by the stage was a row of tables on which were propped gypsy artefacts, drawings and paintings. She wandered round to it.

Smiling at the brightly painted coal scuttles and urns, she glanced at the man standing quietly behind. 'I come from the Midlands,' she said, 'and these remind me of the decoration you see on canal boats.' She was thinking of Rosa who had roses and castles decorating her boat in profusion.

'Yes, well, some of the navvies who dug the canals were Romanies and the Irish Travellers, too. The travelling life on working narrow boats probably suited them and they took to that later.' Was he a Traveller himself? She didn't like to ask.

'Of course,' Anna agreed, 'that would be the connection.' She glanced along the tables and saw some paintings of horses that caught her eye. If they weren't too pricey she might buy one for Kimi as a souvenir of their trip. 'Those are good,' she said.

'Mm. Done by a Traveller but they're just prints.' He hesitated. 'I have some paintings in the back but they're quality.'

'Could I have a quick look?' Apart from anything else, this was the first conversation she'd had since arriving in Appleby hours ago and it would be interesting to see the art. 'I almost certainly couldn't afford them,' she said quickly, not wanting to waste his time, 'but I'd like to see them.'

The man glanced to his left, made a rapid head movement, and a much older man ambled over. 'Just keep an eye out and *chop* if you can but don't give them away.' He nodded at Anna and she followed him up three steps on to the stage and then behind a thick curtain. Framed canvases were propped in small stacks against a sturdy wooden set of step-ladders. He showed her two but she smiled and shook her head and then he drew out a third, smaller frame and turned it to face her. Her breath caught in her chest.

'Who did this?'

'Oh, a Romani I used to know.'

'Was his name Rakes Smith?'

The man's whole demeanour changed abruptly. He stood up straight, very still, and then he turned the painting so that Anna could only see the back. 'No.'

'It's a lovely painting.' Anna realised she had moved too quickly. 'It's just that a friend of mine's fiancee has a photograph exactly like this of his mum and grandfather. It's as though the painting has been done from the photo. That's what surprised me.'

The man seemed to be considering something. 'I know the name,' he said finally, 'but that's not who did the painting.'

'Is it the man in the painting, though? I'm sorry to seem inquisitive – it's just that it's so similar.'

'So what do you know about Rakes?' The man nodded to a chair that was on the side of the stage and Anna sat down. He did not look for a chair himself but there was nothing hostile about him, she felt, he was just wary.

Anna thought about how much to say. 'I'm a genealogist and that's why my friend asked me to look up her fiancee's family because he knew nothing about them and his mother died a little while ago. I did a bit of research and it seems that his mother's grandfather was Lorel Smith and her father was Rakes but there must have been a split in the family because Tom, my friend's fiancée, has never heard of or met any of them.' There was silence for several moments. The man was probably in his late fifties and had a battered but cultured air. She could have imagined him as the owner of a rambling second-hand book shop set down an alley in a quiet market town.

'Bit of a coincidence you being here at the Horse Fair,' he said.

'Not really,' Anna admitted, 'I was hoping to run into someone here who could maybe tell me more but so far no-one has said so much as a word to me, apart from you.' She added quickly, 'I do understand, I mean, I'm just a random stranger.'

'If you're a genealogist you must have a business card – something with where you work on it.'

'Yes, I do.' She rummaged in her bag and brought one out and gave it to him. 'Do you think you might be able to put me in touch with someone?'

'Two questions. Why does this woman want you to trace his family?'

'She wants to give him the information as a wedding present. He feels very deeply the lack of family and any blood connection to anyone now his mother has died. For reasons he doesn't know she wouldn't talk about them but he did find the photograph, the one the painting is so like, and she told him that was her and her father.'

'So he would want to find them?'

'He probably would. But only if they want to be found.' There was another long silence. 'You had a second question?'

'What was his mother's name? Her given name.'

'Her full name was Loretta Snow Smith.' The man seemed to come to a decision and began to put the painting back in the stack. 'How much is it, please?' she asked.

'Fifty if it's going to him – Tom, you said. A hundred if it's for you.' They both laughed. 'The artist is Tony Smith but he only did a few – he's not known. A cousin, but dead now.'

'Are you saying this *is* Rakes and Loretta?' Anna got out her purse and pulled from it two twenties and a ten. Her heart was thudding with excitement.

'Maybe. But I'm not saying more. It's not my family.' The man took the money and then handed Anna back a pound.

'What's this?'

'It's luck money – makes you a Gypsy for a day.' For the first time his face opened into a smile and hope rose in her that he would be able to contact someone, maybe even Rakes or Queenie, but that hope was quickly eclipsed by a different and stronger feeling triggered by his smile and kind gesture that came from her gut, a yearning to really belong, to not be an outsider, but to have a community like these people did. It was such a visceral and powerful feeling that she almost staggered as she rose and the man reached forward and took her hand to steady her.

'I'm so happy to have met you,' she said lamely as he looked around for a piece of newspaper to wrap the picture in.

'I'm Mike,' he said, 'in case me or anyone gets in touch.'

'Ok.'

And then she was on the other side of the velvet curtain clutching her package and needing to get away and be somewhere quiet so she could think. He was back behind the table dealing with a customer so she walked away feeling that anything else said would be redundant and unwelcome.

She didn't want to plunge back into the crowds and there would be no chance of spotting Kimi among them so she turned instead towards the shady arch she'd noticed earlier and saw a chalked sign saying the blessed word, 'refreshments' with an arrow pointing to the church. Inside there was a quiet bustle and the promising rattle of crockery. As she waited, glad of the cool space, a man came in stripped to the waist with a thick gold chain round his neck. He was holding the hand of a little girl and approached the women cautiously asking if there were toilets she could use. One grey-haired woman, the one in charge of the cake-knife, smiled and pointed to a vestibule near the entrance. The little girl ran off and the man nodded his thanks. True evangelism, Anna thought, a thousand times better than words.

When she had told people she was coming to Appleby they had warned her off, telling her she didn't know what she was getting into and to hold on to her purse. The town had closed many of its shops and for all she knew there had been trouble in the past and there might be trouble tonight, but how much of that would be from the Travellers and how much from the tourists? She looked at the little coterie of grey-haired women volunteers, typical of the ones who make possible so much of what is good in the world, big-hearted enough to offer hospitality and a comfort break to all comers.

Her admiration increased as she bit into the moist cake and drank a strong mug of tea. She carefully unwrapped the painting and had a better look at it. The oil paint was done in thick, painterly slabs as though with a palette knife, so that if you looked up close it was hard to decipher the image but when held at arm's length, the scene sprang to life and you could almost smell the lush summer grass and the hot, greasy mane the little girl was clutching. Just a few dabs of paint and there were her sun-flushed cheeks and the cool, violet shade under the brim of her straw hat. The man's face and arms were only slashes of ochre and burnt umber but somehow in the way the angle of the body and the head were painted the artist had conveyed the father's love for his daughter and his pride in her as she sat confidently on the chocolate and cream pony. Anna carefully re-wrapped it and re-tied the string. What could she do now but wait and see what, if anything, might come from Mike?

She was just wondering about whether to take a slice of cake for Kimi when her phone cheeped. 'Are you up for a trip to the campsite?' Kimi asked, 'I can get you there but you'll have to move yourself.'

'What do you mean?'

'No time to explain – you know the Methodist Church we saw? Well, up the side of that is a path, I think it leads up the hill to the train station. Go up that but stop at the first road, I mean a proper tarmacked road that crosses it. Wait for me if I'm not already there. Ok?' The phone went dead.

Anna grabbed the painting, called her thanks to the women and walked quickly out of the cool interior down the path and through the arch to fight her way through the dense crowds on the bridge and then across to the church. But she had to wait a few moments before she could walk up the path because a young boy, maybe nine years old, was leading a string of ponies down it. They were a pretty blond colour and he was taking his job seriously, checking that each one was where it should be in the clattering procession. Anna stood back wanting to take a photo but feeling it would be crass. Once they had passed she hurried up the steep slope but when she got to the road junction, there was no sign of Kimi. There were tired visitors making their way further up the hill, presumably to catch the afternoon train, but the road itself was almost deserted.

She pulled out her phone and started to scroll down for Kimi's number but then heard the drumbeat of hooves coming rapidly closer and before she knew it a trap drawn by a huge black horse had stopped with a flourish of a whip and a skidding on the road.

'Get up!' Kimi called, 'there's plenty of room, come on!'

There was not plenty of room. This was not one of the four-man, two-bench traps she had seen in town, this one had one narrow bench and nothing to lean back on but there was no time to discuss it, she was pulled up and they were off before she had properly got seated. 'Hang on,' Kimi laughed, 'you'll be rolling off the back if you don't watch out!'

Kimi was having a ball. When Anna had a moment to get a good hold on the bench and stop being terrified by the speed they were going, she glanced at her friend and saw that her face was bright with excitement and her hair was bouncing around her head like a pop-star's. On the other side of Kimi was a black-haired man in a white muscle shirt with arms which bunched as he shook the reins or drew them in. The handle end of a long, wand-like whip was stuffed down his boot and its pennant fluttered madly in the wind as they dashed along.

'Charlie!' Kimi shouted to her, indicating the man.

'Hi,' Anna called across but was ignored.

Anna poked Kimi in the ribs with her elbow, she wasn't letting go of the bench, and mouthed, 'What?'

Kimi bent towards her and hissed in her ear, 'He's got a horse for sale! I knew you'd want to come. Just don't get in the way.'

The next few minutes were a roller-coaster ride without restraints. Not only was Charlie's horse tearing up the road at breakneck speed but other horses and traps were careering down the same narrow lane. Yelling people leaping into hedges blurred in Anna's peripheral vision but eventually the trap turned into a field and slowed to walking pace. Charlie drove up a couple of lines of trailers and then pulled into a space between two gleaming caravans and jumped out, knotting the driving reins round a stake in the ground. He strode off behind the van and then reappeared with a huge bowl of water which he put down for the horse. He glanced at Kimi without smiling and jerked his head for her to follow.

So Anna was left alone deeply relieved to be off that crazy ride. She looked around and saw that just one row further up the hill the field opened up into what was, she guessed, a common area, a sort of meeting place, so she walked up towards it hoping there would be someone around. The whole campsite seemed almost deserted except that she could hear some cries from a baby and, in the distance, the noise of a television. A few horses were tied up under the shade of the hedge, dozing and flicking their tails at flies. She didn't want to just stand around awkwardly so she strolled slowly across the open ground wondering how long Kimi would be. Beyond this field, further up the hill, she could see awnings and stalls and a crowd milling about but she was unsure of what her welcome would be so decided to stay put.

'Oi!' someone shouted. She took a couple of steps back and saw that an old man was gesturing at her from the shade of a trailer. He had a knife in one hand but in the other was a stick of some kind which he had been whittling.

She made her way towards him. 'Hi.'

'Who's you one of?' he said with interest.

'Sorry?'

'Oh,' his face fell at the sound of her voice. 'I thought you was one of us.'

'My friend's come up to look at a horse.'

'Ah.' He sat back down on a plastic chair and picked up the stick he was working on.

'Can I watch for a minute?' Anna said, 'If you don't mind.'

'Can't stop you.' After a while he glanced back at her. 'You looks like one of us, *juvie*. Are you sure you ain't?'

'I could be, maybe. My mother, I don't know much about her, but my dad thinks her people might have been Romanies. Maybe in the Midlands – Warwickshire, Worcestershire – I don't know.'

'What name?'

'Walker, but that was her dad's name and he was Birmingham born.'

'Settled?'

Anna was nonplussed for a moment but then understood him. 'Yes, her dad was a silversmith in the Jewellery Quarter in Birmingham. I don't know about her mum – my grandmother. I don't even know her name before she married.' The man was silent then and she watched him work, seeing the knife glide into the stick and turn until slivers curled around the top.

'That's beautiful!' she said as he finished and held the flower up. He put it into her hand. 'Oh, thank you.' She was touched.

'Fiver.'

'Right.' She passed over the money and noted that this time she didn't get any back. 'I'd better go, my friend might be looking for me but it was nice talking to you and thanks for the flower.'

He picked up another stick and she walked away wondering about her mother. Why had she never searched for her family? She had found out a great deal about Harry's biological family and had never needed to investigate George's because he could go back generations. She had to admit there was still some stubborn, angry part of her that was damned if she would get involved with Lena again and get sucked in to her infuriating, selfish life. Her dad had done what he could to heal the wounds from the past but the way Lena had hurt Anna when she was dying was hard to forgive.

Kimi was not back and she had no option but to sit on the ground and wait for her. She wasn't surprised too much by what the old man had said because people often asked if she was Spanish or Italian or even Indian. Neither Ellis nor Faye had inherited her skin-tone or her black-brown hair but she knew where she'd got them from. She was the image of her mother and it was not knowledge she took any pleasure in.

She began to feel irritated with Kimi. It had been at least an hour since she had gone off to look at the horse and there was nothing here for Anna to do, not even a seat. She now had a wooden flower to add to the painting but she was hot and tired and ready to find a nice country pub and a cold beer. Even if the man, Charlie, took them back into town, which he might not, there was still an uphill mile walk to get to the field where they were parked.

She became aware that she was not alone. Standing a few metres away from her but out of her sight-line, until she turned her head, was the whittling man and an old woman. They were both staring at her and speaking quietly to each other. She stood up. 'Hello.'

The woman stepped forward and Anna could see up close that she was very old, perhaps even in her nineties, but her eyes were bright black beads among the deep wrinkles. She was wearing a flowered dress and a pink cardigan despite the heat and on her feet she had gold trainers.

'Yes, you look like your slut of a mother,' she said, and spat on the ground. 'Is she still breathing?' Anna couldn't speak. 'She was the death of Molly May, did you know that? She was evil.'

'Molly May?' Anna croaked. 'Who was Molly May? You knew my mother?'

But the woman just spat again and turned away and the man, after a pause, followed her.

Anna had to leave – she was desperate to get away. She pulled out her phone and called Kimi but the call wasn't accepted. 'Damn her,' Anna muttered, on the brink of tears. She texted, *Walking back to Appleby*, and almost ran through the rows of trailers and cars until she was on the road and striding downhill. It was only when she realised she couldn't see through the blur of tears that she stopped, found a gate and leaned against it to give herself time to calm down.

Obviously the woman was mistaken, and vicious with it. She couldn't possibly have known Lena. In fact, Lena's name had never been mentioned either by Anna or the woman. The name Walker that she'd given the man was common enough and, in any case, her grandfather came from generations of metal workers in Birmingham. It would have to be through her grandmother that there might be any link with Travellers. But even so, even though there could be no connection, Anna felt the sting of her accusations.

She leaned her forehead on the cool metal rail of the gate and let her breathing slow. Then she understood why the woman had upset her so much. Back in the village hall talking to Mike and finding the painting of Rakes and Loretta she had been elated, maybe had even identified a little with the Romani life because of what her father had hinted. She had hoped for those moments that she may indeed belong to a colourful and self-sufficient family who had wandered the countryside for centuries with their ancient culture and tight kinship bonds. She had allowed herself, without realising it, to fantasise a history that her mother might have bequeathed her. Something good, finally, that she could treasure. But, no.

Steve's words came back to her. 'You might have run away with the raggle-taggle gypsies, oh.' For a moment she had wanted to, not run away with them, but be part of them. She sniffed and took a deep breath. At least she had the painting to give to Elizabeth and even a whittled flower to go with it. And there was always the possibility that Mike might be able to put her in touch with the Smith family, so, no, the day had been good, it had not been wasted. She wasn't going to let one deluded old woman de-rail her. She phoned Kimi again and this time was told that she was on her way, was walking down to join her.

Appleby was crammed to a standstill and they decided to slip through the crowds and walk back up to their field, pick up the car and head off for a different village where there might be a pub and a beer and some shade. The sun was dipping a little now but was all the brighter and hotter for it and what Anna really wanted was a shower but the muddy stream that ran down the side of the field literally wouldn't wash. She would take her toiletry bag and towel with her in her back-pack to the pub and at least have a wipe down.

'Actually,' Kimi said, cheerily rubbing a paper towel dipped in water over her face when they got back to the horse trailer, 'I could murder a steak and chips.'

8

It was perfect. The pub itself was attractive enough but at the back was a wide apron of decking and tables overlooking a river rushing by beneath. They sat back after their food had disappeared and sipped at large glasses of rose. 'It's my first one,' Kimi said conscientiously, 'and we're only a hop and a skip away.' The earlier pint of beer clearly didn't count in her tally.

Anna was mulling over the events of the day and realised she hadn't asked Kimi about the horse she had been thinking of buying. 'You didn't like the look of it?'

'It was ok,' Kimi said, smiling to herself, 'a bit younger than I had in mind.'

'What? Skewbald or piebald?' Anna asked to show she'd been paying attention.

Kimi laughed. 'Neither. An Appaloosa.'

'You just keep trying to blind me with science,' Anna muttered, 'just how many kinds are there?'

'Don't worry your pretty little head,' Kimi winked at her. 'I know you're only pretending to be interested.' Kimi's good mood made her pleasant company and Anna was glad she had invited her despite having been abandoned by her at the campsite.

'Have you called Bri? How's she doing?'

'Have you called Steve?'

'I have, actually. When you were in the loo. He's scraping paint off something – I could hear Alice giving him instructions.'

Kimi eased back in her chair and they both watched bats swooping across the river from a barn on the far side. The light was fading but there were still some lingering lozenges of pearl and rose lying like sand-bars against the blue horizon. 'How's that going? Alice, I mean.'

'Not well. Can't be bothered thinking about it, actually.'

Kimi leaned over and tapped Anna on her arm with the bottom of her wine glass. 'What did you make of him?' Her eyes gleamed. 'Charlie?'

'I don't know. He didn't say a word to me. Why, what did you think of him?'

'Mm. I don't know – exotic maybe, feral, possibly?'

Anna turned and regarded her friend more keenly. There was a thickening in her voice and a slight slur that one glass of wine and a beer would certainly not have caused. Kimi was smiling to herself and stroking the arm that held the glass in a gesture Anna had never seen before. 'Kimi? What's this?'

'You have to admit he's attractive. You can't have missed that while you were hanging on to your seat like a wuss.'

'Not my type but, surely, not yours either?'

'Mm. Well, I suppose not.'

'Kimi!'

Kimi only laughed again and then drained her glass. 'Come on, it's getting late – let's head back. I want to see how fast you fall asleep on a mattress of straw after all that moaning.'

Reminded of that, Anna tottered off to the Ladies, cleaned her teeth and used the loo. When she got outside Kimi was waiting for her and started the car. 'You are so old,' she said, 'I'm beginning to wonder if you were ever young and care-free.'

But on the way back Anna thought about how it was Kimi, not her, who had had no adventures before responsibilities kicked in. Kimi had been to a party in her first week as a fresher at university, had been drugged by person or persons unknown and then raped and, finding herself a few weeks later terrified and pregnant had run home and worked at the family firm ever since. Only Anna and Kimi's father, now sadly deceased, had been told about it (surely Briony, too?) and it was possible that Kimi had forgotten Anna knew. Rhea had been the result, a troubled and complex girl who was still in residential treatment for the schizophrenia which had come on strongly during her teen years. These were private matters that Kimi rarely spoke of and Anna kept a tactful silence about. The attraction between her and Briony had been immediate and mutual and they had married only months ago. So, what was this Charlie stuff?

They drove back singing to the car radio, *It's Raining Men*, making up the words they'd forgotten and Anna mused that it had, in fact, been a day full of men of various kinds.

A little later, well-fed and slightly tipsy, Anna stretched out in her sleeping bag and felt the deep softness beneath her shift and crackle. The tailgate had been left down since the night was mild and a breeze lifted her fringe gently like fingers soothing her. 'We must be looking south,' she murmured, 'I can see the Pole Star and the Little Bear.'

Kimi muttered something which may have been, 'Good for you,' but may not have been and almost immediately began snoring softly. Anna lay for a while thinking of Tom's mother and his grandfather and imagining them among the bantering, companionable crowd of Travellers she had seen parading the streets at Appleby calling out greetings to each other. What could have caused Loretta to turn her back on that close-knit, familiar world?

There was a little light in the sky when Anna woke and she saw that it was that breathless pause of the nautical dawn. She imagined the watch on board ships straining their eyes to distinguish the sky from the sea on the horizon. Ushas, Hindus called it – a time of prayer and meditation as the world recreated itself. But before long the moment passed and birds were in full and very loud song. It was much noisier in the country than people told you. She shifted in her sleeping bag and turned to see if Kimi had been woken.

Kimi was not there. Anna yawned and snuggled down – she must be visiting the hedge, possibly, where else could she be? But as time passed and the light intensified Anna couldn't get back to sleep. Where was Kimi? Maybe, she'd gone for a walk. Anna checked her phone but there were no messages so she crawled out of the cosy bag and jumped down from the trailer. Beads of pink were visible through the trees at the top of the field where true dawn was breaking but the field itself was still grey, only the tips of the trees in the hedge next to their trailer picked out in Viking gold. The grass was damp with dew and her feet quickly became cold and wet so she sat on the tailgate and wondered whether she should worry, whether she should get dressed and look for her.

Just as she was about to get up and go back in the trailer to find her clothes, she heard faint sounds from the lane and saw a movement in the mist near the gate to the field. It squeaked and for a moment it seemed as though a mythical creature made of arms and legs and heads was emerging from the fog, but then Anna saw what it really was: a man and a woman on a horse and another horse being led behind. There were only the faintest of sounds, no talking, no rattling of harness, just snuffling and feet on turf and the sight of Kimi leaning her face against Charlie's back and holding him round the waist. As Anna watched, she slipped down and he handed her the rope of the halter so she could lead the second horse. He would have turned away then, but Kimi had quickly moved to his side and put her arms up to him. He leaned down to her. In a moment he was away and down the lane and she was moving as if sleepwalking and, keeping hold of the horse on a loose rope, closing the gate and watching him, presumably, until he disappeared.

Anna shut her mouth and took a breath. She could slip back into the trailer and her bed quickly and pretend she had seen nothing because the gate was at least fifty metres away but she couldn't do it. Then what? She would have to go on pretending that she had seen nothing and that would be impossible. But, what could she say to Kimi? It was none of her business what Kimi did, after all. Even so, she was shocked and probably would make a poor job of concealing that.

Kimi walked slowly up the field with the horse walking quietly behind her. It was a beautiful animal such as Anna hadn't seen before in the flesh. Its mane and tail were a deeper grey against the grey of the dawn, its coat splashed with darker spots like rain on dry slate, but even at a distance Anna could see the fine bones of its head and the delicacy of its legs. Perhaps, after all, Kimi had fallen in love with the horse, not the man, and what Anna had witnessed was merely a thank-you kiss from one horse-lover to another.

Kimi drew closer, still not having looked up to notice Anna, and when she was only metres away Anna said, smiling, 'Two dark horses, then,' which was as good a joke as she could think of under the circumstances. Kimi started, then smiled and walked up to the trailer to tie up the animal and give it a bucket of water.

'I am completely bushed,' she said, climbing past Anna, taking off her boots and sliding into her own sleeping bag. Nothing more was said. Anna stayed where she was to watch the sun rise and to process her thoughts because she knew now that it had not been a courtesy kiss and that Kimi had not just chosen an unusual time to pick up her purchase.

They decided not to return to Appleby but to go home. Anna thought it unlikely that any further contacts would be made and Kimi wanted to get her horse back to her farm. Together they packed up their few belongings and Anna stuffed them into the back of the car while Kimi watered the horse and then led it up the ramp into the trailer. The horse went easily enough after a moment's hesitation but it was only when Kimi pulled down from a high hook a hay-bag stuffed with fresh hay that Anna realised that buying a horse had been the plan all along. And why not? No reference had been made to the morning's episode.

They drove along silently for several miles, both of them hungry now but realising that the first place they could get breakfast on a Sunday morning would probably be on the motorway. As they turned towards Penrith, Kimi spoke. 'Cora,' she said, 'I'm going to call her Cora after my mother. Did you know,' she glanced at Anna, 'that Travellers identify with First Nations people – they have good relationships with them even now and have had for years. It doesn't take much imagination to know why.'

'And your mother was half Cree.'

'So I'm a quarter-breed, yes.'

Anna sat quietly thinking about Gerald, Kimi's father, who was already dying when he asked her to find Kimi's mother and how he had told her of the magical time when, as a young civil engineer in the Canadian wilderness, he had seen a beautiful woman ride bareback out of the forest at dawn and had fallen in love for the only time in his life.

Kimi scanned the road sign and turned on to the M6 taking the curve gently for the sake of the horse being towed behind. 'Did he tell you, my dad, about how he met my mother?'

'Yes. I was thinking of it just then.'

'It's what she was riding that morning – an Appaloosa. It's an ancient breed, you know, they're shown in prehistoric cave paintings.'

Anna grunted her appreciation.

'Ok, it's not far to a stop – will you get me a huge black coffee and a bacon roll, maybe two? I can't leave Cora in the car park on her own and I want to check on her anyway. We had a few tights turns back there but it should be better now we're on the motorway.'

They both felt brighter after breakfast and Kimi played Annie Lennox on her docked phone as they proceeded south in the slow lane at a sedate pace. She seemed not to want to talk and Anna didn't know what to say about the odd Charlie episode so they mostly were silent until they switched to the M5 at Walsall and were only twenty minutes from the farm.

Then Kimi said, 'I've had a brilliant idea.'

'Ok, what?'

'You know that Gypsies find it really hard to get rural sites anymore?' Anna nodded. 'Well, I can build one on my farm. I've been thinking about the three-acre field that lies adjacent to Packhorse Lane – it's pretty flat and there's a good stream runs down the hedge at the back. All I'd need to do would be put some hard-standing down and… '

'Kimi,' Anna said, 'you've got your horse.'

Kimi's grey eyes flashed at her and for a second Anna got a glimpse of the old wildness and wilfulness she had seen years ago before Kimi had met Briony.

'But not my man.'

The silence vibrated.

'I don't know what to say.'

'Don't say anything. I mean it, Anna, don't say anything to anyone. I know you can keep secrets and I'm asking you, as a friend, to keep this one for me. Will you? Will you promise me?' Again, that fierce, challenging look.

What could Anna say? 'Of course I will. But be careful, Kimi, please be very careful, ok?'

Kimi made a meaningless sound.

'Hey, I've just thought, why not drop me off at Barnt Green Station and then you won't have to twist and turn the trailer through the city? I can easily get the train and dad can pick me up.'

'If you're sure?'

But they both knew that to part soon would be a mutual relief. Something huge and dangerous was in the air and Anna needed distance away from it.

But the surprises of the day weren't over. When George picked her up at the station he drove out a short way and then pulled up near a scrap of park. 'Something's come up,' he said, his eyebrows twitching.

'Faye?'

'No, although she has been mooning around. Jack was offered some extra shifts and felt he couldn't refuse.' He scratched his chin.

'So, what?'

'It's that lanky lad from Ellis's band. Bean, they call him.' George patted her hand. 'I'd better just come out with it.'

'Nothing's happened to him?'

'Well, yes, but he's ok. He lives with his dad and apparently it's always been a bit stormy between them but now his dad's thrown him out.'

'But he's only fourteen!'

'Exactly. That's why I thought you wouldn't mind if he stayed at ours for a bit in Ellis' old room. You don't mind, do you?'

'Of course not, Dad, thanks for doing that. He must be devastated.'

'Yes, he must be.'

There was something in her father's tone of voice that made Anna ask, 'What?'

'Well, um, he's not having any trouble making himself at home.'

They walked in to a wall of noise but very quickly Ellis called down from upstairs, 'Sorry, sorry, turning it down now, don't go mad.' Anna needed to go up to her room anyway to dump stuff. She had been hoping for a shower but the bathroom was along the landing and she thought she'd wait until the boys were elsewhere rather than dash across in a towel. She tapped on Ellis' door and then opened it.

'Hi Bean. Ok?'

'Hi, Mrs Ames.' He was balancing on Ellis' bed and appeared to be sticking things to the ceiling. He peered down at her from under a thick fall of greasy hair. 'Is it ok me being here, only, um?'

'Of course it is, Bean. I'm sorry things are bit difficult right now.'

'He's got a new lady and three's a crowd,' he said generously. Anna noted that he seemed fairly sanguine about it so she didn't say any more except to ask if there was anything he didn't eat.

'No, everything – except vegetables and stuff like that and nothing pink. I'm on a no-pink diet.'

'Right, I'll just do the usual and you can choose the bits you like, ok?'

Bean stuck his huge hands under his armpits and beamed down at her. 'You won't know I'm here,' he said.

Downstairs, George was making Anna a cheese and salad sandwich and she had to force herself not to talk about Kimi, well, not about Kimi and Charlie, if such a phenomenon actually existed.

Anna's impression was that he was a lot less interested in her than she in him or was that wishful thinking?

'I'll take the boys over to Safe 'n' Sound in a bit,' George said, 'so we can check on Big B and maybe take him out for a stroll. Did you get anything at Appleby? I mean, information?'

Anna reached across for the wrapped painting and described what it had been like at the Fair, explaining their early return was because of the purchase of Cora but also that she hadn't slept as well in the trailer as she'd hoped and he asked no more questions. She checked for emails and phone messages but, of course, it was far too early to hear from Mike, if she ever would.

After she'd rinsed off her lunch things and popped them in the dishwasher, she phoned Steve. She'd have that shower the minute George and the boys had gone but it would be nice to have a visit to look forward to. All the testosterone in the air at the Fair (and not just from the men) had reminded her how much she preferred Steve's more compelling reticence. Then she remembered as the phone rang at his end that this was the day that Alice's aunt and uncle would be there and she cancelled.

But he called her immediately, whispering into the phone. 'Come down in an hour, will you, Anna, they'll be gone by then and I need to talk. Alice is going to tea with Mina so it'll just be us, ok?'

By the time she'd found a safe place in the wardrobe to stash the painting and the flower and had pulled out fresh jeans and a rather fetching cold-shoulder top, the front door had banged shut and she heard George's car start up. She double-checked out of the window that the boys were with him and headed for the shower with her Appleby clothes rolled into a bundle. She was just about to drop them in the laundry basket when she noticed an unfamiliar odour. At first she thought a dead pigeon had been dropped on top of the washing and recoiled but it was a tangle of socks and below that was a rancid mound of sundry other exotica. She would show Bean the washing machine after dinner and make sure he knew how to use it. She took her own clothes back to her bedroom.

9

Later, cleansed and lotioned, polished and perfumed, she felt she could take a less melodramatic view of what she was now thinking of as Kimi's one-off aberration. She was probably high on horses, truth be told. Anna could remember when she had allowed heated thoughts to visit her own head about one of the university librarians and it wasn't until she had come across him at the supermarket in his running gear that she realised that context is, if not everything, quite a lot. Without the musty book smells, dim reading lights and reverent atmosphere which she loved, she had found him quite unappealing. Kimi would almost certainly think better of the Traveller site idea and Charlie himself now she was home.

Anna pulled on her clothes and added strappy little gold sandals, admiring the way her pink nails showed up against them. To be at Steve's without Alice would be just about the perfect way to spend a Sunday afternoon.

He didn't disappoint. No sooner was she in the door when he scooped her off her feet, nuzzled deep into her neck and carried her upstairs. Thinking back later, she realised that they had not said a word to each other for at least twenty minutes and that was fine.

Afterwards, out on Steve's fancy terrace that he was building, they sat sipping Pimms and watching the seagulls wheeling overhead crying mournfully against a sky where the clouds were stacked high like soggy wedding cakes against the blue. The sound reminded Anna unpleasantly of Bernice's distress but she pushed the thought away. She had told him about Appleby and the painting and now they were silent until he turned to her, lifting her hand and kissing it.

'It's so great being with you, Anna, and I don't want to bring the mood down but there's something I need to talk about.'

She let her glance at him travel over the planes of his face and wondered at how there had been a time when she'd not known and loved him. 'Oh yes, you said earlier,' she replied hastily having forgotten all about it. 'Was it something about Alice's aunt's visit?'

'Yes, well, that's it, isn't it? Julie is Alice's aunt as much as I'm Alice's uncle.'

'Ok, so?' Steve turned his head and looked at her and she instantly sharpened her attention. He was upset. It wasn't easy to tell sometimes with Steve because he almost never threw his emotions at other people but she knew from the subtle darkening of his skin that he was hurt. 'What is it?'

'I told you she married Simon and they moved away to Birkenhead? Well, it turns out they've done well. They're both solicitors, like my brother-in-law was, and the practice is thriving. They've set up a partnership with a couple of juniors and, well, the money is rolling in by the sounds of it. They've bought a big house at New Brighton with an acre of land and now she's thinking of breeding Saluki dogs.'

'Sounds ok,' Anna said tentatively when he stopped. 'So were they just passing through?'

'No, they weren't,' Steve said. 'They want to take Alice.'

Anna's heart leaped. If there was another family home for Alice to visit for weekends, as well as Steve's parents in Derbyshire, that would mean that there would be more times for them to be alone. Why wasn't Steve pleased? Then the words, the way he had weighted them, struck her. 'Take Alice?'

'They can't have kids. They've been through three cycles of fertility treatments and nothing.'

'That doesn't mean they can just turn up and ask to have her, surely?'

'No, of course not.' Steve's voice was weary. 'They're suggesting a series of visits up to them, the first one with me and then, if that goes ok, only with Alice. They say they just want to get to know her but I don't think that's all there is to it.'

'Why, what makes you think that?'

'Julie got so excited after she'd played with Alice for a while that she told her they had already done up a bedroom for her in princess pink and Alice just fizzed over. You can imagine.' Anna was quiet, thinking. 'And,' Steve went on, 'she kept saying how lovely it would be for Alice to be with a proper family and get to do girly things.'

'Cheek. Anyway, she does do girly things now.'

'But I've been thinking, Anna. You know how Alice is with Briony, just adores her, well, maybe she is missing a mother, you know, a female presence.'

Anna was stung. Wasn't she a female presence? But she knew what Steve meant and that it had not been said to discount her. Alice, for whatever reason, didn't like her, was actively rude to her, not to say downright hostile. She focussed on Steve's pain instead of on her own irritation. 'I think you're forgetting that you're Alice's whole world, Steve. She likes to be spoiled and fussed over, of course, but it's you that has been there for her for as long as she can remember. You're not the icing on the cake – you are the cake – Julie and Simon are strangers.'

Steve laughed and took her hand across the iron-work table. 'What am I then, fruit or carrot?'

'Actually, I was thinking beef,' Anna murmured.

'You are totally shameless, Madam,' he said, 'but I hope you're right about Alice. I honestly don't think I could bear to lose her.'

Thinking she would be home much later than she was from Appleby, Anna had planned to make a simple meal of pasta with pesto, mushrooms, walnuts and fried halloumi slices. It was the kind of assembly-line meal that she specialised in, George was the real cook. But when they all sat down Bean stared at his plate with a fading smile.

'Just try it,' Anna suggested, 'you might like it.'

'It's ok,' Ellis put in loyally, and then added, 'you should be grateful, she might have made one of her soups.'

Bean picked at his plate, tried a piece of cheese which Anna thought he probably had mistaken for chicken, and then laid down his fork. 'How about bacon and eggs just this once,' she said, 'when I've finished mine? Would that be better? We haven't got anything else in because George shops on Monday.'

'I don't want to be any trouble, Mrs Ames,' Bean said happily.

'Ok then, just give me five minutes. No, Dad, you finish your meal – you've been holding the fort all weekend. It's fine.' The lad was reminding her of someone but she couldn't think who until Ellis said, 'Big B was ecstatic to see us. A zoosemiotician could write a book on him.'

Bean guffawed and slapped Ellis on the back. 'You're one cool Prof!' he said, and she wouldn't have been surprised if he had dashed round the kitchen joyfully knocking stuff off all the surfaces with his long limbs just like Big B used to do with his tail.

There was a silence for a while as everyone except Bean cleared their plates. 'You're looking very buff tonight, Mrs Ames,'

Bean then announced, leaning back in his chair, as Anna scraped her plate with her fork, 'for an older lady.' Ellis almost choked on his pasta but Bean was on a roll. 'Dad says ladies like to be appreciated.'

George pushed back his chair and took his plate to the sink. 'I'll do these later, Annie,' he said with his back turned to her and she could hear him fighting to contain his mirth.

'I'm a woman, not a lady,' Anna said, as pleasantly as she could, 'and actually it's usually better not to make remarks about their appearance to people you don't know very well.'

Bean was not discouraged. 'Don't put yourself down,' he said kindly and went to the door, 'just off for a tinkle while you do my dinner.'

Ellis stood up and began to clear the table. 'He doesn't mean it the way it sounds,' he said, 'he's brilliant on the bass guitar.' Anna saw that in teen meta-language these two statements were connected as far as Ellis was concerned. 'Hey,' he added, wiping off the table with the dishcloth, 'guess what colour sunsets are on Mars?'

'Um, pink?' Anna pulled the frying pan out of the cupboard and put it on the stove.

'No, blue! Isn't that lollapalooza?' Ellis had given up his previous forays into high falutin' vocabulary in favour of the arcane and obscure.

George paused at the door. 'Did you know that Saturn sometimes has hexagonal storm clouds round its north pole?' he said to his grandson. 'They can be hundreds of kilometres above the cloud deck.'

'You're kidding – how do they know?' Ellis stood transfixed with plates in each hand.

'It was NASA's Casini probe,' George said, opening the door to the utility room. 'Wonders of deep space, new worlds we wot not of.' He scuttled out.

As the bacon sizzled in the pan, Anna's thoughts returned to the unexpected turn of events with Julie and Simon. She had tried to reassure Steve but there was also the undeniable fact that, even for a six-year old, Alice attached importance to her own perceived needs to an unusual degree. Flattery and indulgences went a long way with Alice and Steve might be in for a bit of wild water.

On Monday morning Anna found the usual pile of mail on her desk but felt the need for a brief chat with Suzy first. Suzy was a woman of the world. After enquiring about Suzy's weekend ('totally awesome' trip to Bergen, ergo, Rob re-instated in her affections) Anna came straight to the point.

'I was watching this thing on tv last night,' she said, 'about gay and bi-people.'

'Thinking of branching out?'

'No. It's just that I thought people always sort of knew – well, from adolescence at least – what they were, I mean, their sexual preferences. But, is it possible to realise later in life that, well, that you can go both ways?'

Suzy took Anna by the shoulders and sat her down. 'My God,' she said, 'it *is* you! Tell me everything immediately.'

'No, no, for goodness sake, it isn't me and I was lying about the programme. It's someone I know and I'm just really surprised.'

Suzy relaxed, took a silk scarf out of her bag and in a moment had tied her hair back in a glamorous 40's bandeau. 'It's not that unusual,' she said. 'I knew someone who left her husband after fifteen years of marriage for a woman and she said she and her husband had had a perfectly satisfactory sex-life. She said it wasn't women in general she liked in that way, it was just this one woman that she totally fell for.'

Ted appeared in the office doorway. 'Not to suggest something cruel and unusual,' he barked, 'but, don't you have work to do?' Anna slid back to her desk.

Researchers sometimes did get personal mail among the work post of certificates and so on, usually from grateful clients, so Anna wasn't surprised to see a hand-written envelope. Last week the beneficiary of an estate she had found turned out to be an extremely hard-working carer with four children trying to manage after the early death of her husband from cancer. The estate was substantial and at least the financial worries of the woman were now over. Unfortunately, the letter was not from her.

> *Mrs Ames,* Bella had written, <u>*What*</u> *is your problem? I cannot understand why Guthrie's estate has not been settled. The solicitor says that you are holding things up because the police want you to say that I am his sole heir. You are costing me money and time and distress which is* <u>*nasty and*</u>

cruel of you considering how much I am grieving for my darling boy. I need that money! Get on and do your job or I will be contacting your boss.
Bella Cromer

The mess of factual error and mis-directed rage in this heavily underscored note made Anna feel tired but she did need to talk to Ted about the case now he was back. She pulled up a blank document and rapidly typed a report for him on the situation so far. At the end she put her recommendation which was that Guthrie's case be passed on to an appropriate lawyer. She then printed it and clipped Bella's note with the date received to it and stuck it in the internal mail. To cover everything, she sent a brief email to Ted to alert him to the situation and turned with relief to analysing some very useful certificates for a job she had tracking down a long-lost nephew which had come in the same post.

At half past twelve, just when Anna was going to see if Steve wanted to get lunch, her phone went and Josie told her that a Mrs Cromer was on the line demanding to speak to her. Anna took the call, suspecting that if she didn't the same thing would be repeated all day.

'Did you get my letter?' Bella began without any form of greeting.

'Yes, I did, Mrs Cromer. I have sent it to my line manager with a summary of the situation over your son's estate. He will take the decision how to proceed.'

'What?' Anna held the phone away from her ear. 'What are you talking about? There's only me! There's no-one else, you stupid bitch! Are you completely without any sense?'

'Nothing will be gained by using offensive language, Mrs Cromer,' Anna said calmly. 'I suggest you wait for the process to take its course.'

'It's insane! I am the only possible beneficiary, aren't I? He had no-one else!'

Ted appeared at the office door and beckoned to Anna. 'I'm going to have to go now, Mrs Cromer,' Anna said. 'Please try to be patient.' She put the phone down.

She followed Ted into his office wondering if any of this muddle was going to be blamed on her and preparing herself to make a defence. If anything, she had been over-conscientious, she thought, because if she hadn't gone through Guthrie's travel papers (not of immediate relevance some might think) she wouldn't have found out that he had named Bernice, his aunt, as his next-of-kin.

But Ted was in a sober and rather humble mood which was unusual, not to say unprecedented. He sighed as he sat in his desk chair and everything about him sagged. 'Are you ok, Ted?'

'I've made a mess of things, haven't I?' he said. 'You know – I expect the whole office knows.'

'Sorry, Ted. It must be hard for you.'

'*Mea culpa* or "my bad," as the kids say these days,' he said, 'I can't blame anyone else, least of all Leslie.' This was so out of character for Ted, who had, only a short time ago, been fronting the divorce out with elan, that Anna said nothing. 'I've been doing one of those mediation things with her and a solicitor – you know. It knocked me about, Anna. I had to go away for a while and just take it all in.' So, not off on business, then. 'I had no idea that she knew, that she's always known, and that over the years I've just shredded her commitment to me away with one woman after another and for what? I don't even understand myself. I've always thought the world of her. Why would I do it?' He wasn't being self-pitying, he was genuinely nonplussed, she thought.

The silence in the office stretched out for minutes as Ted sat with his head sunk in his hands hiding his face from her. Eventually, she asked, 'Are you sure it's over? What about if you both went to counselling? Or something.'

'I'd do anything,' Ted said, 'anything, but she says it's too late.'

'It may help you. It may help you understand why you needed those affairs. Sorry, if that's intrusive.'

'I'll think about it,' Ted said unexpectedly, 'I have to do something.' He sat up, sighed and picked up the documents she'd sent him about Guthrie. 'This is a mess.'

'I just think it's a legal issue,' Anna repeated. 'It may be that giving your aunt as next-of-kin on an insurance document isn't of any importance at all.'

'I've been on to Mary,' Ted said. 'Normally, you would be right, but in the case of a lengthy estrangement from the mother, it's more complicated. Anyway, I just wanted you to know it's being handled and you can let his mother know there's a complication and that's the reason for the delay.'

'She won't be satisfied with that,' Anna said, 'She's already been giving me a mouthful on the phone as well as this, hardly friendly, note.' She waved at the document.

'Just tell her that there's some question over who is the beneficiary,' Ted said, 'and let her stew about that.'

Steve had disappeared from his office when she checked so he had probably gone for a lunch-time run. She found Ted's dismay had lingered with her so she decided to get a sandwich from the little Harts' lunch-room she usually avoided and phone Bella to get the unpleasantness over with while she was feeling down. The afternoon could only improve.

Bella came to the phone late, just when Anna was about to hang up. 'What?' she said, breathing heavily.

'It's Mrs Ames from Harts.'

'Well?'

'I've just come from a meeting with my manager,' Anna said, eyeing the gloopy egg sandwich in its plastic caul, 'and I wanted to let you know how things stand.'

'About time. Go on, then.'

'The problem is that there may be another beneficiary, Mrs Cromer. There may be another sole beneficiary.'

The silence that greeted this was like the silence after a child has fallen badly and will soon scream. The longer the silence, the louder the scream. Anna waited, partly because she wanted to see what Bella would say but also because she didn't know what to say herself. She certainly wasn't going to go into details or name Bernice. Bella slammed the phone down.

At five-thirty Anna gathered her things together and left the office to descend the green glass stairs to go home. It had been a much better afternoon and, apart from work, Ted had confided that he had made an appointment with a therapist which must be a good thing. As Anna went through the big doors and down the blue-brick steps she noticed a small crowd of kids on bikes laughing at something on the towpath. She had to pass them to get to the private car park and glanced at where they were looking. In a huge red spray-paint scrawl someone had written: *Anna Ames is a slag.*

Anna retraced her steps and asked Josie to call Ted.

Ted called the police and the police said there was nothing they could do.

Ted called their cleaning company and offered twice the going rate to swab the words off the tarmac towpath before the next day. Then they all went home.

10

George was cooking dinner that night so Anna told him she was going to lie down for half an hour and went upstairs to change into her comfort leggings and loose top. She didn't lie down, though, she needed time to think and sleep was very far away from a possibility. She wasn't alarmed, she wasn't even angry, but she was puzzled. Of course it would have been feasible for Bella to drive from Stratford-on-Avon (if she was there) in plenty of time to write this message and get home again. Perhaps, if Anna had driven to Bella's house the day she broke the news of Guthrie's death, she would have recognised Anna's car in the firm's car park and sprayed that?

But - if Bella was angry or crazy enough to do this, why call Anna a 'slag' instead of a liar or even a bitch as she already had? The sexual connotation of 'slag' was odd, although of course it could simply be the most defamatory insult Bella could think of. What could she possibly hope to achieve by it since the act itself diminished her credibility? But, surely, there was no-one else who would have wanted to do such a thing?

Steve left work an hour earlier than the others to pick up Alice. He had not phoned her or reported the graffiti to Josie so he must not have seen it which probably meant it had not been there. That placed the act between four-thirty and five-thirty. Harts had no cameras that covered the tow-path and Anna wondered if anyone else did. But even if Bella could clearly be seen spraying the words, would the police bother to do anything? A woman off her trolley with grief and behaving in a mildly criminal way perhaps deserved, out of compassion and with an eye to paperwork, to be ignored.

The best thing was that the whole Guthrie inheritance should now be out of her hands although the enigma of his family still niggled at her like a forgotten name that is just on the tip of the tongue. Anna brushed her hair and opened her bedroom door to a savoury smell coming from the kitchen that made her mouth water. Tomorrow she would tell Josie not to put any more calls from Bella Cromer through to her so that made two infuriated and unhinged women, Bella and Mel, who had been banned from contacting her. A record to date.

The next day was a school day and Bean had not appeared for breakfast. Ellis had already unstacked the dishwasher and put the clean things away and had left his cereal bowl soaking in the sink. He was in his school uniform and was checking the contents of his bag: in other words, this was a normal working morning for him. Anna pondered what to do. Should she make him responsible for his friend's tardiness or should she, as the adult, take charge? She decided on a compromise.

'Bean ok?' she asked, saving her last mouthful of delicious Italian-blend coffee that made intelligent life possible at this hour.

Ellis glanced round the kitchen as though he had not noticed that something was missing. 'Oh – ok. I'll go and shout him.'

Anna heard him shout, wait, and then pound up the stairs. Five minutes later, just as she was clearing her plates, Bean appeared unwashed, undressed and giving a good impersonation of the Walking Dead. He slumped at the kitchen table.

'Won't you be late for school?' Anna asked.

'Nah.'

'But you haven't got ready. I mean, you're not washed, and you haven't had breakfast and it's time to go now.'

Bean uttered a hopeless sort of groan, levered himself upright and went out. Anna finished clearing the dishes and putting them in the dish washer and picked up her jacket and bag feeling that if Bean was going back to bed that would have to be dealt with later. She had her hand on the front door when Ellis ran down the stairs with Bean, in full uniform, behind him. They exited together.

She had only been at her desk for five minutes when Josie put through a call to her phone. 'It's some bloke,' she said crossly. Josie was understandably irritated because Ted had agreed to take a Work Experience teenager, not to mentor himself, but to leave with Josie in the far from roomy Reception Work Station (as it was called by Ted if not by anyone else). The girl showed no interest in being there and refused to turn off her phone so Anna assumed it was merely a matter of time before Josie, rather than battle with her for two weeks, came to a compromise which involved the girl hiding it when Ted was in sight and at all other times leaving Josie in peace.

'Hello, this is Anna Ames. Can I help you?'

'Mike.'

Anna inhaled sharply and stopping riffling through her post. 'Oh hi, I'm so pleased to hear from you. Are you ok?'

'You're the lady from Appleby?' The voice was still wary.

'Yes, I bought a painting from you of a man with his little girl on a pony.'

'That's right.' The relief in his voice seemed to indicate that she had cleared security. 'You wanted to know about the Smith lot, right?'

'Lorel Smith's descendants, yes.' There was a pause. 'Did you have any luck?'

'You're not far from Kenilworth.'

'No, not at all. Is that where they are?'

'No,' Mike said quickly, 'I can't say where they are but they'll be there at the July Horse Fair. I could set up a meeting.'

Anna thought quickly. Elizabeth and Tom were getting married in September so that would give her over a month to work on tracing connections if someone would see her and help her with the information. She hadn't known that there was a Gypsy Horse Fair in Kenilworth so she asked about it and Mike told her there was a Fair three times a year. Again she had the feeling of a hidden-in-full-sight world within a world. She asked for details and whom she might meet, perhaps distant cousins or, best of all, Rakes and Queenie themselves – Tom's grandparents.

'Yes, them,' Mike said, and she punched the air. 'They'll see you. They're curious about him, the fiddle player. There's someone else, too, but I couldn't swear to that one.'

'Who?'

'Can't say.'

'Can I get back to you on this number to set things up?'

'Yes, but don't give it to anyone else.'

'No, I won't.'

Anna was about to thank him and end the call when he said, unexpectedly, 'You made an impression where we pulled on.'

'Pulled on?'

'The trailers – the campsite.'

'Oh yes, I went up there with my friend, she was interested in a horse. She ended up buying it, actually, it's beautiful.' She sounded cheerful but she was worried – had Kimi's long and private meeting with Charlie been noticed and remarked on?

There was silence from Mike's end but it was a thoughtful silence so she hung on and then he said, 'She probably paid over the odds – that horse isn't what Gypsies like except for the colour. Not enough hair on it. Anyway, not her – you. You were noticed.'

The scene with the angry old woman rushed back to Anna. 'There was someone who thought she knew me, well, she thought she knew my mother who I do look like, but I expect it was just a case of mistaken identity.'

A longer pause greeted this. 'I'll wait to hear, then.'

'Yes, I'll get back to you soon, Mike, and I'm very grateful.' The phone went dead.

Anna couldn't keep this to herself and leaped up from her desk to find Steve. Already she was mentally taking photos, making notes, pulling everything together into a dossier with the painting and she could see Elizabeth presenting this to Tom and his delighted face. Or – Anna let the office door bang behind her and dashed down the corridor – or, Tom's grandparents might come to the wedding themselves as a surprise! In two minutes it was all organised in the most satisfying manner possible and there wouldn't be a dry eye in the place. She presented a radiant face to Steve as she burst into his office.

'I've just had an amazing piece of news!' she announced.

Steve raised his eyebrows and tipped his head to the dark corner of his office. 'I don't have to ask if it has anything to do with work,' Ted growled from where he was supporting the wall. 'I want to see you later – you've stirred up a hell of a hornets' nest, haven't you? Going the extra mile and all that which nobody told you to, I might add.'

'Ok, Ted, sorry, I think.' She backed away.

'Two-thirty, don't be late.'

She was checking the BMD indexes for any relatives of a recluse who had died intestate when her phone cheeped and she saw it was a message from Faye. As usual, it was a demand in the form of a request. 'Girls nite out Fri meet up home for drinks. Ok.' She texted back, 'What time? How many? Who's providing the drinks?????' Faye messaged, 'LOL, you theb eest.'

Still, that seemed positive, that Faye was not planning to mope all evening while Jack worked but to catch up with her girl-friends. On the other hand, Faye would probably spend all that Jack earned that night. Not my business, Anna told herself firmly. She could run to a few bottles of wine off the bottom shelf of the supermarket but would certainly not be buying spirits. The fact that Faye wanted them to meet at her family home could mean that she was seeing old friends who lived nearby (Tasha would be there, Anna hoped) or that she couldn't be bothered to clean up the flat, but certainly that she was cadging the drinks which would frontload the evening's jollities.

There would be a full house because some of Joan's poetry group were joining George and Ashok (Diane begging to be excused on the grounds that it might be too much of a good thing for her and there were not enough chairs). Maybe they could take some of the kitchen chairs out into the garden? Perhaps George could whip up a fruit punch or something? Time to puncture another pleasing scenario and see what Ted wanted.

He was studying the other side of a flyer for office cleaning products when she tapped on the door and walked in. 'Let me get this straight,' he said, reading, presumably, his own notes. 'Two sisters on the same street, one the birth mother, Bella Cromer, and the other the aunt, Bernice Sitwell, right?'

'Mm.'

'Is the aunt claiming the estate?'

'No.' Anna hesitated. 'Well, I have a feeling she might, or her husband might. When I saw them they didn't know Guthrie was dead until I told them.'

'So who is this Melanie Fisher that I spent ten minutes of my life with that I'll never get back yesterday?'

Anna felt it would be unkind given Ted's fragile emotional state to point out that he wouldn't get any of his time back no matter what he was doing with it. 'She's banned from coming here, Ted. She's a nuisance.'

'She grabbed me on the way to the car park with some story about being Guthrie's fiancée.'

'Yes, that's what she told me and she may have been – even though Chris Barton had never heard of her or an engagement – but that gives her no legal claim on Guthrie's estate, does it?'

Ted put down the piece of paper and regarded Anna mournfully. 'Shacking up, pregnant, joint bank accounts – feel free to nod or shake at any time.'

'None of the above as far as I know. The police could check his phone if that would help. Ted, this is really not our business, is it?

I mean literally, it's not what this business does. Surely this is for a lawyer to sort out?'

Ted pushed the paper about on the leatherette pad he had in front on him. 'I've been to see someone as you suggested,' he said without looking at her.

'Ok. Do you think it will work for you?' Anna offered after discarding several other possible queries of a blunter nature.

'Early days. She seems ok.' Ted picked up the paper and squinted at it. 'Then there's this other one.'

'What other one?' As so often with communications from Ted, Anna felt herself side-swiped into a limbo of incomprehension where she had to scrabble hard to get a foothold.

'Rebecca Sitwell.'

'Pass.'

'You're meeting her downstairs in five minutes.' Ted smiled encouragingly. 'She doesn't seem to be a nutter but, of course, you never know.'

'Who is she?'

'Daughter of Bernice, cousin of Guthrie. Phoned Josie and asked to speak to the MD or CEO or whatever she thinks I am and hey presto.' He frowned. 'Josie's really gone off the boil since that kid came, whatshername? Seelon. Dear me. In the past she'd have put her through the third degree instead of springing her on me.'

'You mean like you've sprung her on me, Ted?'

'Don't pretend you don't like a mystery, I know you better than that.'

'I can't say this one has been a barrel of laughs so far, actually, and I repeat, why are we dealing with it at all?'

In response Ted smiled and tapped the side of his nose, meaning, she supposed, that the reason was his to know and hers to ignore which hardly helped. She stood up and left the office closing the door thoughtfully behind her and wishing she had considered the possibility of the Sitwells having a child, if not several. There was now another female connected with Guthrie for her to deal with. She was feeling a tad gun-shy.

Josie and Seelon could hardly have got further away from each other in the space behind the desk if they had been magnets with opposing poles. Seelon was staring glumly at her phone and Josie was energetically sanding her nails. Across the lobby on the uncomfortable banquette where visitors were placed was a woman, probably in her late twenties. Anna paused on the stair to absorb first impressions before Rebecca raised her head and saw her. Rebecca was sitting quietly reading a newspaper and appeared calm and normal, at least for the moment. Her long hair was tucked up into the kind of knot that runners use to get it out of the way and she was wearing rugged sandals and dark jeans with a grey tunic top. When she raised her eyes over the paper as Anna approached, there was a distinct look of Guthrie about her – a healthy, un-showy kind of good looks. To make things even more reassuring, she was smiling.

'Anna Ames.'

'Hi, I'm Rebecca Sitwell, thanks so much for seeing me.' The voice was pleasant, too, so this may be the first person connected with the case who might not shout, scream or wail at her.

'I'm afraid we only have a small private room for visitors. Is this ok?'

'It's fine. Please don't feel you have to offer me a drink or anything – I'd rather just get on with it and not waste your time.'

They both sat and Anna took out her notebook and pen. 'Please accept my condolences over Guthrie. It must have been a shock when your parents told you.'

Rebecca twisted her mouth and sighed. 'They didn't. Nobody told me. The only reason I know now is because I still read the Avon Courier, you know, the weekly paper, and Guthrie's death was reported in the sports pages. He used to play rugby for the town team when he was still at school and was a bit of favourite of the sports editor so she put a little item in when she heard. I don't know how she knew.'

Even given what she knew about the family first hand, Anna was astonished. 'Um, I don't want to pry, Rebecca, but –'

'Why didn't my mum and dad tell me? Why didn't Auntie Bella?' Rebecca looked wistfully at Anna. 'We've become a strange family, haven't we? It's not normal, I know. I work in Leamington, I'm a para-legal, but there are phones. I'd talked to dad only a few days ago and he didn't mention it. He knows I know now, of course, and he told me you'd been.'

'So, excuse me for asking this, you're on good terms with your parents and your aunt?'

Rebecca looked at Anna thoughtfully, like a doctor trying to form a diagnosis in a difficult case, and said, 'I'll tell you the story but I'll keep it brief. Guthrie was more like an uncle than a cousin to me because he was a bit older. But it was the way he was, too, the kind of person who looks out for the little ones and is the first to take charge if anything goes wrong. I suppose I idolised him not having any siblings of my own. When we were growing up we were always in and out of each other's houses, he taught me to ride a bike – well, I won't go on – I'm still a bit shaken by the news to be honest. Anyway, I thought Aunty Bella was a bit weird, you know, all that seventies' New Age stuff but he thought my parents were a little stuffy because they weren't like that, in fact, my dad was a bit too straight-laced for him, but we all got on ok. Then, when he was eighteen and just about to go to uni in Birmingham, something happened and everything changed.'

Anna sat forward, her pen not needed, because Ted was right, she did like a mystery and it looked like this one was just about to be explained. But Rebecca had paused and was frowning. 'What happened?' Anna asked.

'The truth is, I don't know. I was away on a mountaineering club weekend in the Lake District with my school. When I left home everything was as usual but when I came back everything had completely changed.'

'How do you mean?'

'Guthrie had gone – just gone. Aunty Bella was having fits and wouldn't talk to me and worst of all mum was in hospital – she'd had a stroke and they didn't know if she'd live. Dad was a wreck.'

'But why?'

'I don't know. They would never talk about it but after that I hardly ever saw Bella and if I did she wouldn't look at me or speak to me and when mum came home in a wheelchair she just started shaking and crying if I asked about it and dad told me not to. It was awful – it was the worst thing that had ever happened. The not-knowing was almost as bad as missing Guthrie. We'd had plans, like I was going to go and see him at uni, he was going to take me round and show me the sights – everything. And the kind of person he was, it wouldn't be drugs or anything like that. Then he was just gone. I still can't fathom it.'

Anna remembered the halted boy's room at Bella's and the extreme reaction of the Sitwells. What on earth could have happened? 'But you asked him later? He must have explained, didn't he?'

'How could I?' Rebecca said, tears beginning to shine in her eyes. 'I never saw him again.'

Anna sat up straight in her surprise. 'You never saw him again? Why not?'

'How could I?' Rebecca repeated, 'New Zealand is so far away and I had no address and no money for the fare.'

Anna glanced out of the door at Josie and Seelon to check that she was awake and not desk-napping in case another scene was about to erupt. This apparently normal young woman wasn't making any sense. 'New Zealand?'

'That's where he went. We never saw him again.'

Anna's brain whizzed around like a pinball machine. 'Why do you think that?' she asked.

'Aunty Bella told us that was where he had gone.'

The balls fell into the holes. So that was why Richard had asked so poignantly where in the world Guthrie had died. Had they believed he had been abroad since he was eighteen? But they knew now, since her visit, and had not told their daughter.

Anna leaned forward and took Rebecca's hands in her own. Would what she was now going to reveal help or hurt the young woman? 'I have to tell you this, Rebecca. I don't know why your aunt said that. Guthrie has been living and working in Birmingham for the last twelve years at least, up to the time he died.'

She felt the hands, the arms, the whole person stiffen in shock and saw the blood drain from Rebecca's cheeks. 'No,' she said quietly. 'No.'

'I don't know why you were told that. And did your parents believe he had gone to New Zealand?'

Rebecca slowly nodded her head while tears ran down either side of her nose and dripped from her chin. But Bella knew he was in Birmingham before she had been told he was dead. When Anna had relayed to her how he had died she had not been surprised by his location, only by his death. And now Anna recalled that fleeting cunning expression on Bella's face before she had thrown Anna out. What was going on? Why had she lied to her sister and brother-in-law and niece?

'He was here?' Rebecca said in a faint voice. 'He has been here all along?'

'Maybe – certainly most of the time.'

'I could have seen him!' the last word was a huge sob. 'I could have visited him – we could have been friends like before!'

'I am so sorry,' Anna said, pulling a packet of tissues out of her bag and handing them to her. 'This must be so painful for you.'

Rebecca stood up. 'I have to go. This is too much. Please, can I call you?'

Anna found a card and scribbled her personal number on the back. 'Any time,' she said, 'any time at all – please call. I'm so sorry.'

Rebecca took the card, ran from the room sobbing and was out of the glass doors and away in a moment.

Four round eyes stared at Anna as she made her way back across the lobby. 'Another nutter?' Josie asked, 'Where do you find them?'

'No, this one is different,' Anna said. 'If she ever comes back, call me immediately. She's carrying a very heavy load right now.'

'Not the only one,' muttered Josie, glancing at Seelon who had returned to her phone and was texting furiously with her thumbs.

11

After that unsettling encounter the week plodded along and by Friday afternoon Anna was looking forward to what promised to be a sociable weekend with only the prospect of the riding lesson to add some grit to her soul. Kimi wouldn't let these lessons lapse despite hints and one heartfelt (but ignored) demand from Anna. This had been going on for nearly two years and she showed no signs of giving up. If Anna and Maisie had been left to potter gently round the field for half an hour musing on life and snatching clumps of grass as they would have liked, it might have been bearable but instead they were subjected to Kimi's relentless insistence on improvement. On a brighter note, it would be nice to see Faye and her friends and be part of George's poetry evening. Tomorrow she may have a word with him about the Guthrie situation and see if he could come up with any ideas on what might have happened to blast the family apart so suddenly. He was good at hypotheses, in fact, it was a shared hobby for them to ruminate on any aspect of meanings and motivations – the kind of conversation that had Diane reaching for her car keys.

When she opened the front door, her bags-for-life clinking with bottles, she heard voices in the kitchen and found that Joan was already there seated at the table in deep conversation with her dad. George, in honour of the unusually large group coming to share poems, was wearing his latest Heart Foundation shirt, a black poplin number with his name sewn into the collar. Joan was in a navy and white striped top and navy jeans with the red sandals and looked, as always, neat and conventional, the archetypal sweet old pensioner – which just showed how misleading appearances can be.

'I wasn't expecting alcohol,' George said, watching Anna unpack her shopping, 'I've made a fruit punch. You know how volatile poets are, I don't want to set them off.' He and Joan smirked at each other.

'It's not for you. Faye's meeting her friends here later and wants to have a drink before they go out. I know they'll get a taxi so, why not? I've got nibbles as well.'

'Right, well, I think it's warm enough to sit out at least for the first hour so I'll go and get things set up. There's a cheese salad in the fridge, Annie, just for us three because Ellis and Bean are round at Mike's for the evening.' He grabbed a chair and tottered out through the utility room with it.

Anna made another mug of tea for Joan and one for herself and sat down at the table for a chat. 'So I hear you're off to London for dad's big day?'

'Yes, looking forward to it. I had to have a word with Jakub, though, he was very silly. Wanted to come, jealous of George, all that nonsense.' Although Joan was in her late sixties she had taken a job serving in a Polish green-grocery shop, Nowak's, to offset a financial crisis but had continued because she enjoyed it and the owner's father, Jakub, and she had formed what Victorians might have called a 'close friendship.' Over the months that they had been seeing each other a low-key tussle had developed which always involved Jakub wanting more commitment and Joan sticking with the status quo. Joan liked her own space and her own life whereas Jakub wanted to absorb her into his. A familiar enough pas-de-deux.

'But the friendship's still worth that hassle?' Anna asked, wishing she had bought her favourite biscuits as well as wine.

'Well, the best thing is the creative sex, of course,' Joan replied. 'A bit of a bonus at my age.'

'A bonus at any age,' Anna agreed, lifting her mug to chink Joan's.

'And he's a nice man, really. He knows he's a dinosaur – Piotr's always telling him.'

They sipped their tea in silence for a moment until Joan asked after Steve and Alice so Anna told her about Julie and Simon and that the first visit to them would be the following weekend.

'But Alice would never want to leave Steve, surely?' Joan said. 'She adores him.'

'I know that, but he worries.'

'She can be a little madam. She may have her head turned by all the goodies and attention.'

'That's what he thinks. Not the "little madam" bit – that's what I think.'

Sunlight was laid in bars across the old oak kitchen table picking out the knobbly veins on Joan's hands and the greasy top bars on the assorted chairs. Anna glanced round wondering if this year she really did have to get round to cleaning and painting the room.

An emotional time of year was approaching and she knew that the children felt it, too. The loss of their father so suddenly and so violently would never be forgotten. They had marked the first anniversary of Harry's death by going up to the Staffordshire moors and the Roaches again and finding the outcrop of rock where his ashes had been interred together with their last messages to him. But, without discussion, they had not gone again. Harry wasn't really there, after all, he was here in this house in a thousand memories. Faye and Ellis mentioned him less and less she had noticed but that was healthy, surely. She still said goodnight to his photo by her bed every time she went to sleep but when the anniversary came she needed more and would get out the albums and her own private stash of notes and cards. On the actual day, or the nearest Sunday, the four of them would go out for a long walk no matter what the weather. Such a simple ritual – a chance to talk about him and to offer him, wherever, whatever he now was, the love of his little family.

Around seven thirty in the evening Joan's poetry group arrived all together having car-shared and, since George's old friend Ashok was already in place, they settled quickly into an open session of readings from their own work. Anna ferried out the punch and the macarons George had made but stayed in the house because Faye had not said when her friends would be arriving. By eight-thirty it was too cool to be outside and since the shed was too small to accommodate them all, they came into the kitchen and sat around the table. Anna leaned against the work-top and watched her dad in action. 'There'll probably be a toxic one,' he had said to her earlier, wagging a finger, 'but I shall be ruthless!'

A young man wearing a black Stetson indoors would have been Anna's candidate for the position but the toxic one turned out to be a sweet-looking young woman who announced that she wrote 'fusion' pieces. Anna eyed the bundle of papers in her hand with foreboding – there seemed to be a lot of them. After ten minutes of listening to her read a naively constructed narrative on a fantasy theme while the others stared at the ceiling and shuffled their feet, George intervened. 'I'm so sorry, Lisa,' he said kindly as she paused for dramatic effect, 'I should have explained our rules at the beginning. It's a ten minute slot for each person, you see. We may go round again after a break so you may have another chance to read.'

Lisa stared at him with big eyes and showed him the sheaf of papers in her hand. 'I haven't finished,' she said plaintively, 'there's all this. I've spent weeks on it.' She drooped prettily. The rest of Joan's poetry group looked at George with interest to see how he would handle this, probably so they could use the tactic themselves.

George twinkled at her, his cheeks bunching into red rubber balls. 'I'm afraid those are the rules,' he said. 'Perhaps next time you could bring a shorter piece to share and maybe use this one as part of a collection of your creative meditations on life – it may even be the start of a book?'

Anna almost clapped him. She wouldn't have been surprised if he had suggested a title, too. Lisa looked uncertain and then blushed with pleasure and reverently slipped her work away into a hand-decorated, leather-bound folder. The young man in the Stetson pulled a bottle of whiskey from his back-pack and offered it to George. Anna got the tumblers out of their cupboard.

As if on cue Faye crashed through the front door. This in itself was cheering as she had taken to sliding in dispiritedly lately, so Anna went to meet her. 'It's all in the front room for yours,' she said, opening the door and pushing her in. 'Pops is in the kitchen with some poetry people.'

Faye surveyed the coffee table with its glasses, bottles and plates of snacks while Anna surveyed her. Not since she was sixteen had Faye put on so much slap. She was even wearing false eyelashes with heavy mascara which cast shadows on her cheeks. On her feet were some new black patent shoes with stilts for heels and the tube between head and heels was low at the top and short at the bottom. Worst of all, Faye had had her stunning chestnut hair striped an insipid blonde. What had all that cost?

Anna merely said, 'Are you going anywhere special?' because to lie politely that Faye looked nice would have stuck in her throat.

'Somewhere on Broad Street – there's loads of places.' Faye poured a large drink for herself.

'How's the saving going?' Anna couldn't stop herself saying.

Faye waved the glass at her. 'Don't you start, you sound like Jack. You have to put a downer on things, don't you? I work hard all week and I need some fun.'

Then the doorbell rang and Anna left her to it, but there was something hectic, something joyless in Faye that she was sorry to see.

Saturday was, at least, dry and Maisie and Anna greeted each other with the weary but amicable resignation of battle-hardened conscripts. Instead of mounting up herself, Kimi lead the way into the paddock where Anna saw to her alarm that a jump had been assembled out of red and white poles. This had been attempted before with disastrous results, in fact, Anna still had the scar on her elbow where she had fallen off.

Kimi was in her element in her manure-splashed stable clothes and old boots, her lively hair bouncing about. 'We need to move you up a level,' she was shouting, 'you're too comfortable as it is. You need a new challenge.' She positioned herself in the centre of the ring and indicated with her whip that Anna and Maisie should take the perimeter. 'Just warm up with some sitting trots, ok?' This was Anna's least favourite gait, involving as it did bumping her coccyx painfully on the hard leather of the saddle. On the second circuit she noted Briony was making her elegant way towards them dressed in white slacks with something drifty and pricey on top. She unwisely lifted one hand to greet her and then quickly grabbed the mane.

'Ok, you can stop now.' Maisie, understandably obeying Kimi rather than her rider, stopped before Anna asked her to with the result that she tipped forward and bumped her nose on Maisie's neck. 'I've put the bar down to its lowest – I can't lower it more or she'll just step over it. Do you remember what I told you last time? Gather her up three paces from the jump and then give her a squeeze at the lift-off point.'

'Come on, let's give it a try,' Anna mumbled to Maisie's cocked ear, 'I don't want to either but do your best, eh? I'll try not to get in your way.' But, as they approached the jump Maisie interpreted Anna's gathering in of the reins as a signal to stop and they both drew to a sudden halt metres before the red and white rail. Maisie actually turned her head to look at Anna reproachfully. 'Fine,' Anna muttered, 'I'm going to leave you to it, next time.'

Briony was openly laughing as she rode Maisie towards the paddock rail and then turned ready for the second attempt. She couldn't blame her – Briony had so far resisted all Kimi's efforts to teach her to ride because she had some sense. This time Anna kept her hands in exactly the same place she always had them and merely gave Maisie a little kick as they neared the obstacle. Maisie hopped over it giving Anna a minor jolt but nothing worse.

'There you see!' Kimi cried, 'It's easy when you do it properly.' Anna patted Maisie's neck and circled again. 'Just one more time and then I'll saddle up Cora and we can go for a hack.'

While she was waiting for Kimi, Anna took Maisie to the fence for a chat with Briony. Maisie hung her head over the rail and dozed. 'How's things with you?' Anna asked.

'Busy. Lot of travelling but that's ok.'

'Kimi's not still nagging you about riding, then?'

Briony flicked her pale gold hair back. 'We do our own things,' she said neutrally, 'and that's not mine. How did you enjoy Appleby? Kimi was on fire when she came back – beautiful horse, even I can see that.'

'It was interesting,' Anna said, 'a glimpse into a different world.' She resolutely pushed all thoughts of Charlie to the back of her mind.

'Yes. One of my colleagues is working with a charity helping Travellers at the moment on an illegal eviction order – it happens often apparently. A Traveller family buys a plot of land but then either can't get planning permission to live on it or they're threatened with eviction even though it's their land because the decision is the local Council's and no-one wants Travellers living near them. It's a human rights issue, of course.'

This was far more interesting than the riding lesson and before she had realised it, Anna had slipped off Maisie's back to hear more. 'Actually,' Briony said, 'you may have seen another campaigning group at Appleby – they're called Roma Rights Defenders and they had a tent there – I think it was sponsored by Travellers' Times, the magazine and website? Did you see it? It's a very good thing, they're part of a pan-European activist network to challenge racism against Gypsies, they're almost all Travellers themselves.'

'No, I didn't notice but I'll certainly look them up. I'm sorry I missed them at Appleby.'

Briony leaned her forearms on the wooden rail and said quietly, 'I know I appear as a bit of a cold-faced bitch sometimes, Anna, and I admit I've deliberately created that persona because, frankly, I need to in the world I work in, but this stuff – oppression, injustice, matters to me. You know why probably better than anyone.' Their eyes met and there was silence for a moment as they recalled Briony's nightmare imprisonment in Cook County Jail for the alleged murder of her own child. 'It's not only domestic violence and trafficking and so on that we're fighting – one of the few communities who people at all levels still feel able to abuse with impunity are the Gypsies.'

'So,' Anna said, seeing Kimi riding towards her on Cora, 'what do you think of Kimi's idea to build a site on the farm?'

'What?'

'Oh, forget I said anything,' Anna added hastily, 'just a passing thought, I expect.' Maisie grunted as she scrambled back into the saddle and joined Kimi on Cora who was prettily executing a soft shoe shuffle to show off her newly oiled hooves.

When they went into the big field with a copse at its centre which lay between the farmhouse and the canal, Kimi went up the high end rather than the usual route which skirted the wood and led down to the bottom gate to the next field. She opened the top gate to the road leaning down from her saddle and waited for Anna to catch up.

'Why are we going this way?' Anna asked, fearing the danger of being on a road where cars might zip along and frighten the animals into unpredictable behaviour.

'I want to show you something,' Kimi said, 'don't worry, we won't be on this for long, just listen out and be prepared for any oncoming traffic. Maisie doesn't usually bolt.' Anna sighed and tightened her grip on the reins.

Before long they turned off the road down a rutted track with hedges either side as Kimi picked up the pace which meant both horses had to trot. At least this time she had stirrups and Anna did her best to rise to the occasion appropriately. The track went on for about a hundred metres and then petered out the other side of a five-barred metal gate. Kimi bent down, slid the bolt across and let the gate swing open inwards on its own momentum.

'I have a padlock on it, usually,' Kimi said, 'but I took it off this morning. You don't need to close it behind you, there's no animals in this field.'

Kimi drew Cora up in the middle of the field and patted her neck. They did make a fine sight, the two of them, Anna thought. It was hard to say which was the more striking, although, of course, Cora was the more genteel. Kimi pointed with her crop. 'Stream down that side, not bad at all – good water, there's even watercress in it in season so it must be pretty clean and then look how hidden this space is from the road.'

It was true. The hazel hedges had given way to mature trees like oak, sycamore and alder with some white willows among them so that the field had a private, protected feel to it. The grass was tussocky but that hardly mattered for Kimi's purpose.

'How far to the canal?' Anna asked glumly, feeling that something was expected of her but not able to share Kimi's enthusiasm.

'It's just one field down,' Kimi said, 'but it's a rough piece of land full of thistles and pits and ridges so we don't usually get anyone trying to cross it. It was probably the site of some warehouse or workshop for the canal ages ago.' Maisie had dropped her head and was snatching at grass. 'Don't let her do that! I've told you before. Pull her up.'

'For goodness sake, she's just having a snack.'

Kimi sensed Anna's feelings and rode nearer. 'You think I'm making a mistake, don't you?'

'Have you got planning permission, even?'

'No, but I'll get it.'

Anna tried one last objection. 'Are you sure this is what Travellers want? Have you actually asked around?'

Kimi dropped her head and looked sideways at Anna like a mischievous child. 'Have you forgotten – I have a source, an informant, a point of contact, you might say, don't I?'

Things seemed to be developing far faster than Anna had suspected. 'Have you seen him again, Charlie? Is that what you're saying?' She tried to keep the disapproval out of her voice but didn't succeed.

Kimi coloured and threw her hair back off her face. 'I'm hoping he'll come next week to see it. Bri will be away so we can discuss the site without any distractions. Don't go all school-marmy on me, Anna, I'm not hurting anyone, am I? I'm doing a good thing.'

Before Anna could answer, she gathered up Cora's reins and shouted, 'Watch this!' They trotted a little way before Kimi urged Cora into a bounding canter looping around in a big circle but after one circuit she brought the horse into the centre, sat back, shortened the reins and shouted, 'Hup!' Cora reared up and stood on her back legs treading the air, until after a few seconds Kimi let her down.

'Blimey,' Anna said, as astonished as Maisie at this spectacle.

Kimi trotted her over to join them. 'I found out she would do this on command by accident a couple of days ago,' she said. 'I think she's been a circus horse at some point. Who knows what else she might do?'

'Like her rider,' Anna said under her breath.

They walked together out of the field and Kimi secured the gate. Neither of them, it seemed, wanted to continue the subject of the proposed trailer site so Kimi moved off dangerous ground by asking Anna if she had heard from Mike. Relieved, she told Kimi what Mike had said and that a meeting had been set up between her and some members of Tom's family – relationships as yet unspecified – at Kenilworth Horse Fair. The minute she said the words she regretted them.

'You're kidding!' Kimi said, 'I didn't know about that – I'll come with you!'

'Actually, Kimi –'

'Oh, don't worry, I know you'll do your thing on your own, but I can't pass this up, you must see that.'

They rode side by side up the track until the road was in view and Anna could hold back no longer. 'I know you think I'm interfering in something that's not my business, Kimi, and you're right, but you are my friend and I have to say that I think you're being reckless. Apart from Briony, Charlie may be married or, at least, have a girlfriend or something. I think that Travellers take these things very seriously. You said you're not hurting anyone but – are you sure?'

Kimi halted Cora at the road and peered to left and right. Without looking at Anna she said coldly, 'As a matter of fact, he is married. So what? So am I. If you can't be happy for me, mind your own business, Anna,' and she turned Cora down the road towards the farm at a fast trot.

12

Anna drove home worrying. Of course, the site was a great idea and the location was perfect; it was the motivation that bothered her. What did she want from Charlie? A stimulating bout of passionate sex that satisfied her new-found lust which would conveniently be available right on her doorstep (when he was passing through) or did she have more in mind? What about him? How would he feel about being used in this way or did he feel he was the one using her? In any case, Kimi had been right, it was none of her business. She had warned her and she could do no more. If she pressed on that point Kimi would simply cut her off – she was, to put it simply, unbiddable in any circumstances.

But what about Briony? Anna had known her longer than Kimi and Briony's connection with Traveller life was very different and, Anna thought, a great deal more honourable. If the thing with Charlie carried on, with or without the site, how would Briony react if she found out? It would be bound to wound her deeply. Briony was not someone who gave her heart easily. Hearing her talk today without the usual studied cool manner reminded Anna of how deep Briony's feelings ran and how heroically she had overcome the tragedy of her life, the loss of her child.

When she got home she found George in the kitchen in the act of putting on the kettle, a welcome sight. To add to the pleasure, she saw two halves of a cake cooling on racks and inhaled the aroma. 'You'll make someone a lovely wife,' she said, dumping her bag on the chair.

'I see Bean's gender stereotyping is infecting you,' George said, bashing the tea-bag against the side of the mug.

'Oh, I know, sorry. I've tried talking to him but whatever I say just slips off his brain, somehow.'

'What about a fine? That's something concrete he might understand. He's not short of cash, I notice.'

'I'll have a think about it. Dad, can I ask you something? About Lena – about mum?'

George carried the two mugs to the table, set them down and then returned to the work top to press his finger lightly against each golden base of the sponges. 'Not cool enough to fill yet. Ok.' He sat down. 'What do you want to know?'

'This isn't upsetting for you?'

'Water under the bridge and in the Pacific Ocean by now, love, fire away.'

'I know this is mad, but I don't know her mother's maiden name – my grandmother. I can't believe I've never asked.'

George sucked in his breath. 'Oh, she was a tartar. You think Lena was a hard case but her mum was a greater force to be reckoned with. She didn't approve of me, of course, on principle, and I only met her a few times because the rows when we did meet were horrendous. I didn't say a word, it was her and Lena going at it hammer and tongs. I felt sorry for her husband Reggie – the silversmith, you know - he was a kindly man but reduced to silence and his allotment whenever he could get away with it. Sometimes I'd go and see him there. We bonded over his brassicas.' He laughed. 'I went to his funeral. It was years after Lena had left and he'd become a widower but I kept in touch.'

Something else Anna had never known because she'd never asked. Also, she had always assumed that Faye got her personality from Harry's mother since she resembled her physically but now she wondered if there was a bit of Lena's side in her, too. She could whip up a storm if crossed, that was certainly true.

'This is interesting, Dad, I've never heard you speak of them before.'

George gave a little snort of satisfaction. 'I've remembered! It was Bates – Lena's mum's maiden name – your grandmother, of course.'

'I've come across that name in my reading. You could be right about Lena's roots.'

'Really?' George said. 'Just a minute, let me get started on the filling now the butter's softened.' He returned to the table with a glass bowl heaped with icing sugar, a wooden spoon, a soup dish of butter and a teacup of hot water. As he began to beat in the butter, sweet powder rose up in a little cloud and Anna leaned forward to breathe it in and lick her lips.

'Lena couldn't stand either of them, of course, no-one had any time for their parents in our generation – it was fashionable to despise them. But, I remember she would use words I'd not heard before, like a skirt she got at a jumble sale she said was *kushti,* meaning beautiful, great. It's commonly used now but it was unusual then. I asked her about it and she said she'd picked it up when she was living in a squat in the East End. Now, of course, I doubt she was ever in London, but there you go.'

'Anything else?'

George worked more powdered sugar into the butter. 'Well, I don't know whether this was just her, but when you were a baby she came home one day to find me washing your terry nappies in the washing up bowl and she went absolutely mad, threw it out, and cussed me out with words that I'd never heard – I mean, they were a different language.'

'Why?' The icing was now folding into creamy ridges and peaks and she realised that she had watched her father do the same thing since as far back as she could remember. He added some drops of vanilla essence.

'Well, I didn't ask at the time under the circumstances but since then I've learned that Romanies generally are very clean in their ways and have a separate bowl for each thing so washing nappies in a bowl that also was used to wash plates and cutlery would have seemed very unhygienic.'

'This is fascinating, Dad. Anything else? Can I lick the bowl?'

'Wait till I've finished. Talk about unhygienic. Yes, there was another incident, now I think about it.' He stopped beating and pushed his glasses with their now dusty lenses back up his nose. 'You might remember this. I had to go to a car scrap-yard to see if I could get a replacement radiator cap for that old Cortina we had and you came with me – you were about seven, I think. There were quite a few of them then but not so many now – scrap-yards, I mean, not Cortinas. This one was in Stirchley. Well, the chap in charge had sent a boy off for it but the lad came back with one from a Vauxhall so he got shouted at and they were the same words your mum had used to me so I asked the man what they meant. He said that they were Romani for, well, a more colourful version of stupid fool.'

'Yes, I remember going because I was amazed at the squished cars stacked up in towers. I don't remember the rest of it.'

George got up and took the bowl to the rounds of cake, testing them again with a finger. He slid one off its rack on to a bread board and began to spread the icing with a palette knife. 'When you put it all together, it does seem likely that Lena, or at least her mother, were from Gypsy stock.'

'I don't suppose you can remember her mum's first name?'

George smoothed the surface of the cream and flipped the other half of the cake on top, pressing it gently down. 'Here,' he said, returning to Anna with the scraped bowl, 'you can keep up the tradition since there are no children around. Just a minute, it was an old-fashioned name.' He scratched at his chin, took off his glasses and polished them on the end of his shirt. 'Yes, it's come back to me. It was Mollie May. What's the matter?'

Anna stared at him. 'Dad, at Appleby I met someone, an old woman. She was horrible to me but said she recognised my looks and she said mum broke her mother's heart. She used the name Mollie May.'

They were in Cannon Hill Park and Alice was ecstatic. It was swarming with families and dogs which gave the Arts building and cafeteria and the seating area outside a happy, buzzy feel to which Alice responded. She had been promised a ride on a swan pedalo. The larger of the two boating lakes had been given over to these creatures and there were at least half a dozen already making their stately progress around the little islands. It looked like a restful way to spend an hour and Anna gladly dropped down into the seat next to Steve with Alice in the back. She wanted a buffer zone of distraction so that her brain could process the startling information from the morning without conscious assistance. It seemed to work better that way.

There had been a brief tussle of wills because Alice wanted to work the pedals but a one-minute demonstration proved that would be impossible and the kindly lads on duty had already told her she wasn't allowed. (This kind of prohibition was as white noise to Alice.) Steve trod down on the pedals in the reverse direction, as instructed, to get them away from the dock and then Anna conscientiously joined in on her side. What she had not anticipated was that because she was such a titch this would involve her lying almost horizontal so that her toes could get a purchase on the pedal bar when it was at full extension and this meant the moulded plastic seat caught her in the small of her back. She had also not imagined it would be hard work.

Alice was not impressed. 'We're too slow. Steve! Go faster!' Steve glanced down at Anna's scarlet face and sweaty hair as she struggled beside him. They were not yet even at the island from what she could see when she peeped over the side of the swan's wing.

'Everything all right down there, Captain?'

'Shut up.'

'I do have a suggestion.'

'Keep it to yourself if you know what's good for you,' Anna ground out.

'I'll paddle and you steer.'

'Oh, ok.' She slid back up gratefully and took hold of the little handle. 'I was perfectly fine paddling, though, so if you need a break I'll take over.' Steve winked at her.

'Go faster!' Alice instructed again.

'It is possible,' Steve said, as they skirted a massive swan bearing down on them, 'that we won't last the full hour – what do you think?'

The crazy golf should have worked out better and it would have been literally a walk in the park if Alice had been allowed to cheat. She was so outraged that she wasn't that she kept hitting her ball into the water deliberately for the pleasure of fishing it out again with one of the little nets provided. On the other hand, each hole took so long that Steve and Anna could chat. Couples and families frequently went through as Alice messed about.

'I'm wondering about taking her for a seaside holiday this summer,' Steve whispered, rubbing Anna on her back where the swan had pummelled her. 'What do you think? Would you come?'

'Buckets and spades and candy floss?'

'Yes, it would be fun. We've only really been for weekend trips to beaches before what with one thing and another. I thought Weymouth because of the donkeys. Do you think she'd like it?'

Anna heard a new edge in his voice. 'I'm sure she would, but you don't have to compete, you know.' Alice had finally potted the ball and they picked up their sticks and moved on.

'Two for me!' she shouted and Anna wrote down thirteen on the scorecard thinking she'd lose the tally at the next hole rather than face a tantrum at the end.

'Hey, Alice,' Steve said, pausing before he took his shot. 'Would you like to go to the seaside for a few days in the school holidays?'

'Yeah!' she shouted but added sternly, 'Not now, because I'm going to Auntie Julie and Uncle Simon's and I'm going to sleep in my pink bedroom.' Steve took his shot but Anna saw the wounded look on his face and wished she could find something comforting to say. It would be a bad thing for Alice and Steve, too, if he felt he had to keep giving her special treats to win her back all the time. In her opinion Alice got far too much special attention as it was but, fair enough, a proper seaside holiday with all the trimmings was a good idea given the fine summer it was turning out to be.

When she was a child, George had taken her to St David's in Wales every year to a rented caravan perched on a field above a cliff where a path, which she had believed for ages only they knew about, led down to a cove. No candy floss, no donkeys, but there were the seals that each year they would take a boat trip out to see and there was the wonky cathedral where you could roll a ball down the nave to prove how crazily built it was. In the evenings, or if it was rainy, she would work on that year's scrap book, sticking in feathers or wildflowers she had found with tape and writing out the adventures of the day. They played Snap or Happy Families and often people from the other caravans would gather together round a real fire in the evenings. Someone would have a guitar and the children would run about and play their own games and then the little ones would fall asleep on their parents' laps as the adults chatted and sang into the night. In the morning she and George would wake with smuts on their faces and no-one cared. It was hard to believe now that there were no mobile phones and the only technology was a little transistor radio so George could keep up with the cricket and the news. Anna watched Alice in her pristine designer dress (courtesy Briony's rich friend) as she set up her next shot and tried to imagine her in that relaxed, mucky, care-free scenario. It wasn't easy.

But, the afternoon had been a success for two reasons: it had taken her mind off her mother and Alice hadn't been rude to her once.

It was not until Sunday evening that Anna could sit down with her laptop and search properly. She had never expected to meet anyone who knew her mother, let alone her grandmother, but decades had seemed to implode like a house of cards falling in when George remembered the name.

Lena Walker's birth in Birmingham was not registered and neither was Mollie May Bates anywhere. But, maybe Mollie May was a nickname and not a birth name, or there could be several spelling variations, so Anna widened the time window on the search and began to push the information around wondering if Lena had been named after a family member. Suddenly a result popped up. A Lena Bates had been registered in Stoke-on-Trent. Possibly Mollie May's mother? In the second it took to speculate on that Anna had seen the date of birth on the entry. It was her own mother's. She sat transfixed by the words and numbers in front of her. Lena's biological father was not the gentle silversmith, Reginald. Or possibly they had married after Lena's birth so he could still have been the father?

She turned to the Marriage Index and searched for the marriage of Mollie May Bates to Reginald Walker of Soho Road, Birmingham, and found it was recorded not months after Lena's birth but sixteen years later.

She sat back, thoughts clicking and circling and then brought up Lena's birth certificate on which would be her mother's maiden name. It was not Bates, it was Lee. Anna's chest sucked in a gasp of air. Not only was Mollie May Lee Lena's mother, but Sigismund Bates, an entirely new person to Anna, was her father whom she had married at the age of seventeen in Shropshire. She stared, unseeing, at the keyboard and whispered, 'Mollie May and Sigismund Bates are my grandparents.' It was as though the two had rushed into her kitchen, huge and alien, and demanded she acknowledge them.

So, it seemed that Mollie May had married twice and Lena must have taken the surname of her mother's second husband, Reginald Walker, but that marriage had only happened a couple of years before George had been introduced to them by Lena as her parents.

Not only that. Lee is a very well-known Gypsy name, especially in that area – even Anna, with the little reading she'd done, had come across it many times.

She sat back in her chair and let her kitchen re-appear to her in comforting pieces because she seemed to have travelled a long way away. Here was the cooker, clean if stained, and the wide window out to the garden, just the apex of George's shed visible from this angle. Here was the dresser cluttered with mugs and photos and stuff which had been placed hastily down and was still there years later. Here was she who had stepped into a different zone where the very atoms of her genome had shifted.

George could not have known that Lena was not Reginald's daughter or he would have said so. He had assumed that Lena had grown up with both her biological parents, the people he was introduced to, not that she had been living with Reginald for only a short time when he and Lena met. No-one had told him a lie, he had just assumed the connections as anyone would, as they knew he would. Lena herself had not told him the truth.

So, what had happened? A second marriage was nothing to be ashamed of so why keep it a secret? Perhaps mother and daughter had been in Birmingham for years before Mollie May met Reg.

Anna went back to the indexes and looked up Sigismund Bates and found that he had died in the same year that Lena turned sixteen, just months before her mother married Reginald. There was no record of a divorce but, nevertheless, Mollie May could have left Siggi at any point after Lena's birth and only married when she knew he was dead.

She closed the laptop and stood up. It was too much and there were too many new secrets queueing up to explode at her. Her heart was thumping and the old anger was rising in her. Just scratching the surface of her mother's life brought confusion and pain. Everything about her mother had brought her pain. Now she sensed that another huge revelation was sitting like a ticking box waiting to explode and she didn't want it, she didn't want to know but her mother had a way of not taking no for an answer.

Ellis and Bean clumped into the kitchen and she almost fell on them. 'Are you hungry? Can I get you something to eat? There's sausages. Here, sit down, I'll make you both a cup of tea.'

They looked baffled. 'You all right, Mum?' Ellis asked. 'Only, we just had dinner.'

Bean said, 'Are you having a senior moment? My gran has those.' He spoke to Anna very slowly, 'Do-you-know-what-day-of-the-week-it-is?'

'Very funny,' she said. 'I want to talk to you again about your laundry.'

'We're only here to pick up my game,' Ellis said hastily, 'another time?' and they were gone.

13

Early on Monday morning Anna got a phone call from Rebecca Sitwell apologising for running out and asking if they could meet somewhere. There had been horrible scenes at home at the weekend and she needed to talk all of this weird stuff over with someone sane, she said. They arranged to meet in a café on New Street the following Saturday as Rebecca was coming in by train from Leamington to shop and that would be a convenient place.

It was not a busy time as Anna was waiting for documents to come before she could continue with her other cases so she decided to go over all that she now knew about Guthrie Cromer. There were far more questions than answers, the first one being, had he colluded with his mother in the New Zealand lie and, if so, why? She pulled out his slim file and looked again at the information she had: employment dates, birth certificate, death certificate, pathology report, insurance policies citing Bernice Sitwell as next of kin and the photo of him in his rugby team. She wrote out the dates for birth, marriage and death of all the key family members, including Guthrie's father, Philip Wright, to see if any patterns emerged but none did beyond what she already knew from her visits and from Rebecca.

Something had happened in Guthrie's eighteenth year which had blasted his mother, his aunt (and uncle?) and his cousin, like lightning striking a tree. She did not include Melanie Fisher but did wonder if she had been responsible for the graffiti on the tow-path rather than Bella. It might be more her style and she had been furious when she had left after the last meeting.

Then something caught her eye. The birth certificate for Guthrie listed the hospital in which he had been born which she had skipped over before, assuming it was in Stratford or nearby. In fact, when she looked it up, it was in Wales. A Google search brought it up but the website noted that the hospital's maternity unit had closed in 1998 when the larger hospital in Powys had absorbed it. It was now an Emergency Clinic. She pulled up a map on her computer and saw that it was only ten or twelve miles over the Welsh border but in what appeared to be a very rural area. The calculated driving time from Birmingham would be about two hours so she could make it by late morning. She picked up her desk phone to call Ted and then used her own phone to speak to Steve and George.

The motorway and dual carriageways leading to the Welsh border were unblocked and Anna made good time but decided not to stop for coffee until she had found the Long Edge Emergency Clinic. It was a decision she regretted forty minutes later when she had crawled along narrow lanes behind slow traffic but eventually the village announced itself and, a moment later, there came the cheering sight of a pub which told her that morning coffees were on offer.

The pub was almost empty and the young bartender, whose badge helpfully told her was called Denis, was willing to chat so she asked him about the old hospital. 'I was born there,' he told her, 'all the locals were. People here were very upset about them taking the maternity to Powys because it's so far away. Mam said it was lovely having a baby there because you'd know the nurses and quite a few of the other patients so they could have a good gossip.'

'So, would any of the people who worked there then, when it had a maternity ward, still be around?' At this, his expression shut down a little.

'Why do you want to know?'

Anna got out her card and gave it to him. 'We're trying to find out about a baby that was born here in 1983,' she said. 'Anything would be helpful.'

Denis relaxed and smiled. 'Might a bit of dosh be involved?'

Anna smiled back at his arch tone. 'You've guessed it.'

'Have your coffee. I'll phone my mam and see if she knows of anyone, ok?'

'I'm very grateful. But can I ask you something else? Is that a cranberry muffin I see before me?'

She sat in the bow window and relished the delicious coffee and lumps of cake making a mental note to go for a fast walk when she got home. Bobble, Big B, had been good for giving her some exercise, at least, poor mutt. It seemed that Safe 'n' Sound were no nearer to finding him a home and she knew how Ellis felt about that after raising him from a pup. It was impossible for them to have him back after the accidents he had caused – he was not a suburban dog for all the sweetness of his nature.

'Ok, then, you're in luck.' Denis was standing in front of her grinning.

'Great!' Anna prepared to finish her coffee quickly.

'No rush,' he said, 'you're not in Brum now. They're coming here, mam and Dilys, to talk to you. Take your time. I'll get you another latte, she'll be having her usual de-caff cappuchino. I don't know what Dilys drinks in that line. It's usually a pint when I see her at night.'

Anna only had time to review her facts and questions before two women entered the pub and made straight for her. One was as tanned as a handbag and wore a low-cut top over a short denim skirt with flip-flops. The other was taller and older with that direct gaze that characterises professionals who routinely deal with emergencies involving challenging behaviour. Faye's Year 11 tutor had had much the same look. They sat down with Anna, calling to Denis to get off his phone and hurry up with the coffees.

Initially the chat was off Anna's topic as it transpired that Denis's mother, Bethany, had just got back from a Caribbean cruise and moments of drama from that were shared. Dilys then told her latest tale of how a motor-bike and delivery van accident two days ago had resulted in body parts being strewn across the road just out of the village. Although she was now a health visitor, she had become involved as she had stopped at the scene to see if she could help on her way to check an ulcerated leg.

Anna could happily have let these anecdotes flow on, lurid and yet oddly cosy as they were, but Dilys halted herself when her Americano (black) was finished. 'Now then,' she said, 'you've not come all this way to hear us chunter on. How can I help you?'

After she had explained who she was, Anna came to the point about Guthrie Cromer. 'I'm wondering if you can tell me anything about his birth?' She gave the year.

'Exact date?'

'She's got a bloody fantastic memory,' Bethany said admiringly of Dilys. 'She's the best quizzer in Wales.'

Anna gave it to her and the names of Guthrie's parents. Dilys paused for only a moment. 'We didn't get many non-locals in the maternity unit for obvious reasons,' she said, 'so, yes, I do remember them. She was like a frightened rabbit, poor love, looked younger than her years and cried and cried after the birth. It takes some like that. The dad, he was glad to be out of it – he didn't want to even be in the room. They were too young to be parents, I thought. Maybe the baby wasn't planned, if you know what I mean. Lovely little chap, though.'

'Do you know why they were here? Why they had come to Wales from Stratford when she was so heavily pregnant?'

Dilys pursed her lips. 'Now, that I don't know. I asked him, while he was mooching about smoking, why he'd allowed her to travel when she was about to pop and he said they'd thought a little holiday in Wales would do her good and they hadn't realised she was so close which was a lie because it was February and cold and wet as you can imagine and no woman forgets her due date even if the man does.' She looked knowingly at Anna. 'I wouldn't say this is right for them but people did used to go to out-of-the-way places to give birth in the old days if they didn't want the pregnancy known.'

'I don't think Guthrie's parents made any secret of it,' Anna said thoughtfully. 'His birth was registered as usual just a few days later and the home address in Stratford given.'

'Well, I don't know, then,' Dilys said.

Anna was wondering about the change in Bella from frightened rabbit to the rather intimidating person she now was – maybe that had happened after Guthrie left. 'Do you remember anything else about the mother?'

Dilys stared out of the window. 'I remember her hair – everyone remarked on it. It was beautiful, very long and dark. When she came in she had it just tied back anyhow and you didn't notice it, but after the birth we washed it for her and combed it through and it fell down around her little shoulders like a film-star's. The baby had a good head of hair, too, although of course, it might not have lasted. They were a picture together.' Anna remembered the thick grey skein of hair that Bella had twisted up into a knot when they had met.

She thanked the two women, left Denis a good tip and asked where the nearest petrol station was. There was no point in going to the Emergency Clinic now. It was quite in character that Bella would have taken it into her head to do something as daft as dash off to the wilds of Wales just when she was due to give birth. She was possibly planning something 'natural' away from her doctor's control and had rapidly gone off the idea when the pains started. So, it had been a wasted journey, but enjoyable, as it turned out.

As she drove back she realised that she had been hoping that something would emerge that would mean she didn't have to talk to Bella and Bernice (and Richard) again but now that seemed inevitable. But what could that have been and how could it have helped? A pointless question since anomalies and oddities were just exactly what researchers looked for and investigated. Not every turned stone reveals more than bare earth, though. If it had been up to her she would have been tempted to drop the whole thing now, but Ted was worrying at it, not wanting to let it go. His attitude had changed since he had first given her the job, for instance, his approving this rather tangential excursion to Wales, and she didn't know why. She spent some time considering various options for the interviews which would now have to take place. Should she ask to meet Bella and Bernice together, perhaps with Rebecca as mediator, or should she speak to each one individually and if so, who should she talk to first? Rebecca had said that things at home were volatile so maybe she'd wait until Saturday to get her input. She seemed like the only stable one of the whole bunch although Anna had liked Bernice, too, before the hysterics.

As she turned on to the slow road into the city centre her thoughts shifted to the brief conversation she had had with Mike about meeting Queenie and Rakes in Kenilworth. They hadn't wanted her to come into the Fair itself but rather to meet at a gastro-pub not far away from the town. Anna had been disappointed, imagining the get-together taking place in one of the gleaming chrome trailers she had seen at Appleby, but she understood their caution and a time was arranged. She would take the photograph which Elizabeth had copied for her of Loretta, Tom and herself at the Symphony Hall.

She had passed the news on to Kimi hoping that she would not be joining her but Kimi had merely said that she had made her own arrangements. From her tone of voice she had not forgotten or forgiven Anna's warning.

It had been a long day and Anna was glad to get home after work.

Ellis was sitting at the kitchen table doing homework but as soon as she came in, he stopped. 'You all right, Mum?'

She flopped down at the table. 'Tiring day. I think it's going to be a fish and chips night – I can't face cooking and Pops won't be back from London till late, wearing his laurel crown, no doubt.'

'Mum?'

'What?'

Ellis stared at the table and then at her. 'Something funny's happened.'

Anna had been about to drag herself upstairs to change but settled back in her chair. 'How so?'

'When I was at school, I found this in my bag.' He pushed a creased envelope towards her on which her name was typed.

'From your teacher?'

'I don't know, but they don't do that. They tell you when they give you anything to take home and it's not like that, a sealed envelope. And I wasn't given it, I found it.'

Anna slit it open and pulled out a single piece of paper. On it was typed her home and work addresses, her work phone number, her car registration number and the names of George and Ellis. To this was added:

> *'We want you to know that we can do anything to you at any time, Anna Ames, you bitch. Watch and wait, not that it will do you any good, because we are coming to get you if you don't stop what you're doing.'*

'What is it, Mum?'

Ellis was far from stupid and she had been taken to task by him before for not trusting him with worrying information but should she show him this? Then she realised she had to because how else could they work out how it had been planted.

'It's a threat,' she said, 'not a very original one and quite melodramatic but as you say, odd. It's the sort of thing people usually tweet if they want to troll someone so I'm guessing this person doesn't know how to, or knows I'm not on social media.' Bella's seventies' domestic scenario was in her mind. She was unconvinced by the second person plural and felt sure that it had been used to attempt to add power to the threat. This must be a sole operator. The florid tone would be like Bella, certainly.

'Let me see.' Ellis read the note and looked at her. 'Has anything else happened?' So, she told him about the graffiti on the tow-path.

'How could that have got into your bag, though?' Anna asked. His school bag was a back-pack with many pockets but he had found this in the second largest one which was also the easiest for someone to access without detection. At school, it would have been very easy for another student to put something in as the bag was always lying around in the form room or a teaching room and he was not always with it. He kept his phone and his money and bus pass on him, not in the back-pack, so was not particularly careful about it figuring no-one would ever steal text-books.

'It could have been on the bus,' he said, 'or even in the queue for the bus. We were jostling around quite a bit this morning because it's Dan's birthday and Bean and me were trying to give him the bumps.' As she was uncomfortably processing the logic of this, Ellis voiced her thoughts. 'But someone would have had to follow me for ages to have that chance. I mean, normally, it's just on my back.'

'Are you ok, Ell?'

'Mm. Worried about you.'

She stood up and kissed the top of his head. 'I'll tell my boss tomorrow. It's silly stuff, really, but now it's happened twice I think it should be documented. I'm afraid I have upset a client about an inheritance, Ell, and she's a bit unbalanced so, even though I did nothing wrong, she might think she'll lose it because of me. That's all. It's not like she's a criminal or a gangster or something.' He still looked anxious so she added, 'She's even older than me!'

'Ok, in that case, I'll be on the look-out for a zimmer bandit,' he said, and went back to his maths.

14

Anna woke in the middle of the night and listened for noises. A door clicked closed. It was only George coming back from London – a train must have been cancelled or delayed – but she could not go back to sleep. She knew in that moment (her subconscious brain must have been working on it) that Bella would not be capable of tracking a teenager for days until she got an opportunity to plant a note on him. She was old, she was chaotic and histrionic, she lived in Stratford, not Birmingham; she was not the sort of person who discreetly tracks a smart teenager and gets away with it. This was not a comforting realisation because it only left Mel and Mel was young, obsessional and aggressive so altogether a scarier prospect.

The thought that such a person might have been hovering near her son for days, within touching distance of him, made Anna shiver. She thought of the long, pale bony fingers on which the ring had flashed and the white powder on her face. Mel might be sick enough to have fantasised the whole relationship with Guthrie, whom she may have known in reality only marginally, or not at all. If she was sufficiently disturbed she could be dangerous. Anna doubted if the police would be at all interested but she could try. Mel had Anna's work mobile number and might have tried to troll her online without success – or, maybe she worried that she might be traced – maybe, she'd been caught doing such a thing to someone else before.

Sleep was now impossible so Anna got up, slipped on her cotton robe and crept down the stairs to find the kitchen light had been left on. Her dad must have been exhausted when he got in and forgotten to turn it off. But it was Bean sitting at the kitchen table eating a huge bowl of sugary cereal which he insisted was the only breakfast he could manage.

'Can't sleep?' she asked, moving towards the kettle.

'Nah. I will in a bit but I've been gaming. Solid session.'

'You must find it difficult to keep awake at school,' Anna said.

Bean grinned. 'I take power naps. Like execs.'

She sat down and waited for the kettle to boil wondering about a piece of toast but not wanting to prolong the conversation with Bean. Perhaps she could take it back upstairs. 'How's your dad doing?'

He yawned. 'Sweet. His girlfriend's hot.'

'I'm thinking of fining you for sexist remarks while you're staying here,' Anna said, failing to strike the right tone.

'What do you mean? I'm not sexist.' Bean was now offended.

The kettle had boiled and Anna got up to make her tea. 'Would you say a man was hot?'

'No, I'm not gay!'

'I'm just trying to explain what a sexist remark is,' Anna said wearily, stirring. 'If you wouldn't say something to or about a man, you'd only say it about a woman, it's probably sexist.'

'Like saying, "She's having a baby" is sexist?' Bean retorted.

'Oh, for goodness sake.' Anna stood at the worktop and sipped her drink wishing she hadn't started this.

'If you're going to do that,' Bean said, now animated with a new thought, 'I think you should get fined for swearing.'

'I don't swear!' Anna said hotly, before she could stop herself.

'Yes you do. You're always saying shit and damn and crap. My dad says that it's the sign of an impoverished vocabulary.'

'What dictionary of clichés did he read that in?' Anna muttered. 'Isn't it time you went to bed?'

'You started it,' Bean said, rising from the table and leaving his cereal bowl in a puddle of milk, 'but you don't like people giving it back and that's women all over, my dad says.' He escaped into the hall but not before Anna had raised her mug into hurling position.

It was so fine on Saturday that Anna chose an outside table to wait for Rebecca so she could watch the cosmopolitan crowds go by and speculate on what clothes might suit her that worked so well on other women. A burkha probably came closest. She really did have to start exercising seriously – just planning to do it didn't seem to be working. Her phone beeped with a text from Steve. *Just arrived*, it said, *wish me luck*. She sent back a smiley face and added a heart and a black cat. Silly. Thinking about it, though, Alice had been much more mellow with her since Julie and Simon had come into the picture so maybe the discovery of new and agreeable family was helping the little girl to feel less threatened.

'Hi,' Rebecca said, 'Sorry I'm late.' She sat down and hung a shop bag on the back of her chair. 'Just been stocking up on running gear – there's a sale on.'

'No problem,' said Anna, 'I was just thinking about going for a run myself.'

Rebecca glanced at her and wisely let this pass. 'I must apologise again for how emotional I was before. You must have thought me very rude.'

'I thought you were very shocked as well you might be,' Anna replied. 'It's never pleasant to be lied to, but in those circumstances it was appalling. Would you like a coffee?'

'I'll just go and get a juice,' Rebecca said, 'back in a minute.'

A group of lads in Aston Villa shirts surged past laughing and shouting and Anna smiled at their exuberance. They were followed by a much quieter procession of Chinese tourists in sensible shoes who were clutching souvenir bags from the BMAG shop. Rebecca came back and sat down, unscrewing the top of her juice bottle. 'Do you mind if I get straight to it?' she asked Anna. 'Can I tell you about last weekend?'

'Of course.'

'I hadn't actually been home since I found out about Guthrie's death, so I didn't know how they were taking it. We'd had words on the phone because I was upset, of course, but you can't tell a lot from a phone conversation – not with my parents because they're usually pretty reticent about anything difficult. They got worse after my mum's stroke, because they're always together, I suppose.'

'Your dad doesn't work?'

'When it happened, the stroke I mean, he got a job analysing insurance data that he can do from home and still look after mum so neither of them gets out much, apart from mum's allotment and a bit of volunteer stuff. She's a gardening nut – that and seeing to her babies – the four-legged ones!' She looked about her at the lively street scene. 'Their world shrunk when Guthrie went and my mum got ill – they seem to only take an interest in me, which is a bit of a burden sometimes.'

'But it was different last weekend?'

'Totally. They were so angry with each other. When my mum's angry she shrieks and wails, it's awful to hear, but my dad goes really icy and just says a few pointed words that make her crazy, you know?'

'Do you mind me asking what they were angry about? I can understand that they would be grieving and distressed about losing their nephew and being lied to, but why angry with each other?'

'I know. I don't understand it myself. She kept calling him gutless and a coward and he kept saying she owed everything to him and what would happen to her if he left. She's not really that person at all – it was very strange.'

'So it wasn't about Guthrie, really?'

'In the end I got fed up with it. I shut them up and said I had something to tell *them* and even if they didn't care about Guthrie dying I bloody did, and I told them about the New Zealand lie and that it was Aunty Bella's fault that we lost him when we could have visited him anytime in the last twelve years.'

'What did they say?'

'It was scary, Anna. They just sagged and went silent – they fell apart in front of my eyes. Mum didn't speak for hours, she just sat in her chair staring at the wall and dad, he cried, he cried and cried. I've never seen him do that before. I had to leave that night but before I did I was hugging mum, trying to get her to respond, I was worried she would have another stroke, but she just kept whispering "I'll kill her, I'll kill her," over and over as though she didn't even know I was there.'

Rebecca sat quietly and Anna didn't want to speak either. Bernice and Richard had already known that Guthrie had died in Birmingham, they knew because of Anna's visit, but they had not known how long he had been living there because Richard had thrown her out before she could tell them. They must have assumed that he had only recently returned. The sun shone, the voices of the crowd rose and fell, phones jingled and somewhere not far away a busker was beating out a rap.

Eventually, Rebecca picked up her shoulder tote and pulled a buff envelope from it. 'I brought a photo for you to see so you don't think we were always weird,' she said. 'It's how we used to be before Guthrie disappeared – it's when we were a normal family.' She passed the 5"x7" glossy across to Anna who immediately recognised Richard, as thin then as now, and Bernice's fine bone structure although in this photo she was standing and laughing, her long dark hair blowing in the breeze. Rebecca was a leggy sub-teen, sticking her tongue out at the camera, and Guthrie was standing behind her looking much the same as in his rugby team photo. Bella must have been taking the photo because the only other person in the group was a rather stout woman with short, fair hair.

'Who's this?' Anna asked.

Rebecca frowned at her. 'It's Aunty Bella. You've met her, don't you recognise her?'

'But she's blonde.'

'Yes. She didn't bleach it or anything, she's always been blonde – well, until she went grey.'

Anna tried very hard not to show her reaction. 'So, Guthrie's father, when did he die?' She must know this but she'd forgotten and now it was important.

'Oh, it was sad for Guthrie and for Bella, I suppose. He died just around the time Gus was born, I'm not sure exactly when. He never knew him. Luckily for her, Bella I mean, she'd been given the house from her grandma who she was named after when she went into a nursing home, so she had that, and she got some insurance money from the accident Gus's dad died in, and then she's always had little jobs, you know, so she managed. Of course, mum was living with her when Guthrie was born, she was still at school. Their dad, Bella's and mum's, died of cancer and their mum died not long after when they were just children so Granny Bella raised them.'

Anna let the words flow over her, grateful that she had time to think. There was no reason to say anything to Rebecca at this point so she shelved the bombshell of information Rebecca had unknowingly given her and asked instead about the best way to set up another interview with her parents.

'Quite honestly,' Rebecca said, 'the way they are at the moment, I think it would be a mistake to try to talk to both of them at the same time.' She thought for a moment. 'Next Saturday my dad is coming to Birmingham to see a Blues game, it's almost his only outside interest, so I stay with mum while he's doing that. You could come to the house, or better still, if the weather's nice we could meet in the park not far from them. That way she's out of the atmosphere, you know? She seems better out of the house – more like her old self.' They made the arrangement and rose to leave. Unexpectedly, Rebecca hugged Anna saying, 'I don't feel so alone with it all now – thank you.'

Anna set off towards the Art Gallery thinking that a quiet visit to Burne-Jones might give her the thinking space she needed. The BMAG was moderately busy but she slipped quickly through to Gallery 14 and grabbed a folding stool so she could sit opposite King Cophetua perpetually adoring the rather bored Beggar Maid.

She liked the huge mixed-media cartoon for several reasons. She liked the fact that the Beggar Maid was not over-impressed with the King and that he was so patient and humble (he had even taken off his crown) so it was ideologically right-on, not just for the late nineteenth century, perhaps even more so now. But, best of all, she liked the handsome King C and she had to admit that her eyes rested on his face more often than the centrally placed but vacuous Beggar Maid. Fair enough, though, there had been more than enough images for the Male Gaze to enjoy in the last thousand years, so she felt entitled to her pleasure.

It was only when she was seated, with her eyes effortlessly following the directions the painter proposed (for the most part), that she took a deep breath.

Bella Cromer was not Guthrie's mother, Bernice was. She really was his next-of-kin. Apart from anything else, it explained Bernice's powerful reaction to the news of his death because he was her son. The reason for the initial subterfuge could be the familiar scenario of an under-age girl's baby being given to an older relative (usually the girl's mother) who would claim it as her own. Padding would be involved, a disappearance (perhaps for months) before the birth, and many, many lies. This certainly still happened in the 1980s and beyond although it was far less common since attitudes to illegitimacy had softened so much in the last half century. But then, Anna reflected, attitudes to under-age sex had hardened, hadn't they? Bernice would have been only fifteen when she was pregnant so in modern times the child's father, assuming him to be over sixteen, could have been put on the Sex Offenders Register. And who was the father? Pointless to speculate. The description Dilys had given was so generic as to be useless.

Again, the fresh information raised more questions than it answered, the chief one being why, in these more enlightened times, Bernice had not claimed Guthrie, although her belief that he could not be found could be a reason, and there was still the old question of what family tsunami had happened when Guthrie was eighteen. Anna thought about Rebecca and imagined it could only add to her grief and distress to know that Guthrie was even closer to her than she had thought – had been, in fact, her half-brother.

Anna decided that while she was here she would greet a couple of favourites and walked off to see Arthur Gaskin's Wild Swans and the 16th century vellum map of Europe carried on the ships of all Sicilian navigators, which was a thing of beauty and had Sicily very firmly at the centre of the world. But, she thought, that's how we are, isn't it? We draw maps of our personal landscape with ourselves at the centre. Bella wasn't alone in doing that.

She strolled slowly out of the gallery and into the sunshine wondering how Steve's weekend was going so that she didn't have to think right now about how she would handle next Saturday's interview with Bernice. As she was walking through the Piccadilly Arcade to the station, looking up to admire the paintings on the ceiling, her phone jingled. It was Tasha, Faye's friend, so she stopped walking and went to the window of a jewellery shop to take the call.

'I'm sorry to bother you, Mrs Ames,' Tasha said nervously, 'but I'm worried about Faye.'

'It's no bother,' Anna said, 'what's the problem?'

'You know we went out last Friday night?'

'Mm.'

'Well, she was acting so wild, so over the top. She's always the life and soul, you know, but she was drinking a lot and, well, flirting with boys we didn't know. It's not like her. Usually, if a guy approaches her she cuts him down but it was her making the advances.' Tash paused. 'We were a bit embarrassed actually. Girls don't usually flirt when they're out together – it's sort of an unwritten rule. You know, this is our time.'

'She was wearing a lot of make-up – I noticed that.'

'Jack phoned while we were at the bar and she didn't take his call.'

'Ok, Tasha, I really appreciate you telling me. I was a bit worried on Friday night because of the way she looked so I'll see her and talk to her. Thank you.'

'Um,' Tasha hesitated.

'I won't tell her you said anything.'

'Oh, good, thank you. Bye.'

15

When she got home, the first thing Anna did was look up the obituaries in the now fully digitised Avon Courier for Philip Wright's exact date of death and there it was: a full six months before Guthrie was born in the Welsh cottage hospital. She picked up her phone and called Bernice.

'Sorry to be mysterious, but I'm just following something up,' she said. 'Do you remember what caused Bella's husband Philip's death?'

'Why?'

'Could be nothing, just loose ends.'

'Well, it's embarrassing.'

Anna sighed. 'Really, Bernice, I've heard everything.'

But she was wrong, she hadn't heard this one. 'It was accidental death by erotic asphyxiation the Coroner said.'

Dear God, Anna thought, what a family. So, probably, the man who was with Bernice at the birth was the baby's father but that scarcely mattered now. What did matter was that because of Philip's death Bella had no-one to contest (or betray) her plan to take Guthrie from Bernice. The only people who would know would be the two sisters and a man who was probably only too happy to get shot of the whole embarrassment. Did Richard know that his wife had had a child when she was so young, Anna wondered? They hadn't married until she was twenty and he was twenty-four so it was entirely possible that he didn't know and believed, had always believed, that Guthrie was his wife's nephew. Assumptions are made when we don't even know that's what they are, she thought, remembering George and Lena.

On the way home Anna had another thought. Bella had certainly known that Guthrie was living in Birmingham, she had expressed no surprise that he had died there, but there was a hint that she knew what he did. She had speculated that a grateful client might have left him money (before she knew Anna's true purpose in contacting her) so she might have known what he did for a living. Assuming that they were not keeping in touch – and that did seem to be the case – how did she know? Perhaps Anna should revise her dismissal of Bella as the one stalking Ellis. It would have taken considerable ingenuity to stalk Guthrie since he had no social media profile (Anna had checked) and was not even on a professional site like Linked-In. He had no landline and a Google search revealed nothing, even to the tenth page. Of course, there was the electoral register – he had not changed his name. She could have simply found his address and followed him to find out where he worked.

Steve texted again when she got home, this time to send photos of Julie and Simon's house (huge) and garden (extensive). He had added an exclamation mark. Anna took a photo of a bottle of wine and two glasses on her kitchen table and sent him that with a kiss.

She was due to see Elizabeth in the afternoon to bring her up to speed with events and give her the painting and the wooden flower and was looking forward to it but since Tasha's call she wanted to do something about Faye, too. She phoned her but the call was rejected. It was only lunchtime, after all. Perhaps George was in his shed.

He had the door open to let in the summer air and curled on the rag mat by the door was a black cat. 'Hello,' Anna said to it, 'Who are you?' It politely stood up and arched its back to be stroked. 'Where's this come from, Dad?'

George was in pre-magazine production fervour. He had a system of coloured paperclips to indicate the suitability of various poetry submissions for the next issue so there was a stack of papers with these attached and another stack of notes which he would edit together to be his newsletter that also appeared in the mag. Ashok did the art work on the covers so he didn't have to bother with that. The stacks of work were in the middle of his desk surrounded by all the usual detritus that landed up there. He looked up over his glasses. 'What? Oh, her. I don't know where she lives but she often visits since Big B left.'

'She's a bit skinny, should I get her something to eat?'

'Do you want her to move in?'

'Ok, I won't,' Anna said reluctantly because she liked the sleek look of the cat which resembled the emoji she had only recently sent to Steve.

'Did you know that black male cats are the hardest to find homes for?' George asked. 'Do you suppose that's racism or superstition?'

'Maybe a paucity of witches.'

George stopped organising and sat down. 'Come in then and tell me what's on your mind, Annie, instead of hovering there and interrupting Macavity's nap.'

Anna went inside the shed and sat down on the old rocker so that her legs were caught in a wedge of sunlight from the door which the cat was also enjoying. 'Wasn't Macavity male?'

'I'm protecting her from Bean's misogyny by re-labelling her gender.'

'Ha.'

'So what is it?'

How many times in her life had she come, like this, to mull over a problem, a hurt, or even some aspect of the meaning of life with her dad, to be met with his undivided attention? Thousands of times. How lucky was she. She tried not to see how thin his shoulders were getting and how his spine was developing a stoop.

'Tash phoned me about Faye and I was worried myself.' She filled him in.

'Maybe now Jack's working at weekends she's lonely,' George said, 'I don't suppose she's ever felt that lost, hollow feeling before and she doesn't know what to do with it.'

'It's basically a money problem,' Anna said, admiring the neat curve of the cat's curled tail. 'I've been thinking about the lump sum that Gerald Draycott kindly left us to take care of Harry, but we didn't get a chance to use it for that and you said, and you were right, save it for his children. Has the time come, Dad, to use that?'

'Half of it is Ellis's, of course. Are you thinking of a deposit for a house?'

'Mm – they're talking about it.'

George propped his bristly chin on his fists and stared at nothing for a few minutes. Macavity stood, stretched so strenuously that she shivered, and came to be petted by Anna who rubbed her under her ears and along her back, estimating how much flesh she had under her fur. She was probably a healthy weight for a young female, but certainly on the slim side.

'We could do that although it would only cover ten per cent of the very cheapest house nowadays,' George said, 'but we need to think it through. Jack is doing his best for them, he's really stepping up to his responsibilities and he may feel undermined if we just hand over cash. It may hurt his pride. His parents can't afford to do that and neither could we if it hadn't been for Kimi's dad's generosity.'

'And it would reward Faye's bad behaviour, too. I do see that. The last thing she needs is to get what she wants by upsetting everyone. But, on the other hand, if we do have the means to help and don't do it, would that be right? You and the in-laws helped Harry and I get started – we never could have done it without you.'

Anna felt a soft pressure on her thighs and saw that Macavity had leaped up and landed with the lightness of a ballet dancer. She stroked the delicate face and admired the yellow eyes. Macavity admired her back, purring like a rasp.

'Let's have a think,' George said. 'We need to handle this carefully. I do agree that they need the money now, or soon, there's no point in hanging on, houses aren't going to get cheaper – but doing it the wrong way could cause resentment.'

'Ok. I'll look into mortgages, too – isn't there some help-to-buy scheme for first timers?' She didn't want to move because Macavity had now settled into a warm cushion on her lap, but she knew her dad wanted to get on. She lifted the cat up and held her in her arms for a moment and then gently put her down on the floor. George was right – the gift had to be tactfully given.

Anna phoned Faye again in the evening and this time she answered sounding quite bright and chatty so she asked her to meet on Friday evening for a meal out and was able to go to bed feeling happier than she had. As far as Guthrie's estate was concerned she could do nothing until she had talked to Bernice. Elizabeth had been charmed and delighted by the painting and by the news that Anna might meet Tom's family very soon at Kenilworth. That left the unpleasantness with Kimi to deal with at some point but Anna found herself unwilling to engage with it just yet because she still thought Kimi was behaving badly and whether it was any of her business or not, she didn't want to spend time with her at the moment.

On Sunday night Steve texted: *We're home, she's in bed, can you come down?* and, of course, she went.

'Come into the living room, I've got some Cabernet Sauvignon opened.' They settled on the couch and Steve put a glass in her hand. 'Honestly, Anna, if I didn't have you to talk to I'd go nuts.'

'And then there's my pneumatic charm. So how was it? Tell all.'

'They were very nice to Alice, very, very nice – me, not so much.'

'What are they like?'

Steve leaned back and sighed. 'I like him, Simon, more than I like her to be honest. He doesn't talk as much as Julie but he says more, if you know what I mean.' Anna nodded and sipped her wine. 'Julie, well, she's a bit high-maintenance. He told me she had the workmen out ten times after they'd fitted the new kitchen just to do things like scrape off a stray hair of paint or re-set a tile because she'd changed her mind. He seemed to think it was admirable but I don't.'

'How about Alice? How did she like them?'

Steve frowned and she snuggled her head into the hollow of his shoulder. 'She was quiet at first, nervous, I suppose. You know how she can be excessively polite when she's out of her comfort zone?' Anna struggled to think of an example of Alice being even normally polite. 'You remember, when she first met Briony in the farm kitchen and she was so impressed by her, she put her hand up to ask a question?'

'Oh, yes, ok.'

'But she was soon back in charge, demanding to see things, bouncing on her pinker than pink bed, insisting that I go with her everywhere and then telling me to go away when she had got them under her thumb.' He laughed.

'So what did you do with yourself?'

'When I'd been dismissed? Read a book I saw in Simon's study that he recommended. It was an American thriller about a man whose wife and children are murdered and he goes on the run but you don't know if he did it or not. Very gripping. In fact,' Steve smiled down at her giving himself double chins, 'I remember more about the book than about the visit.'

Anna grunted in amusement. 'Ok, then, cut to the chase – does Alice want to go back on her own?'

'I asked her that on the way home and watched her face in the rear-view mirror. She thought quite a long time and looked a bit worried and then she said she did want to go again but only if I came with her.'

'Not bowled over, then?'

'It seems not, not completely, anyway.' Steve shifted and turned towards Anna, kissing her upturned face. 'Enough about me and mine – how was your weekend?'

Anna pulled his head down for more, enjoying the heat and musk of his body and the softness of his lips and wondering how deeply asleep Alice might be. When they stopped for breath, she said, 'It's been rather a surprising weekend one way and another, actually, but the surprise I'm hoping won't happen now is for Alice to come down.'

Steve rose from the couch and trapped a chair under the door handle. 'I've done my duty and bitten my lip for two days and I claim my reward.'

'Quite right, too,' Anna said, 'get over here.'

16

The working week passed as usual, still no call from Kimi, and the Friday night meal out with Faye was so pleasant that Anna decided to leave saying anything about the money situation until she and George had worked out a plan. Saturday turned out to be fine in this lovely summer they were having, so a text from Rebecca confirmed that the three of them would meet in the fresh air.

Anna got out of the car in Stratford-on-Avon and stood for a while studying the billboard map of the layout of the park. There were curving paths and a pool, a war memorial and a children's play area but Rebecca had said they should meet at the café as there were outdoor tables so Anna set off to find it. The park was more pleasant than the map promised because the paths were mostly tree-lined and the park's features were set among well-kept flower beds. The café was busy but there were still some empty tables and Anna recognised Rebecca's strong, athletic figure approaching from a different direction pushing her mother's wheel-chair. As they drew closer together and waved, Anna saw that Bernice wasn't doing well at all. Unlike the bundle of cheeriness she had presented at their first meeting, she now seemed to have shrunk inside her skin like a rag doll.

The greetings were subdued. 'I'm sorry you've had more shocking news,' Anna said, deciding that chit-chat would be an insult given how devastated Bernice must feel.

Bernice merely nodded, glancing away, and Rebecca said, 'Mum told me they believed Bella about New Zealand because the university wrote to Guthrie after he'd left and asked whether he was planning to take up his place since he had not signed in during registration in Freshers' Week. She showed us the letter.'

'I don't want to distress you even further,' Anna said, 'but can you tell us what happened that caused Guthrie to go away? Unless you've already explained to Rebecca?'

'No, she hasn't,' Rebecca said quickly. 'She said she'd tell me today.'

Bernice was wearing a thin top with a drawstring at the neck and began to pick at the tie. 'I don't really want to talk about it,' she said. 'It's all been awful.'

'Please, Mum.'

'Turn me round so I'm not facing into the sun, then,' she said rather peevishly, and Rebecca did. 'Alright. You do deserve to know, pet, since it's all coming out now.'

Anna wondered how Rebecca would cope with the big revelation that was about to be made but she was a steady young woman. The family at the next table got up and left which meant the three of them were now surrounded by a scattering of empty drink cartons, dirty plates, soiled napkins and space.

Bernice said, 'Guthrie was eighteen and we were all at Bella's waiting for his A Level results to see if he'd got good enough marks to go to uni. He'd been accepted provisionally, but he had to get the marks. Rebecca was away doing something with the school. He said he'd phone us when he got them - he'd gone to the school, you see, with his friends. But he didn't do that.'

'Why not?'

'He came home instead to tell us that he'd done well, he'd got the marks he needed so we were all pleased, of course, and congratulating him, but he didn't seem so pleased himself. He seemed nervous, not excited, so Bella asked him what was the matter, why wasn't he happy about it? Then he told her, told us, that he didn't feel ready to start uni and that a friend of his was going to New Zealand and taking a couple of years to travel the world and he wanted to do the same. He said lots of people had gap years, or a few years off, before studying and that's what he wanted to do. He said he'd been saving his wages from working Saturdays at the garage for the airfare and then he would work his way round like the Aussies do.'

'That must have been a surprise! How did Aunty Bella take it?' Rebecca was hanging on every word.

'She went mad. You know what she's like, she doesn't hold back. Well, she shouted and screamed and said she had never had the chance to go to university and he owed it to her and she wouldn't stand for him going away. She said wild things like she'd lock him in his room and I think that was what did it. He was a man, not a boy. He charged off up the stairs and she broke down and sobbed but before we knew it, he was back down with his sports bag saying he was going and she couldn't stop him and he left.'

'Did you and dad go after him? Did Bella?'

'He had a little car then, do you remember? He took off in it – sold it later, I suppose. He had his passport and we could never have found him. Then, a month or so later, Bella told us that he had sent a postcard from Auckland saying he was staying there and wished us all well but never wanted to see us again. She said it had upset her so much she'd burned it. I thought we would have to have her sedated, she was in such a state.'

'But you were the one that had a stroke when he left,' Anna said quietly.

'Oh yes, but that would probably have happened anyway,' Bernice waved her hand as if to waft such an idea away. 'It was just coincidence, the doctors said, but all the upset wouldn't have helped.'

Anna felt the adrenalin drain from her body and numbness take its place.

Rebecca was now crying silently and Bernice, herself in tears, put out her hand to hold her daughter's. 'I'm sorry, love, but you can see now why your dad and I believed Bella when she lied to us about where he was?'

Rebecca hugged her and wiped her own face and Bernice's. 'I'm sorry, Mum, it's just so wicked.'

Anna said nothing. Bernice had had time to prepare this story and had thirty five years of practice at deception. 'Perhaps you could get your mum a cup of tea?' she suggested.

'Oh yes,' Bernice said, 'that would be lovely.' She blew her nose on her handkerchief and Rebecca went off to join the queue. She turned to Anna, looking much more relaxed. 'Families, eh? You must see it all.'

Anna moved closer to her. 'Yes, we do,' she said. 'Sometimes we find that people are not who they say they are. For instance, sometimes an aunt is really a mother.'

Bernice froze. 'What?'

'You were Guthrie's mother, weren't you, not Bella?'

'How?' Bernice shot out her hand and gripped Anna's. 'Don't tell Bella you know, don't tell Rebecca, don't tell anyone, anyone! They mustn't know! Promise!'

Anna felt the stinging pain of Bernice's grip but the terror in her voice was worse. 'Why not?' she begged, seeing that Rebecca now had the tea and was putting in milk at the counter so they only had moments to talk. 'Bernice, Guthrie left a great deal of money – your life could be so much better, easier – '

131

'No, no, no!' Bernice cried, 'give it to Bella, give it to her, all of it! You don't know what she's capable of – I don't want it – please!' Then she must have seen Rebecca was approaching because she stopped and froze again.

'Oh, Mum,' Rebecca said, arriving and setting down the tray and looking into her face, 'I'm sorry that remembering all this has upset you. Let's just enjoy the tea now and talk about something else.'

'Yes, love, yes, let's do that,' Bernice said. 'It's all so long ago and there's nothing to be gained by dredging it all up.' She shot a piercing look at Anna.

But after talking about the unusual weather and Rebecca's job, the subject of Guthrie's disappearance was raised again. 'I don't understand,' Rebecca said, 'why he didn't ever get in touch with *us*. We believed we couldn't find him, but he knew where we were. He just wasn't the sort to bear a grudge for years like that, was he, Mum? And, in any case, we hadn't done anything wrong.'

'I don't know,' Bernice said, looking round vaguely. She hasn't prepared for this question, Anna thought. 'Maybe he just wanted a fresh start.'

'No,' Rebecca said firmly, 'I know what must have happened. Aunty Bella must have lied to him, too. Told him never to come back, never to contact us. She's spiteful enough to do that. She would have said we didn't want anything to do with him or something like that, made up some story.'

Bernice stared at Anna. '*Was* Bella in contact with him?'

'I don't know,' Anna said. 'I do know, as I told you, that he used your name as next-of-kin.' The warning was clear in Bernice's eyes at this, but Rebecca was on a different tack.

'Oh, that shows he still cared for us!' she cried. 'Whatever Bella said, he still thought of us as family!' Bernice nodded, but Anna could see that she was at the end of her limited stamina – her chin was trembling and her hands fidgeted uncontrollably. It would be cruel to impose further strain on her.

'I'll go now,' she said, getting up, 'thank you for seeing me.' She held out her hand and Bernice gripped it tightly, her eyes burning in her scared face.

Anna hugged Rebecca and walked away down the shady path to her car. On Monday she would tell Ted everything she had discovered about this case because it had grown too big, too complex, and, to be honest, too frightening, to handle on her own. For the first time in her career she wanted to kick the responsibility upstairs for someone else to deal with it. What was Bella capable of that would cause her disabled sister to give up a small fortune out of fear?

As soon as she got home Anna sat down with her laptop and started to compose her report to Ted. She wrote down everything of significance: dates of meetings and biographical information, conversations, speculations, statements made by all parties with verbatim comments in italics. She thought about adding the two threats to her but decided against it – there was no evidence that Bella had been responsible. While she worked, George, Ellis and Bean pottered in and out of the kitchen, but left her alone. It took her two hours and when she had finished she re-read it and then made a summary with bullet points. It was too late for lunch and, in any case, she was too wound up to eat. She picked up her phone.
    'Rosa? Are you up for a visit?'
    'Great, but bring some milk, would you, I've run out.'
    It wasn't that she needed to tell her about the case, she had no intention of doing so, it was that she wanted the comfort of Rosa's colourful boat and cheerful company. As she drove over to Selly Oak she tried to remember how many years it had been since Rosa had come into their lives. Harry had been too ill for George to cope with on his own and Rosa had been wonderful with him and since then she had become a kind of oasis of sanity for all of them – even Ellis still liked to go to the canal mooring from time to time although Faye hadn't been for ages. Alice loved her, running to her to be hugged and telling her important secrets in the private fore-cabin where Rosa slept, and much as Anna understood that, it saddened her that the little girl was never that way with her.
    Anna parked the car, slipped through the gate on to the tow-path that served the moorings and walked slowly along enjoying the rose-bay willow herb springing up to hide that season's graffiti on the old brick walls lining the path. She hoped Rosa was alone. Fond of her half-brother as she had become, Len was a demanding presence and she wasn't in the mood for him. The relationship between Len and Rosa was endearing but puzzling. Len had declared himself to Rosa not all that long ago and she had, in her own way, reciprocated, but that seemed to have made no visible

change in either of their living arrangements. Rosa stayed on her narrowboat and Len stayed in his council flat in the city but when they were together they seemed perfectly amicable, affectionate, even. Not for her to question that.

'Hey,' she called when she reached Rosa's boat, 'Anyone at home?' The open doors to the cabin were now full of Rosa herself, drying her hands on a tea towel.

'Step on,' she said, 'I've just finished icing some cupcakes.'

'You say the nicest things,' Anna laughed and gingerly stepped across on to the side and the deck. 'Here's the milk.'

'Good, I was gasping for a cup of tea. Sit yourself down and I'll put the kettle on.'

Anna sat on a crocheted cushion on the deck and leaned back against the hot, painted wood. A rented boat chugged past with waving occupants looking smug to have booked a week when the weather was so perfect. The sound of the busy Bristol Road a quarter of a mile away could be heard but it was just a hum except for the screaming emergency vehicles on their way to the Queen Elizabeth Hospital. Anna closed her eyes and inhaled the smell of green water and calor gas. A breeze lifted hair from her forehead with a pleasant soothing effect. 'Do you want any help?' she murmured, hoping not to be heard.

Rosa plonked a mug down beside her and a plate with a luscious cupcake topped with swirled icing and shaved chocolate. She sat down on the opposite side of the boat, which tipped and then righted itself. Rosa was not only generous in her nature. 'Aren't you having one?'

'I never feel like eating something I've cooked until later, I won't go short. How's things?'

'I love the hair,' Anna said, 'it's your most exotic look yet – well, that I've seen.'

Rosa reached up and patted the spiky creation of lime green braids bound at their tips with scarlet rubber bands. 'It pulls my scalp a bit – I might have to take them out. Only Gemma from two boats down is learning to do them and I said she could practise on me.'

'So how's my brother?' Anna asked, 'I can never get hold of him. Does he actually use his phone?'

'Well, you know Len,' Rosa smiled. 'He's not really of this century, is he? I imagine him in saggy tights and a tunic with one of those pixie hoods.' This was such an apropos image that Anna spluttered her tea. 'He drops by a few times a week so I'll let him know to get in touch.' Anna bit into the moist, sweet cake and moaned. 'So what have you been up to?' Rosa asked again.

'Oh, you know, the usual.'

'So why are you so het up?'

'I'm perfectly relaxed,' Anna said, and then added, 'Ok, there's something going on at work but I can't talk about it. It's doing my head in but I've decided to get someone at a much higher pay grade to worry about it.'

Rosa took another sip of tea. 'Right-oh. Well, I have some news for you.'

'Good or bad?'

'Er, good and bad, I suppose, but mostly good. Kara's been over to tell me that she and her dad are both off to Glasgow.'

'No, really?' Kara and Robert had been the subjects of a recent investigation by Anna that had taken them all on an emotional roller-coaster but Rosa had been a large part of Kara's recovery while she had stayed on the boat after the horror was over. Robert had been given a place at Clyde Marine Training to be a Merchant Navy navigator. 'It makes sense, though, for her to go up there – I'm sure she'd get a great reference from Church View and there are carers wanted everywhere. It's so nice that they want to be near each other.'

'Yeah. A happy ending.'

'Or beginning. What's the bad news?'

'Dean.'

'Oh. Sorry.' Rosa's brother was the opposite from her in every way: drug user and dealer, thief, liar and thug. This was how Anna saw him. Rosa saw him as the frightened little kid who'd been knocked about by their dad and put in a Young Offenders' Institution to learn bad ways.

'He's inside again, but at least I can get to see him now my van's back on the road. The cup-cakes are for him – I'm going up there tomorrow.'

Rosa had no illusions about Dean but she was that rare person capable of unconditional love and Anna admired her for it. Easy to love a nice person, easy to pretend a horrible one has no faults if you want to, but to see someone's faults clearly and still love them – that was heroic. Anna tried to remember what Jane Austen had said: not that we must love people, but that we must 'develop the habit of learning to love.' Rosa was one of the few people she knew who didn't need that advice.

She watched two boys with a golden Labrador walking down the public tow-path on the opposite side of the canal eating chips out of paper. 'Speaking of difficult relatives,' she said, 'my mother's raised her ugly head.'

'Tsk, Anna,' Rosa reproached her. 'Isn't she dead?'

'But she won't lie down.' So she told Rosa about the old woman at Appleby Fair and the things her dad had told her and what her research had revealed. 'I'm pleased about having Gypsy heritage, that's something, but it isn't pleasant to know she was so hateful, even to her own mother.'

'So you don't know why they gave up the travelling life?'

'No. I'm not sure I want to if it was something nasty.'

'I've got Traveller blood myself,' Rosa said, 'quite a few of the long-time canal people have so we might be related!'

'That's a much happier thought,' Anna smiled. She stood up. 'Thanks, Rosa, you've worked your magic and I am no longer twitchy and fit to be tied, as the Americans so succinctly have it. I hope your visit to Dean goes well.'

Rosa folded her in into her tie-dyed T shirt and leaned her cheek on the top of Anna's head. 'Take care of yourself. Just watch out.'

17

Ted read the report, put the paper down on the desk and regarded Anna anxiously. 'I'll take this from here,' he said. 'Just leave it with me.'

'I was hoping you'd say that. I didn't fancy another round with Bella.'

'No, no, it may be a police job now, but I'll talk to Mary Willis first.'

'The police? What crime, Ted? Bernice was very frightened – don't let them go barging in.'

'Impersonation? Intimidation? I don't know. What would be good is if there was DNA evidence that Guthrie was Bernice's son. No problem getting his DNA, of course, and they could insist on hers but I'm not sure if it would show the difference between a mother and an aunt. Do you know?' Anna shook her head.

'She admits she's the mother and doesn't want the inheritance. Could we just recommend that Bella gets it? That's what Bernice wants.'

'It's a tricky one, but, I'm happy to say, not our decision.'

'I could look up the DNA thing.'

'Ok, but just out of interest, all right, don't do anything. I don't want you involved any more. We still don't know who's been harassing you.'

'Thank you, Ted.' He didn't seem to want her to go so, after a moment, she added, 'You ok?'

Ted wiped his face as if it was covered with cobwebs. 'The therapy's bringing up a lot of stuff. Stuff I haven't thought about in ages. I thought we would talk about the marriage but she hasn't mentioned it. She keeps wanting me to talk about my dad.' Anna remembered Ted telling her once that he had been in and out of prison most of Ted's life and no use when he was at home. 'So maybe being irresponsible is genetic, eh?'

Anna ignored his attempt at laughing it off. 'You're doing a good thing, Ted, a lot of people wouldn't have the courage.'

He pushed the report round on his desk with his fat, hairy fingers. 'I saw Leslie the other day.'

'How was it?'

'She was surprised I was in therapy but I think she was pleased.'

The phone on the desk rang and Anna got up to go but when she was outside she realised that she did not feel a weight had been lifted from her shoulders by Ted's ownership of the Guthrie estate problem as she had expected – she felt, if anything, more anxious. Bernice had been so insistent that no-one must know that she was Guthrie's mother and now someone did and the police might be involved, but what else could Anna have done? She sent a text to Bernice to say that she had had to tell her boss but he would be very careful with the information, and hoped for the best.

But by the end of the week the worry over Bernice had faded since nothing had been heard from her (or Ted) and meeting Queenie and Rakes at Kenilworth was exciting enough to drive everything else from her mind. Elizabeth had wanted to come but Anna felt it was best not to over-heat the first meeting that had been brokered by Mike because she had no idea what to expect or how wary they might be.

She picked through her wardrobe on Saturday morning trying to decide what might be appropriate for the occasion; something that wouldn't be too casual or too dressy (not much choice in that end of the range). Eventually, she chose a simple black cotton shift dress with strappy tan sandals and her favourite colourful scarf to wear around her shoulders. She added the gold chain Harry had given her, some stud earrings and a slim bangle and grabbed a posher tote bag than her battered black work one.

In the kitchen Bean and Ellis were chortling over their phones. Curled up on one of George's cardigans on the wonky chair was Macavity. 'Did one of you let the cat in?' she asked, pulling her notebook, tablet, folder of documents, purse and phone out of her old bag and stuffing them into her red one.

Bean whistled when he saw her and she glared at him. 'That's just the sort of thing I mean, Bean,' she said, realising immediately that the unintended rhyme had made her sound ridiculous, 'it's just not how you should behave towards women.'

'Why? It's a compliment,' Bean said.

'Mum,' Ellis said patiently, not raising his face from his phone, 'absolutely no-one could ever think of you as a sex object –

Bean didn't mean it like that,' which annoyed Anna in a different way.

'Are you going to fine me?' Bean asked with relish, in much the same tone as a masochist might ask if someone had a whip concealed about their person.

'You couldn't afford so much money,' Anna said, 'so I'm going to take pity on you and hope you see the error of your ways before you alienate every young woman you ever fancy.' She checked the cash in her purse and added a brush to the bag.

'You like it really, though?' Bean said thoughtfully.

'No, actually, I don't, but I don't suppose you'll believe that.' She glanced at her watch. 'Ell, I've got to go now and I'll be gone most of the day – Pops knows – but can you boys cut the back grass so he doesn't have to?' Ellis, deep in his phone, nodded.

Bean leaped up and opened the hall door for Anna, adding as she passed, 'A nice lipstick would look nice.' She glanced at his face and was irritated to see that he was serious.

'Bye,' she said to the room and then went back in. 'Ellis, usher that cat out – nicely,' but Ellis only shook his mahogany hair and there wasn't time to pursue it.

Queenie and Rakes Smith had said they would meet Anna in a roadside pub-restaurant, one of a well-known chain, which was clearly a popular place for Saturday family lunch. The noise level hit Anna's ears like a blow as she pulled open the doors. She had not imagined that she would need to know how to recognise them because she had failed to foresee this clamour. Nevertheless, she pushed through the hot dining room to see who was there. She was looking for an older couple but they could have brought other family members and there were dozens of such groups. She pressed through until she saw a large conservatory, also packed, and then, tables outside.

It was a relief to step into the pub garden and out of the din. Some of the tables had shade umbrellas and most had ashtrays full of stubs and many tables were occupied but it was quiet and at the far side, the furthest from the building, there were trees and a table beneath one of them at which sat an older man and a woman looking intently at her. She quickly made her way over to them.

'Mr and Mrs Smith?' The woman was plump with diamante combs holding back wavy grey hair and alert eyes behind rimless glasses. She wore a floral dress and dainty gold jewellery but her face announced that she would not suffer fools gladly. The man had risen from his seat awkwardly when Anna spoke, shook her hand, and then sank down and she wondered if his knees bothered him. He had the ruddy look of a countryman who had spent his life out in all weathers and though he was in his seventies his thick black hair was only edged with grey around the ears and in stripes from his temples.

Anna sat down, not sure how to begin after the initial greetings. It was Queenie who spoke first. 'Our Etta's gone, then, Mike said?' Of course, that would be the very first thing she would want to know – was it true that her daughter was dead.

'Yes, I'm so sorry. Do you want to know more about it – I can tell you a little?'

Rakes leaned forward. 'She was our only gal, our only one.'

'I wants to know,' Queenie said stiffly, holding herself together, 'all of it, if you don't mind.'

So Anna told them what Elizabeth had told her; how well Loretta had done, how well she had raised her son, Tom, and how, tragically, she had drowned in the English Channel. They were silent when she finished but Rakes put his arm around his wife's shoulders and they leaned their heads together.

'Mike says her boy wants to know us, maybe,' Rakes said after a few moments.

'Yes,' Anna agreed eagerly, glad to have some happy news for them, 'he feels the lack of family very much. His mother didn't talk about you, sadly. There was only the photograph and then I looked you up when his fiancée asked me to.'

Queenie sighed and seemed to come to a decision. 'We usually keep our gobs shut about our business but I will say what happened – why she went off and never wanted us no more. It's been our curse, our lifelong sadness.' Rakes nodded gravely.

It seemed that the family, like many others, had been victims of the harsh laws brought in in the 50s and 60s to prevent travelling families stopping at their usual sites so that they would always be moved on, sometimes after only five minutes rest. It meant they couldn't do their itinerant work on farms following the harvests from beets to apples and laying hedges and hawking things they'd made to the local people. Councils were ordered to provide sites but many were unsuitable and the one they had been moved to was in a city, in a triangle of useless land between a motor-way flyover and a railway line. It not only had toxic chemicals in the ground, it was noisy, dirty and had not so much as a blade of grass but they had to go somewhere. They all hated it and the children, unused to cities and being penned in with nothing to do, had just as bad a time at school where they were often bullied. They were not allowed to have their horses and the sanitation arrangements were primitive and disgusting. Later, after only a year, they moved off that site and were settled for a few years in a council house until, in their later years, they bought a comfortable modern trailer and now travelled as much as they could.

'Etta was sixteen when we got moved there to that dump,' Queenie said, 'but we knew she would soon be wed because there was a chap had his eye on her and they was engaged. It was a good match, we was friends with his family, and we all thought the world of him. The dress was being made and all the families coming and she would be pretty as a picture.'

'Teller?' Anna put in.

The two old people were silent and then Queenie shook her head. 'Not him, no.'

A waitress appeared at the table and set down platters of fish and chips for Queenie and Rakes with a pot of tea for two but they barely acknowledged them. Anna asked for a coffee.

'Do you have *chavvies*, Missus?'

'Yes, a girl who's just left home to live with her boyfriend and a teenage boy.'

The two exchanged glances. 'It's different with us,' Rakes said, 'gals don't go with chaps till they're wed.' Anna was not surprised. 'So when Etta come to us not a week afore the wedding and told us she was expecting, we was upset and I was going to have it out with the boy and let him know what I thought of him. As for her she knew she'd shamed us without us saying a word, but still she defied us and told us she didn't care what we thought. I did *snope* her then, but not hard.'

Anna knew how it had been in the seventies and eighties for some teenagers – free love, kaftans, weed and communes but even then, of course, that kind of life-style had only been for a small minority. George and Lena had only been week-end hippies. Had Loretta been influenced by all that heady looseness in the *gorgia* world? She understood that the Romani moral code was a strict one but still, Loretta was going to marry the man very soon, so surely it wasn't that bad.

Queenie had been watching Anna's face as she was silently staring out past the tree occupied with her memories. 'You're thinking we was too harsh? But it was what was said next that did it.'

The fish and chips were growing cold but neither person seemed interested in the food. Anna's coffee arrived and she sipped at it not saying anything because Queenie was now quietly crying. Rakes leaned into her and murmured something in her ear.

'No, she can know. Tom is our grandson and he has a right.' She dabbed at her eyes with the paper napkin and sighed. 'We was all shouting and then it come out. She told us it wasn't his, her intended, it was for a fairground fella, Teller Budas she was having a fling with and said she loved. "Is you mad?" I said. Well, that was the bitter end.'

'I told her that she was no daughter of mine and to take her stuff and go. She'd shamed us all and we didn't want her.' Rakes put a trembling hand on to the table. 'And she went and we never saw her or heard of her again up to Mike called us. When a family has a runaway like that among us Romani it gives the family a bad name, but losing her was worse.'

Queenie sniffed back her tears. 'So she married him, Teller?'

'Yes,' Anna said, 'but he left her not long after Tom was born.'

'She was on her own? She had no-one around her? His family?'

'No. But she did well for herself,' Anna repeated, seeing now how this fresh information made them feel so much worse. 'And Tom had a happy childhood and now he's making his way as a violinist, he's becoming famous.' But still they sat slumped in sadness. 'It will be so wonderful for him to know he has grandparents alive and well.' Anna reached out and touched their hands. 'All parents make mistakes,' she said, 'I certainly have, but there's a future for your family now – a chance to re-connect.'

'He won't want to know,' Rakes said. 'We don't live in that world.' He stood up stiffly and Queenie also got to her feet. 'We're obliged to you for coming here and telling us, missus, but we'll go now.'

'Oh, please, think again!' Anna cried. 'He would very much want to know you, please don't leave like this.'

'It's been a shock for us,' Queenie said soberly, 'We're not saying no, we got your number from Mike, but we need to go away now to our own place and have a think.'

'All right, I do understand,' Anna said, 'but before you go, can I just show you a photograph? It's of Loretta and Tom and the young woman he will be marrying soon, Elizabeth.' She grabbed her tote and pulled out a cardboard-backed envelope and drew the glossy photo Elizabeth had copied from it. She handed it to Queenie. The couple stared hard at the image.

'He's a *kushti mush*,' Queenie said.

'He certainly is,' said Anna, and then, taking a risk, 'he looks a bit like his grandfather, I think.'

'And that's our Etta.' Queenie traced the outline of her daughter's face on the photograph with one trembling finger. She looked at Anna. 'Can you get us one?'

'It's yours. Elizabeth got it for you to have.' She gave them the envelope.

They shook Anna's hand and walked away together and Anna sank back on to her seat. After a few minutes she phoned Elizabeth to tell her how it had gone, but as she left she felt wrung out and disappointed. She could only hang on to Queenie's promise to think about meeting Tom.

It seemed a shame to be so close to the Horse Fair and not visit it so she turned out of the pub and made towards the town centre looking for car park signs. Very quickly the road became congested and then grid-locked. A man in a high-vis tabard was walking along the line of cars from behind and she realised that he was turning people back the way they'd come.

'No more parking,' he was calling, 'you need to U-turn and go out again.' As he approached Anna she asked if there was any alternative but he just shook his head and insisted that she reverse and turn back. As she did she thought she glimpsed Kimi in the crowd pressing along the pavements and she craned her neck to see. 'Move on!' she was told firmly, 'Keep going,' and she had no choice. She could see nothing in the rear-view mirror except a mass of heads and it would be dangerous not to watch the traffic with cars being manoeuvred in front of her as well as behind as drivers grasped the situation.

As she drove away and looked for the Birmingham road she thought it was quite possible, probable, that Kimi had come to the

Fair and it made her sad and angry, but to have this silence between them was painful and she decided that at the first opportunity she would try to heal the rift. No-one else might know what was going on and Kimi might need someone in her corner, if only for a sympathetic ear. Goodness knows, Kimi had been in Anna's corner before under far more dangerous circumstances and the truth was, however she behaved over Charlie was none of Anna's business as had been pointed out so forcefully.

18

On Monday morning, noticing that she had forgotten to charge her work phone, Anna plugged it in and went through the motions of sorting out her mail but ten minutes later she glanced at it and saw that there were three messages. She tried not to give out this number too easily as sometimes clients became nuisances but there were times when she had to. She opened the message box and saw that the first two were requests for information from other researchers, one from a London firm and one internally from a colleague working from home. But when she read the third message her heart constricted as though Bernice's fingers had reached inside her body and squeezed. She read it again.

You didn't promise but you must. She killed Phil. Don't tell anyone about me.

Bernice could not have got Anna's message saying that she had told her boss and if she hadn't, if someone else had read it and deleted it, who would that be? It could only be Richard. He would have easy access to his wife's phone.

After long seconds the most shocking part of the message exploded in Anna's head. Bella had killed her partner Philip? Of course, Bernice could be mistaken or deliberately maligning her sister (why?) but it was recorded that he died of erotic asphyxiation – maybe it hadn't been so erotic. Rebecca had told Anna that Bella had received insurance money from his 'accidental' death. Why would Bella want to kill him? The answer came immediately. Philip may not have been willing to go along with the deception over Guthrie's birth or if he had agreed, he would have been in a powerful position to control Bella. If she had set it up carefully enough the police would be only too willing to hand it over to the Coroner to determine cause of death and, given a convincing enough back story, Bella would probably be believed. What reason would the authorities have for doing otherwise since she had nothing but a modest lump sum to gain from his death?

Anna picked up the office phone and called Ted. He advised her to do nothing – it was all allegation and conjecture apart from the actual fact of Guthrie's birth in the Welsh hospital and Bernice's confession.

She thought for a moment and then phoned Bernice who answered immediately. 'Are you alone?' Anna asked. Bernice was. She had not received the text and became agitated when Anna told her that she had passed on the information.

'You probably think I'm being hysterical,' she said, whispering into the phone, 'but, really, Bella is not quite sane and she can be vengeful. We just daren't provoke her.'

'But what can she do?' Anna asked. 'Guthrie, sadly, has gone. What other hold has she got over you?' Bernice said nothing. 'Wouldn't it be better to tell Rebecca everything? Isn't revealing the secret your best insurance policy against anything happening to you? You're at risk as long as you are the only person who knows the truth, except me, of course.' She didn't mention the veiled threat she'd had. The last thing she wanted to do was alarm Bernice further.

'Except for Richard,' Bernice said, 'but he's terrified of her, too.'

'He believes she killed Philip?'

'He knows she did.' She sounded as though she was finding breathing difficult. 'Bella made him help her rig up the rope.' Anna took a deep breath, forcing herself not to be too shocked or sucked in by this latest twist in the family horror. 'He didn't know what she was planning, of course, but she said no-one would believe that he hadn't been a willing accomplice. It's been going on since then – the threats, the bullying. She says if it ever gets out she'll burn our house down with us in it or find some other way to murder us and we believe she would.'

They had been brainwashed into submission – coercive control syndrome. Two things occurred to Anna simultaneously. How did Bella know Richard at that stage and, more practically, why didn't he and Bernice just move away?

'So, did you consider moving house?'

'Oh no, because then I wouldn't have known Guthrie, I wouldn't have watched him grow up and had the joy of him coming to our house all the time so I could cook treats for him and even hug him when he was little. He was my life.'

'But, when he went away and you thought he wouldn't come back, what about then?'

'Oh Anna, the only place Guthrie could find me, if he did come back, was at that house. How could I leave?' Of course, Anna thought, Bernice had to stay put under miserable circumstances on the off-chance that her son may return. What a contrast with Lena! 'But it wasn't just that,' Bernice went on desperately. 'Since the stroke Bella has been paying our bills – Richard's salary is nowhere near enough to live on but he has to be at home for me.' Trapped. Bernice had made her prison into a flower garden but it was still a prison.

'So, how did Bella know Richard back then, Bernice? You said he helped her.' Anna didn't want to interrogate the poor woman but she had to make sense of this strange story.

'Richard?'

'Yes, how did Bella know him and when did you tell him about the plan over Guthrie?'

Bernice sounded confused. 'I don't understand. What do you mean?'

Anna remembered how Bernice had played for time when Rebecca had asked her an unexpected question in the park. Was she still concealing things? 'I just wondered when you told him about who Guthrie's real mother was, if you did, that is?'

'But he's always known. He's Guthrie's dad. He set up the whole Welsh thing – he was there when Guthrie was born. Bella threatened to tell the police about him having sex with an underage girl, you see, because he was nineteen when I got pregnant and I was only fifteen.'

Her voice went on but Anna wasn't listening. This meant, if it was true, that Rebecca was Guthrie's full sibling. She had researched, as far as her understanding of genetics went which wasn't very far at all, the feasibility of matching Guthrie's DNA to Bernice's but had only got as far as realising how complicated it might be to get a definitive result. Bella would certainly not give a sample. But this changed everything – the difference between a half-sibling and a full sibling could be clearly demonstrated as far as she could tell. Among the other genetic information there would be "completely identical" markers in the DNA of the brother and sister which no near relative would have. All they needed to prove that Guthrie was Bernice and Richard's son was for Rebecca to consent to a DNA test. But, it was not for Anna to tell Rebecca the truth of

Guthrie's conception and birth. Bernice, and, it now appeared, Richard, must tell their daughter that.

She chose her words carefully after waiting for Bernice's flow of examples of Bella's bullying to stop. 'I think you should tell your daughter everything,' she said simply. 'Apart from the fact that she deserves to know, it will mean that Bella no longer has any power over you. No-one is going to pursue Richard over the Age of Consent issue given the situation. In fact, it would mean that for once you have power over her so she will back off. You could move if you wanted to, live a normal, peaceful life and a lawyer could almost certainly get you Guthrie's assets which would improve all your lives.'

In the silence that followed, Anna started to scribble a memo to herself to ponder several key questions. What should her own role in this be? Had she already over-stepped by giving such specific (and un-asked for) advice? How far would Harts (Ted) go with pursuing the DNA match when Guthrie's parentage was still only Bernice's word against Bella's? They were already in liminal territory, to put it mildly. Ted would be very cautious about a possible counter-action from Bella saying that the company had acted outside its remit and beyond ethical boundaries. But, really, if he did axe any further involvement in the case, would it matter? Rebecca and her parents could hire a lawyer and take this up on their own – poor Guthrie was still in the morgue, after all.

'I can't tell her because she'll hate me,' Bernice said finally.

Of course! 'Because,' Anna said tentatively, knowing she was on dangerously unprofessional ground, 'when Guthrie found out the truth when he was eighteen, he left and you never saw him again.'

'Yes.' Her voice was now so small Anna could hardly hear it.

With a huge effort of self-control Anna pulled herself back and made herself say neutrally, 'It's your decision, Bernice, yours and Richard's.'

When she got home that evening, still rattled by the conversation with Bernice, she found the utility room unusually full. Mostly it was full of foam and their large plumber whose backside reared up from the floor. George was making an effort to sweep the mess out of the back door and Bean was staring wide-eyed at the scene. Ellis dashed up behind her. 'It's not as bad as it looks, Mum, there's no real damage done. Anyone can make a mistake.'

'Help Pops,' Anna said, turning to go upstairs and get changed.

'Sorry, Mrs A,' Bean called, 'but, look on the bright side, your floor's getting a good wash.' He waggled his head at her to indicate this was a joke.

Anna looked past him to George sweeping the soapy water and saw that there were beads of sweat on his forehead and heard the ragged intake of breath into lungs not completely healed from a recent bout of pneumonia. The situation with Bernice and Bella was volatile and unstable and could blow at any moment in any direction and there was nothing she could do about it – only Bernice could do something and she wouldn't. But she could do something about this. The bottle of dishwashing detergent was still on the washing machine – it was clear what Bean had done, and in other circumstances it might have been funny, although the amusement would have drained away faster than the water when the emergency call-out bill came.

'Dad, give Bean the brush, you and me are going out to the pub and we'll have dinner there.' She pulled a ten-pound note out of her purse. 'Ellis, this is for you two to get a take-away.' Her voice betrayed to Bean nothing of the anger she felt but Ellis and George were not deceived.

'We'll sort it all out, Mum, it'll be like it never happened when you get back.'

'I've put all the stuff that was on the floor outside to dry off,' George said, giving no argument and handing the brush to Bean. 'Let me just go and change my cardigan.'

'Take-away! Nice one!' Bean said. 'You're ace, Mrs A.'

Chris, the plumber, was packing up his tools and winked at Anna in sympathy. 'Not really what you want to come home to, is it Anna? Should be ok now but give me a call if there's a problem.'

Anna saw him out and went upstairs to put on jeans and a top. She sat on her bed and stared out of the window watching the nearest little branches of their tree wave towards her and away again and the ivy leaves tremble around the frame. Why was she so disturbed, so anxious? Normally, she could ride out most work-related problems and was used to little crises at home – in fact, since Faye had left there had been far fewer dramas. Then she realised – it was not the things in themselves so much as that familiar underlying dread, that intuitive sense that things were not right, possibly dangerously so, that was churning within her. She had ignored this feeling before and regretted it. She sat gazing out at the wisps of cirrus cloud drifting like feathers across the deep blue afternoon sky and scanned for something important she was not paying attention to; something menacing but maddeningly elusive.

George tapped on her door and after grabbing her bag from the kitchen they went out of the house and walked across the park to the pub. 'You held it together well,' he said, after they'd found a table in a sunny corner outside. 'Bean can be rather trying.'

'I'll have to talk to his dad again at some point, I suppose, although the phone chat we had when Bean moved in didn't fill me with confidence. Do you know any more about the situation? I don't like to quiz Ellis but maybe I should.' George shook his head.

'So you got the mag out?'

'Yes, all done. Ashok thinks it's the best we've done this year.'

'That's good.'

They sipped their beers.

'What's the matter, Annie? Is it Alice?'

Anna smiled. 'No. Actually, she's been fairly ok with me lately. The other day she even asked if I would like a biscuit to go with my coffee. Major progress. I think that maybe having more of her own family making a fuss of her is helping.'

'I know there's something bubbling away inside. You can always talk to me.'

'I know that, Dad, and believe me, it means a lot. I am a bit worried but I can't really put my finger on it. There's the situation I told you about with the two mothers but that's not going anywhere and the work I was doing for Elizabeth and Tom has stalled, too, because the grandparents aren't sure whether they want contact, or whether he'll want contact. He will, of course, but because he's so successful I think they feel anxious about rejection. So it's like things are kind of suspended and – '

'They're beyond your control.'

'Yes. That's awful, isn't it? It's not that I want to control them, I just want there to be the better outcomes there could be, not this paralysis of fear and hesitation.' She picked up the menu and glanced over the options. 'But it's not even that. It's a feeling that

I'm somehow being careless, thoughtless, missing something important but I don't know what it is.'

'You haven't mentioned the abuse you've had,' George said softly. 'That must be preying on your mind.'

Anna groaned in frustration. 'But there again, I don't know what's going on. None of it makes sense. Is it Bella? But what does she have against me? She just thinks that I'm causing the delay over her getting Guthrie's money but even she must realise now that I don't have that power. She doesn't know that I know about Guthrie and Bernice and, come to that, Philip.' George made a questioning face and so she told him what had happened that morning.

'It's all very upsetting stuff, isn't it?' George said, 'No wonder you're a bit on edge.'

She ordered for them at the bar and then settled back at the table with two fresh half-pints. 'Maybe you need a break, Annie. Why don't you go out to the farm and have an evening with Kimi? There's certainly no ambiguity about her and you've been friends for years.'

'She isn't talking to me.' George leaned forward to query this but she stopped him. 'I can't tell you why, Dad, but I will phone her tonight and try to sort things out. I do feel bad about it. Basically, I was sticking my opinion in where it wasn't wanted.'

'We all do that,' George said promptly, comforting as ever. 'No progress on finding out more about Lena, I suppose.'

'Again, it's waiting for someone to get in touch. Mike said he would put the word out and I did put out queries online but it's a long shot that anyone would contact me.' She had not told George about her recent discoveries about her mother and Mollie May because she hated him to know that he had been deceived from the day he met Lena as well as being abandoned by her.

'I was telling Diane about your interest in Travelling people,' George said, 'and she had an idea that might be worth considering.'

Their food arrived and they chatted easily as the evening deepened into gold so by the end of the second half pint and a salmon salad Anna was feeling more relaxed. As they crossed the park towards home, she slipped her arm through his and they played a game he had made up when she was a child. 'If I was the Emperor of Persia,' she began, 'right now I'd whistle up a white horse and a carriage to carry me home and plonk me in a warm bath of asses' milk.'

'If I was the Emperor of Persia,' George said, 'right now I'd have a court apparel-carrier bring me a warmer cardi.'

Anna rubbed his arm and laughed as her phone beeped. She fished it out, noticing with irritation that it was her work phone which she must have dropped in her bag by mistake. She would check she had her personal phone with her in a moment. There was no ID on the screen but it was only a message so she opened it. She stopped in her tracks and George stumbled for a moment.

The message read: *Every step you take, every move you make, we'll be watching you!* followed by a devil emoji.

'It is getting a bit cool, Dad, let's put our best foot forward, eh? See what miracles of cleanliness the boys have achieved?' So the pace was quickened and Anna only allowed herself to look behind them once. The park was almost empty.

Later in the evening she phoned Kimi and was rewarded with a curt 'What?' in response to her greeting.

'I hate this, Kimi,' she said. 'You were right, what you do is none of my business and I miss you.'

'Ok, then – lucky for you I don't hold grudges. Actually, Anna, I wouldn't mind a bit of company. Things aren't going brilliantly and Briony's still away but I forbid you to say "I told you so," ok?'

'As if I would.'

19

She was deeply asleep when the sound of knocking woke her. She lay still for a moment and then leaped up and wrenched open the door. Had her dad or Ellis been taken ill? Had the police come about Faye? Where was Steve?

Bean stood before her with a huge mug of milky tea in his left hand. A miasma from sweaty nooks and crannies eddied around him as he pushed it forward. 'Brought you a morning cuppa.'

Anna grabbed her summer robe from the back of the door and struggled into it, still fighting the panic. 'What's happened? Is everyone alright?'

'Milk, no sugar. I remembered.' He grinned. 'Everyone's fine. You worry too much, Mrs A.'

Anna looked at her bedside clock. 'It's five o'clock in the morning. What are you thinking of? I was fast asleep, Bean.'

'No worries,' he said, in that irritating way he had where it was somehow assumed he was doing her a favour instead of being a nuisance. 'I don't mind.' He hung his head a little. 'I've been talking to my mum. Can I come in?'

'Oh, for goodness sake,' Anna grumbled, 'if you must. I'll never get back to sleep now.'

'Sweet.'

She pulled out the dressing table stool for him to sit on, drew the curtains so that the dawn came in and got back into bed, heaping the pillows up behind her. The house was set so that from her room at the front she could see the sunrise (not that she had wanted to on this occasion) and the sunset hit the back. Bean set down the Wallace and Gromit pint mug and slopped another puddle on her bedside table. Anna ignored it, gritting her teeth.

Bean was looking around. 'This is a nice room,' he said. 'It's much bigger than mine.'

'It's not yours, though, is it? This is not actually your house, Bean.' Given how annoyed she was with him, this was about as pleasant as she could be. She even managed to stop herself asking him when he was going home.

'I just talked to my mum,' he repeated.

'At this hour?'

'She's in Turkey so she's up getting ready for work.' He picked up the framed photograph of Harry she kept by the bed. 'Is this Ellis' dad? Is he the one that died?'

'Put it down, Bean.' Anna folded her arms and glared at him. 'What do you want to talk to me about?'

'Oh yeah. I told her what you said about my dad not knowing how to treat women.'

'Bean, I never said that.'

'She said you're right. She said he doesn't get women. I mean, he gets plenty of them but he doesn't…'

'Understand them.'

'Mm. She said he's incapable of a proper relationship because he's a poor eater, or something. What did she mean?'

Anna's numb brain struggled with this. 'Do you mean *puer aeternis*?'

'I asked her what she meant and she said, "Ask your father," so I'm asking you.'

Anna's head was beginning to ache and her mouth was dry and sour. 'It's Latin for eternal child. It means he hasn't grown up.' Bean's forehead wrinkled. 'It means he's immature – expects people, especially women, to do what he wants, make him the centre of attention like a little kid.'

'Oh,' Bean said, his brow clearing, 'well, yes, who wouldn't?'

'Do you know what, Bean?' Anna said, 'I think I'd like a bit of peace and quiet now so I can get my head together before I have to go to work.'

'Do your thing,' he offered magnanimously. His bony haunches struggled to keep balance on the stool while he gazed around.

'That means you have to leave.'

'Oh, ok. I'll hit the sack then, I've been up all night playing.'

'You'll have to be up for school in two hours!'

Bean stood up and stretched his arms above his head revealing a little nest of sticky hairs in each armpit. 'Don't stress, Mrs A, it's cool,' he said, 'ta for the chat. Drink your tea.'

The room was now suffused in pink and when Bean left she got up and went to stand by the window watching with pleasure as torn candy-floss, sugar pink against the turquoise sky, drifted past without a care in the world. After a moment she turned to go out to the bathroom and when she came back the light had changed and the day had begun.

There was nothing from Bernice or any other member of that family waiting for her at work and the hours passed routinely except for a lunch break spent accompanying Suzy to John Lewis to buy an extravagantly expensive perfume and a lunch of superfood salad. At three George phoned to say Andrew's church was collecting food to take to the food bank, he'd seen a notice on the board, and did she want to contribute, too? She said she'd pick some things up from the supermarket on her way home and pop in to see Joan at the greengrocers for a few minutes. When Joan heard about the food bank collection, she had a word with Jakub in his office and before she knew it, Anna was struggling along the High Street back to her car with four stuffed bags of fruit and vegetables to add to her own haul of tins and packets.

'How have we come to this, Dad?' she said, finding him in the kitchen, 'what's happening in this country?'

'Too much for too few, too little for too many,' George said immediately, with a poet's brevity.

'Have you taken yours down?'

'No, it's all still in the car.'

'Ok, I'll get the boys. It's always a problem parking around there at this time so they can help me carry it all down.' There was no doubt that they were in because she could hear them thumping about.

Sure enough, it had been right to walk as all available on-street parking spaces were full and Anna guessed the little car park attached to the church would be, too, since there were only three hours to drop off donations which would then be collected by the food bank van. People were milling about chatting as she and the boys made their way through to the Church Hall. It was a relief to put the bags down when they got there. She rubbed the sore ridges across her fingers.

'Can I go now?' Ellis asked. 'I've got to get to a practice at the Club.'

'What are your plans, Bean?' Anna asked. He shrugged.

'Anna!' She looked round and saw Elizabeth making her way towards her, holding out her arms. 'It's great to see you and especially great today because Tom's here! You can finally meet him. Come on.' But he wasn't in the Hall or the Church so Elizabeth turned into the grave-yard and looked around.

'Is that him?' Anna asked, seeing a tall, dark-haired young man standing by a grave some distance away, apparently reading the inscription.

'Oh, yes, come on, I'll introduce you.' Elizabeth stepped quickly between the graves and slipped her arm around his waist, turning her bright face up to his. 'Hey you,' she said, 'you disappeared.'

'Sorry.'

'No, it's fine. I just want to introduce you to a friend, Anna. She's a fan of yours.' This put Anna in an awkward situation since she had never heard him play and, in any case, wasn't given to being a groupie. But when Tom turned to face her she saw that he was more embarrassed by the introduction than she was.

'Hi,' he said, flushing slightly.

A voice, pitched high and sharp, rang out across the grave-yard. 'Elizabeth! Where do you want the fresh stuff?' Elizabeth smiled at them both and sprinted off. They turned back to look at the headstone. It read: *Sarah Beswick, Beloved Wife of Josiah and Mother of Sophia, We Will Part No More.*

'Beautiful but sad,' Anna said quietly. 'It seems from the dates that the daughter and the husband pre-deceased the mother.'

Tom was quiet for a minute and then said, 'Do you believe in an after-life?'

'I don't know,' Anna said. 'Do you?'

Tom put his hands in his pockets and sighed. 'It would make you feel less lonely, wouldn't it?'

He was still grieving. Elizabeth was so full of energy and excitement about their coming wedding that she had missed it, very naturally. Anna's previous impression of Tom came entirely from the photograph of him with his mother and Elizabeth at the concert. She remembered that she had felt he was an unusually fortunate young man to be blessed with talent, good looks and early success. He had blazed with self-confidence, she thought, but now she saw that he was far more complicated than that. It's easy to forget that photographs so often only tell a surface truth about a second in time.

'I'm sorry about your mother,' she said. 'Elizabeth told me.'

He glanced sideways at her and she saw how pale his skin was as though he rarely was outside in the sun and fresh air. He looked around them at the ranks of headstones, some tilted and mildewed, some almost shockingly bright and new. 'Families,' he said.

'I never really had a mother,' Anna found herself saying, 'so I grew up with fantasies of what she would be like. My favourite was probably Judi Dench.'

He smiled. 'So you had only one parent, too?'

'Mm. A very good one, though.'

'She died when you were a baby?' He seemed genuinely interested and although the conversation had so quickly become both serious and intimate, she felt no need to protect herself from him. There was an authenticity about him which made him both vulnerable and accessible.

'No, she left us when I was a toddler.'

He turned fully to look at her then. 'My father abandoned me, well, us.'

'Do you ever imagine him?'

He looked down at her, maybe searching for the right words. 'He was a doctor – I don't know. Sometimes, when I felt miserable, I imagined him as cold and arrogant, because I couldn't conceive how he could have done that – left my mum to fend for both of us with no money – she was so young. I would have little vengeance fantasises. I would find him and make him beg forgiveness, you know, the sort of thing kids think.'

'But now?'

'Oh, now.' He seemed so sad that Anna had to stop herself from reaching out for him. He was so young himself to be left, as he imagined, completely alone. There was an unusual quality about him which she had not experienced before from anyone; sensitivity spiked with passion, almost ferocity, that was so understated that it could only be detected in the timbre of his quiet voice and the almost invisible tremor of his mouth and only then if you paid close attention. It was as if he was himself an instrument made for feeling, perhaps a little too tightly strung. 'I don't think about him now,' he said. 'He may have had a reason for what he did.' She knew a sticking-plaster rationalisation when she heard it.

'I'm much older than you but I'm still angry with my mother,' Anna said, kicking at a clump of grass, 'and it doesn't seem to help that she's dead. My dad tries to get me to forgive her because he knows it hurts me but I can't seem to do it. I can't seem to let her go.'

They began to walk slowly back across the graveyard, finding a narrow path and following it rather than risk stepping on old graves. When they reached the wall of the church Tom said, turning serious eyes towards Anna, 'Mostly, I feel untethered.'

'Yes, I can understand that.'

Then Elizabeth was calling for him and he took her hand and said, 'Thank you,' so simply that it brought tears to her eyes.

There was an old memorial bench by the path and she sat on it and thought over the conversation, letting her own emotions play out. At the far end of the grave-yard where the new graves must be, she could see a couple placing flowers and cleaning off the stone – a tribute of love for the dead, not the bitter offering of resentment which was all she seemed to have for Lena. Her thoughts returned to Tom and after a while she came to the decision to talk to Elizabeth about revealing the search for his family and telling him that two of his grandparents had been found. But would he feel better or worse if they never contacted him? Would it be better to leave him in ignorance?

As she walked down the drive to the gate she became aware of Bean loping behind her. 'Are you all right?'

'Can I walk home with you?'

She fought the temptation to remind him again that it was not his home. 'What's the matter?'

'There's this girl at school, Mrs A. She thinks I'm stupid.'

'Ok.'

'I really like her, though. How do I make her like me?'

20

There was a fine mist in the air from a prone stratus cloud when she arrived at the stables but Kimi was outside staggering to the furthest stall with a hay bag. Cora, on trend with her grey hair and liquid eyes, peered out of her half-door stall but all she could see of Beauty was a bay rump. Maisie was tucking into her snack so Anna called a greeting to which the mare responded with a brief ear flick so she left her to it.

'Have you eaten?' Kimi demanded.

'Yup. You?'

'No, but there's a tub of spag bol left – enough for one.'

They walked quickly across the yard and into the farm kitchen. 'Go to it, then,' Anna said, unable to judge Kimi's mood since she was routinely abrupt. She watched as Kimi pulled the tub from the fridge and banged it into the microwave. In Briony's absence Anna suspected that Kimi would not wash her hands, much less change her clothes.

'Wine?'

'Just a little one.' She decided to talk about Kimi's favourite subject as a peace offering. 'How's Cora settling in?'

It had the desired effect as Kimi turned a sparkling face to her from the cupboard where she was getting a bowl. 'What a star,' she said, glowing like the mother of a child prodigy. 'I showed you her rearing on command, right? Well, she does all sorts of things, like she can lift the latch on her stable door – I've had to put a bolt on it – and she'll lie down, roll over and die.'

'Worth every penny, then,' Anna said, but Kimi caught the tone and glared at her, so she added hastily, 'So you think she was circus trained?'

Kimi slopped the spaghetti out of its tub in to her bowl and picked up her fork after pushing one of the glasses of red wine over to Anna's side. 'Must be, but you can see from her teeth that she's only five, so it can't have been long ago. Charlie bought her in Kendal but he doesn't seem to know anything about her. She's not really a Gypsy horse, they prefer the stronger cobs with a lot of feathers round their feet.'

The taste of the food didn't seem to be registering with Kimi as she ladled it into her mouth, the pasta ends like little whips flicking tomato sauce over her cheeks as she sucked it in. Anna suspected she never ate like this when Briony was there but she wanted to keep the conversation pleasant and neutral so she pushed it a bit further. 'So, have you got any plans for her? I mean, to show her or something?'

'Not sure. I haven't found out everything she can do, yet.' She scraped the bowl and stood to put it in the sink. 'Ice cream?' Anna shook her head. She re-filled her own glass when Anna put her hand over hers and then went to the freezer. 'Charlie might have some ideas.'

'Ah, I thought –'

Kimi settled back to the table with a mound of chocolate ice-cream to which she added caramel sauce and nuts. Anna guessed that she was, at most, size ten which just proved the unfairness of life. 'What?' she demanded, 'You thought we'd broken up?'

'I don't know, I thought maybe Kenilworth wasn't such a good experience.'

'Oh, he was just pretending to be done with me.'

'Why would he do that?'

'His wife was watching like a hawk. She even had a go at me.'

'Had a go at you? What did she say?'

'You can imagine what she told me to do but then she grabbed me so I had to, you know, deal with her.'

'Kimi!'

'I didn't hurt her – it was only a scuffle. She got a good handful of my hair, though.' Kimi laughed. 'Look.' She dipped her head and parted her springing hair and there was a patch the size of a finger-nail near the crown which was still shiny and red.

Anna stood up and went to the sink pretending she needed to run herself a glass of water. She found herself aligning instinctively with Charlie's wife and didn't blame her for a moment for trying to drive her rival away; not only that, Kimi was rich and propertied and headstrong and, in this case, totally selfish. She looked out across the yard. It had stopped drizzling and the sky was an arrangement of low, grey-bellied clouds parting to show delicate brush-strokes of white against a far blue – the kind of sky that almost transports you to the heights it reveals. She felt a spasm of sorrow.

'You're trying to steal the person she loves, possibly the father of her children,' she said, without turning round.

'Oh, don't start that again – all's fair in love and war.'

'No, it isn't,' Anna said sharply, surprised at her own anger, 'otherwise there wouldn't be poisonous divorces that wreck lives and war-crime trials.'

'Bit dramatic,' Kimi observed coolly. 'Is a button being pushed?'

Anna turned round then. 'You've got so much,' she said, 'it's not right.'

Kimi stood up and stuck her hands in her jeans' pockets. 'For God's sake, I don't want to marry him. It's just sex, it's just a bit of fun.'

'For you, maybe, for him, perhaps, but for her – no, Kimi, it can't be fun for her.'

The kettle started to roar for the cafetiere. 'Anyway, he's not returning my calls and I have no idea where he is now so –' For the first time Anna heard a different inflection in Kimi's voice and saw that her shoulders were drooping as she filled the jug. 'Don't go on. I'm not stupid.'

'What about the site idea? What did he think of that?'

'I didn't actually get to talk to him. He saw me and walked away. Don't say anything – I haven't given up yet.'

There was no point in continuing. 'So, how's Briony? Where is she?'

'Oh, probably tucking into quails' eggs *en croute* in some luxury hotel,' Kimi said bitterly, reaching down two mugs from the cupboard above the kettle. Kimi didn't run to cups and saucers or even anything that matched. It was hard to think where she'd bought the odd assortment of crockery she possessed unless she'd spent a day combing charity shops which was certainly possible – she had as little interest in beautifying her home as she had in adorning herself. Briony was also uninterested in the home beautiful despite her glamour.

'Is that what this is?' Anna asked. 'Are you punishing her?'

Kimi got milk from the fridge and put a little in her own cup, none in Anna's and then stood stiff and defiant, the jug in her hand, facing Anna like a shield-bearer on the front line of battle. 'Why can't you understand? *I* don't know what this is, *I* don't know what's going on. I thought I was in control of everything. Just stop judging me and be a friend.'

Anna leaped from her chair, stung by the bullseye accusation in Kimi's plea and hugged her. 'I'm sorry,' she said. 'I won't do it any more, I promise.'

Kimi released herself and opened the kitchen door. 'Let's take the coffee outside and you can tell me what's going on with you. How's the Alice thing? Is she still being a pain?'

It was a relief to move off the subject of Charlie but even more so to realise that Kimi had been dumped whether she acknowledged it or not; a situation where Anna felt her friend had got off lightly all things considered. She remembered Joan telling her about an affair she had had when she was young and how she had described it as like having flu – a fever that went almost as quickly as it had come - a far cry from love. Perhaps that was all this was.

Later, driving home and squinting through low evening sun, Anna thought about Tom standing sadly alone in the graveyard among the dead. Was he the result of an attack of lust when the teenage Loretta lost her virginity to a mad affair with a passing stranger only weeks before her wedding? As she turned a bend in the road she was blinded for a second by the reservoir transmuted to gold and she pulled into a layby. Across lush and sparkling fields the light on the water was dazzling and she brought up Aretha Franklin's voice on her phone - surely the only one to accompany such unearthly beauty - letting herself be transported.

But her serene mood crashed as soon as she slowed to turn into her own drive. Across the garage doors was scrawled the message *U R SCUM.* It could have been worse but for one thing. The abuse had now reached her actual home.

Passing through the hallway she could hear crashes and screams from the front room but she went on and filled a bucket with hot, soapy water and grabbed the big car sponge. On the way back she set the bucket down and opened the door. Three heads turned briefly so she could identify Bean, Dan and her son and then snapped back on to the screen on which some digital apocalypse was playing out.

'What's up?' Ellis said, 'Woah! Got you!'

'Did you hear anyone come up the drive?'

'What?'

She closed the door and went out of the front and down the steps but before she began to wash off the letters she gingerly touched the gel, smelled her finger and then licked it. Squeezy mayonnaise. It was easy to wash off but it left a slight trace in the paint which meant the acidic vinegar had had time to begin to eat away at the surface. Lucky there hadn't been a car on the drive. She dropped the sponge in the bucket, wiped her hands on her jeans and walked round to next door but the old couple on one side had heard nothing and on the other side no-one was at home. Then she noticed that the newly-occupied house over the road was a hive of activity so she went over.

A skip had been in place on the end of their drive ever since they had moved in and at this moment the man was chucking plasterboard into it. George had gone to greet them with one of his lemon drizzle cakes on the day they had arrived and since then they had waved and smiled at each other so she felt no need to introduce herself.

'Hi, have you got a minute?'

'Sure. I could do with a breather.' His hair, skin and clothes were thick with plaster dust and anyone in their right mind would have worn a mask, she thought. 'What's up?'

'There was some graffiti on my garage door – not paint, just mayo – but I wondered if you'd seen anyone messing about? I've been out and the boys are oblivious.'

He wiped the back of his hand across his mouth and spat. 'Sorry. Um, yeah, I did see a kid about an hour ago but I thought he was playing with yours. Some gang rivalry is it?'

'How do you mean?'

'I shouted at him when I saw what he'd done but he hared off towards the park. Kids that age are always having spats, aren't they?' He coughed. 'At least it's not obscene, eh?'

Anna shrugged. 'No, there is that, especially since it's probably marked the paint.'

'Ah, well, what you have to do…' and Anna stood on his drive for a quarter of an hour while he explained about stain-blocker and so on. She didn't mind because it gave her a chance to re-think what had been happening. A kid? But the foul language of the first message spray-painted outside Harts couldn't have been, surely? Although, of course, it could. Anyway, what teenager would know or care where she worked? The second was the letter left in Ellis' school-bag and he would have thought nothing of another boy of his age hanging around the bus stop or his bag at school but the phone message had been on her work phone and how could a school-boy know that number? Now this, which at least wasn't sexual, had definitely been done, it seemed, by a youth. Were there two completely unrelated attempts to intimidate her? Or, were all of these messages weird pranks committed by a hacker, maybe jealous of Ellis, who could get information but couldn't troll her since she had no social media presence? Far-fetched.

'I could do it for you.'

'What?'

'Paint the garage doors. As long as you're happy with gun-metal grey, that is.'

Anna wrenched herself back. 'Oh, no, thanks. I think you've got your hands full here, and I quite enjoy painting.'

'Yes, I like a project,' he said smugly, 'only on a bigger scale. You won't know this house when I've finished.'

And you won't know your poor neighbours because they won't be speaking to you, Anna thought, and crossed back to her own drive.

21

Elizabeth, it turned out, was impatient to reveal all to Tom believing that he would find Romani family connections as romantic as she did. He would shortly be performing with an Early Music ensemble at The Barber Institute on the University campus so she invited Anna, and whoever else would like to go, to hear him and then come to the Vicarage for an after-event celebration with just the family. The more excited Elizabeth got about it all, the more apprehensive Anna felt but couldn't think what else to say. She had no way of contacting Queenie and Rakes except through Mike and Queenie had specifically said they needed time to think and then she would contact Anna.

All this was relayed to Steve while she helped him build a permanent seating area on the now finished terrace. He was happy to go with her to the concert but shared her concern about Tom's reactions because most people, told that they have close family alive, immediately want to contact them (or want nothing to do with them). There would be a visceral impact on anyone but particularly on someone like Tom, who believed himself to be quite alone.

'Grab the other end of that two-by-four, would you?' Steve said, glancing across at Alice and Mina building a den out of an old curtain and some garden chairs. They carried the plank from the lumber pile to the saw-table.

'I was thinking acid thoughts about the chap over the road turning his house into a construction site yesterday,' Anna said, 'do your neighbours mind?'

'I shouldn't think so,' Steve said, looking round for his tape measure. 'I've never done anything before this and laying the stonework didn't make a noise. It's Saturday morning – fair enough for DIY I would have thought.'

'Mm.'

He took a pencil from behind his ear and narrowed his eyes at Anna. 'So when were you going to tell me?'

She grimaced. 'You saw it.'

'Actually, Alice did. She was coming up the road with Mina and her mum yesterday just as you were about to clean it off. She asked me what it meant and I said it meant the garage doors needed washing.' Anna grunted, amused. 'So, how many more have there been?'

'That I haven't told you?' She rubbed some sawdust off her hand carefully and saw where the splinter had stuck in the ball of her index finger. She began to pick at it. 'Just one – an audio message on my work phone – well, a refrain from a Sting song.'

'The stalker one?' Anna nodded. 'Let's go inside for a minute, I've got some stuff in the kitchen.'

Inside the cool, uncluttered space he cleaned her finger and then, so gently she could hardly feel it, drew out the sliver of wood with tweezers, dabbed more antiseptic on, dried that with a paper towel and put on a plaster. Then he kissed it. 'No-one's done that since I was a little girl,' Anna laughed, touched by his tenderness.

Steve filled the kettle. 'So what are you thinking?' She told him what the man over the road had seen and what hypotheses she'd been considering but when she mentioned the possibility of two separate people he shook his head. 'You've never had anything like this before – it would be too much of a coincidence – although the last thing could have had something to do with Ellis. Have you asked him?'

'I'll try to catch him later. He's out a lot at the moment.' They stood looking out at the garden and listening to the two girls shouting orders at each other until the kettle boiled. 'So is it next weekend you're going up to Birkenhead again?' Steve raised his eyebrows in assent. 'Is she thrilled?' At the sound of their voices, or maybe through some sense that she was being discussed, Alice raised her head and then stood up facing them and staring at them intently. Was she going to dash into the house and say or do something provocative to get rid of Anna? They both waved but she stood as still as a halted deer, her silver hair floating around her head, and then she turned and knelt again to heap up grass cuttings into a bed.

'It's hard to say. She was when it was set up but then, after she'd Skyped Julie last night, she seemed a bit less keen.'

'Oh, what was said?'

'I don't know – I just left them to it. Julie's not interested in talking to me, which is fine, but Alice was a little subdued after it. When I asked her if she was ok she just said could she take her own pillow because theirs was too squishy.'

'Fair enough. Do you mind if I push off when I've drunk this? I've got a load of laundry to do and I'd like to catch Ellis in the brief interval of his being around between waking up and leaving the house. He's getting as bad as Bean, although thankfully hasn't given up washing.'

He came with her to the front door and tucked her into his arms. 'Don't ever not tell me about this stuff that's going on, Annie,' he murmured. 'We need to think about it properly.'

'Ok. Let's talk when we go out tonight. I've never been before but it sounds brilliant.'

'The Glee Club? Neither have I, but I like the line-up.'

'You've been talking to my dad, haven't you?'

Steve lifted her face and kissed her. 'Yes, he did have a word and it was the nudge I needed. We both deserve a break, though, and dinner and a good laugh should set us up nicely.'

When she got home, Ellis was at the kitchen table whitening a tennis shoe and there was no sign of Bean so she seized the moment. 'How's it going?' she asked, sitting down and picking up a washed cotton lace to thread into the other chalky plimsoll.

'We're up against Coventry this afternoon.'

'Good luck. What about school? I hardly see you these days.'

'Ok.'

'Sorry to ask this, Ell, but is there anyone you've fallen out with or who's fallen out with you?'

He rubbed his nose with a white thumb. 'Why?'

'A kid wrote on our garage door yesterday with squeezy mayo, of all things.' She laughed nonchalantly, she hoped. 'I just wondered if there was something going on.'

He was instantly alert. 'Have you been getting more messages, Mum? Have you told the police?' The sight of his tense face made her wish she hadn't said anything.

'Honestly, Ellis, it was just childish – nothing worrying.'

He pushed the tennis shoe a little. 'Ok, well, there is something, but it's nothing to do with that. I know I'm being mean.'

She finished the lacing and set the shoe down. 'You've never been mean in your life so spit it out.'

'I wish Bean would go home. He's been here ages, nearly two weeks, and I don't get any time to be on my own and do my own stuff. He's all right when we're all in the band but –'

'I was going to call his dad anyway so I'll do it today but before I do, is there anything I ought to know about his situation? All that his dad said before was that they needed some space from each other for a while but is it more than that? Does his dad treat him badly or is there anything else going on?'

Ellis picked up the second lace and shoe and began threading it. 'Don't think so, he's always going round there. His dad's got a new girl-friend, though. The trouble is, he likes it here, I expect he misses his mum.'

Anna pushed back from the table and stood up, fishing her phone out of her back jeans pocket.

Later she went to hang out the washing and found George and Macavity sharing the shed in companionable silence. The cat raised her triangle face and narrowed her eyes at Anna in greeting so Anna rubbed the few white hairs under her chin and was rewarded with a resonant purr but then George suddenly slapped down his book and the cat shot off from under her hand.

'What?'

'I completely forgot. A man phoned for you on your work phone earlier on, didn't give a name. You left it on the table and I answered it before I realised it was yours.'

'That's ok,' Anna said, trying to remember whether she had given Rakes and Queenie her personal number or her work phone, or both. 'What did he say?'

'Nothing, just that he would appreciate a call back.'

George was frantically sorting through a pile of closely-written scraps of paper on his desk, frowning and muttering, but she leaned across and pulled an envelope from under the lamp that had numbers scribbled on it. 'Is this it?'

'Oh, thank goodness. Diane says I'm getting more absent-minded but I think it's that I'm tuning her out more which is worse, of course.' He pushed his glasses back up his nose. 'Although, I am always picking up the remote instead of the landline and then wondering why I don't get a dial tone.'

Macavity had returned and was now nuzzling down on Anna's lap so she felt no urgency to leave. She trawled her memory of the Gypsy narratives she'd been reading for a morsel her dad would enjoy. 'Did you know that sometimes Hindi speakers can understand Romani because it's so close linguistically?'

George was immediately engaged. 'Fascinating. I wonder if they mind that we, you know, us *gorgias*, have learned a few words? Shared language is so binding, isn't it? I think that's why teenagers invent new words – they need to have a private community where they can be literally incomprehensible to the people outside, especially if those people are in control of their lives.'

Anna stroked the silky black head and Macavity rumbled pleasingly. 'Gay people used to do it, didn't they, before they were legal? What was it called?'

'Yes, Polari, but that was different again. Before gay people took it up it was the language of the streets – prostitutes, beggars, travelling entertainers, even wrestlers and sailors around the Med for centuries. A lot of it comes from Italian. But Romani is a more ancient language; it's probably millennia old. Some say that Gypsies are descended from the Hindu soldiers who fought against the Mughal Empire taking over and had to run for their lives when they found themselves on the losing side.'

Anna looked out into the sunny garden at the sheets blowing on the line – gathering in sun-dried linen smelling of the sky and having a purring cat on your knee are among the quieter of life's pleasures but no less sweet for that. She carefully placed Macavity back on the chair after standing up. 'I can just imagine my mother taking on the Mughals. I'll go and phone this mystery man.'

She took the phone into the front room so she could watch through the window for any repeat vandalism but didn't have long to wait before it was answered.

'Hi,' she said, 'this is Anna Ames. You called?'

'Oh yes, thanks for getting back.' The voice was deep, almost guttural, with a country accent that she couldn't identify. 'I got your number from Mike – that you bought that painting from?'

'Yes! I'm glad to hear from you. Is this to do with Tom Budas?' There was a pause and Anna wondered if she'd blundered. 'I mean, Queenie and Rakes Smith?'

'I did hear about that, but no, Mrs Ames, this is a different lot.' Again, there was a pause and she could hear a muted babble in the background which could be the television or that he was calling from a crowded place. There was a shout and then laughter and then he said, 'I'm Bill Bates.'

Anna's legs gave way and she sat heavily on the arm of the sofa. 'My mum's family? Lena's? My family?'

'We think so.'

'Her mother, my grandmother, was Mollie May Bates?'

'And your grand-dad was Siggi.'

'Yes, yes!' Anna's heart was hammering. 'Thank you so much for phoning, Bill, thank you, you don't know what this means.'

'All right, darling, it's all right – don't take on. Listen, I'm your grand-dad's youngest brother's son so I'm a cousin to you but you do have closer-in-age cousins.'

Anna could hardly breathe. 'Ok, that's great, ok.'

'I've got a bit of land out the other side of Droitwich where we built a little place to keep our trailer and horses and such and me and the wife want you to come out so we can meet and talk over things. Get to know each other. Are you interested?'

'Bill, I would love it. Could I bring my dad, too? He'd really like to meet you.'

'If he wants to come, he'd be welcome.'

Her hand shook as she wrote down the address and directions and a date and after the call had ended she stood for some time staring sightlessly into the street. Her mother's family had reached out to her, wanted to know her, it was unbelievable, wonderful, but at the same time terrifying.

Whenever families who are estranged, for whatever reason, come together secrets explode and misconceptions, good and bad, are exposed and it can be dangerous. Her (now permanently) absent mother had been an enigma all her life but the fantasies Anna had woven to explain her disappearance had been a cocoon of comfort, a possible kindly explanation. Anna had imagined her as an explorer, a free spirit, a rare and precious talent who could not be pinned down to conventional life but who had never stopped loving her little girl. When she had met Lena in the flesh all of that had been blown sky high and she was left with a reality that had hurt her – still hurt. What now, she wondered, what now?

22

It was like being in love, this assignment with her family, because when mundane practical matters weren't occupying her, thoughts of them would instantly pop up. She would find out every last thing she could online to prepare. She laughed too much at the Glee Club and chattered too much to Steve and when they made love later she sensed his slight wariness at the intensity of her passion.

But Sunday afternoon brought the visit from Bean's father and she reluctantly came back to the present. When she opened the front door to him he bounded towards her and took her hand. 'Anna!' he cried, covering it with his other hand which was a gesture she didn't care for from a man she had never met. She indicated the front room.

He stood by the fireplace looking round. 'Wow. Great room – you're quite the home-maker, aren't you?' Anna didn't even bother to glance at the walls and assorted clutter. It had been lovely when she and Harry had decorated it and shopped for auction house furniture two decades ago. She decided not to offer a drink, or at least, not yet.

'Please sit down. I just thought we should have a word about Bean because he's been here for quite a while now.'

Bean's dad (had she ever known his name?) leaned back on the sofa. 'Don't worry about it, it's fine.' Now she knew where Bean got it from.

He was wearing Converse high-top canvas boots and jeans so tight that he winced as he re-positioned himself on the sagging sofa. Everything about his image that could be managed had been, so there was the sculpted hair-do, the tattooed arm, the trim waist. He looked like the male model in a catalogue that got sent to her with wearying frequency because five years ago she had ordered something for Harry.

She remained standing by the fireplace. 'Well, no, it's not fine. I think it's time he went home now. He's a nice lad but it was only supposed to be for a few days.'

Bean's dad put on a comic expression of angst. 'What's he done? He can be a muppet sometimes.'

Irritated, Anna became a little firmer. 'He hasn't done anything – it's just that this is not his home, is it? His home is with you.'

Now he switched the agonised expression for a mournful one. 'He thinks the world of you, you know. He needs a mother. I do my best but it's not the same. He's been so much more, um, together since he's been here. Now I've met you I can see why and it means so much, a wonderful woman like you to nurture him.' He smiled sadly.

'It's time he left, Mr, er – '

'Jed.' He had had his teeth whitened. 'Short for Jedai as in Knight.'

Bloody hell, Anna thought, and folded her arms. Where was Faye when she needed her? 'I'm going to have to insist that you take him home,' she said, trying not to sound like a headmistress, but it was as if she had not spoken.

'I'm writing a novel, you know,' Jed now confided, passing a hand lightly over his gelled hair, 'because I have so much to say about the paradox of contemporary masculinity. You're a book-lover, aren't you?'

'So it would be best if you take him back today since it's school tomorrow. You can call him now and arrange it. They're practising at Mike's.'

His look changed to one of calculation as the posing was abandoned. 'To be honest with you, sweetheart, I was hoping you'd have him for a couple more weeks. I've got a chance of a holiday rental in Spain and was planning to go with a friend.'

'No,' Anna said, unable to stop herself bristling. 'Here's an idea. Why don't you wait for the school holidays and take your son somewhere instead?'

'What's he been saying?'

'Nothing. He admires you. Take him home.'

Jed struggled up from the couch. 'I got you wrong, didn't I? Jeez, there's no pleasing some women.'

Anna moved towards the door and he had no choice but to follow her. 'So, around seven, ok? He will have eaten and I'll make sure he has all his stuff.'

She closed the front door quietly behind him and made a Kali face at it.

Bean came home later looking soulful. 'You're throwing me out,' he said, his eyes swivelling to George's mixed grill spitting on the hob. He looked so droopy and lost under his clump of greasy hair that her heart melted. It wasn't his fault that his dad was a pillock.

'Well, you had to go home some time,' she said, giving him cutlery to place round the table, 'but feel free to pop in.'

'Really?'

'Yes. You can tell me how you're getting on with that girl you like.'

He dropped two forks on the floor, picked them up and placed them where she and George sat. 'Really? Can I?'

She retrieved the forks, put them in the sink and got two clean ones. 'Yes, of course. Just check with me first, ok?'

'Sweet.' He blushed and she almost relented but thought of Ellis.

'Lay a place for Faye, would you?' George said, turning, 'She phoned earlier.'

Anna's heart lifted. She hadn't seen Faye for a while and she missed her despite the worry over how she'd been on the girls' night out, or because of it. 'Is Jack working tonight?'

George slid a fish slice under the lamb chops and flipped them expertly on to a hot metal plate which he posted into the oven. 'He is, but I think she may be on the scrounge, too. It's hard to tell.'

'Just tell her no,' Ellis said, coming in and slumping at the table with his phone. 'She's such an adultescent millenial. She took my best compasses last time. Why?'

Glancing at his watch, George gave the sausages a last turn and prodded the green beans. 'She's doing Venn diagrams on their kitchen table.'

With her usual impeccable timing – too late to help, too early to miss out – Faye arrived in the kitchen in a flurry, dropping her bags on top of Anna's on the old chair and wrenching open the fridge door to check for goodies. Bean lowered his head a little and watched her covertly. It was so good to see her animated in the old way, face bare of make-up and glorious chestnut hair bouncing on her shoulders.

'Your hair's back to its proper colour,' Anna said. 'Have you re-dyed it?'

Faye grabbed a bottle of beer from the fridge and inspected the contents of George's huge skillet. 'Mm, that smells great,

Smurffy. It was only paint, Mum, foils would cost a fortune.' She swiped Ellis lightly across his head. 'Hey, bro, what's up?'

'Have you brought my compasses back?'

'Next time – don't be such a nerd. Who has *best* compasses?'

'People with GCSE Maths – you didn't even ask. Just because you were ergophobic at school doesn't mean I am.' He looked away from his phone to stick his tongue out at her.

Faye grabbed his face and planted a huge kiss on it making him splutter with disgust. 'Don't know what that means, don't care. Where did that cat come from?'

Macavity walked over to George and twined herself round his legs, purring. He flushed guiltily. 'It was only scraps,' he said. 'It would have gone to waste. Come and get your plates.'

After dinner Faye disappeared outside and Anna followed her hoping for a chat but she was more interested in the contents of the little tool store backed on to George's writing shed. 'What are you looking for?'

'Didn't we have the old pots of paint here from when you and dad were decorating? I'm sure I remember them. Wait a minute.' She pulled out a folded tarpaulin coated with dead leaves and spiders and groped through the cobwebs and dust until she could lift out one can after another, the metal ones rusty and the plastic ones filthy. As she took them out she shook them and made two piles. 'Half of these are empty or dried up,' she complained, 'why haven't you thrown them away?'

'Because there isn't anywhere to throw them, any more. The tip won't take them and you're not supposed to put them in the general rubbish.' Anna picked up the newest tubs, one splattered in yellow and one in white. 'I need these for touch-ups, they're from when I did the bedroom. What do you want paint for anyway?'

Faye tossed back her hair and announced, 'Minimalism is dead, Mum.'

'If you say so.'

'I'll take these, then.'

Anna stacked the useless tins and tubs into the back of the tool-shed and stuffed in the tarp while Faye piled up the others in her arms. 'I was hoping we could have a bit of time together this weekend, love.'

'Why? Can I borrow that big garden bag for these?'

'I thought we might go down to the markets in town and browse around. You used to love doing that. Do you remember all those vintage clothing stalls?'

'Or,' Faye said, 'you could help me trawl the furniture charity shops. We could get twice as much if you bring your car.'

Anna followed her up the garden debating whether to say something about yet more unnecessary expense. Faye crammed the bag of paint tins in the back of her car under the gaze of Bean who was standing on the front step with a packed sports-bag and a dismal expression. Anna waved her goodbye and went up the steps to go in through the front door. 'Why are you standing here?' she asked.

'Dad's on his way and doesn't want to run into the man-hater, he says.' Anna rolled her eyes and Bean added, 'I don't think that, I think you're nice.'

She looked up at him. 'And you're nice if you think for yourself. We don't have to believe everything our parents believe. And remember, girls of your age are just as confused as you are.'

'Ok, then.' A horn beeped.

'See you soon,' Anna said, not looking round, and closed the front door behind him.

Later, laying aside her book before she drifted off to sleep, she thought of what the week might bring. She and George and Ellis, too, would be making the journey to see her cousin Bill on Wednesday evening. This meeting with her family, the strangers who were her family, preoccupied her almost all the time now. They were her first thought in the morning and at night she had to read until her eyes felt as though they were rolling in grit before she could get to sleep. George had been excited at the news of Bill's invitation and then thoughtful, but she could see he was as stirred at the prospect of meeting them as she was. Telling Ellis had been easy because he had never known his grandmother and she spared him the dramas and kept it simple because the main interest for him was visiting a Gypsy home. She couldn't prepare him because she didn't know herself what to expect. She turned on her side and sighed into the pillow.

At nine o'clock Monday morning Bernice Sitwell phoned. Anna took a deep gulp of her double-espresso latte and prepared to stand ready, knees flexed, hands stretched out like a goalie waiting for where the penalty shot would be aimed and trying to catch it. Bernice had wrong-footed her several times already.

'Bella's impossible,' Bernice said immediately, 'it's like she's demented. She's been round here yelling at us and threatening us about nothing. I know she doesn't know anything about you and us meeting, it's all just venom because she hasn't got her hands on poor Guthrie's money so Richard and I have talked it over and we think you're right, that we should tell Rebecca everything but we want you to be there.'

'But, it's not my – ' Anna began.

'Oh, will you? Rebecca likes you,' Bernice pleaded, 'you can talk better than us and then she won't go off the deep end. It's your idea to tell her, after all, and we're so beside ourselves here.'

Anna didn't miss the emotional blackmail but the truth was that she did want to be there for Rebecca when Guthrie's parentage was revealed. Not because she was worried the young woman would do something rash but more because she would be deeply hurt to find that she had been deprived of a brother because of the Byzantine machinations of the two sisters. 'Ok, I'll come, but not in work time, this is not part of my job. You must understand that it would have nothing to do with Harts?'

Bernice sounded vague when she answered, 'Of course – I know.' Her voice now acquired an angry tremor. 'But what Bella did telling us he was in New Zealand, that's what we've been reeling from as well as the loss of him. I can't get my head round that he was only an hour's drive away, my own son! I always thought he would come back – that there would be a knock on the door one day.' Anna could hear the poor woman crying and then she asked, 'Have you ever lost anyone dear to you? '

The unexpectedness of the question knocked Anna over. Anyone dear to her? She was instantly kneeling on a rocky hillside with Harry's body in her arms, the gash in his neck still weeping blood.

'Yes,' she whispered.

'I'm breaking my heart here, Anna.'

Of course she was – it was a tragic situation. To know that Guthrie could have been found, the rift perhaps healed, a loving closeness restored would drive anyone to distraction. Anna forced herself to suppress her own surging emotions and concentrate on

Bernice's situation. 'It will be very emotional for Rebecca to find he was her full brother.'

'Just as long as she doesn't blame us. We didn't do anything wrong.' The self-centredness of this remark, the apparent unconsciousness of what a bombshell this would be for their daughter took Anna's breath away and surprised her coming from a woman who seemed so full of maternal love.

'I think it will be a huge thing for her.'

Bernice seemed to acknowledge this. The arrangement was made for the following Sunday because Anna had committed Saturday to Faye and Steve would be away on the Wirral for the weekend so she would be free that day. On a practical level, it would mean that in due course Rebecca could be approached about the DNA test and that might settle the whole business of Guthrie's legitimate beneficiary.

Anna was about to call Ted but decided to go to his office and see if he was there. The tension which Bernice's phone call had induced had made her body tight and desperate for movement so she sprang up and made for the door wishing she could go outside and walk it off for half an hour but as she left the main office she saw that Steve had come to his own office door and flicked his head to indicate that he needed to talk to her inside.

'What's up?'

'I know you're busy, Anna, but I just wanted to quickly run something by you. Have you got a minute?' She nodded as he ran his hand through his hair making it stand up on end like a yard brush. 'Alice said something to me last night about going up to Julie and Simon's next time and I don't know what to make of it.'

Anna perched on one of his swivel chairs. 'What?'

'She said she didn't want me to leave her there and come home, she said she wanted me to be around but not at the house with her.'

'Do you know why?'

'No. Nothing I can make sense of. She wants to go but there's something troubling her about it. It may be just a feeling she has, something she can't articulate because she's just a kid and doesn't have the language, or she may be ashamed of feeling insecure or homesick with them. She said to me, "I'm not a baby, you don't have to stay," as though being there without me was some kind of test, but then she said, "You won't go properly away, will you?"'

'It would be natural for her to feel a little lost there, though, wouldn't it? She doesn't really know them very well. So, she may want to appear brave and confident but needs to know you're not far away.'

'So you think her fear is a normal stage in becoming more independent?' He seemed relieved at this and sat down on his own chair, but was still turning it from side to side, considering.

'You don't think anything bad is going on, do you?' Anna couldn't help saying.

'Oh God,' Steve cried, 'I don't know – how do you know? All I can do is keep telling her to phone me anytime and I'll come and get her. I can't believe anything awful is going on with them, though, although I don't particularly like them, and I don't want to over-protect her. I've booked myself in to a hotel in a village about two miles away.'

Anna stood up. 'Try not to worry, it's probably nothing. You'll be there, nearby, and even if she doesn't like the food she's offered she knows you will turn up in five minutes to take her away. It is the first time you've left her like this so you're bound to be nervous, too.'

Another researcher now appeared at his door and Anna slipped out past her to go to Ted's office. She was remembering Alice's odd frozen intensity in the garden as she had stared at the two of them, her uncle and herself (the wicked interloper) standing side by side in the kitchen looking out at her on Saturday morning.

There was no-one in with Ted so she tapped on the door and he nodded her in. The business with Bernice, well, with the whole family, was making her uneasy and she needed to put Ted in the picture so that he would know she was being straight with him; he may even have some useful advice for her.

'I told her it would be a purely personal visit,' she repeated after telling him the gist of her earlier conversation with Bernice, 'that it would have nothing to do with Harts.'

'Mm, but you are from Harts, aren't you – that's why and how you know them? I don't know if that distinction would hold up in a court of law.'

'I can phone back and say I can't do it, if you insist, Ted, but I'm worried for Rebecca.'

'And she's the one that might give the DNA?'

'Mm.'

Ted sighed and leaned back in his chair rolling his tongue round his teeth and she noticed that he looked a little better, a little less haggard and hopeless and was pleased. 'I think I'm going to do a Pontius Pilate on this one,' he said eventually. 'You are a free agent, after all, you can see who you want in your own time and I'll make a summary record of this conversation and not deny that we've had it but it must be clear to all of them, as you've made it clear to Bernice, that you're not acting for this Company.'

She stood up. 'Ok, Ted. I'm glad I told you, though.'

He grunted. 'Makes a change.'

23

On Wednesday she arrived home early at four and was greeted by Ellis and George both in a state of high excitement. They ate slices of fruitcake and Anna ran upstairs for a shower but within fifteen minutes she was down again in a light flowered dress and flat sandals to find them hovering in the hall waiting to go. George was carrying his old wicker basket with two plastic containers inside. 'Can't go visiting family empty-handed.'

It was a close, sticky afternoon on a day threatening thunder and Anna noticed that her hands were sweating as they slipped on the steering wheel. It was a good time to be driving out of Birmingham as the roads were fairly clear as they left the city behind and headed out along a dual carriageway to skirt Droitwich. At first Ellis kept up a stream of questions but as they drew closer they all fell silent wondering what lay ahead. Impossibly old-fashioned images sprang to mind – highly decorated traditional Vardi vans, camp fires and cooking pots, dogs and horses that jostled in Anna's imagination with the chrome and lined out motorised mobile homes she had seen at Appleby and the top-of-the-range SUVs. Eventually they turned into a lane and could see from the screen that they were near their destination. Who would greet them? Certainly Bill, but would his wife Cherry be there, too, and how did she feel about the visit, and about Lena?

Anna slowed the car when they saw a gate post ahead with a US-style mail-box bolted to it topped with a bald eagle and a track turning to the right to disappear behind a stand of beech and birch trees in full leaf. The car crawled up the bumpy unmade track and turned at the bend. Ahead of them, set square on, was a neat red-brick bungalow with conservatories sticking out from either side and to the left a low-roofed barn. Three trucks, four cars and a quad bike were scattered about the space in between the two buildings and a lurcher, a springer spaniel and a little terrier bounced towards them barking and wagging their tails. Anna parked the car to the side near the barn and they all got out.

From behind the bungalow a nut-brown man with a frosting of silver hair appeared with his arm raised in greeting. 'Come on, come on,' he shouted, 'we're lining up for you!' Anna laughed and moved forward first and he caught her up in a quick embrace.

'Heck, you do look like your ma, and who's this handsome young *mush*?' Ellis flushed and grinned and was pulled into another hug the minute Anna had been released. 'And you, Sir, are very welcome,' he went on, addressing George and putting out his hand.

Vibrating with bonhomie, her dad shook Bill's hand and proffered the basket. 'I'm very pleased to be here,' he said, 'thank you for inviting me.'

'And what's this?'

'Lemon drizzle and shortbread. Made today.'

'By his own fair hands,' Anna put in. They followed Bill towards the house but he walked around it along a little crazy-paved path.

'Hey, Cherry!' Bill shouted. 'They've heard about your baking and they've brought their own.'

A woman erupted from the back door drying her hands on a tea-towel, 'You'll get a slap one of these days, old man,' she said, moving quickly towards Anna and taking hold of her shoulders to study her face. She was large and firm-fleshed, deeply tanned and rosy from cooking and Anna felt for a moment like a child under the gaze of her bright eyes. 'So you're our Lena's girl,' she said, and then, enfolding her, 'Welcome home, chick.' But as Anna's eyes pricked with tears, Cherry moved on and was hugging Ellis and then George.

'Come on, come on,' Bill said again, sweeping them forward down the path out of the back garden, 'they're all waiting for you and we've laid on a proper Gypsy feed.'

Beyond the garden was a small field, invisible from the road, and Anna, George and Ellis halted at what they saw. A fire had been lit some time ago so now it was burning hot and low and over it, from a tripod, was hanging a huge iron pan. 'Barbeque, Romani-style!' Bill joked, 'only we've been doing it for a bit longer so it's *shushie* stew. That's Romani *chib* for bunnies. You've got a lot to learn!' He laughed.

Around the fire were folding chairs and sawn off sections of tree-trunk on which were sitting a dozen or so men and women. Children ran down from ponies grazing where the field met the trees but stopped to stare, their eyes wide. Bill walked round the circle introducing them with a sarcastic comment from Cherry for each man: 'This here's Dommie, your grand-dad's great-nephew,' Bill said of a burly man dressed in smart jeans and a check shirt, 'Always here when the pot's on,' Cherry added, ' And this is his missus, Mona, and…'

Anna's little family, which had believed itself to be only that, met so many relatives that the names and the faces blurred and all they could do, all they wanted to do, was smile and hug and be hugged until it came to an end and they found they had been seated and drinks had been put in their hands. As everyone began to chat and explain and make connections, a thin boy of maybe twelve or thirteen with a sharp haircut approached Ellis. 'You want to see our horses?' he asked and Ellis was out of his seat in a moment.

'Where do you keep your beasts, then?' The question came from an unsmiling man with a roll-up cigarette in the corner of his mouth who narrowed his eyes at Anna. She couldn't remember who he was.

'I haven't got any,' Anna said, 'I wouldn't have enough grass for a donkey in my back garden.' At that, he looked past her, erasing her wordlessly like the man had at Appleby but in the next moment she was seized and hugged by someone's aunt.

As things settled down and Cherry and some of the other women went back and forth to the kitchen, attention shifted from the novelty of the visitors and it could be seen that not all the adults sitting around, some smoking, some talking quietly, were as thrilled to see her as Bill and Cherry had been, but, Anna thought, that was understandable. They were, after all, townies, strangers, and the more remote the family tie the less interested and the more suspicious people were bound to be. It was also possible that there were ancient tensions as in most families and, she reminded herself, Mollie May had left them and that must have caused resentment.

Cherry plonked herself down next to Anna announcing, 'That's it, I shall work no more the day, you can all see to yourselves.'

Anna was wondering who Bill had meant when he had said on the phone that Anna had closer relatives than himself when a little white car drove cautiously up the pitted track and parked in the yard. Bill put down the ladle he was stirring the pot with at the sound of the car and now jumped up and told Anna, 'Here she is, your cousin Geena, she said she'd be here but she's always late. Come on.' Anna glanced round and saw that George was deep in conversation with an older man whose name she'd forgotten so she went with Bill back around the house into the yard. Coming towards her was a woman who looked as though she'd just stepped out of a solicitor's office in her black suit and neat shoes with her thick, dark hair whipped up into a mass of curls on top of her head.

She stopped when she saw Anna approaching and the two stared at each other. Immediately there was intense interest, a thrill of recognition, a vibrancy between them that was quite different from the ready affection of Bill and Cherry. She stepped forward, not knowing whether to hold out her hand which seemed too formal or to embrace which would be, oddly, too casual for this first meeting. 'I'm Anna,' she said, to say something, 'I am so happy to meet you, Geena.'

Geena nudged her shoulder bag back and stretched out both hands. 'Oh, me, too! I've been so excited all day! My mother and yours weren't just first cousins, they were childhood best friends,' she said, 'and even though we didn't know you existed, I feel as though I've been waiting all my life to meet you.'

When they drew apart Geena said, laughing, 'I didn't even have time to get changed! What will you think?' She had the same hooded dark eyes as Anna's own and the same latte skin although her features were otherwise different – a more delicate chin, thinner lips. She could see that Geena was making a similar inventory of her and said, 'We do look alike, don't we? No one else in my family looks like me.'   No one alive, anyway.

For the next hour there was eating and talking after Geena begged some of her daughter's clothes from Cherry and re-appeared in white trousers, a T shirt and trainers to sit next to Anna and talk. She was an advocate specialising in Travellers' housing issues and not for one second did the conversation lag between them despite both of them packing away the rabbit stew. In fact, the others were making jokes about them chattering like teenagers and using up all the air and so on and George and Bill took photos on their phones. The field turned golden as the evening deepened but then Geena put her hand on Anna's arm and said, 'There's something I want to show you. It's not far away – will you come?' and Anna immediately stood up.

Bill had been in full flow to George explaining how Siggi, Lena's father, had disappeared when Lena was young. 'He was a bit of a lad, Siggi, and Mollie May was a woman that took no prisoners so we reckon he'd had enough nagging and took off after a *gorgia* he'd been seeing down Chepstow way. Well, a bit after, Mollie May took off herself and Lena with her – couldn't take the wagging tongues they said – and that was the last we seen of any of them until this one,' nodding at Anna, 'turned up out of the blue. And you told me Lena had a boy, too?'

It was hard to imagine the huge, shambling Len as a boy. 'Yes, Len. Different father. I've been trying to get hold of him to tell him about all of you but he's a bit elusive.'

Geena said, 'I want to show Anna one of our old stopping places at Cooper's Wood – we won't be gone long.'

Anna looked at George but he waved brightly and she could see Ellis was now astride one of the cobs and clearly having fun so she slipped her arm through Geena's and they made their way out to her car. This is what it must be like, Anna thought, as Geena turned the car into the lane and glanced warmly at her, still chatting, this is what it must be like to have a sister.

It seemed that Geena had decided long ago she didn't want a Romani husband. 'Some of them are great, like Bill, but some of them are a bit too set in the old ways, you know, where the men do what they want and the women have to put up with it. A bit too handy with their fists, too, some of them.'

'Mm, it's not a problem limited to Travellers.'

Geena nodded. 'I do have a partner and my ma knows about him but they don't. I keep my private life private.' Geena's mother, and her father before he died, had been settled in Wythall for years so Geena had gone to school and done well but they had kept close ties with the families both parents had known when they had been travelling, always going to weddings and funerals and seeing them often at the horse fairs.

After a few miles Geena turned off on to a narrow lane and then came to a halt in a small gravel car park by an access stile into a wood. A sign had been put up to say what flora and fauna might be seen in the wood and to let visitors know the penalty for littering. 'It wasn't like this then,' Geena said, 'this was a space where trailers could pull on but now the Council's taken it like so many other stopping places.' They got out of the car and Geena led Anna down a path through the trees. They walked slowly, Anna asking questions and Geena answering.

'In the early spring,' she said, 'Lena and my ma, Phyllis, would go into these woods with the other kids and their mums and gather snowdrops to make into little posies with a bit of greenery to back them and take them into the town to sell them. Later, it was those little wild daffies, you know?' Anna nodded. 'I'm talking about the fifties now. The men made wooden flowers, too, and pegs and they'd take those.' They walked slowly, feeling the pleasurable crunch of the gritty soil on the path. 'If they were lucky, a town lady might let them tell her fortune, you know?' Geena laughed but then grew serious. 'But some of them were very deep-minded, it wasn't all play-acting. Some men, too, they have the gift.'

'So the men would be working for the farmers, harvesting?'

'Mostly, and the women and the children did that, too and other farm jobs. But when the laws were passed closing most of the stopping-places in the late fifties and sixties and people were so against Travellers they couldn't do that anymore and that's when the farmers started getting seasonal workers over from Europe, students and such. Our families used to do all that. Now, they say English people are too idle to do farm work, but I don't know.' They walked off the path deeper into the woods seemingly at random but Anna felt that Geena was taking her somewhere, had a destination in mind.

'Ma always goes on about how idyllic it was living out in the fresh air among nature, what a carefree life they had, but I think they were often cold and hungry and, of course, school was a nightmare for the kids if they did go. She was a bit of a campaigner in her time and I'm proud of her but I'm glad I was born when I was.' She paused and then added matter-of-factly, 'My dad couldn't take to the settled life so he took to the bottle instead.'

'I wish I knew what had happened to my grandfather, Siggi Bates,' Anna said, 'I've looked on quite a few websites like *findagrave* and *deceasedonline* because he's not listed under registered deaths but, of course, he could have changed his name or gone abroad and even if he was buried in this country, records aren't a hundred per cent complete.' Geena looked sideways at her.

For a while they walked in silence listening to the calls of the birds and an occasional sigh of breeze rattling the leaves. It was cool in the wood and a relief to be out of the sticky evening sun. The storm seemed to have passed over without breaking although the air was still leaden and oily and the back of Anna's dress was damp with sweat.

Geena stopped and pointed to a wild rose growing on its own in a small clearing. 'Look at that dog rose,' she said. There was something in her voice that caught Anna's attention. She turned and faced her looking serious. 'Anna,' she said, 'do you want to know the truth about what really happened to Lena? I can tell you, because my ma told me, but it's bad.'

Immediately Anna's heart began to hammer in her chest. She had known all along, hadn't she, that there was a dark story lurking somewhere in Lena's past, and hadn't she dreaded knowing it? But now, with this newly-found cousin, bright, compassionate Geena, in this quiet wood, it was impossible to say, no, I don't want to hear it, let's walk away and go back to Bill's and swap anecdotes.

'Is it what Bill said?'

'In a way, but in another way, no. Bill doesn't know what happened and my guess is that those who did never told.' Anna slid down into a sitting position on the soft turf and Geena mirrored her a few yards away, wrapping her arms around her knees. 'If at any time you want me to stop, just tell me, ok? But I noticed the few things you've said about your mother and what she did to you and it may, in the end, help you to know this, to understand her a little.'

'I'm ready.' Was she?

Geena leaned back against a silver birch and looked up through the branches to the sky so the shifting light played across her face as she spoke quietly. 'Lena was fifteen and Phyllis fourteen and they'd been out all day calling with the other women, you know, trying to sell things in the town, and then had the long walk home and it was hot and they were tired. Probably a day like today. Well, down the other side of this wood where the land drops there's a stream and it widens out and deepens and the *chavvies* of the families that stopped here loved to go there and splash and swim a bit. Some of them caught a few fish they could take back for the pot. Anyway, on this day, Lena wanted to go on her own but she wasn't allowed because when they all got back to the camp it was her job to start the dinner and make sure the day's wash was done and all that. But she didn't want to do it. She was very headstrong and it caused problems with her ma, with Mollie May, and it was worse that Siggi thought the world of her and wouldn't ever have a word said against her. You can imagine the rows.'

Anna's throat had closed and all she could do was nod. One harsh parent, one spoiling one – difficult for a child to know where it stands.

'So, on this particular day, Lena snuck off alone because she wanted to go to that pool and cool off and Phyllis begged her not to but she went. Well, of course, Mollie May was furious and cursing her for running off but was too busy to go looking for her. When it started to get dark Phyllis went off on her own to find her. The poor girl wasn't far into the woods but she was hiding in a bush too scared to come home. Ma said she took one look and even as naïve as she was, she could see what had happened. Lena had blood down her legs and she couldn't stand or walk properly. Ma got her into her trailer while the others were round the fire and put her to bed and washed her down with a cloth but Lena never said a word, she just stared and shook from head to foot.

'Ma told Mollie May that Lena had gone to bed because she was tired, that she wasn't feeling well, but her ma jumped up and said she'd make sure she wasn't feeling well, leaving her to do all the work. Siggi was there, too, and he followed her in and there was a lot of shouting, ma said, although not Lena, and she thinks Siggi might have hit Mollie but then it all went quiet. Well, the next thing was that Siggi came out of the trailer and he nodded to his close cousins that always worked together and they went off into the woods. Ma said she had never seen Siggi look that way – he was a laughing sort of man and very well-liked but that evening she said he had a face like Satan.

Everyone was very quiet round the fire because they knew something bad had happened. After a while one of the men with Siggi came back and without a word he got his shovel out of his trailer and then he went back into the woods. Lena and Mollie May stayed in their trailer and not a peep came from them.

'About two hours later, when it was dark, the two cousins, I don't know their names, they came back and the one with the shovel went back to his trailer and shut the door. The other one went to Lena's trailer and knocked and stepped inside and the next they knew Mollie May started screaming but then it was cut short and it was quiet and the man came out and went back to his own trailer without a word to the others.

'Ma was desperate to see Lena and comfort her but she couldn't get to her until very early the next morning when she tapped at the window and Lena opened it a crack. Ma said she looked like a ghost she was so white. She told Ma that she had overheard that her dad had killed the man, the tramp, that had raped her but the man had a knife and had done for Siggi, too. The tramp died quickly from the cord Siggi strangled him with but Siggi, he bled out because he wouldn't let them take him back. He knew what would happen – he knew he would be put in prison and he said he would rather die out in the woods - so they sat by him and watched him bleed until he was dead, too. Then, they buried both of them.'

Anna kept her eyes fixed on the forest floor, on the dry leaves and the baby ferns and last year's rotting cones. There was a fire burning in her chest.

'There were quite a few *mumpers* about then,' Geena said, after watching Anna anxiously, 'some of them were men who'd come back from the war to nothing and took to the road but others were messed up in their heads and lived in the hedges and the forests like animals.'

'So what happened to mum and granny?' Anna asked, sickened and hungry now for it to end.

'They left the next morning. Bill was right about that – they left with just a suitcase each not having spoken a word to anyone there and they were never seen again.' Geena got up and sat by Anna, putting her arm round her shoulders. 'That rose bush?'

Anna raised her head and looked at the pale pink blooms sprouting pristine from the arching briars. 'Yes?'

'That's where your grand-dad is buried.'

Anna's blood stilled in her body. The sprawling rose bush had guarded him for over half a century, she thought, its talons repelling any casually inquisitive animal or person. She stood and went to the shrub and broke a sprig from its thorny stem and held it cupped in her hand. Geena sprang up and came to her and they stood for a long time while Anna thought of nothing but the sound of wood pigeons far away and the prick of thorns in her palm. She would find a box when she got back and keep that blossom in it.

Later, as they were driving home, Anna heard what had happened while she and Geena had been away; how the boy called Jamie had promised to teach Ellis to ride and handle horses and how a couple of the men had brought out a board and danced on it while the ones round the fire had sung and clapped the rhythm. Anna was grateful. She didn't have to talk and they had had an evening far exceeding their expectations. She kept her eyes on the road and wound down the windows on both sides so that cool air lifted their hair and refreshed them.

'Mum, you'll never guess what?' Ellis was leaning over from the back seat and shouting in her ear.

'What?'

'I told Uncle Bill about Big B and he said that was a good name because there used to be a bare-fist fighter from Birmingham called Big Brum whose real name was Isaac Perkins and he was famous and he might have been a Romani because that's a favourite sport for them. So now he's got a proper name. It's good, isn't it? He said, "Bring that towser out" so they can meet him. It would be a perfect home for him, Mum. Can we?'

'Of course. Well done, Ell.' But her reply was automatic because what had side-swiped her was Ellis giving Bill the honorary title of Uncle. Maybe this family would mean as much to him as to her. Technically, he did have a half-uncle in Len but somehow that title had rarely been used, especially not by Len himself who could tolerate Ellis but couldn't stand Faye.

But throughout the animated chatter the image of Lena lying on her death bed, as she had last seen her mother, never left her mind's eye for a second as though all the excited talk that was going on in the car was just confetti blowing across that bitter face and at any moment a dark eye would open and be turned on her despised daughter. Lena had been raped in a Worcestershire wood only two years before she met George who still believed that she had grown up in Birmingham as Reginald and Mollie May's daughter.

She said she was tired when they got back even though she knew George would want to share impressions with her after Ellis had gone up but she couldn't do it. She needed to be alone. She went through the motions of getting ready for bed, responded to a text from Steve asking about the evening with a cheery little message, but then turned off the bedroom light and dragged the bent-wood rocker over to the open window. Sleep would be impossible.

How welcome, how desperately needed must George's romantic interest in Lena have been to her? He was kind, he was steady, he was too tactful to ask questions, too credulous to need explanations or detailed histories. He simply took what she and her mother and actual step-father appeared to be on trust. They had met in the Bull Ring market where he had a stall at weekends selling used books for a little extra money and she had been triumphant at making him blush by asking if he stocked *Lady Chatterly's Lover*. They were both eighteen. It seemed from what Geena said about

Siggi that she had been used to being adored and indulged so George must have filled a familiar role for her and she must have still been grieving for the loss of that first unconditional love, apart from the horror and guilt she must have felt over how her father died.

Anna stared out at the few bright stars that could overcome the amber mist of Birmingham's street lights. But then a sudden thought made her flush with adrenaline. Had Lena become pregnant from the rape? Had there been not a baby, but an abortion? 'Oh God,' Anna said out loud, 'Oh, God.' No clinics then, no, it would have been a dangerously illegal back-street job. Anna got up and walked back and forth in the bedroom trying not to let speculation overwhelm her. The facts were bad enough, she didn't need to make it worse.

So, Lena must have loved George at least for a while because he would have been just what she needed; not only kind but someone who could take her away from her blaming mother and from all those memories. When Anna was born the young couple were living in the small flat which was all George could afford on his printer's wages but by then what was Lena feeling? How different her free-wheeling travelling life had been from a couple of cramped rooms in a poor inner-city neighbourhood where she knew almost no-one and was too quickly trapped, as she had felt, into the drudgery of motherhood. No support and fun from a huge extended family, no help from her mother whom she would avoid at all costs, only dependency, penny-pinching and loneliness and most of all, no freedom. For a woman like Lena it would have seemed like finding herself in prison.

That thought triggered Geena's account of Siggi's death. He would rather bleed to death in the woods than face hanging or jail for life. But was that really his choice? It didn't seem to make sense. Why would the police come looking for a vagrant, a tramp, or care if he was alive or dead? Surely the others would have protected Siggi and concealed what he had done? She must see Geena again soon and, if possible, meet her mother, Phyllis, Lena's childhood friend. As she resolved to do this, a deep weariness overtook her and she only just made it to the bed before she fell asleep.

24

As soon as she woke the next morning Anna knew she could not tell her father what Geena had told her. It would be the first major secret she had ever kept from him, but she couldn't risk hurting him with fresh knowledge of how he had been deceived.

She planned to phone Geena that evening but it was only ten thirty when her private phone rang and she saw Geena's name. 'Are you ok? Was it too much for you?' Geena asked immediately, her soft Worcestershire accent already unforgettable. 'I've been worrying ever since you left last night and thinking I should have waited or not told you at all.'

'I am shocked,' Anna admitted, 'but I'd much rather know. Thanks for being concerned, though. I've decided not to tell my dad because I don't want to upset him but it does give me a lot to think about.' Anna glanced round the office and checked that Ted wasn't on the prowl. 'But there is something that's puzzled me now it's all sunk in a bit. Why was Siggi worried about the police arresting him over the killing of a tramp that probably nobody in authority knew or cared about? He could have been taken to hospital and told them the stab wound was an accident when he was cutting wood or something.'

'Yes, I can see how that wouldn't seem to make sense to you,' Geena sighed. 'I told you how there are some Romani who do seem to have the gift of clairvoyance, didn't I? I don't expect you to believe it but I've seen several things where no other explanation fits.'

'Ok.'

'My mother told me that Siggi believed that his future had been cast because an old granny, who was much feared for her gift, had said when he was a boy that she'd seen his fate and that he would one day have to make a choice which was to die young and free or old and trapped. He must have thought that the time to make that choice had come. If anyone *had* told the police they would have come down very hard on him like they would on all Gypsies and life imprisonment would have been worse than hanging.'

Ted appeared at the office door. 'I've got to go, Geena, my manager is here wanting me but please, let's get together soon, ok?'

'We'd better! My mother is bouncing up and down wanting to meet you!'

Anna laughed. 'I'd love to meet her, call me when you're less busy and please don't worry – you did the right thing. Bye.'

Ted had been held up by a query but when he looked round and saw that Anna was free he raised a hand and waved her to him in a gesture oddly reminiscent of the Queen greeting her loyal subjects. Anna went over and he handed her a folded piece of paper. 'Guthrie Cromer's assets,' he said, pursing his lips, 'don't leave it lying about but I thought you should know what's involved.'

Anna glanced quickly at the total amount. 'But he was only thirty-five!'

Turning away, Ted said, 'Looks like he had a few investment side-lines of his own – all legit but it makes you think, doesn't it? I'm in the wrong business, that's for sure.' Nevertheless, he walked off with his shoulders back shooting sarcastic comments to left and right in his old jaunty style.

As she worked on Bona Vacantia cases for the rest of the morning Anna wondered what to say to Steve about Geena's revelations. Normally she would tell him such things but it seemed wrong to tell him something she was not about to tell her father so she decided to play it by ear. As it happened, when they left the building for a quick lunch at the canal-side café she had another piece of news to share with him. Elizabeth had left a message asking again if they would join her and her family to hear Tom play at The Barber Institute on Friday evening – an informal affair of Conservatoire friends getting together for a scratch concert. He had particularly asked, Elizabeth said, that she would come and Steve would be welcome, too. Afterwards there would be drinks at the Vicarage.

'This week is turning into quite a social whirl,' she mumbled, telling Steve her weekend plans while they both bit into salad baguettes.

'While I'll probably be kicking my heels in a hotel worrying about Alice!'

'There must be some lovely walks round there – I'm sure you'll be fine.'

'I'll see if my neighbour can baby-sit for Friday but if not, do you mind if I ask Ellis?'

'Of course not, but Jack will be working probably so Faye might do it.'

And so the brief lunch-time passed with nothing much needing to be said about the meeting with her Romani family except that they had all enjoyed themselves very much and the pleasure of finding Geena was a huge bonus.

The afternoon was busy and by the time Anna got home she was spent and ready for a shower so the sight of Bean folded up on the front step like a delivery was not a welcome one.

'Waiting for Ellis?' she said hopefully.

'No, Mrs A, I'm popping in like you said.'

He followed her into the kitchen and collapsed at the table as though his extra-long legs could bear no more. She sorted out drinks for them both and sat down with him. There was no sign of George, or Ellis for that matter, and she realised she had no idea where either of them was, so taken up with her own feelings had she been. 'So, what's up?'

'I've got a bit of a problem,' he said. She nodded wearily for him to continue. 'There's two girls like me and I don't know what to do.'

Things had clearly moved on rapidly. 'Is one of them the one you like?'

Bean looked confused. 'What one's that?'

'Never mind. So what's the problem?'

His Adam's apple bobbed as his eyebrows knotted together. 'One's brainy and – er – not super fit, you know?' He glanced at Anna who remained impassive. 'And one's a real babe but she's got a rep.'

Outside the sun would be warm and the air fresh and it was all Anna could do to stay in the chair but she had promised, like an idiot, that he could drop in and talk about such things. 'How do you mean, a rep?'

'They say she only goes out with boys so she can trash them on Twitter.'

'So what do you think?'

He stared seriously at the scarred table top. 'I'll go with Chenelle – she's got a massive hooter but at least she's not a ball-breaker.'

Anna rose from her chair. 'Good plan, Bean,' she said.

He loped ahead of her down the hall and wrenched open the front door. 'Ta for the words of wisdom, Mrs A – I'll tell you how it goes.'

She stayed under the shower longer than she had meant to thinking about the previous evening. Geena had told her what had happened to cause Siggi's death and the rift between Lena and her extended Travelling family because she thought it would lessen Anna's painful feelings about her mother, make her feel sorry for her, perhaps, but had it? She put back her head and let the water bounce off her face.

Certainly, the rape must have been an appalling shock for Lena and Anna did cringe at the thought of the teenager being attacked like that when all she had wanted was an innocent dip in a country stream. Then, to know that her father had lain dying in the woods because he had gone to take revenge on the stranger who had attacked his adored child must have stoked her heart with grief and remorse. It was more than possible that Mollie May had not spared her daughter the accusation that Siggi had died because of Lena's wilfulness. Her mother might have even blamed the girl for inciting the rape in some way as was often the thinking at that time. That evening both their lives had completely changed and Mollie May had chosen for them to become exiles among strangers while they created a rag rug of lies. George had never mentioned Lena reading, Anna realised, and wondered whether she had even been literate when he met her. If they couldn't read or write the only way to survive would have been manual labour or marriage for both the woman and the girl.

Mollie May had found the shy (and compliant) skilled craftsman, Reginald Walker, and that had been her way out of poverty and hard work. No wonder Lena had come up with a similar plan. All of this new insight was good reason for compassion and a change of heart towards her mother as Geena expected and yet that had not happened.

She stepped out of the shower and towelled herself vigorously trying to break the resentful thoughts which ashamed her. As she dressed she heard George's car draw up in the drive and the doors slam and then there was his voice and Ellis's passing through the hallway and into the kitchen. A tide of gratitude rose in her and she quickly dressed and ran down the stairs.

Over dinner of stuffed peppers and salad with garlic bread on the side, Ellis entertained them with his account of the band's first paid gig which had been the previous Saturday night when one of their classmates had hired them for her birthday party. Each boy and the singer, Kirsty, had been paid £10 and they felt that this marked the beginning of The Dream coming to pass which was bound to include international stardom and, in the case of the instrumentalists, an excess of female adulation. Dan had started writing their bio for press releases. A good measure of how successful it had been, Ellis felt, was that the neighbours who arrived to complain about the noise stayed to 'prat about dancing like old people' and had hinted that another booking might be on the cards.

Anna went over to the fridge to check what supplies George might have laid in and pounced on a cache of choc ices. She made a strong cup of coffee to have with hers being of the opinion that nothing on Masterchef could beat the combination of melting chocolate and ice-cream combined with a liquorice-strength mug of hot Italian blend.

They sat and licked their wooden sticks companionably until Ellis got up, announcing that he had a history test the next day and needed to revise. 'Thanks for booting Bean out, Mum,' he said. 'You don't have to worry, he's ok at his dad's.' Anna found she had been sufficiently callous not to give Bean's welfare a thought but didn't admit it.

She was finishing rinsing the dinner things and stacking them in the dishwasher when she glanced round the kitchen, checking for anything she'd missed, to find that George was pouring out two glasses of wine. This was unusual for mid-week.

'Are we celebrating, Dad?'

'In a way.' He picked both glasses up. 'Let's have these in the garden, shall we? It's supposed to rain tomorrow but it's a beautiful evening so we should enjoy it.'

Anna followed him out, on guard against revealing too much if he wanted to talk about their visit to Bill and Cherry last night. He had already pulled two chairs out of his shed which looked even shabbier in the low sun but Macavity was curled up on one of them. Anna picked the cat up and sat down, placing her, still purring, on her knee.

George settled himself, looking down the garden towards the thick foliage of the oaks which separated them in summer from their neighbours' windows, and took a sip of wine. 'Good to meet Lena's family, your family, last night, wasn't it? I liked them very much.'

'Yes,' Anna said, stroking Macavity's hot fur, 'Geena's lovely, as well as Bill and Cherry. We got on very well.'

'Ellis enjoyed himself, too, and it could be a perfect solution to the problem of Big B. Diane had hinted at it herself a while back when you were hoping for a meeting.'

'Did she? Yes – it's very good.'

George sat quietly for a few minutes and then said tenderly, 'You don't have to protect me, Annie, I know there's something you're not saying. You were very quiet after you got back from being out with Geena.'

'Oh, it was all a bit overwhelming. To find that I have a huge family I knew nothing about and to meet a first cousin who actually looks like me.'

'Mm.'

Macavity stirred and lifted her head to show yellow half-moons of appreciation. Anna rubbed her under each ear. 'I'm sorry I missed the singing and dancing, though.'

'There will be many more times, no doubt.'

Anna was wondering how soon she could get up and go down to Steve's for an hour or so, when George said, 'Bill and I had a chat about your grandfather, you know.'

'Oh, yes?'

'I asked him how old Lena was when Siggi disappeared.' Anna stopped stroking Macavity and looked at her father. 'She wasn't a child, she was a teenager, Annie. She was almost sixteen when she and her mother left.' He let a moment pass and then added, 'Did you know that?'

'Yes, Dad.'

'I think you'd better tell me what Geena told you. We've never had secrets, you and I, not important ones, and I'm not such an Ancient of Days that I can't take a bit of unpleasantness. Unless, of course, you'd rather not tell me.'

Anna sighed and felt the tightness leave her shoulders and stomach. 'Ok, Dad, I'll tell you – it would be a relief to be honest. I should have known I wouldn't be able to keep it from you, but there's no way this can't shock you, perhaps even more than it shocked me.'

Re-telling the events that took place that night so long ago in a pretty wood deep in the Worcestershire countryside, Anna saw again in her mind's eye the dappled forest floor, the rose bush with its arching branches standing alone in a golden clearing like an ancient tapestry, and heard Geena's soft voice telling of the brutality and tragedy of Lena's violation and bereavement.

When she had finished, George sat still for a long time with his head bent and his fingers interlaced as though he was at a Meeting. When, at last, he spoke his voice had the roughness of unshed tears in it. 'Poor girl, poor girl,' he said. 'What a heavy load she was carrying and I had no idea.' Far from being angry at the deception Lena, Mollie May and even Reginald had practised on him, George only felt compassion. Anna's shame at her own hard heart deepened.

'But it explains why she needed so badly to move on,' he added after a while, 'because that had been her whole life, moving on. When we were together the only really happy time we had was that trip we took, you know the one before you were born, when we were going to Katmandu in a camper van but ran out of money in Cairo?' He laughed. 'Of course she was happy travelling. New companions, new sights, new challenges – she understood that way of life, didn't she? I see that now. It was being stuck in a little flat in a city she couldn't cope with!'

Anna's anger against Lena rose like bile in her throat but she stopped herself from crying out: *And me - she chose not to cope with me!* 'Are you all right, Dad?' she asked instead.

'Oh, quite aerated. It's a lot to take in, but yes, I'm ok. I'm glad you told me because there were things about our relationship I've often wondered about but that make sense now.'

'That's good. Is it ok if I pop down and see Steve?' She rose up, placing the cat carefully down on her seat and beginning to leave so that there was no danger of him detaining her, no danger of there being a spiteful outburst because she couldn't contain it any longer.

'Yes, yes, off you go. Macavity and I will make sure the sun sets on time.' His glasses flashed above his red nose and frowsty beard as he grinned up at her as though he didn't mind or even understand that the love of his life had dealt with him so treacherously. Anna walked away swiping the tears from her cheeks.

After Alice was asleep she went out on the terrace with Steve and told him everything and he sat her on his knee and wrapped his arms round her like he had done once before and rocked her gently. When she got home, exhausted but comforted, there was a message from Rebecca on her phone which she had left on the kitchen table, asking her to call back whatever time she picked it up. If it had been any other member of the Sitwell family she would have ignored it.

'Hi, are you ok?'

'Oh, thanks for phoning back. Mum and dad want to see me on Sunday and they said you're going to be there. What's happened?'

'I think they just want to explain something to you from the past.'

'What?'

'I'm sorry, Rebecca, I can't tell you.'

'Is it bad?'

'Um. Surprising, I'd say, but not bad.'

'And you won't tell me?'

'It's not my story to tell.'

'Well, I'm glad you'll be there.' She hung up.

She found George fast asleep on the sofa in the front room surrounded by boxes of photos and old albums. She bent and picked up one of Lena she had never seen before. She was wearing a scarlet dress and ropes of beads and was laughing at the camera. Her dark hair was shoulder length and she wore the heavy eye makeup fashionable at the time. It was uncanny how Anna resembled her. Had she been carrying Anna then? She decided not to wake her father and risk embarrassing him and left the room silently.

25

The concert at The Barber Institute, which included two of Anna's favourite Baroque pieces, was sheer delight and Tom appeared at ease and animated with the other musicians. He was clearly in his element. In the interval Anna and Steve stood around in the elegant foyer sipping wine and getting to know Elizabeth's family. Andrew's wife, Adrienne, was not at all as Anna had imagined her from the photo on the mantelpiece. For one thing, she was short and for another she was almost diffident, not the take-charge personality Anna expected from a woman whom she knew was quite a big wheel in the Diocese. Elizabeth's aunt and uncle on her mother's side, who were also present, were a different matter. They had made the trip in from Cheltenham to meet Tom and yet seemed unenthusiastic about the evening.

'We'll only come back for a few minutes,' Vivian said, 'we're driving down tonight.'

'You're very welcome to stay,' Andrew offered, but the man shook his head.

'Meeting the Finance Committee first thing.'

Anna and Steve, after they had been glanced over cursorily, had been ignored by the couple which made her spiky. 'It's great to see Tom doing what he's so good at,' she said to Elizabeth, slightly turning her shoulder to exclude Vivian.

'So you won't be able to start a family for years, darling? What do musicians earn?' Rosemary put in over Anna's head.

Sunny Elizabeth laughed. 'I'm only twenty-five! Heaps of time for all that. Besides, I can easily support Tom on my salary.' There was a frosty silence.

'Shall we go back in?' Andrew suggested and they joined the slow-moving crowd who were filtering through tall wooden doors into the auditorium.

'Are you all right?' Anna whispered to him. 'You look a bit tired.' He just smiled and ushered her in before him.

Steve took her hand when they sat down. 'Is Elizabeth really going to tell Tom about his Traveller family tonight?' he asked under his breath, 'Couldn't she wait till the aunt and uncle aren't there?' Anna just shook her head meaning that there was nothing she could do once Elizabeth got an exciting idea in her head.

The others had arrived at the Vicarage before them and the rain meant that everyone was indoors but when they were shown into the living room there were only Vivian and Rosemary seated on the couch staring glumly in front of them while Tom had his back turned to the room and was watching the downpour bounce off Andrew's garden shed, or so it appeared.

Annoyed that the aunt and uncle were making no effort to get to know Tom (which had been the object of the evening) Anna took Steve over and introduced him. If anyone could make someone as clearly ill at ease as Tom was feel more relaxed, it was Steve. If the concert hall was Tom's Elysian Field, then a drinks party and small talk was obviously his Gehenna. Elizabeth and Adrienne were going to and fro with glasses and plates of nibbles and Andrew was nowhere to be seen.

Anna walked over to the couple on the couch. 'Hello again,' she said, 'Did you enjoy the music?'

'Are you one of Andrew's parishioners?' Vivian asked in a bored tone.

Anna would have loved to say something like, *No, I'm his Whore of Babylon*, but that would hardly help matters. 'No,' she said, 'at least, only in a technical sense, but I hear he is a valued pastor and priest.'

Rosemary turned her head to look at the door. 'What are they doing in there? We can't hang around all night.'

Anna joined Tom and Steve at the window, fuming inwardly. It was taking Steve a while to draw Tom out. Classical music was not one of Steve's passions and he was having a hard time trying to find a point of contact. Eventually he hit on a question about how well Tom liked Birmingham's Symphony Hall and got quite a lively reply about how excellent the acoustics were but this exchange didn't last long. Just as she was wracking her brains to find something else to talk about, Elizabeth entered the room with her mother and Andrew close behind, a familiar package under her arm. The parents were looking as apprehensive as Anna was feeling. She would certainly have told them every scrap of information Anna had passed on to her so they would know what was coming.

'I have an announcement!' Elizabeth said, taking the centre of the room. Everyone turned towards her. 'Tom, there should be a drum roll but you'll just have to imagine it.' Tom smiled uncertainly.

She unwrapped the parcel to reveal the painting that Anna had bought from Mike at Appleby. 'It's part of my wedding present to you, darling!'

'Passable,' Vivian said, glancing at the painting. 'School of Augustus John, I would say.' He turned to Tom for the first time that Anna had seen. 'Are you fond of art?' Tom looked confused.

'No, no – it's the subject of the painting,' Elizabeth went on gaily. Anna heard Steve give a small groan behind her.

'Darling,' Elizabeth said, stepping forward and drawing Tom into the centre, 'this girl is your mother and this man is your grandfather!'

Tom's confusion intensified. 'I assumed they were, Lizzie, I showed you the photograph. Have you had this painting done for me? That's kind of you.'

'No, I didn't. Anna found it and guess where?' Tom shrugged hopelessly while Vivian looked at his watch. 'Appleby. At the annual Travellers' Horse Fair! It was done by a Romani artist and Anna found it and bought it. She's been researching your family, Tom, as I asked her to and guess what? Your mother's family and probably your father's too, are Romani Gypsies! Isn't that thrilling?'

Tom pushed past everyone and crashed out into the back garden. Vivian and Rosemary raised their eyebrows, gave each other meaningful glances and announced their departure but not before Vivian said to his sister: 'Now do you see what we mean? It's not too late.'

Elizabeth, suddenly marooned and abandoned, stood in the middle of the room looking stunned. 'What just happened?' Andrew went to her and put his arm round her shoulders as Adrienne escorted her brother and his wife out. Steve found his way to the kitchen and out into the garden and Anna watched him through the window as he joined Tom in the streaming rain, bending his head to the young man's bowed one.

'What did I do?' Elizabeth begged Anna. 'What went wrong?'

Anna went to her. 'Maybe just a bit too much, too soon, but I expect he'll come round.' She heard the front door close. 'I'm sorry that your uncle and aunt don't seem to approve of him.'

'Oh them.' Elizabeth collapsed on to the couch. 'I don't care about them – they're dreadful snobs but if they've upset Tom I'll never forgive them!' Anna bit her tongue. She was struggling with her own conjectures. She couldn't believe that Tom was a prejudiced person and yet at Elizabeth's announcement he had bolted like a frightened horse. But, she knew from her work that family connections go so deep into our hearts, and especially Tom's perhaps, that any new or surprising information can set off a tsunami of emotion. Not just from her work, either, she reflected grimly.

Adrienne appeared now with a tray of mugs and set it down on the coffee table. 'I think tea is the thing we need,' she said sensibly, 'and Tom and Steve will be drenched. Andrew, go and get a couple of blankets down, would you?'

Five minutes later the back door opened and the two men could be heard making their way into the living room. Tom looked as though he was about to burst into tears and Steve had that warning expression that said: this person is fragile, handle with care. Elizabeth ran to her fiancé. 'Oh God, Tom, I thought you'd be pleased – I'm so sorry to spring this on you!' The rain trickled down his face and his dark eyes stared at her. Adrienne wrapped the blanket Andrew had brought round him and gently pushed him into a chair. The other blanket was handed to Steve who drew it round his shoulders trying not to shiver.

'No,' Tom said, as though beseeching Elizabeth, 'No –'

'So stupid of me,' Elizabeth rattled on, kneeling now on the floor and holding his legs. 'I wanted to give you a family and Anna found out so much and I couldn't wait to tell you.' At this, Tom switched his gaze to Anna and she saw again that fierce intensity in his look.

'No,' he said again, more insistently, 'listen to me. Please, listen to me.'

Anna slipped on to the couch next to Steve, rubbing his chilled arms, and Andrew leaned his elbow on the mantelpiece while his wife stood close to him, her arm round his waist.

Tom bent over Elizabeth and held her face with his slender, trembling fingers. 'You couldn't have given me anything I would want more.'

'What?' Elizabeth sat back on her heels.

'All my life,' Tom said, 'I have loved Gypsy music. All my life, Lizzie! The first time I heard it was the Bucharest Chamber Orchestra with the Romani violinist Ion Voicu in the late sixties, a vinyl record I got from a jumble sale. After that I bought everything I could find that I could afford. It spoke to me in a way other music didn't – that's why I took up the violin. There's a soulfulness and a joy in it that just seems to vibrate in my core.' He came to an abrupt stop and Anna guessed that he was used to eyes glazing over when he spoke of what meant so much to him. But here, all five faces were engaged, waiting for him to say more.

'So, when I had to choose a research subject I picked the influence of Gypsy maestros on our greatest music for the last five centuries.' He looked eagerly at the small group listening. 'It's a story that has been forgotten because very often the well-known composers didn't feel they had to acknowledge by name the Gypsy virtuosos and composers that they heard so I wanted to give credit to those extraordinary musicians who had such a huge influence on people like Haydn, Beethoven, Schubert, even Brahms and, of course, there are Dvorak's Gypsy Songs.' His eyes brightened and his voice became more animated. 'Did you know that Lizt in his Hungarian Rhapsodies tried to imitate the style and technical brilliance and charm of the Romani he heard play? They weren't just ordinary fiddlers, these men, they were extraordinary talents but so few people have heard of them.'

'Django Reinhardt,' Anna murmured, remembering.

Tom nodded at her. 'Yes, jazz improvisation and even contemporary classical pieces have Gypsy influences. Sandor Lakatos, the sixth generation of brilliant Gypsy violinists only died in Budapest in 1994. And, of course, there are some wonderful musicians now. But – oh – I'll stop. I could go on and on.' He had been leaning forward but now he sat up straight, not quite back in the room with them, as though he was still hearing the soaring voices of ancient instruments and that intensity in his nature, Anna now understood, was passion. What was it his grandfather had called him? A *kushti mush*, a fine man. Even with soaked hair plastered to his pale skin, yes, indeed.

The room fell silent. 'Wow,' Elizabeth said. Romani *Rai,* Anna thought, letting the alliteration roll round pleasurably.

'So I didn't rush out because I was upset, it was because I was overwhelmed, I was blown away! There isn't a heritage that I would love to have more than this. Thank you, thank you.' He turned to Anna. 'Please, tell me everything.'

So Anna told him about the Smith grandparents she had met and what had happened with Loretta and Teller and how she had not been able to trace him but still hoped to find out where he was.

'Your father was a fairground entertainer,' she said, 'and possibly, given his last name, from one of the Balkan countries, so he may have left the UK long ago.'

Tom was quiet. 'Mum never told me anything of this. Why? Was she ashamed of what had happened? But why would she be?'

'Different times,' Andrew said quietly. 'Harsher times in some ways.'

'But one thing is sure,' Anna said, 'Loretta's parents loved her and have bitterly regretted what happened but they had no way of finding her. They know about you but I think they're worried that you might not want to know them since you live in such a different world.'

'But I don't feel that way at all – I must meet them!' Tom cried. 'Can you get in touch with them?'

'Not directly, but I can speak to Mike who's the one who sold me the painting and contacted them before.'

'Please,' Tom said, 'please pass on to them how much I want to meet them.'

Eventually, the questions were answered, as far as they could be, and Anna and Steve rose to leave. Faye would be staying at Steve's so there was no need to worry about Alice but Anna felt drained. Tom's reaction had been so extraordinary that she wanted to process it but she needed, more than anything, to sleep.

At the door Elizabeth, still in high gear, said, suddenly remembering, 'Weren't you interested in finding some Travelling family of your own, Anna?'

Anna kissed her. 'Another time. Goodnight.'

26

Faye had a list. They were to start at the charity furniture shops in Northfield and then move on through the city suburbs to end up near to where Faye lived. 'I know exactly what I want,' she instructed her mother, 'so I don't want you to make suggestions. Just follow me round and help me pack the cars.'

The first haul was two mismatched chairs with scratched varnish and uncertain seats, a mirror, a stained coffee table and a lamp without a shade. 'So what does Jack think of this?' Anna ventured as the lamp was added to the stack by the till. But, narrowing her eyes to do a final sweep of the shop, Faye ignored her. After the third shop both cars were full and Anna felt that a coffee somewhere would be in order and that the task had, happily, not been too onerous but, no, Faye set off, ordering that she follow, and they stopped outside a garage on the edge of a dilapidated industrial estate close to the flat. Faye unlocked the padlock, pushed up the metal door and then began unloading the Micra which had the smaller items.

She looked across at Anna. 'Come on, this is just the first load.'

Anna went across to her. 'Faye, stop. What's going on? I know you've got a lot of stuff but you've already spent over eighty pounds. I'm worried. Most of this, be honest, is tat.'

'Oh, for goodness sake, Mum, stop stressing. It's ok.' She strode to Anna's car and started lifting the tables out. 'Two more trips should do it – there's only a dozen more shops worth checking.'

Anna stood her ground. 'You've been saying how hard up you and Jack are – how you're saving for a deposit and the poor guy's working all hours and I just don't understand.'

Faye, rushing back for another little table, glared at her. 'When have I *ever* been extravagant?' she demanded, which required such a detailed answer that Anna didn't even want to start. 'Why can't you trust me and just *help*!' Anna reached into the car and dragged out a chair by one leg. 'Watch it! That cost me four pounds, Mum!'

By mid-afternoon Anna was exhausted and Faye, tousled and grubby, was jubilant. She went for a high five but Anna had already turned away and sunk down into her driver's seat searching for a mint in her glove compartment.

'Where are you taking me for lunch, then?' Faye asked.

It was the weekend of the trip to the Wirral for Steve and Alice and he was texting regularly. The little girl had gone in to her aunt and uncle's house willingly with her rabbit under her arm and wearing her favourite *Frozen* back-pack containing essentials for the stay. After about ten minutes (having heard the exciting itinerary for her visit: beach, crazy golf, ice-cream, cinema) she had dismissed Steve who had sheepishly made his way to the nearby hotel to check in and get something to eat. Alice had exhibited no fresh signs of concern on the journey or on arrival and he was feeling a bit put out, having wanted to spend the weekend finishing off the terrace.

Anna contemplated going out to join him for the rest of the day and the night, but after her exertions with Faye (and faced with the prospect of another emotionally fraught Sitwell family encounter the next day) she found she hadn't the energy to make the drive. She decided that while she was hot and sweaty she might as well tackle another section of the garden but when she went through the kitchen she heard the sound of *El Condor Paso* and realised that Len was visiting. She opened the utility room door and stepped out.

Under Rosa's influence Len had taken to wearing Nehru shirts which he bought in 4X size from a shop on the Soho Road. Today he was adorned in maroon, the sleeves rolled up to reveal his huge, pale forearms as he held the flute to his mouth. He was sitting with his back to her on the stout bench that Steve had made for them after the old creaky one had collapsed. Long tendrils of mousy hair waved about as he swayed back and forth.

Anna stood and watched him for a while as he went through his repertoire. When she had first met him, only a few years ago, he had played from ear a miscellany of tunes from TV jingles, film melodies, old songs he'd heard and so on but since his little band had formed and had some modest success touring around, his technique and range had improved. In short, she was proud of her step-brother. True, Lena had not abandoned him like she had her daughter, but then neither had she nurtured him, so jealousy was never on the cards. When Anna had first known him, annoying and smelly as he had been, she had thought she had never met someone so neglected but now, especially since he and Rosa had become friends (or whatever they were) he had calmed down and settled himself. When he lowered the flute she called out and went to sit next to him on the bench.

He patted her head. 'All right?'

'More or less. You?'

'Rosa said to come round.'

'Yes.' She paused, not sure where to begin. 'I've been looking into Mum's family.'

'Dead.' Len shook saliva out of the flute and wiped it on his sleeve.

'Did you ever meet Mollie May and Reg?'

'Who?'

So Lena had never taken her son to meet his grandparents, although they were certainly still alive when he was born and living in the same city, so it was likely that she had cut them off, too. This meant that far from living a globe-trotting life of adventure (as Anna had always imagined until she discovered the truth) Lena had walked out on her and George and her own mother only to continue living in Birmingham, part of the crepuscular club scene it seemed, and carelessly made another baby. It made Anna's blood boil.

After she had finished the story, including the visit to Bill Bates but not including Geena's harrowing narrative, Len sat still for some time staring down the garden. 'So you and me are Gypos?'

'I wouldn't use that word, but, yes.'

He manoeuvred his bulk a half-turn towards her. 'She wasn't a happy woman,' he said. 'I didn't see it before but I see it now. You know, since Rosa. I feel sorry for her.'

'Oh, Len. She was so careless with you, so selfish. How can you?' First her dad and now her brother.

'She wasn't all bad, Sis. You just got on the wrong side of her.'

Anna jumped up. 'Oh, did I? What, by looking after her, visiting her every day, making sure she had everything she needed, being there when she died? How did I get on the wrong side of her?'

He stood up, too, patting the air to soothe her. 'Don't get upset. It wasn't your fault.' He looked anxiously towards the house. 'Have you got a bit of bacon? I've been waiting for you for ages.'

Anna took a deep breath. 'Ok, I'll get you a bacon sarnie and a beer and you can tell me what's been happening with you. Sorry I got emotional – it's got in amongst me a bit.'

Len preceded her into the kitchen and planted himself at the table while she pulled out the big frying pan and set it on the cooker. His broad slab of a face, not far from the same colour as the bacon in the wake of this highly-charged family encounter, was looking concerned. 'What you need is a hobby, like knitting,' he said helpfully. 'So you don't get so het up over nothing.' Anna lifted the heavy frying pan thoughtfully and then set it back down.

Mike must have called Queenie and Rakes as soon as she phoned him because at six-thirty that evening, just as she was about to open a bottle of red, they got in touch. The greeting, though, was not what she had expected.

'You're one of Bill Bates' lot, then?' Rakes said.

'I am, I'm happy to say. We met them at his place last week. We had a very good time.'

'Oh yes. Bill's alright. You told him and Cherry about seeing us?'

She was taken aback. 'No, no, I didn't. I thought what you told me would be private and I didn't know you knew them.'

'We go back a long way, me and Bill. We picked apples together in the Wye Valley when we was *chavvies*. We was always out in nature, we knew where the badgers lived and we used to watch them playing with their young ones, and the foxes.'

Behind Rakes' voice Anna now heard Queenie muttering, '*Dordi*, let me speak to the woman before we all die of old age.'

'Hello, Queenie!' she said, hearing the rustle of the phone being transferred, 'Tom is so happy to know about you. Honestly, he is. He can't wait to meet you.'

'We're not house-dwellers,' Queenie said after a moment, 'we don't have a place like Bill does.'

'Queenie, if you were living in a paper bag, Tom would be tapping at it the first moment you'd let him.' It was a relief to hear the burst of laughter that greeted this. 'He's a lovely young man, anyone would be proud to have him in their family and you and Rakes are just the people he needs.'

'Did you say about our Etta and Teller?'

'Yes.' So then she told them about the music and about how overwhelmed he had been to hear that he had family living and that they were Romani.

'I expect he thinks we live in a painted Vardi with a queenie stove and a bloody horse and roasted hedgehogs,' Rakes muttered.

'Well, we would if we could, wouldn't we? But the trailer's smart enough, I should think,' she replied tartly. 'So when's he coming to see us? Will you bring him?' Anna punched the air with her free hand.

The couple felt that seeing Elizabeth as well would be too much and Anna could tell that they wanted their grandson to themselves, at least for the first meeting, and she couldn't blame them. They were staying on a rural site not far from Tewkesbury so she got their phone number to be able to contact them directly after talking to Tom. They sounded nervous but excited and Queenie couldn't stop herself from letting a sob out as she instructed, again, that Anna would make sure that Etta's boy would know he was welcome.

Anna sat at the table sipping her wine after the call was done and before she phoned Tom, she called Mike to thank him. 'All this networking, where's my finder's fee?' he asked. 'That's what you nosey-parkers call it, isn't it?'

'How about a bottle of whisky?'

'Make it a big one and you're on, lady.'

Tom responded immediately and gave Anna some dates, she phoned the Smiths and then phoned him, and within fifteen minutes the meeting was arranged. She would need to leave work early again but so what? She felt like doing a jig round the kitchen. When Tom had thanked her she told him the truth: 'I wouldn't have found my own family if I hadn't been looking for yours, so I should be thanking you.'

27

A sporty little Mini-Cooper was parked outside the Sitwell house when Anna arrived so she assumed that Rebecca was already there. It was noon, an awkward time to meet in Anna's opinion, even on a Sunday. The door opened before she had a chance to ring the bell and she was shown into the front room.

The day was dry and hot but no windows had been opened, presumably for fear of any raised voices being overheard in the street, and Richard had stationed himself in the bay window like a sentry as though Bella might appear at the gate at any moment. Bernice was already there in her wheelchair, rigid with apprehension, and someone could be heard clattering in the kitchen. It was so different from their first meeting that Anna's mood sank.

Bernice wheeled herself to her and grabbed her hand. 'Don't let her fly off the handle at us!' she whispered urgently. 'Don't let her leave us!' She was being put at the centre of this family mess which she was expected to control but it was hard for everyone and she understood the terror that gripped Bernice over Rebecca's possible reaction to the news. As she looked round she saw that the room itself was more comfortable than all its current occupants with its welcoming sofas and well-tended plants.

'I can't,' she began, and then Rebecca came in with a tray of glasses.

'We thought you'd like something cool, so I bought some elderflower cordial. Is that ok?'

When they were seated, Anna found all three were looking at her so she said, quietly but firmly, 'I'll need to get back before too long, so please, Bernice or Richard, please start when you're ready.' They looked at each other in panic.

'You tell her,' Richard said to Anna, bobbing his head in a reptilian movement as before.

'I think it should come from you,' Anna said decisively.

Rebecca stood up. 'Oh, for goodness sake, Mum, Dad. Just tell me! My imagination's been running wild – everything from me being adopted to one of you having a criminal record! I can't stand any more suspense!'

Bernice said quickly in her breathy voice, 'You're not adopted,' and Anna dropped her head.

'What?' Rebecca shouted. 'What!'

'It's about Guthrie,' Richard said and then stopped.

'He's not your cousin,' Bernice added, 'I mean, he wasn't your cousin. Don't get angry, Becky darling, don't be cross with us.'

Rebecca's confrontational demeanour suddenly changed and she pulled across a little footstool to sit by her mother, taking her hand. It was a role reversal that Rebecca may have enacted many times throughout her life, Anna realised, from exasperated daughter to consoling parent. Bernice had, possibly unconsciously, engineered the switch by refusing to be the adult, insisting on being the frightened child given the task of revealing her big secret, so the jolly, managing exterior that Anna had seen at their first meeting must conceal deep insecurity. But Rebecca was a good-hearted woman and had realised that her mother was distressed so the affection that must normally flow in this family group eased the atmosphere. Bernice seemed steadier now that she had her daughter to hold on to – or to hold back. Anna felt for both women as they struggled across one of the most fraught thresholds in their lives.

'So are you telling me that Guthrie wasn't Bella's son?' Rebecca asked gently. 'Are you telling me that he wasn't related to me at all?'

'No, love. He is, he was related to you, but he's not Bella's son.'

Anna hardly dared take a breath.

'Dad?'

Richard stood, more immobile than his wife, silhouetted by the light from the window. His voice was guttural when he spoke. 'He was your brother.'

At first their words came slowly but as Rebecca sat silently, the staccato pace became fluent and then chaotic as each parent talked over the other, explaining, describing, desperate to make her understand how frightened they had been, how cowed and cornered. They talked and talked until they were repeating themselves, running themselves into the sand and all the time the young woman sat as still as a stone. When they finally exhausted themselves and sighed and whimpered to a standstill, Rebecca turned to Anna with cold eyes.

'Is this true?'

Anna nodded.

'Is this the real reason Guthrie left that day?'

'I don't know,' Anna said.

Rebecca turned back to her mother. 'Tell me.'

Reassured by her calm voice, Bernice explained how it had been. It was true that Guthrie had come back to tell them he was going to take a gap year starting in New Zealand, that part was true, and it was true that Bella had over-reacted and upset him but what they had not told her was that in between Bella clawing at him and demanding he stay and him leaving, Bernice had let it out that she was his real mother.

'I always was going to tell him when he was eighteen, you see,' she said to Rebecca, 'so it was, sort of, on the tip of my tongue anyway. He was so upset and he was leaving and I couldn't bear it and it just came out.' She glared at Richard. 'Your dad was no use, quaking in his boots at what Bella might do.' Richard retracted his chin into his chest.

'How did Guthrie react?' Anna asked after a moment, surprised that Rebecca was saying nothing.

Bernice was now crying and making no effort to wipe away the tears. 'He went mad. He said we'd all lied to him all his life and Becky was the only decent one of the lot of us and then he went. I never saw him again. We believed what Bella said – she's the one,' Bernice gripped Rebecca more tightly, 'she's the one to blame for all of this!'

Rebecca stood up without a word and strode out of the room and down the hall to the front door, flinging it back with a crash. Bernice gave her visceral seagull shriek and Richard stumbled to his feet to go after his daughter but Anna got out before him and ran to catch up with Rebecca as she marched down the path. 'Don't leave them!' she called, 'Talk to them, don't go!'

But Rebecca was not going to her car. At the pavement she turned right and Anna hurried along behind her trying to keep up while Richard halted at his own gate, seeing where she was headed, not daring to follow.

When she got to Bella's front door Rebecca banged on it and yelled, 'Open this door, you mad bitch or I'll smash it in!'

Windows were open up and down the street because of the heat and Anna, hovering and uncertain whether to try to intervene (would it be any use?) behind Rebecca, saw heads popping out. She wondered how well-liked Bella was and guessed not much. There was no stopping Rebecca and no point in trying, she decided.

Throwing back her head Rebecca searched the upstairs windows and Anna, following her gaze, thought she saw a slight movement of a curtain. A cement Buddha, his features eroded by lichen and grime, squatted by the side of the path and Rebecca picked this up and slammed it into the door.

'Stop it!' came a furious voice from inside the house, 'Go away!'

'I'm not going away until I've torn your fucking head off your shoulders!' Rebecca shouted, pounding at the door until the wood began to splinter. 'I know everything, I know *everything* and I'm not like mum and dad! I'm not afraid of you, you liar, you bully, you...'

'I'm calling the police!' came from the other side of the door.

'Call them!' Rebecca cried, 'Save me a job!' Whack into the door again. 'I know about Wales, I know about Guthrie, and get this, you psycho, I know about Phil!'

Silence.

Panting, Rebecca dropped the Buddha and stood with her hands on her hips shaking. Then she went close to the shattered panel on the door, pushed open the twisted letter-box and hissed: 'Not one penny of Guthrie's money will you get, I'll see to that, so pack a bag and start running or wait for the police to come for you but don't ever go near my parents again or I will kill you.' Then she turned away and Anna saw in her face that the fury was spent and she was on the verge of tears.

They walked together back up to Bernice and Richard but Rebecca was too distraught to stay long and they were too overwhelmed and terrified to respond to what she'd done. They were blown apart by what had happened. Anna and Rebecca left the house together and stood by the Mini-Cooper for a few moments while Anna answered questions about where Guthrie's body was and what officials Rebecca should contact. The young woman's face was stiff as though she would never smile again.

'I need a drink,' Rebecca said at last, 'but when I start I may not stop so I'm going home.'

Anna had no desire to go back into the Sitwell house and unlocked her own car thinking that she may pause before leaving Stratford at some kindly pub just to sip a lager and unwind. She was relieved that Rebecca didn't want company and understood why –

there would be time to talk things over once the authorities had been informed.

As she drove away, she wondered whether Bella could, in fact, be charged with any crime. Phil's death, even if it was murder, was over thirty years ago and Richard would be the only testifier to her guilt. His own self-interest and this opportunity to take revenge for years of intimidation would probably render him useless as a witness and she doubted the police would take it up further than a cursory investigation.

What else could Bella be accused of that Bernice and Richard hadn't colluded with that could result in a criminal charge? Nastiness, lying, threats and intimidation would be set against the money she paid and they accepted every month to keep them afloat. They would be seen as merely another dysfunctional family snaring each other in nets of misery. But, DNA tests would prove Guthrie was a full sibling to Rebecca and that both were the children of Bernice and Richard so, added to the fact that Guthrie had named Bernice as his next-of-kin, there should be no problems over the inheritance of his estate. They could now move house and try to start a new and happier phase of their lives.

In the pub she called Steve but he didn't pick up so he might be out of earshot of his phone although that was unlikely given that he should be on the alert for a call from Alice. Eventually she finished off the liquid in the bottom of her half-pint glass and picked up her bag to make the drive back to Birmingham. In any case, it was over now. There was no part for her or Harts to play because Rebecca was more than capable of taking everything forward. It wasn't until she turned off the dual carriageway into Birmingham to cut across to her own neighbourhood that she became aware that the sense of foreboding was still there deep in her gut; the awareness that live wires were dangerously close together.

No more unpleasant messages had been left so she may never know what that was all about but it seemed incredible that a woman over sixty would have been responsible for organising them and there had been no follow-up of any kind from Mel, thank goodness. Probably the tension she felt was nothing but a redundant sloshing around of cortisol in her system left over from all the recent adrenaline shots.

She tried to think about seeing Steve that evening but the hot morning had given way to a sweaty afternoon and she found herself thinking instead of the teenage Lena flogging along a dusty country lane on a day like this, tired and mulish after her work and scheming her escape through the wood to the balm of the pool.

A message pinged as she was turning into her drive which was Steve saying that he was already home. Alice had called him after breakfast and demanded to be fetched. George and Ellis were out and after her shower and a change of clothes she sauntered down the road wondering what had spooked the little girl, if anything. She wasn't used to staying with anyone apart from her grandparents without Steve and she could simply have been shy in the unfamiliar surroundings even though shyness was not normally a problem with the child.

Steve was slicing a brown crusty loaf in the kitchen and Anna's stomach growled – lunch had not been on the Sitwells' agenda. She picked up a slab, coated it with butter and gobbled chunks of it. 'It's to go with the soup,' Steve said mildly, sawing an extra piece. He added, 'She's playing upstairs, she's a bit subdued. I don't know what's going on. Can you give the pot a stir, it should be ready.'

'It's a bit hot for soup, isn't it?' She moved the long-handled wooden spoon slowly enjoying the way the thickened liquid swayed round it.

'Special request.'

'Did you check with Julie and Simon about why she wanted to leave?'

The chunks of bread were now heaped into a wicker basket and Steve was clattering bowls and plates. 'They said they didn't know and I believe Simon, he seemed genuinely surprised and a bit upset, but I'm not sure about Julie. She blushed and seemed flustered. Alice?' he called up the stairs, 'It's ready.'

Steve had laid three places so Anna prepared to be rejected and despised as usual but Alice merely climbed on to her stool glancing at Anna from under pale spiky eyelashes. When Anna picked up her spoon to start on her soup, Alice even pushed the bread a little nearer to her.

'Thanks.'

Nearing the bottom of her bowl of pea and mint, Alice decided to talk. 'You're a mummy, aren't you?' she said to Anna, 'But you're not my mummy.' This seemed a little naïve from a six-year old so Anna merely nodded and continued to eat her soup wondering if Alice was stuck for a conversational opener.

'She's Faye and Ellis' mother,' Steve said.

Alice regarded him scornfully. 'I know that,' she said, 'I'm not a baby.'

'Wasn't it fun at your Aunt Julie's?'

'They want me to go there and live with them,' Alice said, scraping the last slicks of soup from her bowl. 'Can I have an ice-cream?'

Steve flushed. 'And did that upset you, or did you like the idea?' Anna could hear the tension in Steve's voice and thought that Alice was sharp enough to pick up on it as well.

She propped her elbows on the table and blew air out noisily like a balloon collapsing. 'Can I have an ice-cream? There's some in the freezer. I'm too hot.'

Steve got up and picked one out for her. 'What would you like to do this afternoon?'

'Play snakes and ladders in the garden!' Alice shouted, 'I'll get them!' But she stopped herself at the door and turned to look at Anna. 'You can play, too,' she said, adding cautiously, 'for a bit.'

But Anna had only just thrown a six when her phone went and she saw that it was Rebecca so she excused herself and walked a little way down the lawn. 'Hi,' she said, 'is everything ok?' Someone was shouting at her so loudly that the words were distorted and she held the phone away from her ear to try to make sense of it. It certainly wasn't Rebecca. 'Slow down, please,' she said, 'I can't make out what you're saying.'

The babble was replaced by sobbing. 'She's dying! She's dying! We shouldn't have told her!'

'Bernice? What are you saying?' Surely Rebecca hadn't tried to take her own life? Or had she driven while she was drunk?

'Bella – she was waiting for her, hiding – she stabbed her with a carving knife outside her own front door when she got home! The neighbour found her. Oh God, oh God help us!'

'Where are you? I'll come now, tell me where you are.'

The ambulance was tearing up the M40 with sirens blaring on its way from Leamington to the Queen Elizabeth hospital in Birmingham, the best major trauma unit at that moment for a stab-wound, and Richard and Bernice were trying to catch up in their car. Rebecca was being taken to the same hospital where their son,

Guthrie, lay ice-cold in the morgue. Bernice had grabbed Rebecca's phone from her bag hoping Anna's private number was on it.

Anna ran from the car park to the Accident and Emergency entrance and arrived as Bernice was turning away from the swing doors where she had been barred from finding her daughter. Her face was ashen. 'They won't let me go in. They won't tell me anything.'

'Where's Richard?'

'Parking the car. He's so angry with you, Anna, but it's not your fault. We should have done everything differently! Now we've lost Guthrie and we may lose our darling girl.'

Anna paced back and forth trying to contain her panic over what had happened to Rebecca and berating herself over not having foreseen this outcome. That premonition, those sparking wires had been Bella's madness and Rebecca's rage and she had carelessly not seen that they might touch and cause an explosion. Her gut had been screaming at her but her brain hadn't understood.

'Have the police got Bella?' she asked.

Bernice looked past her so she turned and saw Richard whose face darkened at the sight of her. He snapped. 'What are you doing here? Haven't you done enough damage?'

Anna asked Bernice to phone when they knew how Rebecca was doing and left.

28

Where could she go to think, to try to get some perspective? George and Steve would comfort her, tell her it wasn't her fault, but she needed to sort it out in her head before she could share it with them, whenever that would be. She needed to walk and walk and let the tumult in her brain settle into some kind of sense. She texted Steve to say there was no news yet and she didn't know when she'd be back and drove out of the city until she crossed a hump-backed canal bridge with fields either side and pulled off the lane to park. She set off striding down the tow-path.

She had no idea where she was but it was quiet (it was beautiful) and she could concentrate on nothing but the blood pumping in her legs and the banging of her heart making her breathe huge gulps of air. She listened for birdsong above the crunch of her feet on the gravel path and looked up at the sky to see what it was doing. A woman at the helm of a passing narrowboat raised a hand to her and she automatically lifted her own in return.

An hour later the shaking was so bad that she climbed a stile into a field and collapsed out of sight into the scratchy grass and weeds under the hedge. She rolled on to her back, sharp stones prodding her skin, nettles prickling her arms and closed her eyes.

What if Rebecca died?

She forced herself to go through each stage of the story in order – each decision, each new piece of information, each appalling twist and turn and then she interrogated herself like a prosecutor. The questions burned her heart. What if she had never visited Bernice, never known Rebecca, never gone to Wales? What if she had done nothing, closed the file, taken all that she had initially discovered on face value, not delved into those travel insurance documents? What if she had accepted Bella Cromer as Guthrie's mother and legal next-of-kin as had appeared to be the case? The answer was searingly obvious. If she had done so, Rebecca, so strong and healthy and her parents only remaining child, would not now be fighting for her life in the ICU.

Eventually she forced herself to her feet feeling stiff and sore and climbed over the stile to walk back the way she had come. There was nothing she could do to make things better – all she could do was hope. And pray.

At eight-fifteen that evening Anna was outside in the garden pushing the lawn mower up and down so that no-one could try to talk to her above the noise when Bernice phoned. She sounded exhausted but said that Rebecca was stable and out of danger and they had seen her and spoken to her. The relief was so great that Anna barely managed to mutter her thanks before she sank to her knees.

There were six messages from Steve so she texted him to tell him the news and say she would see him at work. She put the mower away in the tool store, managed to smile at George as he typed away in his shed saying she was having an early night, and walked into the house and up the stairs to lie on the bed.

At midnight she woke, still fully clothed, and stood at the window for a while watching a gibbous moon sidle across a navy sky. The front door creaked as she carefully pulled it open and clicked behind her but no light came from upstairs and she walked quickly down her drive and on to the pavement. There was no-one in the grave-yard but in any case she was not afraid. The porch benches had nothing more than dust and dry leaves on them and she sat on one, leaning her back against the stone door arch and drawing her knees up to her chin. This would have been where supplicants would have come in ancient times and where parishioners might have paid their dues. She touched the still-warm wood of the seat and felt the whorl of grain beneath her fingers. It was only when the tightness in her chest had eased at last and her mind had stilled that she unbent her knees, got up and went home.

Ted was horrified when she filled him in on what had happened. He leaped up from his chair and paced up and down blowing out his cheeks and rubbing his head. 'Are they blaming us?' he demanded.

'No, he's angry with me but Rebecca isn't. She was well enough to phone me from her bed this morning and ask me to go in. I'd like to go now, Ted.'

'Yes, go.' He stopped pacing and stared at her. 'We need to properly talk this through, Anna. Not your finest hour.'

'I know.'

'You might mention the DNA, though,' he added. 'Not to be insensitive but it's a perfect opportunity.'

'Can I just see how she is?' she said meekly.

Ted came round his desk and astounded her by patting her shoulder. 'I'm not sure I can cope with a humble Anna Ames,' he said kindly, 'don't beat yourself up too much. I'd probably have done the same.' Anna very much doubted it.

She had expected Rebecca to be prone, hollow-eyed and pale, so it was more than a pleasant surprise to see her seated in the padded chair next to her bed and texting furiously. She looked up as Anna approached, shrugged and smiled. 'Not dead yet.'

'Don't joke about it!' She dropped the running magazine and fruit on to Rebecca's bed tray and fetched a stacking chair for herself. 'I'm so sorry that I didn't think what might happen.'

'Oh, she meant to finish me off but she hadn't calculated that she's old and weak, for all that she's mean as hell, and I'm young and strong and have fast reflexes, thank God.'

'So how bad is it?'

Rebecca indicated the shoulder she had not shrugged. 'She got me in my deltoid so that's sore but it's just a flesh wound. It'll take a while to heal but luckily I'm right-handed so I can use the phone and the computer and shouldn't need to take more than a week off work. Some of the blood I was covered in that freaked the neighbours came from her when I turned the knife on her and slashed her arm. It was an automatic reaction, I used to do karate, but I'm sure there was no serious damage or she would have collapsed but she ran off.' She could have been relating a sporting injury, she was so composed.

'But you were unconscious, your mum said? Why was that?'

'Oh, that.' It was a relief to see her face break into a wide smile. 'After I got the knife from her and struck out at her arm, I lost my balance and fell. I must have hit my head on the step because I know she was off as soon as I attacked her back.'

'So is that ok?'

'Apart from a headache like I was partying last night with a Russian rugby team, yes, it's fine.'

Anna sat back in the chair feeling tension drain from her body. 'Your mum and dad were so worried. I even went for a long walk so you can tell what a state I was in.'

Taking a grape from the bunch Anna had brought, Rebecca sighed. 'I know. They were so scared of her – I hadn't realised, you know? I just thought of her as a bit of a weirdo. I had no idea how she'd been controlling them through the old carrot and stick for ages – all my life and for years before that.'

Anna nodded. 'Bullying and deceiving them while making sure they were dependent on her for money. A nasty combination.' Anna hesitated before going on. 'And how are you coping with what they told you about Guthrie?'

In the act of taking another grape, Rebecca's hand fell back. 'It hurts. To be honest, I'm still in shock. I can't seem to get a grip on all of it.'

'No rush. It's a huge thing to get your head round.'

'Mostly I just feel sad – for them and for me. So many wasted years.'

'Yes.'

'But there is one thing I've been thinking about and you may be able to help me.'

'I'll do anything I can. I feel so guilty about how things turned out.'

Rebecca regarded her with bewilderment. 'Why? A nasty, festering abscess got lanced and if it hadn't been there would have been more decades of misery and bondage under Bella's thumb. Bella wouldn't have ever told mum and dad that Guthrie was dead, you do realise that, don't you? She had nothing to gain from them knowing, so they would have been waiting in that house all their lives in the hope that he would turn up one day and they could be reconciled while Bella spent his money.'

'I hadn't thought of that. Thank you. So what can I do?'

'Could you arrange for me and poor Gus and mum and dad to have DNA tests done? I want it beyond all doubt that he is my full brother and their son. That way they can inherit, can't they? They can live debt free and move house to wherever they want.'

'Of course. I'll get going on it immediately.' Anna stood up and took the chair back to its stack. When she returned she noticed that Rebecca was a little paler than she had been and was probably unwilling to admit that she was tired now.

But when she turned to leave, Rebecca asked another question which stopped her in her tracks. 'Where is Bella? Do you know? The police came to interview me but they wouldn't say. I don't think they've found her.'

Anna's heart chilled. She had assumed that Bella would be in police custody but it seemed not. Where was Bella, then? She had been with Rebecca on Bella's path yesterday, Bella had seen her. Who would Bella search out to be her next revenge victim before she was arrested, jailed and unable to kill anyone? Anna made herself walk, not run, out of the ward but the second she was outside she whipped out her phone. Ellis would be in school and Faye at work, both safe – she called George.

He answered his phone breathlessly. 'Just a minute, love, I'm walking and talking as they say. There's someone at the door.' Anna screamed at him not to open it. 'Why, what's happened? I'm going into the front room to look through the window – that's ok, isn't it? Whatever is the matter, Annie?'

'Don't let yourself be seen, Dad!'

'I'm peeping behind the curtain like a nosy neighbour,' he said, chuckling.

Anna's heart was racing. 'It's serious, Dad, don't let yourself be seen and don't answer the door!'

'It's the postman with a parcel.'

Anna breathed out. 'Oh, ok.'

'I'm going to sign for this parcel, hello Sanjiv, all right? Then you're going to tell me what's going on. Bye then – not you, love. You stay on the phone.' She heard the door click shut and slid down into the cold comfort of a plastic chair.

When Anna got back to the office she went immediately to see Steve and closed his door behind her – something she had never done before. He whirled his computer chair round. 'What's happened?'

When she had finished he sat quite still for a while thinking. 'If those threatening messages came from her, then she knows where you work, where you live, she knows about Ellis and she probably knows your car registration.'

'Yes.'

He leaned forward and took her hand pressing it firmly – a little too firmly, which betrayed how anxious he was despite his calm voice. 'You mustn't be alone and George shouldn't leave the house or have anyone come until she's caught. You need to pick Ellis up from school and take him home so I'll drive you.'

'But Ted – '

'Go and tell him now what's happened and what we're going to do. There's no point in alarming Ellis by picking him up early so we'll wait until the end of school but – '

'I'll text him and let dad know.'

'I'm going to contact the Birmingham police and put them in the picture, I don't suppose you have a photo of Bella?' Anna shook her head. 'They'll liaise with the Stratford police who have probably already searched her house and most people have at least one photo of themselves on display in their homes so they can email that.'

Anna bent her head forcing herself not to sob with relief that someone she could trust entirely, someone capable and clear-thinking was by her side.

The day seemed to stretch endlessly while she got through police interviews and a meeting with Mary Willis and setting up arrangements for DNA testing. She would not be able to relax until Ellis was with her and they were safely home. He had responded to her message with a question mark and a thumbs-up emoji so she had just texted back that she would explain later but not to leave the school building. She had also called Faye and explained why she shouldn't drop by, had she been planning to.

'Are you all right, Mum?' Faye asked quietly, 'I do need you around, you know.'

'I know. Same.'

Ellis was waiting with two of his friends inside the school gate like the sensible kid he was and jumped in Steve's car in a moment. Anna grabbed him and hugged him to her until he gently pushed her away. 'So, what? Give.'

It took the whole journey home to go through the story of the Sitwells and answer his questions. By the time they had reached the house he had fallen silent and Anna was worried it had all been too wretched and frightening for him.

'It'll be ok,' she said, 'we just have to be careful until she's locked up.'

'So, I can't go to the tennis club? I've got a match on tonight I didn't want to miss, but it's ok if I can't.'

'Pops and I will take you,' she said, 'and cheer you on.'

Steve shot a glance at her but he could see she was determined that Ellis wouldn't lose out and knew she would be careful so said nothing except, 'Keep in touch.'

29

Ted had told her to take the next day off. He had received her news in silence, told her to watch her step and then gone into Steve's office and closed the door. Later, she got an email from him saying that he would be screening her clients much more carefully in future which she took as an apology for making her take the Guthrie Cromer case, not that she had wanted or expected one. It seemed to her that mistakes had been made all round. But she needed the day off if only to take Ellis to school and be around George for the day.

She slept badly that night although when she woke she couldn't remember the dreams that had made her thrash about and rise up gasping. Probably just as well. She found she couldn't settle to anything so by late morning she went out into the garden just to have something physical to do to settle her nerves.

A couple of hours later George laid out a salad and newly baked bread on the kitchen table and called to her to come in. She pulled off her gardening gloves and washed at the kitchen sink but then thought she had heard the post so went into the hall to see. There was nothing on the mat so she opened the door and looked down the drive. A small figure dashed out from under the house eaves and shot off down the road. She leaped after him but in the few seconds it took to get round the cars to the pavement, he had gone. She looked up and down the road but no sign of him although a people-carrier was taking the far corner at speed. She turned back to the house and saw, as she expected, another message on the garage door. This time it was done in spray paint.

There was a crude drawing of the two-finger gesture and the word, *Hor*.

She trudged inside and locked the front door behind her.

'It was a child like before,' she told George as they picked at the lunch. 'Surely that's not the sort of thing Bella would set up, is it?'

'Will you tell the police?'

She groaned. 'I just think it would muddy the water – you know, set them off on a wild goose chase.'

'Not to mix your metaphors or anything.' They both smiled – relieved not to be serious for a moment.

'Let's sit in the garden for a while,' George said, getting up, 'I can clear this later and there's something in a happier vein I'd like to discuss with you.'

The cut grass, yeasty in the afternoon sun, exuded a clean, green smell and the borders and beds showed a hint of definition thanks to Anna's need to relieve her anxieties. Macavity strolled up the garden from her mysterious other life and waited for George to seat himself before leaping gracefully up. All three lifted their chins and narrowed their eyes to enjoy the play of light and colour.

'Go on, then,' Anna said eventually as Macavity rumbled under George's stroking hand.

'It's about Big B. I've been keeping Diane up to speed with all our exciting family news, well, not all of it – I mean about Bill and Cherry and the others.'

'Mm. We should have invited her along, really.'

'No, I think what we did was right. Not too many on the first go. Only you and Ellis are blood relatives after all.'

'They loved you, though.' Anna had such emotionally charged memories of that visit that she left it at that. Geena had sent an affectionate message asking to meet for lunch and a visit to her mother once the conference she was organising was over and it still felt strange that she would be able to actually talk to someone who had known Lena so well.

'Well, anyway, Diane wondered before if they would be interested in having Big B to live with them. He's got to go somewhere – goodwill is running out among the volunteers at Safe 'n' Sound because he eats so much but no visitor has even hinted at wanting to have him. So I phoned Bill and sounded him out and we had quite a chat.' George looked sideways at Anna. 'I did tell him about what had happened and why we had had to let him go.'

Anna was silent, her mind now crammed full of images of a cliff edge, rocks, a child, a dog and then Harry, motionless and blood-soaked on the ground far below. Then another body prostrate in the road, the same dog. Mike had recovered, her husband had not. She shut it all down.

'What did he say?'

'He only asked one question which was, "Has he ever been vicious?" I said, absolutely not, he's got a gentle nature and never deliberately hurt anyone. He's what he is, a large sight-hound, it's in his blood to chase.'

'So how was it left?'

'It turned out he had been thinking about the dog, too, ever since Ellis mentioned him. You remember Ell was tickled when Bill told him that there had been a bare-knuckle fighter called Big Brum in the old days?'

'Oh yes, Isaac Perrins, I'd forgotten.'

Macavity stretched and turned her face blissfully into the sun. 'He suggested a couple of months' trial out there. They haven't got any small children around usually and he could be tied up if any visit to be on the safe side until they can trust him. Cherry was on the lookout for a big dog as their old greyhound died last year.'

'They've got others,' Anna reminded him.

'Apparently she likes to have four different sizes,' George laughed. 'She likes a set.'

'It would be a wonderful home for him.'

'I think Bill wants to see how he is around the ponies although he didn't say that. Dogs and horses sometimes get on well and other times they really don't and they have to put their horses first.'

'Best not mention it to Ell, then, in case it doesn't work out?'

George pushed his glasses up his nose. 'No, I think we should tell him. He's not a kid any more. We all have to learn to live with ups and downs.'

Anna stood up. 'Well, there's one down I think I can spare him. I'm going to go and slap some undercoat on that garage door. He'll think it's to cover the stain from before.'

George gently disentangled himself from Macavity and they went together to the paint store. Anna rooted around and dragged out a tub with brown dribbles down the sides. She shook it and it slopped so it was still good. 'You know what he'll say when he sees this?'

'"Shit colour,"' George and Anna said in unison, which was the second light moment of a day when there hadn't been too many.

After dinner Steve appeared at the front door. 'Alice wants to see you, could you pop down for five minutes?'

'You could have phoned,' Anna said, tucking a crumb of lemon pie into her mouth.

'Mm. I'll walk you down.'

She didn't argue but called to George, who was stacking the dish-washer, that she would only be gone for a few minutes. 'What is it, then? She's never done that before.'

'I know, I'm mystified myself.' They squeezed round the cars. 'Interesting colour for a garage door.'

'It's just undercoat I had. I needed something to do.' Muddy water and a wild goose chase didn't need to be mentioned, she decided.

'Are you ok?' He took her hand and it felt good.

'I am now.'

It was a calm, golden evening and she wished that the two of them could just take off and walk for hours and forget everything. It was a huge relief that Rebecca would recover fully and there was the up-coming meeting between Tom and Rakes and Queenie that should be a happy thing (with luck) but recent events had cast an anxious shadow and Anna couldn't seem to get past it. What if Bella was never caught? But if she was, what if she only served a short sentence since the injury to Rebecca had not been as serious as first thought? If she felt vengeful now, how would she feel after suffering prison for months?

Alice was waiting in the kitchen and had prepared, as a good hostess should, by filling a Wallace and Gromit beaker with blackcurrant squash and placing a custard cream on a plate from her doll's house. This was unlooked-for cordiality and Anna braced herself. Alice had always possessed a sense of occasion and was now seated on her own stool with hands clasped before her and a serious expression on her waif's face. Her fine, dandelion-clock hair was wilting in the heat but her eyes were very alert.

'Please sit down,' she said, and Anna obediently sat. Alice pushed the refreshments towards her and waited while Anna got them down although squash had ceased to be a favourite with her some forty years ago.

'Thank you, Alice, that was very welcome. It's so hot, isn't it?' The formality of the child's demeanour was triggering an automatic small-talk reflex, she realised, and decided to cut it out. 'Is there something I can do for you?'

'Yes,' said Alice.

'Ok. I will if I can.'

'Mina and me are going to start dance classes with Little Stars. Steve says it's ok. I want you to take me.'

'I can take you,' Steve said, puzzled, 'I've already had a word with Mina's mum and we'll take it in turns.'

Alice turned her head and gave him a quelling look and then faced Anna. She'll probably end up being a head-teacher or a judge, Anna thought, if not a corporate raider. 'I want Anna to take me and stay and bring me home. It's an hour.' She added reluctantly, 'I'll give you half my pocket money.'

'Oh, darling, there's no need for that!' Anna cried. 'I would be more than happy to take you and watch you dance and bring you home. Just let me know the time and the day and I'll come and pick you up, and Mina if you like. Maybe, we could get an ice-cream on the way home?'

Alice solemnly inclined her head, slid off the chair and ran upstairs.

Steve and Anna looked at each other in bewilderment. 'I think you just got an invite to the prom,' Steve said.

Later in the evening Faye phoned to check on them, which was kind of her, but every time her phone went Anna hoped it was the police so when Kimi rang later she called her back on the landline to free her mobile.

'I'm in the stables,' Kimi said, 'just wanted to catch you up with things. Oh, are you ok?' Anna mumbled something, knowing Kimi was just trying to be polite. 'I've been thinking things over – you know? Maybe I did go overboard a bit with Charlie and I hate to say it, but you may have been right. He's made no effort to contact me and the more time passes the more annoyed with him I get. He's taken me for an easy lay, hasn't he?'

'You've got Cora,' was the only thing Anna could think of saying to boost Kimi's mood, 'he didn't swindle you over her, did he?'

'Suppose not. She is a beauty. I know I paid too much for her but, you know, in the heat of the moment and all that.'

Anna couldn't resist it. 'Sounds like there were a few hot moments, kiddo.'

'Yeah, yeah.' Kimi paused. 'I suppose this means I'm what they call "bi". That's a surprise.' For Kimi to share this insight into her own nature was extraordinary so Anna decided not to press on the comment but to move on.

'But you and Briony are ok?'

'She's promised not to go away so much and she did bring back a gorgeous saddle blanket from South America with Cora's name embroidered on it. She had it made specially.'

'So you're letting the idea of the site go?' Anna said, fetching the dishcloth to wipe a coffee circle from the table.

'It would be asking for trouble wouldn't it, being as it seems I can't resist handsome rogues.'

'They're certainly not all rogues,' Anna replied, and told Kimi about her recent visit to Bill and Cherry and meeting cousins and so forth. She decided not to talk about Geena.

'Nice,' Kimi responded dully at the end of quite a long monologue from Anna. 'Better go and bed the beast down, then. Briony, not Cora, of course.' Anna laughed politely. But it was a relief that Kimi had got to the other side of her odd adventure and she was happy that the couple were back on track.

She drifted restlessly around the kitchen and then sat down at the table to open her laptop. It was pointless, she knew, but she scanned the news feeds that might be local enough to be relevant looking for some breaking stories. Bernice and Richard had a family liaison officer staying with them and Rebecca was still in hospital. She wondered what would happen when she was discharged, which wouldn't be too much longer now. She couldn't very well go back to her own home unprotected when Bella was still at large.

Frustrated by her fruitless search she switched to Ebay vaguely thinking of their crippled kitchen chair that should be replaced at some point and surfed the images listlessly until she sat up and stared. There was a picture of the chair she had dragged out of her car on the charity shop trawl. She recognised it because she and Harry had had one like it years ago, but this chair was painted aqua and covered with intersecting circles, also painted in retro colours of orange and pink. What was it George had said Faye was doing with Ellis' compasses? Drawing Venn diagrams on her kitchen table. Overlapping circles. The image of the chair gave a link and Anna clicked on it. Up sprang picture after picture of chairs, tables, stools, mirrors, picture frames and so on and each one was done with the same pattern of overlapping circles of different sizes and in different colour combinations. Each object had been photographed against a black or white background (or probably photo-shopped) and the effect was fresh, young, on-trend. The brand name was *Circles*of*the*Mind*.

Anna clicked on the chair she had first looked at to find a price and sucked in her breath when she saw it. What? Would anyone pay such a price? She knew that this particular chair had cost Faye four pounds so the mark-up was phenomenal. Without thinking she picked up her phone and called her daughter.

'Yeah,' Faye acknowledged laconically, 'it's a sort of cyber pop-up shop.'

'The stuff looks brilliant Faye, but the prices! You'll never sell anything if you ask so much.'

Faye was watching Masterchef as Anna could hear (although she never cooked) and could barely be bothered to reply. 'Chill, Mum. Raking it in.'

'Honestly, Faye, I can't believe that!'

'Jack's given up his bar job, we're into full-time production now at the weekends and there's a couple of guys from work doing some for us. We've had two more trips round the shops in Walsall and Worcester. We're branching out next weekend and going to an auction house near Coventry.' She yawned. 'Why do you never cook endamame beans, Mum? There's a whole world out there, you know.'

'You're actually selling?'

'Oh, nice. Such confidence in your brilliant daughter. Yes, we're selling stuff. In fact, we've sold out of what's on Ebay.'

Anna congratulated her and ended the call. Blimey. She went out to find George and tell him the news. 'Have you had time to look into first-time mortgage loans, Annie?' he said. 'I think we should speed up our plans.'

'I'll do it now.'

She brought up a financial advice website and was clicking on the appropriate tab when her phone jingled. It was Steve. 'Hey,' she said, her eyes following the words on the screen, 'you ok?'

'Have the police called?' Anna looked at her phone and saw a missed call.

'Um, could have done. What's happened?'

'Birmingham police have just rung me. They've found Bella.'

Anna leaped up and took the phone to the window. 'Where is she? Have they arrested her?'

'No point. She's dead.'

'What? How?'

'They think she must have done it within a short time of stabbing Rebecca. She must have driven back to Stratford and made her plan on the way. Perhaps she believed she had killed Rebecca and the police would be coming for her. She chose a point in the river near the weir but the body has only just been found because she had weighted her pockets down with stones. It's taken a while for it to get washed up at the bank.'

'How dreadful.'

'Yes. Fortunately, an off-duty paramedic found it when he was walking his dog. It would have been terrible if a child had come upon it after days in the water.'

'I can't believe it, Steve. I thought she would go abroad or hide or something. Not this.'

Steve's voice was grim: 'Well, it sometimes happens that violent people, deprived of their control-objects, can turn on themselves because violence is their only solution to problems.'

Anna gazed down the garden where the sky was edged with a bruise of purple as the night approached. 'I should feel relieved but I'm just shocked.'

'There was an ironic twist, too. The stones she'd put in her pockets to weigh her down were those therapy ones people use.'

'What do you mean?'

'They were painted with flowers and the words: *Peace, Love, Family.*' Anna sighed. Steve went on, 'Do you want to come down here? I can't leave Alice, she's asleep, but there's a glass of wine with your name on it?'

'That sounds so good but I need to tell Ellis and dad and maybe have a word with Rebecca, too. Another time, darling, lots of other times.'

'Sleep well, Anna. I love you.'

30

As much as she had been looking forward to going with Tom to Gloucestershire to meet his grandparents, she found that once the adrenaline rush of recent events had gone, she was feeling flat and a little despondent probably because the pain of the family tragedy around Guthrie had become real. It was not a mood that would help him and she tried to rally herself.

Tom was quiet himself as they drove along until she hit on the idea of telling him about her own family encounter with Bill and Cherry. Kimi had been bored by it since families were of no interest to her but it turned out to be just the thing Tom had needed to hear since he and she were in a similar situation in finding extensive family among the Travelling people whom they were only just getting to know.

'I don't know what to expect,' he said. 'I'm worried they'll think I'm up myself.'

'You've never come across like that to me.'

He flashed her a smile and the power of it, as before, silenced her for a moment. He had no idea, did he, of how dazzling he sometimes appeared to others? Now that she knew him better she realised that the glossy photo Elizabeth had showed her at the beginning only revealed one facet of Tom's complex nature and that alongside the joy he had in playing and performing was the serious child practising alone in his room and yearning for connection, for some thing or someone to share his passionate nature with. He had Elizabeth who would be loyal and encouraging and, of course, loving, but she seemed to have few shadows in her soul whereas he was only too aware of rejection and loss. She was curious to know more about him and asked him about his schooldays.

'I was a bit nerdy, I suppose,' he said, 'but it was ok. I did alright in most subjects and we had a fantastic music teacher. I started off with a tuba because that's what the school orchestra needed but I always wanted to play the violin and when another kid came in and took that on, the teacher told mum about private tuition and he let me play in the string section once I was good enough. Then I got into the National Youth Orchestra which was amazing.'

'Sports?' Anna asked, watching out for the junction they needed to take to travel west.

'Not really. I can play footie a bit – defence.' Anna let the conversation drop and checked her silent satnav. They had been driving through the gently curved hills of the Vale of Evesham with its patches of lush woodland and clustered villages, each one heightened by a church tower or spire. Red-tailed kites swooped above them and she wished that they had time to take the B roads and get off the noisy motorway.

'I was a lonely child, I suppose, but I hardly knew it,' Tom went on. 'I didn't realise what normal families were like until I had college friends and met some of theirs.'

'Define "normal families",' Anna muttered, thinking of Kimi's warring tribe and most of the families of people she knew, including her own, all of whom had difficulties, schisms and even tragedies to come to terms with.

She badly wanted to ask him how he was assimilating what he now knew about his mother's past and her decision to cut them both off from family. Did he blame her, Loretta, for what she'd done or did he understand? She had been in many ways a good mother to him but he may very well have mixed feelings about her now. But she couldn't ask, it was too intrusive and he was too vulnerable. Perhaps in the future they could have that conversation.

'Right,' she said, 'it's not far now. Do you want to stop for a breather?'

'No, I'm nervous but I want to get there, I want to meet them.'

Tom had brought gifts for them: a framed photo of himself with his mother at the sea-side when he was a child and a CD of some of his favourite performances. He had hesitated, he said, between a CD and a flashdrive so had brought both but would present them with the CD. Anna thought it more than likely that they still had a player. He had also brought, carefully wrapped in tissue, a hand-knitted Fair-Isle sweater which had been his mother's and which she had possessed ever since he could remember. It had gone with them on every move despite the fact that he had never seen her wear it and he hoped he knew why.

The road became a lane and then the satnav gave up. Anna drove forward slowly, avoiding ruts and keeping a sharp lookout for anything coming in the opposite direction. The lane was wide enough for a trailer but only just.

Unfenced woodland appeared and they both laughed. Rakes must have done it. There was a large cardboard sign nailed to a post, on which was written in red paint: *Anna, pull on here.*

Beyond the sign was a wide unpaved track through the trees and she crawled up it, hoping her tyres could take the rough surface patched here and there with gravel. Then they were in a large clearing with a dozen trailers parked in a semi-circle and a score of cars and motor-bikes. Children were playing in an inflatable pool, running about and splashing each other, and dogs of all kinds were wandering around panting or asleep in the shade under the cars. Up the far end were some wooden picnic tables where a clutch of teenagers, boys in one group, girls in another, had established their camp with huge soft-drink bottles.

They got out of the car and looked around but only for a few seconds. Rakes appeared calling and waving and they made their way towards him. Anna hung back as Tom and his grandfather met. There was a moment of silence as the two men stared at each other and then Rakes stepped forward and took Tom's hand.

'Our Etta's boy,' he said, choking a little. 'I never thought I'd ever lay eyes on you.'

'I never thought I'd ever have a family,' Tom replied, equally moved, 'but I always wanted one.'

'Well, you've got one now and always will have.'

Anna looked about. 'Where's Queenie?'

Rakes dragged his eyes away from Tom. 'She's feeling a bit shy. She's there in the trailer waiting for us like a *divvy*. She's spent all week shining it up when it was spotless already. Come on, boy, let's see her before she blows a gasket.'

As they walked across the grass the children stopped playing and stared at them and even the teenagers spared a few minutes to wonder who they were. The trailer Rakes led them to was a beauty, picked out in cream and maroon with gleaming chrome trim. Beside it was a folding table and half a dozen chairs. 'I'll just wait here,' Anna said.

Rakes ushered Tom up the steps and they disappeared inside but after ten minutes Queenie came to the door and called her in. The old lady was, of course, bubbling with tears. Inside, the trailer was spacious, pretty and comfortable with its fresh white lace curtains, glass-fronted cabinets full of Crown Derby and cut-glass treasures and on the kitchen worktops were laid out plate after plate of cooked meats, bulging sandwiches, and pastries.

Queenie bustled about making sure Tom had his tea the way he liked it and that he was comfortable in that chair, or would he prefer this chair, until Rakes told her to stop fussing and sit down. She couldn't take her eyes off Tom, neither of them could, but Tom was just as fixed on them, his normally pale skin flushed.

After a while the initial chatter died down and all four of them simply sat smiling at each other. 'Let's take this outside,' Queenie said, 'I want everyone to see our *kushti* boy.'

'Another time,' Rakes said to Tom as he carried the huge teapot out, 'we'll have a proper Gypsy meal round a fire.'

Tom ran back to the car to get the gifts he'd forgotten and they sat in the sun round the table laden with food and passed around the photo while people drifted by to say hello and be introduced and maybe take a little snack and then move on. It was tactful and gracious, Anna thought. These were people who knew how to live in close community without treading too much on each other's toes.

When they were alone, Tom lifted the tissue-wrapped bundle and handed it to Queenie. 'I may be wrong about this,' he said, 'it may mean nothing to you, Granny, but mum took it everywhere we went and kept it wrapped up with a bag of lavender tucked inside.'

Queenie, who had reddened with pleasure at hearing him call her Granny, slowly unwrapped the paper but as soon as she saw what it was, she stopped and bent her head uttering a little cry. Tom got to her before Rakes, with his stiff knees, could. He knelt beside her and put his arm around her shoulders and she leaned her head against his chest. 'Oh, my dear gal,' she whispered, 'my dear little gal. She didn't forget me.' She turned her face to Tom's and he kissed her cheek and stroked her hair. 'Look,' she said, 'look at this.' She folded back the paper and lifted the sweater so that it unfolded to reveal the intricate stitches she had knitted. 'I made her this when she was fourteen because she saw the pattern in a shop and liked it and kept on at me to do it. When I'd finished she said it was the most beautiful thing she'd ever had and she would keep it forever.'

'And she did,' Tom said. He turned to Rakes. 'And you know she kept the photo of you and her on that pony from when she was just a little girl.' Rakes nodded, dropping his head so his face couldn't be seen.

Tom kissed Queenie again and then stood up. 'Do you have any photos of the family?' he asked. 'I'd love to see them.'

'Of course we do,' Queenie said, 'we got the albums out for you! Go and get them, my *mush*, and put on the kettle for a fresh pot.'

'I'll help,' Anna said, getting up, too.

Tom pulled his chair close to his grandmother's and they began to swap memories of Loretta and before long Anna could hear laughter as anecdotes were rolled out.

'Here,' Rakes said to Anna, 'I think this is more like it than the teapot given the occasion,' and he produced a bottle of Scotch. 'There's glasses in that cupboard.'

The shadows under the trailers began to stretch to the east as the sun moved across the sky and the dogs and children disappeared. Televisions could be heard from inside trailers and now it was groups of women sitting at the wooden tables nursing babies or doing each other's hair or just chatting together.

'We want to have a do before your wedding,' Queenie was saying, 'so we can all meet each other, you know. She's a lovely looking woman, your bride-to-be.'

Tom looked shocked. 'But you will come to the wedding? You must.'

'That's a new suit for you,' Queenie said to Rakes sternly to hide her feelings, 'them big lapels and flares have gone out now, you know.' She turned to Tom. 'Thank you, darling, we will come but we still want to have a get-together before. We want to show you proper Gypsy hospitality.'

A shadow fell across the table and Anna shaded her eyes to see who had joined them. She couldn't see his face against the sun but it was a tall man with a bag slung over his shoulder.

'Tez,' Rakes said, also shading his eyes. 'All right, boy?' There was a new, careful note in his voice.

'Sit down, don't be frit,' Queenie added quietly, 'have a bite to eat.' But the man scuffled his feet and dropped his chin. Tom looked up from the album he was studying.

'You're Loretta's boy,' the man said gruffly to him.

Tom put the album down and stood up. 'Did you know her?' he asked.

'For a bit.' He moved a few steps sideways so that his face was now visible to Anna. It was a lined and leathery face and he seemed unwilling to look at Tom. 'Good luck to you, then. I'll be getting along now.'

Queenie raised a hand to stop him. 'We was talking about a bit of a do for our Tom and his intended since he'll soon be wed. You might play your fiddle for us, eh?'

'I dunno,' the man said.

Tom stepped towards him and, perhaps as a defensive reflex, the man pulled his head back. Anna couldn't help gasping. She glanced at the old couple and saw that they were watching keenly.

Tom looked puzzled. 'This can't be right, but you look familiar.'

Anna, Queenie and Rakes sat still as rocks.

'I should go now,' Tez said.

'I play the fiddle, too,' Tom told him, putting out a hand and almost touching the man's sleeve, 'well, the violin, same thing. Do you have yours with you? Would you play something?'

The man looked desperately to Rakes for help but Rakes only nodded. After hesitating, he slipped the thick cloth bag off his shoulder and took out a battered case and opened it, slipping the instrument from its velvet nest and then the bow. Tom stepped forward quickly and looked at it as it lay in Tez's arms. Anyone could see it was old. The wood was a deep mahogany colour, glowing with use and care, and Tom couldn't resist moving even closer to reach out and lightly touch it. He was standing very near to Tez now and their profiles mirrored each other exactly. Queenie uttered a small sigh.

'Please play,' Tom said.

'This was my great-grandfather's,' the man replied, 'from the old country. My dad give it me before he went back there to die.' He raised it to shoulder height and Tom moved back to give him space.

As the music soared every trailer emptied until a crowd had gathered near them on the grass. Anna had never heard anything like it; the violin sang with joy and pain and longing and Tez became a different man, his back straight, his eyes blazing, his foot tapping to the complex rhythm. At last he finished with a frenzied crescendo and the crowd clapped and whooped but Tom didn't speak. He was as pale as she had ever seen him.

'May I?' he asked, and took the violin from Tez before he realized what was happening.

Tom raised it and tucked into the chin-rest that was still warm from the older man's skin. He tilted his head to one side looking down at the instrument as the bow slid experimentally across the strings and then he began to play. Anna realised that he was taking the melody that had wound through Tez's piece and adding to it, not boastfully, but tenderly, thoughtfully, as though they were in a conversation together and this was Tom's reply. It was breath-taking virtuosity and the crowd listened in silent awe in the mellow afternoon sun. It seemed to Anna that even the birds stopped singing and the breeze hushed. Tez watched Tom's face and flying fingers until the music stopped in a sweet resolution of the harmony and counter-point and the young man stood, trembling, staring at Tez.

After a moment Tom let his arm fall and said, 'You're my father.'

The other man dropped his head. 'I'm a disgrace to the name.'

Instead of replying, Tom bent and carefully put the violin in its case and then stepped towards him and wrapped his arms around him in a tight embrace. Tez was rigid, the cords standing out in his neck and his teeth gritted, his entire hard-used body shaking. Tom stood back a little, but still held him by the shoulders.

'The violin, the music, it's my heart and soul. It's who I am,' he said. 'You gave it to me, it comes from you, and I'm proud that you're my father – I'm proud and grateful.'

Then Teller Budas buckled and almost fell to the ground but Rakes and Queenie were there to help Tom hold him and after a while they began to laugh at themselves, at what a comical picture they made, sobbing and tugging at each other while the others surged closer and cat-called and shouted.

'Get that whisky, Anna, for the love of God, and bring out every glass we have!' Rakes ordered and Anna jumped up to obey, kissing Tom's cheek as she passed.

31

George, Ellis and Steve sat for a long time over dinner that night while Anna told them what had happened and showed them the photos she had taken on her phone. Alice had tucked herself in next to Steve and was colouring with crayons. But when she'd finished and they were clearing up the kitchen, George was quiet and Anna wondered what he was thinking.

'You know,' he said, rinsing off the cutlery under the mixer tap, 'I never realised what a wrench it must have been for Lena because how could I? I didn't know what she'd come from, what it must have meant to leave everything she knew.' He bent and dropped the forks into their slot. 'I wish she'd told me. I might have been able to comfort her.'

Anna put the mayonnaise and the remains of the fruit salad in the fridge. She didn't trust herself to say anything, not this time because she was angry with Lena, but because she was beginning to agree with him. One of the most terrible punishments in any closed society would be exile. Now, with multiple communication networks and easy travel it would be unpleasant but not the end of the world, but for them, for Lena and Mollie May, it literally was the end of their world. To be without the people you knew and who knew you, familiar food and customs and the places where you had grown up, where you expected to die, to have no home, that would be loneliness beyond imagining and yet that is what had happened to Lena through no fault of her own when she left the ancient Romani life. At fifteen, violated and bereaved, she had become a displaced, stateless person.

'Time to get this one to bed,' Steve said. 'Will you come down later?'

Anna glanced at Alice but the child only said, 'Don't forget tomorrow,' and waved goodbye.

When the kitchen was clear and George had gone out with Ellis to visit Big B at Safe 'n' Sound and give him a wash and brush for his visit out to meet Bill and Cherry, Anna sat down at the table to phone Rebecca. There had been a message from her earlier requesting a call but the day had been so full and emotional, she had not had time before now.

'Brilliant news, Anna,' she said, 'I wanted you to know asap. The DNA all checks out and the solicitor says there won't be any problem about the inheritance because even if Bella had inherited, it would all come to mum anyway now she's dead.'

Rebecca's tone seemed a bit flippant in the circumstances and she gave a muted reply.'I'm glad it's working out.'

'We're cremating Bella when they release her body,' Rebecca went on more soberly, 'but it will be a very brief service for just us. What good thing could anyone say that wouldn't be pure hypocrisy?'

'Are you ok?'

'A bit giddy, up and down, you know. We're all the same but we can help each other when the jitters attack.'

'It's been a shocking time.'

'It certainly has – we all need a bit of ordinary now. Anyway, we'd like you to come to Guthrie's funeral, please. Remember, we wouldn't even know he'd died if it wasn't for you and you've been there through all this, putting up with us.' Anna said nothing. 'We're going to give him a proper send-off with as many people who knew him as we can get hold of. Most of his old rugby team, the Avon Avatars, are coming, believe it or not. I'll let you know the details when it's sorted but please come if you can.'

'Of course I will,' said Anna, wondering about mentioning Dilys, who had delivered him at the maternity home in Wales, but she could do that another time. She was tired, drained.

There was still an hour of proper daylight so she changed into an old T shirt and shorts and took the paint can out to the front of the house. The brown looked disgusting (what job had they bought that for?) and she needed to decide what the top coat colour would be but first she had to finish the undercoat on the second door. As she stroked the brush up and down she pondered again the series of abusive messages.

The most likely explanation for the two on the garage door were simply that some vengeful stranger had sent a child to the wrong address. A case of mistaken identity. The one outside Harts, the first message written on the tow path, could have been Melanie – she was weird enough and angry enough to do it. But what about the others? The note in Ellis' bag, the threatening lyrics on her phone? They were personal, they were targeting her. Melanie could have done those but it seemed unlikely. Well, if they stopped she wouldn't do anything but if one more happened, she would have to go to the police. Bella had, against her will, rattled her.

She finished the last stripe and stood back. Maybe a greeny-grey? Maybe ask Rosa to do castles and roses? She'd see what paint Faye had left them and that idea reminded her to go inside for a bit more financial sleuthing before going down to Steve to lie in his arms and let the world go by.

Deciding to be early to pick Alice up for her dance class, Anna first tapped at the front door but then, when there was no answer, went down the side passage and through the gate to the creamy slabbed terrace, each day more Italianate and now with huge terracotta pots of scarlet trailing petunias and dwarf cypresses.

Steve and Alice were sitting close together with their heads bent over a book which Alice was reading out loud. She looked like a wood nymph cradled by a bear, so frail did she appear and so strong and brown was he. The pair of them could have stepped out of a fairy story. Anna stayed where she was and leaned against the trellis frame watching them.

'And then they put *another* mattress on top of that one,' Alice read in her piping, skylark voice. The Princess and the Pea. Of course. It was her favourite story, which was hardly surprising given that the heroine turned out to be high-born as proved by her extraordinary delicacy, a character Alice identified with in preference to those foolish girls who allowed themselves to be taken advantage of (like The Little Mermaid) and came to a bad end. Anna remembered liking the story herself and reading it to Faye who had been bored by it. She narrowed her eyes. Wasn't that her own book that Steve held? Yes, it had a spilled cocoa blotch on the cover so it would be over forty years old. Faye must have passed it on to Alice from their stash.

In an instant Anna saw herself as a child, not slight and pale like Alice, but dark and sturdy, and sitting close to her on a rickety bench in their tiny yard George, the young father, with his hippie beard and cheesecloth grand-dad shirt listening to her read. The same book. The very same words. Two little girls each with the person who meant most in the world to them.

No wonder Alice had resented her when Steve had laughed with her and kissed her. How would she have coped if George had brought home a woman that he clearly cared for? It had never happened. She had never had to face even a moment of competition for George's unconditional love. (In fact, as a teenager, she had begged him to go out on dates wanting the house to herself for her own romantic experiments, but it had never happened. Only a few years ago, when her mother died, she realised why. He had never stopped loving Lena and no-one else had measured up.)

Alice had tried to drive her off with aggression and insults but without success. Had she now decided on appeasement? Anna felt her heart soften. Poor kid, she would have probably done just the same given the same terrible predicament. Sharing people you love is hard at any age.

'Oh hi,' said Steve, 'is it that time already?'

'Stay there,' Alice ordered her, 'I've got to get my bag with my leotard and dance shoes.'

Steve got up, smiling, as she rushed off. 'It's her new favourite word – leotard. This is a very big deal, Anna, you know? Can you cope?' He put his warm hand on to her neck and lifted her hair off the nape, kissing it. She leaned into him.

All the windows in the studio were open but it was still stiflingly hot. The assortment of mothers, fathers, grandparents (and Anna), who were sitting on hard chairs down one side, shifted uncomfortably as the hour went on and fanned themselves with the Health and Safety Guidelines which they had been given to take home, read and sign. Even some of the excited little girls (and two boys, thanks to Strictly) were wilting but Alice was made of sterner stuff.

'Your daughter's not cracked a smile once,' Anna's neighbour said. 'She's really concentrating.'

'Mm,' Anna murmured, not bothering to contradict her and relieved that she had not been taken for Alice's granny, 'she takes life very seriously.' Having said it, she realised that it was true and in many ways admirable. The girl had strength of character. There was no doubt that Alice was brave and resourceful, too, but Anna had been so taken up with resenting her hostility that she had forgotten.

Mina's mother arrived to take her off to some family meal so Alice and Anna wandered back from the class towards the car park alone. 'Can we go to Joe's?' Alice asked. 'I want an ice-cream sundae.'

'Please,' Anna said automatically.

Joe's was a new addition to the High Street; it had taken over one of the vanquished retail outlets and turned it into a fifties-style American diner. It had become a hang-out in the afternoon for the under sixteens after school and before home – a brief respite from different kinds of pressure. A booth done out in red plastic and stainless steel was free so they slipped into it and ordered.

'So,' Anna said, 'you did really well. Did you enjoy it?'

'Yes,' Alice said firmly, 'I'm going to be as good as Gemma Atkinson soon.'

Anna stared out of the window at the dusty road and the rush-hour traffic. If moral laxity and general irresponsibility had been the flaws of some of her mother's generation, would narcissism corrupt Alice's? Harsh, she decided. The sundae and Anna's honeycomb cone arrived and they got stuck in.

'Anna?' Alice asked after a few minutes, waving her long spoon in the air, 'Will you be my mummy?'

There had been a delicious nugget of crunchy honeycomb that Anna had been savouring but now choked on. Fortunately, she had also ordered glasses of water. She wiped her eyes. 'What?'

'Auntie Julie says that all little girls should have a mummy as well as a daddy and she wants to be mine but I don't want her to be. She says it's against the law for Steve to have me when he isn't my daddy and he's not married. She said I might get taken away.'

Fury rose up in a red tide. Alice always liked to put on a 'not-bothered' face but she must have been worrying for weeks about what Julie had been telling her. No wonder Julie had been embarrassed when it got too much for Alice and she asked to leave – she should be ashamed of herself. It took more than a minute and several sips of water to calm down.

She leaned forward and said as smoothly as she could, 'No, darling, it isn't against the law for Steve to have you because your own mother and father asked him to look after you if anything bad happened to them. Sadly, something did, so Steve is your legal guardian as well as your uncle. Auntie Julie shouldn't have said what she did, it isn't true.' And she knows it, Anna added to herself.

Alice pondered this, licking her spoon. 'She just wants me all to herself, I expect.'

'And what do you want?'

'They're all right but I like it better at home with Steve and I like my room.'

Anna sat back against the sticky plastic. 'I see,' she said, smiling and raising an eyebrow, 'you only asked me to be your mummy to get out of having to live with Julie?'

Alice stirred the slush at the bottom of her glass. 'Maybe.' But then she did something that she had never done before and that Anna would never forget. She winked. 'Can we go now? I don't like this melty stuff and I want to show Steve I can do a pirouette.'

As they walked along the baking pavement to the car, Alice slipped her hand into Anna's.

'There's a parcel for you,' George called from the kitchen when she got home, 'I put it in the front room.'

'Is it ticking?'

'It's from Rebecca, I think.' He appeared wiping his hands on his apron and curious to see what was in it. He handed her the vegetable paring knife to cut the sticky tape. Anna laughed when she folded back the cardboard wings and took out one object after another.

Rebecca had given her a full set of summer and winter jogging gear with a pricey pair of trainers as well. In a small box Anna found a Fit-Bit watch. The note said: *Had to guess the size, don't be offended (!) you can exchange them if you need to. See you out there!*

Ellis crashed the front door and popped his head in to see what was happening. Anna had pulled the tight top on over her T shirt and was trying to get into the leggings.

'No, mother,' he said, appalled, 'not round here. I know people.'

'It could be Venus,' George said, 'it's low enough.'

'If that's the pole star,' Anna pointed, 'then you must be right. I wish we could see more but at least we're looking in the opposite direction from the lights of the city centre.'

'That's definitely the Great Bear.' He pointed almost straight up. The constellations were unmasked by cloud, the moon low on the horizon, and it was a joy to be lying on rugs on the grass and to be cool.

'One day I'd like to go to a desert,' Anna said, 'and see the night sky properly in all its glory.'

George said, '"*Become the sky*

Take an axe to the prison wall
Escape
Walk out like someone suddenly born into colour
Do it now.'"

Anna turned to look at his profile. 'Yes. Is that you or Rumi?'

George grunted. 'Both – no, him, of course, I'm saying it for him because he can't be here.'

The earth spun a little more.

Anna said, 'I've been thinking a lot about mum lately.'

'I'd noticed. What set that off?'

'I'm not really sure but maybe something about how obsessive Bella was about Guthrie, she would never have left him, and Bernice, how she stayed in the same house miserably, just on the off-chance he might come back.'

'Whereas Lena left you before you could even talk. I see.'

Anna stared into the vast cosmos. 'They turned out to be a mess, but, you know.'

'And then there was Alice rejecting you.'

'Mm. I understood why she was like that in my head, but not until very recently in my heart, and it did hurt but we're ok now.'

They lay in silence for a while listening to the sounds of the night – laughter and music from a barbecue a few doors down, a neighbour's dog yapping at some intruder, the constant soft moan of traffic on the main road. It wasn't yet cold enough for the dew-point so the ground was dry. There was a gentle pressure on her side and Macavity slipped into the space between herself and her father, purring loudly. George cupped her head and scratched her chin and she settled against him.

'So how are you feeling about Lena now, with all that you know?'

'I think that when she had me she was all over the place and coping with a small child was just too much.' She took a deep breath. 'It had only been a short time since she'd been badly hurt in so many ways and a bold spirit like hers must have hated being a victim. I think it wasn't so much that she wanted to leave us, it was more that she wanted to live her life. It had got stopped before it started and she must have longed to be free and see what she could make of it. She went the wrong way about it, perhaps, and I think in the end she knew that deep down and was ashamed.

'I took on face value the hurtful things she said to me when she was dying but now I wonder if it really was only to hand over Len that she made herself known to me. She may have wanted to get close but we both got defensive and it didn't happen. Maybe she wanted her people around her like Romani do, like anyone would. She couldn't be taken round the old stopping places but she might have longed to have her own flesh and blood with her at the end.'

'You can't reproach yourself with how you were. You took care of her until her last breath,' George said quickly.

Anna watched the lights of a plane cross the sky on its way to Birmingham International. 'I could have been more understanding, more compassionate to her, but I'm not beating myself up over it. She was a difficult woman and it was an impossible situation but now I do feel I understand her choices a little and it's a relief to be free from that low heart pain, if you know what I mean, that resentment and sadness.'

'I'm glad.' George reached past Macavity and patted her arm. 'My eyes are more used to the dark now – I think that's Ursa Minor, isn't it, above Polaris? Can you make it out?

'Oh, look! A shooting star!' Anna cried.

Macavity, alarmed by the sudden loudness of her voice, jumped up and ran off and a little while later they both got up, shook the dried grass cuttings from the rugs and went indoors. Anna picked up her phone from the kitchen table while George put the kettle on for his bed-time cup of cocoa.

'Text from Kimi.'
'Is she ok?'
Anna read the unusually lengthy message:

Forgot to tell you, hope you don't mind, I gave your business card to Charlie and pretended to be you (used a burner phone to call him). I didn't want him knowing what family I come from, he would have charged double for Cora since we're so filthy rich and it might have been awkward in other ways. Are you up for a ride Saturday?'

So that was it. Since it was a case of laugh or scream, Anna laughed. 'Yes, she's ok, Dad, but I think she owes me a very expensive meal out.'

'Good night, then, chick. I enjoyed star-gazing with you.' She watched him make his way out of the kitchen trying not to slop his cocoa. His scalp shone through the tangle of grey hair and his cardigan hung, misshaped, from the stoop of his back.

'Yes, me too, and Dad? Thanks for everything.'

She took her cup of tea to the back window and looked again up into the night sky. With the kitchen lamps on she couldn't see the stars but she didn't have to because there was no doubt that they would always be there.

'Good night, Mum,' she said softly, raising her mug, 'rest in peace.'

*

Thanks

Again, I am so grateful to my family, friends and readers for your encouragement (and other useful comments of a more bracing kind). I think this one will be the last but I've said that before. Catharine Stevens has been, as ever, an enthusiastic and encyclopaedic source of genealogical expertise so if there are any errors they are entirely my own. Thanks, too, to Terry Quinn and Peter Calver for their patience and expertise in checking my work.

When I was a child, a relative told me that the reason for my dark eyes and brown hair (in contrast to my blue-eyed, blonde sisters) was that on the night I was born a Gypsy woman gave birth in the same maternity ward and the two babies were mixed up. I found this possibility thrilling. So thank you to that person, too.

I also want to thank the people I met at Appleby for allowing *gorgias* like me to enjoy the rich experience of a Horse Fair.

Books Anna might have read:

Our Forgotten Years: A Gypsy Woman's Life on the Road by Maggie Smith-Bendell (University of Hertfordshire Press, 2009)

Beneath the Blue Sky: Four Decades of the Gypsy Traveller Life by Dominic Reeve (Abacus, 2012)

Gypsy Boy by Mikey Walsh (Hodder and Stoughton, 2009)

No Place to Call Home: Inside the Real Life of Gypsies and Travellers by Katharine Quarmby (Oneworld Publications, 2013)

Geraldine Wall has lived and worked in the UK, the USA and the Cayman Islands and now lives in Birmingham, England. She has been a factory night-shift worker, a cinema usherette, a teacher, a lecturer and an advocate for victims of domestic violence as well as having the huge good fortune to have become a mother and a granny.

Email: geraldine.wall@blueyonder.co.uk

Printed in Great Britain
by Amazon